NEVER ALONE

ELIZABETH HAYNES

First published in 2016 by

Myriad Editions
www.myriadeditions.com

Second printing
3 5 7 9 10 8 6 4 2

A CIP catalogue record for this book is available from the British Library

ISBN (pbk): 978-1-908434-96-8
ISBN (ebk): 978-1-908434-97-5

Praise for *Never Alone*

'Haynes is one of those "just one more chapter" all-night-reading writers. Her acute understanding of human nature under stress is delicious, her plotting ingenious and trustworthy. *Never Alone* is a terrific book.'
Alex Marwood

'A masterclass in suspense. The final chapters are the most sublime I've read in ages. So brilliantly tense.' Clare Mackintosh

'I knew from the first page that *Never Alone* was going to grab hold of me and not let go – and I was right. The tension and intrigue ramp up throughout the book, right until the final terrifying moments.'
Rachel Abbott

'A tale of love, jealousy and obsession. The characters crept under my skin more and more as the story unfolded, revealing layers of intrigue and mystery and finishing with a climactic ending. A superb rollercoaster of emotions.' Mel Sherratt

'Atmospheric and beautifully written – impossible to put down. I tore through it, gripped all the way to the pulse-pounding ending. Brilliant.'
Mark Edwards

'A gripping and tense story that had me on the edge of my seat. A grown-up version of *Into the Darkest Corner*, this story is full of lust, suspicion, mistrust, desire and guilt. An exceptional psychological thriller.' Tracy Fenton, THE Book Club

'Haynes doing what she does best – cleverly, subtly weaving the terrifying into everyday life. What makes it all the more chilling is that this could happen to any one of us.' Lisa Cutts

'Haynes is genius at finely tuned suspense. *Never Alone* frayed my nerves and gripped me from the start.' Lesley Thomson

'A thrilling, atmospheric, creepy and unsettling page-turner.'
Sam Carrington

'Full of menace, and de

Praise for Elizabeth Haynes

'It's hard to put the uniqueness of Elizabeth Haynes' writing into words. Her stories grip you by the throat and force you to acknowledge that this is what real crime and real horror look and feel like, as well as real love, hope, fear. Suddenly, much of the other crime fiction you've read seems, in comparison, rather like stories made up by writers. Haynes is the most exciting thing to happen to crime fiction in a long time.' Sophie Hannah

'Haynes' powerful account of domestic violence is disquieting, yet unsensationalist. This is a gripping book on a topic which can never be highlighted enough.' *Guardian*

'Check the locks on your doors and windows and surrender to this obsessive thriller.' Karin Slaughter

'Haynes does a great job in ratcheting up the suspense... and there are many lip-biting moments.' *Daily Mail*

'A chilling, page-turning read that charts domestic violence without flinching and portrays OCD with insight and compassion.' Rosamund Lupton

'All the fascination of a good horror film combined with the terror of a bad nightmare. Features one of the scariest villains I've ever encountered.'
Amanda Ross, creator of the Richard and Judy Book Club

'A terrifying and convincing portrayal of an abusive relationship and a damaged woman's heroic attempts to recover from it.'
Publisher's Weekly

'A psychological thriller packed with tension and suspense. This is a debut of such strength you have to wonder if Haynes is the next Minette Walters.'
Rhian Davies, CWA John Creasey Dagger judge

'Compelling and disturbing.' *Mystery Women*

'A *tour de force* debut novel that is both creepily disturbing and yet beautifully rendered.' *New York Journal of Books*

'Everything you could possibly want from a thriller: an intelligent and feisty heroine, a mysterious packet, complicated relationships and a great cast of characters who are not always as guilty or as above suspicion as they might at first appear. Do you want to add tension and intrigue to your everyday life? Read this novel. Now.' *Book After Book*

'Fear about the loss of control is at the heart of readers' obsession with crime… That she lends Genevieve power over fear, her body and the men for whom she dances has enabled Haynes to create a character with more complexity than is usual in genre thrillers.' *Independent on Sunday*

'Unputdownable, this thriller with a heart of gold reads like a breath of fresh air.' *Red*

'Wonderfully and grimly fascinating... *Human Remains* could be one of the thrillers of the year.' *We Love This Book*

'A deeply unsettling psychological thriller.' *Bella*

'A tense and thought-provoking debut novel with dark moments. Its portrayal of obsession will send a shiver down your spine.' *Shotsmag*

'This racy jeopardy thriller proves that Haynes' much-praised first novel was no fluke.' *Morning Star*

'Full of suspense and intrigue and keeps the reader hanging on its every word. Very highly recommended.' *Eurocrime*

'There are few writers who could write such disturbing prose so beautifully.' *Books and Writers*

'Fast-paced and chilling… Lock all your doors and settle down for one of the most gripping reads of the year.' *Pamreader*

'[Haynes] might have been expected to produce a conventional procedural. Instead, she plays with the form and, in doing so, subverts it... her initial success was no accident.'

Sunday Express

'A brilliant book... I literally could not put it down.'

Crime Scraps Review

'If you're not one of the thousands of readers who've been knocked sideways by this thriller then start here.' *Lovereading*

'A disturbing, exciting and powerful story that is beautifully and eloquently written. Prepare to sleep with the light on!'

Spirit FM

'To say this was nail-biting is a complete understatement. I loved this book from the first page.' *Bleach House Library*

'All the fascination of a good horror film combined with the terror of a bad nightmare.' *The Age*

'An unforgettable story.' *Suspense Magazine*

'A scorching read. As the tension grew, the pages turned of their own accord. All in all a very satisfying psychological thriller.'

Second Helpings

'It's now safe to say that Elizabeth Haynes is no longer just a rising star. She is a star.' *The Bookbag*

For Sarah M'Grady

Part One

Exile is a curious thing. It starts off and you think it's fine, you think you're not bothered, but at some point it starts to burn.

I kidded myself that this was what I wanted – I needed the space, I needed time to get my head straight; I needed to find myself. That's what they say, right? So I ran as far away as I could, and then I started to wonder what I was running from.

Running from myself? Running from my own mistakes?

Hard to admit that.

But it's impossible to sustain, exile, that's the thing. Because the feeling of home is too strong a pull, and sooner or later the cord snaps tight and you find yourself working your way back.

And that's when it starts to get really, really difficult.

When you realise that the people you left behind have changed.

When you realise that you should have stayed away.

Sarah

Not for the first time, Sarah Carpenter stands at the top of the hill and thinks that this would be a good place to die. It feels like the end of the world, so high up that even the trees don't bother to grow. It's just tussocky windblown grass, clouds racing overhead, drops of icy rain when you're not expecting them.

You could die here and nobody would notice. You could lie down, and nobody would ever find you. The wind would continue to blow and the sun, sometimes, would shine, and there would be rain and snow too, picking at your clothes and your flesh until there was nothing left but bones. Even in January, though, with the weather unpredictable and sometimes even dangerous, it's not just Sarah who comes up here. There are wildlife rangers, fell-walkers. Someone would find you, eventually.

But today – there is not a soul up here. Just Sarah and her two dogs, who have, for the moment, disappeared out of sight.

She is completely alone.

Below her, the slope down to the dry stone wall that marks the boundary of her property is steep and treacherous. There is a field, of sorts, patchy, rutted, the tough grass yellowing and breaking away at the steeper parts, earthy cracks forming uneven terraces. In the field, squatting like a troll, is the derelict croft that once sheltered shepherds, before the farm was built. Below that the gradient begins to even out and there is her garden, stunted trees and a vegetable patch, nothing growing there now. Four Winds Farm huddles into the hillside as though the wind might rip it off its foundations and blow it down into the valley.

'Basil! Tess!' Sarah calls, and her words are stolen from her mouth by the wind. She can hardly feel her face now. Time to head back.

Whether she has heard or not, Tess the collie appears from behind her and Basil is not far behind, wagging his tail and looking overjoyed at the fact that he has found something foul to roll in. His blond coat has a long streak of something black from shoulder to flank.

'Oh, Basil, you little sod.' She doesn't have time to give him a bath, not today. Stumbling over the tussocks, she debates hosing him down outside and leaving him out until he's dried off. But it's freezing, and, looking at the clouds overhead, it might even snow.

She checks her watch: it's nearly half-past eight. Perhaps, if she's quick...

She leaves Basil whining outside the back door while she dries Tess with a towel in the utility room. Out of the wind, her cheeks are stinging and her ears humming with the sudden quiet in the house. Tess looks at her with big brown eyes and raises one doggy eyebrow as if to point out that she should expect nothing less from a Labrador.

'I know,' Sarah says aloud, as if Tess had actually spoken. 'He's an idiot. What can you do?'

She gives Tess a biscuit and the dog scampers away to her bed in the kitchen. Doors shut inside for damage-limitation purposes, she lets Basil in. He's not sure whether he's pleased to be allowed in or anxious about what might be coming next, which gives her the advantage. She takes him by the collar and hauls him into the small downstairs shower room.

He hangs his head and gives out a little whine.

'It's your own fault,' she says. 'Today of all days, Basil, how could you?'

Still, she thinks, massaging him with lavender-scented, doggy-calming shampoo, *at least he'll smell fresh for our visitor.*

He's early. That's good.

'Basil, shush! That's enough!' It's as though he's never heard a car before: he's barking, tearing around the kitchen. Tess, glancing up from her bed, isn't as bothered. Sarah watches from the kitchen window as the dark blue Ford Focus pulls round in the turning circle outside the house and comes to a stop facing the garage. Her heart's thudding. *Well, of course it is. Deep breaths, girl, come on. Be sensible about this.*

She opens the door and stands there, holding on to Basil's collar, while he gets out of the car and she gets her first proper look at him. Tess is curious enough to get up from her bed and she stands next to Sarah, craning her neck to see what's arrived.

Aiden Beck. It's been over twenty years.

'Hi!' she calls, brightly, gives him a little wave.

The sun's shining, and just for a change the wind has dropped. It's not often you could call across the yard and rely on someone hearing you. She doesn't tell him that, of course.

Basil's tail is wagging and now the car's parked it's safe to let him loose.

'It's okay, he's friendly.'

'Hello, Sarah,' he says. His smile is still beautiful. He's rubbing Basil's head, patting his side. The dog's beside himself with joy. Tess has turned and gone back inside already; she's not so easily impressed.

Aiden comes over to her, kisses her on both cheeks, a hand on her upper arm. He doesn't look any older, and she's about to tell him so, but stops herself just in time. *Nothing personal*, she tells herself. *You thought about this.*

'You look great,' he says.

'Thanks,' she says, about to deflect the compliment with something disparaging about her jumper, but she's promised herself that she will think before she speaks, and it seems to be working. 'Did you have a good journey?'

He's driven from somewhere, of course, but she has no idea where. There was no real planning, no time to discuss his complicated travel arrangements. She thinks he flew back yesterday. Presumably he's been in a hotel somewhere; maybe he stayed with friends. It's none of her business.

'Yeah, it was fine. It's good to see you again; it's been too long...'

'Come in, come in,' she says then, not giving him a chance to finish. She's trying not to stare at him, trying not to be obvious while she's drinking him in, all the little details: the lines around his eyes, the stubble on his cheek and chin.

She leads him into the kitchen, which is spotless. She's been cleaning the whole house since Friday, when this whole crazy idea started.

'I – um – I thought you could go and have a look around the cottage while I make tea,' she says. The key is on the kitchen table, next to the bowl of lemons and limes. She hands it to him. He's looking surprised. It felt like a good idea, this: give herself a few minutes to recover. She knew she'd need it, and already it's feeling awkward. Her face is burning.

'Oh – okay. Are you sure?'

'Yes, of course. I need to make a couple of phone calls. Take as long as you like; have a good look round. I'll put the kettle on.'

He goes back out the way they came in. The kettle is full and has only just boiled, because she flicked the switch when she saw the car negotiating the tight bend into the gate. She stands at the sink and watches him cross the yard, heading down the slope towards the cottage that had been an outbuilding and, before that, a piggery. They had converted it into accommodation for Sarah's father-in-law, but, as it turned out, James Senior had died two days after being admitted to hospital with pneumonia, and he'd never even seen it. She had been thinking about getting a tenant, or maybe advertising it as a holiday let, but her heart hadn't been in it. She didn't want someone she didn't know living on her doorstep, and the thought of having a random selection of holidaymakers didn't appeal either. So the cottage had been sitting vacant, pristine, for a long time. Sarah had visitors, of course, friends, family – but everyone always stayed in the house.

On Friday, everything had changed. It had taken her by surprise, a rare Facebook post from him, set to 'friends' only.

Coming home next week, been a while!! Anyone know of any nice one- or two-bed furnished flats to rent, preferably Yorkshire or North, let me know?

He had had few replies, mostly of the 'let's have a beer' and 'I'll keep my eye out, have you tried the paper?' variety. Then she'd added a comment: *You can always stay in my cottage. I've been looking for a tenant. Send me a message if you're interested.*

It had taken her an hour to come up with that. Not wanting to sound too keen, just the right level of nonchalance. Five minutes later, she heard a ping:

Hi, Sarah, great to hear from you, how have you been? Thanks for your kind offer of the cottage, I might just take you up on that. I could come to see it on Tuesday if that's any good? A x

She'd replied quickly:

Yes, that's fine, here's my phone number, I'll be in on Tuesday.

Yesterday, there had been a text from an unrecognised number:

Hi Sarah this is my new mobile number. Will be with you about 11am tomorrow if OK. Thanks again A x

She had been sure something would go wrong. He'd call again, tell her thanks but he needed to be somewhere less remote, or he'd decided to go back to Japan, or wherever it was, after all, or he was going to stay with friends until he found somewhere permanent. She shouldn't get her hopes up. All this cleaning, while it couldn't hurt, was pretty pointless and she was wasting her time...

And yet, here he is. She stares at the yard, still, although he has long since let himself into the cottage and shut the door behind him. She gets the teapot down from the shelf, warms it, fetches mugs and the tin of biscuits down and puts them on a tray. Should she put the biscuits on a plate? Or be brave, and get out the cake she'd made? This morning it had felt like too much, too obvious that she was making an effort to welcome him. Too desperate. She leaves the biscuits in the tin.

While the tea brews, Sarah calls Sophie. She answers immediately, as if she has been clutching the phone in anticipation. 'Well? Is he there?'

'Yes,' Sarah says. 'He's looking round the cottage.'

'You left him alone?'

'It's not a big place. I think he can probably manage to find his way around.'

'You should be chatting him up!'

'He'd run a mile.'

'I doubt it. The cottage is lovely, and you are too. I wouldn't be surprised if he moves in today. Has he got all his stuff with him?'

Sarah looks across to the car parked outside the garage. 'I don't know – maybe. He's not said anything.'

'And? Is he just as gorgeous as you remembered?'

'Oh, give over. It's not as though I haven't seen pictures of him over the years...'

'Well?'

'He's not really changed much, put it like that.' *And my heart's not stopped pounding*, she wants to add. *And it's as though the last twenty-four years haven't happened. Do I feel the same way? No, it's worse. Much worse.*

Sophie gives her girlish giggle, the one that makes you think she's twenty-three, not forty-three. 'It sounds as if it's going well. I'm glad to hear it, and I can't wait to meet him and see this man you've been obsessed with your entire life.'

'You keep your paws off.'

'Don't worry, darling, I only have paws for George, you know that.'

Basil, who has been waiting at the door, starts barking again. Sarah glances up and sees Aiden crossing the yard towards the house. He is talking on a mobile phone, smiling.

'Soph, I'll call you later, he's coming back. Basil, for Christ's sake shut up! Bed!'

Basil whines and obliges, but then leaps up again as the door opens and Aiden comes into the kitchen. Sarah puts her mobile down on to the kitchen table. 'What do you think?'

'It's great,' he says. 'I can't believe how big it is inside.'

'Cunning use of white paint, I think,' she says, transferring the tray with the teapot on it over to the table. 'Have a seat.'

She pours the tea while he watches her. There is some tension in the air already, or is she imagining it? Is it her? He's gearing up to tell her that he's just here to look, he needs to be nearer to London actually, nearer his friends. He has friends, of course. Even though he's been away for years.

'I wanted to say how sorry I was not to make the funeral.'

She stops, mid-pour. Looks at him in surprise.

'I meant – Jim's funeral, of course. Although I would have come to his dad's too, if I'd been here.'

'Oh. That's okay. I wasn't expecting you to come all the way back from abroad.'

'But I should have come. He was a good friend. What a shock to lose him so young.'

Sarah wonders if he's expecting her to be upset, or to cry. It's been three years since Jim died, and actually, when it happened – six months after the car crash that had put him into a persistent vegetative state – it had been almost a relief. Her grieving had been done slowly, painfully, beside a hospital bed. 'Yes, it was. He was... a great father.'

She can't quite bring herself to say more than that. And even when Jim had been alive and well, despite being happy and settled and everything else that came with a twenty-year marriage, it had been Aiden she'd thought about before falling asleep, Aiden she'd fantasised about when the mood took her.

He can never know that. Ever.

'Thanks,' Aiden says, as she passes a mug across the table towards him and carefully avoids his touch.

Basil has settled under the table, his large behind on Sarah's foot, which means his head must be resting on Aiden's. Tess is watching the scene from the sanctuary of her bed in the corner, her gaze wary.

'So...' Sarah begins, then stops, with no idea how to continue. Why does this feel so awkward?

'So,' he replies, and laughs. 'Tell me about the cottage. What about rent, bills, stuff like that?'

'Oh, I wasn't going to charge you anything. It's on a separate meter, so I guess you could pay the bill for electricity. And you can stay as long as you like.'

He gazes at her across the table and she's aware of his eyes, that they are green. Somehow she'd forgotten this detail, despite picturing him in her mind so often.

'That's a very generous offer, but not one I'm prepared to accept,' he says.

It's an oddly formal way of phrasing it, and the way he's looking at her is almost cold. 'Oh,' she says.

'You could probably make five hundred a week if you let it out as a holiday cottage. As a residential let, maybe eight hundred a month?'

'Maybe,' she says, 'But I'm not keen on having a stranger living there, and I don't like the idea of a long-term commitment. Your using it would be ideal.' To give herself time to think, she changes the subject. 'So what are your plans? Have you got a job? I don't even know why you're moving back.'

Aiden shifts in his seat, moves away slightly. Basil jumps up, then heads over to his food bowl in case something might have fallen into it since the last time he checked. 'It felt like the right time. I was thinking of doing some freelance work for now, until I find something permanent.'

'I'm being nosy, sorry.'

'Not at all. It's a valid question. What's it like living here? Do you have good internet coverage?'

'I've got broadband. The wireless even works in the cottage, but the signal's not as strong. You might want to get your own router.'

'I could work from home,' he says.

Sarah's heart beats faster again. *He said 'home'. He thinks this place is home.* 'Absolutely.'

'What's the village like?'

'It's great – lovely friendly people. It's got a few shops, coffee shops and tea rooms, a post office, a Chinese, a chippy, but I steer clear of that one. The pubs are nice. The restaurant in one of them is particularly good, but you have to book. There's a new village hall, lots of things going on... events... you know.'

He considers this, drinking his tea. At last he puts down his mug. 'If you don't like the idea of commitment, we can dispense with a contract. But I'll pay you eight hundred a month, with a month in advance as a deposit. If you need me to leave, you can give me, say, a week's notice. How does that sound?'

'But we're friends,' she protests.

'It doesn't mean we can't have a professional understanding over this particular issue. And I'm afraid I'm going to insist on it.'

He's so serious that she finds herself breaking into a smile. 'Are you really?'

'Yes.'

And she gives up. 'All right, then.'

He offers her his hand to shake, and the deal is done. Her heart is beating hard enough, she thinks, for him to hear it. *Eight hundred a month.*

He smiles, finishes his tea. Then looks up at her from under his brows. 'You're sure this is a good idea?'

'Why wouldn't it be?'

He doesn't answer. She has a horrible feeling it's because he knows quite clearly how obsessed she is.

'I promise I won't trash the place, or have noisy parties without inviting you,' he says.

'And I promise I won't ask you to fix the septic tank,' she replies. His hand is warm, his grip firm.

So it begins.

Aiden

When the tea is finished, she offers to show you the rest of the house. You accept. You need to see it, to picture where she lives, sleeps, works. How she spends her days. More than that, you need a way to keep the conversation going. You hadn't expected this to be quite so awkward.

Sarah leads the way from the large kitchen into a living room that's half the size, with a big corner sofa unit that's looking threadbare under the white cotton throws. The throws have been put there for your benefit, you realise, as one of the dogs makes a leap for the corner seat that has an indentation in it exactly to his dimensions. She shouts at him to get down, which he does, looking confused. She has a small television in the corner and a large bookcase covering one wall. You like this proportion and what it tells you about her.

As well as the living room, there is a garden room and a conservatory. A downstairs loo and shower, a utility room with the back door leading off it.

'The cottage has got a washing machine,' she says. 'But if you need to dry things you can always bring them in here.'

'Thanks,' you say, trying to picture yourself coming in here with a laundry basket when she's not here. Or when she is.

'The door's usually unlocked,' she says.

You give her a questioning look.

'I've never worried about it. I don't think anyone locks their doors round here.'

She leads the way up the narrow staircase to the first floor. You are distracted from the close-up view of her arse in those tight jeans by the original artworks on the walls. They are her illustrations for *The Candy Cotton Piglet*, her first and most successful book. She won awards for the series that followed. The illustrations look so much brighter than the books themselves, and you tell her this.

'You think?' she calls, from the landing. 'I don't think I even look at them any more.'

You join her upstairs. The house is set into a hillside and is clearly old, with sloping floors and low ceilings. She shows you two of the five bedrooms, one of them still obviously belonging to the absent daughter, Kitty, who must be at university. What about the son, Louis? There doesn't seem to be much left of his room. He went away to study, then you seem to remember he dropped out after a year. The same year that Jim died. You wonder what happened after that.

'How are the kids?' you ask.

'They're fine,' she says. 'Kitty is doing well. She should be coming home for a visit soon; you'll get to meet her.'

'Where's she studying?'

'Manchester. She's doing civil engineering.'

'And Louis?'

'This is the bathroom,' she says, standing to one side.

It's clear from her wide smile that she's particularly proud of this room, and it is very nice. A roll-top bath stands in front of the window, down two steps. There's a shower too, and oak beams. The bath is in front of the window and there aren't any curtains.

'Bit public, isn't it?' you say, before you think about it.

She laughs. 'Nobody around for miles,' she says. 'And if there were, I don't think they'd be interested.'

You want to disagree but you've seen the flush that's creeping across her cheeks and you know she's embarrassed herself, so you restrict your response to a polite smile. Besides, she's given up on the tour. 'There are another three bedrooms,' she says casually. One of them will be the master bedroom – hers alone now, you think – but she has no need to show that off.

'Where do you work?' you ask.

'I've got a studio behind the garage. Jim used it as a workshop, but I had some skylights put in and I took it over. I'll show you another time.'

She heads back downstairs. After a moment, in which you look down the narrow hallway to a door at the end, slightly open, you follow.

'When are you going to move in?' she asks.

'Straight away,' you say. 'If that's not too cheeky.'

'Of course not,' she says. 'The place is yours now.'

You head out to the car. She doesn't offer to help and you're glad to be on your own again. You drive the Focus back up towards the cottage, which has its own parking space next to the front door. The boot is full: two suitcases, a holdall and a suit-carrier. You unlock the door of the cottage again and enter, this time with a proprietorial air. You collect the luggage from the car and leave it in the hallway, closing the door behind you and standing for a moment, listening to the quiet.

At last: you can breathe.

Nobody knows where you are. Nobody, except Sarah. You are safe here, thanks to her.

Her generosity is astonishing. Perhaps even alarming. But then, she has this cottage and you can understand her reluctance to have a stranger live in it. You're just surprised that she's willing to let you take it over, since you're practically a stranger too. And it is a great space, exactly what you need: a large open-plan living room with a kitchen area at one end; big patio doors that show off a view down into the valley, with nothing but fields, sheep and dry stone walls for the next two or three miles. The furniture is modern and functional, which must be deliberate. Everything is white and clean, all blond wood and natural fabrics. The bedroom is surprisingly spacious, with a double bed, an iron bedframe. She's even made up the bed, with a dove-grey duvet cover and pillowcases. A small pile of towels sits at an oblique angle on the end of the bed. They look brand new. The bathroom is small and there isn't room for a bath, just a shower. You don't mind. A pot plant sits on the windowsill, the depth of which gives you an idea of the thickness of the exterior walls. The plant is green enough to be made of plastic, but, when you investigate, it's real; the compost is slightly damp. You'll have to remember to keep it watered; you don't want to kill it.

Your watch says it's half-past twelve, although you're not hungry. You barely slept last night, and you're too tired to eat. It would be easy to go to bed now, you think, looking at the iron bedstead that looks so comfortable, but if you do that you won't sleep tonight. You have to stay awake until bedtime. Before that, there are many things you could be doing.

You spend an hour unpacking. Suits, shirts on hangers in the wardrobe. Toiletries into the bathroom. The bed calls you again.

You head back outside, leaving the door unlocked. Better get used to it, you tell yourself. One of the dogs barks as you walk across the yard towards the main house. It's an excellent warning, of course. You knock on the front door.

'You don't need to knock,' she says, opening the door. 'You can come straight in.'

'No, really,' you say. 'I can't just walk in.'

She's smiling, amused. 'Everyone else does.'

'I'm going to go and get some provisions,' you say. 'Where's the nearest supermarket?'

'There's a Co-op in town. In the square – you can't miss it. If you want to do a big shop you'll have to go to Thirsk.'

'The Co-op sounds fine. Do you need anything?'

'No,' she says. 'If you need anything for the cottage – or if there's anything in there you don't want – just let me know. I keep the bed made up, but you might prefer to have your own sheets... I don't know.'

'It's great,' you say.

There's a pause then, because you're looking at her, and you lose your train of thought. In your defence, the tiredness of the long drive and everything that preceded it is overwhelming. Your eyes have glazed a little, remembering something from a lifetime ago.

'My friend Sophie is having a bit of a get-together tomorrow night,' Sarah is saying. 'You're welcome to join us. It's just in the Royal Oak, in town.'

'Oh,' you say. Caught out. 'That sounds nice. Thanks.'

'Only, you know, if you're not busy. See how you feel.'

'Thanks,' you say again. 'You've been really kind.'

She smiles and you head back up towards the car. *A bit of a get-together*, you think. It sounded like a casual invitation, and to anyone else it might have seemed she'd felt obliged to ask you, now you're here. But you're not anyone else. You're good at reading people. You know that, however dismissively it was phrased, Sarah really wants you to go. It's warm in the car and you open the windows as you indicate to turn into the lane. You start to think about what to wear, what to bring. Who Sophie is, and what Sarah's friends might be like, how they will react to you. And what might happen afterwards.

In your back pocket, your mobile phone vibrates. You check the number and smile before answering. Three calls, already? It looks as if you're going to be busy.

Sarah

Aiden offers to drive, so that Sarah can have a drink.

It's a very casual offer, but by the time they have crossed the yard to his car, got in and buckled up, Sarah's cheeks are burning and she has such a surge of emotion that she thinks she might actually cry. He didn't mean anything by it, she tells herself, cross at her reaction. She's not even sure if he knows all the details of Jim's accident; he wasn't in the country when it happened. He sent flowers, a card with a really kind letter inside it, his memories of Jim – but all he knows, all he really knows, is that there was a car crash and Jim died after six months without ever fully regaining consciousness. He doesn't know what caused it.

'You're very quiet,' he says. 'Is everything okay?'

She can't bring herself to look across to him. They are halfway down the hill, the headlights illuminating the hedgerows either side of the lane. 'It's nothing,' she says, then adds brightly, 'You'll like Sophie, everyone does. And George is all right too; he comes across as a bit of an arrogant arse but he's OK when you get to know him. He's an MP. Not ours, though. You need to turn left at the bottom.'

He knows, of course, where the square is. Already she is wishing she hadn't suggested this. She loves Sophie, she is her best friend – really her only friend – but the socialising thing, it's awkward. She never quite feels comfortable. As soon as she gets out of the house, no matter how much she's looked forward to it, she instantly wants to go home again.

'How have you been getting on?' she asks, to change the subject. 'The cottage, I mean. Have you got everything you need?'

'Yes,' he says. 'It's great. Very... quiet.'

This makes her laugh. 'What about your job?'

'I need to make some new contacts up here, but yes – that's looking good.'

'What is it you do again?'

There is a pause while he waits to turn into the car park and she thinks maybe he wasn't listening, but then he says, 'It's like a therapy business. Setting up franchises, that kind of thing. Facilitation.'

The car stops and he turns off the engine. Turns to look at her.

'I'll tell you all about it another time,' he says. 'You look absolutely beautiful.'

The sudden compliment takes her by surprise and chokes her. Nobody has told her that for a long, long time. Only Sophie, but then Sophie thinks everyone's *gorgeous, darling*, and it's not the same. Not the same at all.

As they walk across to the pub, Sarah fights the emotion back down again. *It's hormones*, she tells herself. *Get a grip!* Aiden holds the door for her and she goes inside, into the warm pub with its low ceiling and uneven carpeted floor, and there is Sophie in a black dress that shows off her long legs, and she is smiling and elegant.

'Sarah, darling! And this must be...'

'Aiden Beck. Pleased to meet you.'

She kisses him on both cheeks, managing to give Sarah a quick wink as she does so. Sophie introduces George, who is already, by the look of his ruddy complexion and enthusiastic handshake, well refreshed. Becca is there, with Daniel. Laura and Marlie, Paul and Amy, Ian and Diana. Sarah says hello to the ones who catch her eye.

Aiden goes to the bar.

'He's a bit gorgeous, isn't he?' Sophie says in a loud whisper. 'How are you getting on?'

'I've hardly seen him,' Sarah says. 'He only moved in yesterday. He's been busy, sorting things out.'

And Sarah has been avoiding him – not intentionally; it's just that she doesn't have anything in particular to say. She doesn't want to harass the poor man. She doesn't want to give off the impression that she's lonely. She isn't; she has the dogs, and Sophie, and her work. And Aiden is an old friend, nothing more.

A small voice inside reminds her that he just told her she was beautiful, less than five minutes ago. It felt like a very personal thing for him to say, after so many years. She wonders if he actually meant it, or if he says it to every woman he's friends with.

Aiden

You love things like this: the opportunity to meet all these new people in an environment in which they are all unguarded, feeling safe. They do not realise how much they reveal about themselves, and how quickly.

The exception to this is Sarah, who is not at all comfortable. She has some degree of social anxiety, you think. It's endearing. Considering her career, which was at one point stellar, and how she was at university, how determined and focused and calm, she is very different now. It's as though she has been wrung out by the world and discarded. You think that's what getting married and having two children does to you – you become a wife and a mother, and the core part of you is… what's the word?

Desiccated.

You have seen this time and time again, with clients who have visited you, trying to find themselves. Trying to irrigate the dry land, trying to find a way to grow.

Irrigation is your speciality.

That thought makes you smile.

Her friend Sophie is intriguing, though. She is charming, and mildly flirtatious, looking you in the eye and touching you gently on the arm when she's talking to you, but she does that with everyone, except her husband. He is a bore, of course, holding court with the other friends who have joined them, laughing like a drain at his own anecdotes and filling everyone's glasses.

You have been trying to think what it was that you said, just before you got in the car. Something happened, some memory or something you said made her sad. It came off her in waves, the desolation; you could almost smell it.

She won't admit to it, if you ask. She won't tell you. It doesn't matter; you know better than to push someone when they're in that vulnerable state. You can wait. You'll find out soon enough.

And the other thing that's bothering you. Her son – Louis. She avoided your question neatly, distracting you with the bathroom. She doesn't want to talk about him.

You remember seeing photos over the years, via the infrequent letters and then on Facebook, the children growing up. Holidays, first days at school, parties; Louis with his arms thrown around his mum's neck. They were close, always close. What has happened there?

Sarah and Sophie are gossiping, heads together. Of the two, you can see that Sophie, tall, with glossy dark hair and an almost effortless elegance, is the more traditionally attractive.

They both look at you.

'I'm going to find us some menus,' Sarah says. 'Would you like another drink?'

'I'm fine, for now,' you say. 'Want me to come with you?'

'No, I'll manage.'

You watch her as she walks across to the bar.

'You know, I can't help feeling we've met before,' Sophie says to him, drawing his attention back to the present.

'I don't think so,' you say, and smile. 'I'm sure I would remember you.'

'I'm good with faces,' Sophie says. She returns the smile but it's not quite made it up to her eyes. 'You've been abroad all these years?'

It feels as if she is trying to catch you out.

'Pretty much.'

Sophie half-turns to follow your glance to where Sarah is leaning over, trying to attract the attention of the landlady who is flitting between the lounge and the bar. 'I'd better go and give her a hand,' she says.

She had been about to say something else, and she'd checked herself. This Sophie has her guard up with you. She is opaque, frosted; maybe you will have the chance to work on that, while you're here. You suspect it would be worth your while.

Meanwhile, Sarah is not like that at all. You can't stop looking at her. She glances up and sees you watching, and for a moment you've caught her, and you can see right inside.

Sarah

Sarah goes around to the other side of the bar, where it's quieter, to ask for some menus. They hadn't planned to have dinner, but it turns out that nobody has eaten and they're all hungry, so Sophie and George have collared two tables that don't have a *reserved* sign on them. What they really want is chips. This is the equivalent of slumming it, for them.

Sarah is glad of the moment away from them, a chance to breathe, to clear her head. She wishes Aiden hadn't offered to drive. She has had two glasses of wine and actually she'd rather not have any more; she wants to be focused, wants to choose her words carefully, wants to not make a fool of herself.

Something makes her look round, and Aiden is watching her. He doesn't look away.

'Sarah?'

She turns quickly and before she has fully registered who it is – bright, intense blue eyes, a beard, rough brown curls cut short – he has pulled her into a bear hug. A proper, breath-stealing squeeze.

'I thought it was you. How are you?'

'Will!' she says, having in that precise moment found her voice again, 'I'm fine, thank you. How are you?'

Will Brewer – of all the people to see here! She thinks for a moment about the last time she saw him. Louis's twenty-first birthday party... And then Louis had moved out; she hadn't seen Will since.

And now? Here he is. He seems ridiculously pleased to see her, his grin wide, showing impossibly white, even teeth. 'I'm great,' he says. 'Great. God, it's good to see you.'

'So,' Sarah ventures, her heart still bumping at the shock of seeing him again, 'have you been away?'

'I've been working abroad,' he says, still smiling. 'America, India... I've just got back from Cambodia.'

'That sounds really exciting,' she says, thinking, *He's not very tanned.*

'Aye, it is. I've had an amazing time. Weird to be back, to be honest.'

'So what are your plans?'

'Ah, just catching up with everybody. It's been ages. How's Louis doing? I'll have to see if he wants to come out for a beer.'

'Well,' Sarah says, 'you should give him a call.'

When Louis was doing his A-levels Will had always been around; they'd go drinking together, went travelling in Europe one summer. The summer after Jim's accident he'd even lived with them for a bit and Sarah had been grateful for it, because by then Louis had started withdrawing into himself, somewhere she couldn't reach. Will always seemed so calm, so thoughtful; she thought he was good for Louis. Someone to listen to him, if he wanted to talk.

Sarah feels another sudden lurch of emotion at the thought of her son, who hasn't spoken to her since Christmas and then only because he was forced to. And, before that, months without any contact at all.

At that moment, when she and Will are staring at each other and smiling, and Sarah is thinking about Louis, and his twenty-first birthday, Sophie appears at her shoulder.

'I need another drink. George is being a twat.'

'Soph,' Sarah says, 'do you remember Will?'

It's quite funny, she thinks, to see it happen in front of her eyes like this. Will's gaze moves from Sarah's face to Sophie's, like a train switching to another track. And Sophie, who had been pulling a face, reacting to whatever crap George has just come out with, visibly straightens and beams.

'Hello, Will,' she purrs, offering him her hand.

'Will is Lorraine and Bill's son. Remember? He's friends with Louis.'

'Of course,' she says, 'how are you?'

Sophie doesn't remember him. Lorraine and Bill aren't really Sophie's type of people: Bill is a mechanic, used to own the garage up the road in Holme, and Lorraine was once Sarah's cleaner, back when she was really busy and didn't have time to do anything but work. She watches as Will tells Sophie where he's been, sees the way her eyes light up.

He's just a boy, she thinks, *but he's not, any more, is he? And he's good-looking, too.*

Sarah leaves them to it. The fact that Will is talking to Sophie, and not to her, is something of a relief.

Aiden

You have spent the past twenty minutes discussing cricket with someone called Ian, who is married to Diana, who seems to lead a hectic life consisting of baking, the library and the church. They're not religious, though, as they've both made a point of saying. They like the church because it's a place that everyone can get together. You don't have to believe in God to go. In fact it's probably easier if you don't.

The evening has been both more informative and more entertaining than you were expecting. You always like meeting groups of people who know each other. It's intriguing, as an outsider, to be able to observe them and see all those things most people miss. The glances, the body language, the rise and fall of the conversation. At first sight, this lot seem entirely at ease with themselves and their environment: a happy group of friends who've known each other years. They think you can't see beneath the smiles and the pink cheeks and the in-jokes to where all their resentments and disappointment swell and fester, but you can. You don't know the nature of them yet, and most of them probably aren't very interesting anyway, but that won't stop you finding out.

You're not in any hurry. Already you can feel yourself fitting in, nestling into the gaps they leave.

Becca and Daniel, inseparable, finishing each other's sentences, are a bit annoying, but the rest of them are fine. Ian seems all right, with his never-ending tales of sporting glories. But then, when you sat down, you noticed that Ian chose to sit as far away from Diana as he could, and that she has noticed the same thing and has not spoken at all since. She is smiling at a story Becca is telling about the local amateur dramatics society, but she is holding herself stiffly, as if she's forgotten what to do with her limbs and doesn't want to get it wrong. Ian has ignored this and carried on talking about the test match. Is he really that callous, or is he just an idiot?

And Sarah's best friend – Sophie – is a different story. She's undeniably attractive, with a lithe grace that makes you think she might have been a model once, or a dancer – and yet she is reserved. Holding back. She doesn't trust you. She is sizing you up, watching you through sleepy, cat-like eyes. You wonder what she thinks of you so far. You have been, of course, on your absolute best behaviour, but that might not make a difference, especially if the look she's giving you means what you think it does.

She has spent a long time at the bar, but now she is back with another two bottles of wine. She holds out a glass for you, not for the first time, but you stop her.

'Driving,' you say. Again.

Her eyes are bright, her cheeks flushed. Something has happened.

'I ordered chips and cheesy chips, and olives and bread,' she announces to the table, then she sits down next to you. 'So, Aiden. Tell me how you and Sarah met?'

You look at Sarah and for a moment your eyes lock. She looks away first. 'Aiden was friends with Jim,' she says. 'We all met at uni. More than twenty years ago.'

Interesting, you think, that Sarah chose to answer the question that Sophie directed at you.

'I seem to remember telling Jim he should steer clear of you,' you say, smiling.

Sarah laughs, which is a relief.

'Doesn't sound as though you were much of a friend,' Sophie comments.

'It wasn't that. I could see he was besotted with her. I just knew I was in danger of losing my best mate, that was all. Of course, Sarah just ended coming out with the two of us all the time, poor thing.'

'Did you manage to control your jealousy?' Sophie asks.

Her question is loaded in every possible way. You give the only answer it's possible to give that retains a grain of truth. 'I had nothing to be jealous of.'

Sophie glances at Sarah and her grin is one of self-satisfaction. It feels as though you've given something away without realising it. She is going to try and stir things up, you can feel it. You are going to have to watch her closely, or try to get on her good side. You could do this, of course. You haven't spoken to George other than that brief introduction, but from the way he's behaving you already know she would stray if she could.

Her type always do.

Turns out that coming back isn't that bad after all. After tonight, it feels like a whole world of possibilities has opened up in front of me.

These women, the two of them; beautiful, hungry for it. I could have either of them, if I wanted to, if I put my mind to it.

Sweet Sarah; I've known her for years, after all. Do I want to go back there again? Maybe not. Things were different back then, weren't they? But she is going to be useful.

Note to self: don't screw things up with her.

And sexy Sophie? She's a player, isn't she? I can tell. But beneath the charm, the smile, the clear eyes, there is something much darker, more intense, waiting for me.

She wants to play.

Sarah

An hour later, the piece of bread Sarah has eaten has done little to soak up the wine she has consumed and she realises, almost with surprise, that she is drunk. She has been listening to George tell the story of the MP who had asked him whether he could claim expenses for his four-berth racing yacht on the grounds that his constituency included three inhabited islands.

Everyone has heard this story, apart from Aiden, who isn't listening.

He is resting his hand palm upwards on her knee, under the table, and she has her fingers curled around his. When did that happen? How long has she been holding his hand? Almost as if he senses her awareness, he gives it a little squeeze and withdraws.

Immediately she feels as if she might have imagined it.

She glances up at him. He is laughing at George, but as she watches he looks across the table to where Sophie is sitting. She follows his gaze unsteadily. Sophie is talking to Will Brewer, who is perched on a low stool, his legs spread, elbows on his knees, all his attention focused on Sophie. She says something and he laughs, sits back, rubs his thumb over his eyebrow. He can't take his eyes off her.

George, thankfully, seems oblivious to it. Not that it should matter, given his history. This time last year, George admitted to a two-year affair with a former model he met at a charity fundraiser. Sophie knows this to be not the only time he has strayed, although it was the first time he admitted it. Just before Christmas, Sophie voiced concern that George was at it again. Nothing has been proven, or admitted. And it's not as if she would do anything with the information anyway, since she has set a precedent of forgiveness and turning a blind eye.

Sarah thinks Sophie deserves better.

She looks back at Aiden. 'Would you mind if we headed back soon?' she asks.

When she gets up to say goodbye to Sophie, Sarah stumbles slightly, corrects herself with a hand on the back of George's chair.

'Come here,' Sophie says, wrapping her in a hug. 'I'm so glad you came.'

'Me too. Thank you for asking me.'

Over Sophie's shoulder, she can see Will waiting for her to let Sophie go again. She closes her eyes. 'I'm drunk,' she says.

'Be careful,' Sophie murmurs.

'I will. Don't worry. Aiden's driving.'

'I know,' she says. 'That's not what I meant.'

Aiden

It's bitterly cold outside in the car park. You support Sarah with your arm around her waist.

She doesn't say anything until you're in the car, strapped in.

'Thank you for not telling Sophie,' she says.

'About what?'

'About you and me. Back in the day.'

The headlights of your car pick out an elderly Jack Russell terrier and his equally elderly owner crossing the entrance to the car park. You wait while the dog crouches for a pee. The old man holds up a hand to say thank you.

'Long time ago,' you say.

'Even so. She thinks Jim and I were some kind of perfect couple, just because –' She stops abruptly.

'Just because what?'

She doesn't finish her sentence. Perhaps she's forgotten what she was going to say.

You pass a motorbike heading in the other direction, but after that you turn right up the hill, and there is not a soul on the road. You think of Jim, and whether the night he crashed was like this.

'Who was that lad that Sophie was talking to?' you ask.

'Will Brewer,' she says. 'He used to hang around with Louis, years ago. I've not seen him since Louis's twenty-first.'

'He's been away?'

'His mum and dad split up. His mum went to Morecambe with his younger sister; his dad went back to Scotland with his older brother. Will got kind of left behind. He's been a bit of a nomad ever since.'

She is gazing out of the window, although what she's looking at you have no idea. It's pitch-black up here, just the car's headlights illuminating the winding lane. You change down a gear as the gradient steepens.

'Is he friends with Sophie?' you ask.

It's the part of the evening that has intrigued you most: the unexpected arrival at their table of the young man, casually dressed in jeans and a checked shirt. You took that in and the rest of it: the wild hair, the beard, the leather bracelets and the silver nose-stud. He wouldn't have looked out of place at a festival, or selling knock-off sunglasses on a beach somewhere. But sitting next to the impeccably dressed Sophie?

'No, they just met,' she says.

You don't say any more. You pull up outside the main house, turn off the engine, sit for a moment. From inside the house, you can hear the dogs' muffled barks. Nothing else.

'You were holding my hand,' she says.

You look at her. She turns her head to face you.

'Yes,' you say.

There is a brief pause.

'You want to come in?'

Sarah

Pushed against the side of the kitchen table, Sarah thinks: *I want to remember this.*

She has forgotten what this hunger feels like. She has forgotten the feel of another person's hands on her skin, being held, gripped by someone stronger than she is, being kissed hard by someone who tastes, faintly, of wine and distant memories. He smells of some aftershave, clean sweat, warm skin. His cheek is abrasive against hers. All of these things are like a whisper of the past coming back through the fog, falling away again.

Her fingers are numbed by the alcohol, clumsy.

'You're sure?' he asks, against her throat.

'Mmm,' she responds, as if she's forgotten how to speak along with everything else.

'Come on, then,' he says, stopping abruptly and leading her by the hand, out of the kitchen.

She catches a glimpse of Tess, watching her. She imagines Tess's expression is vaguely judgemental and this makes her giggle.

'It's cold up here,' he says, in the bedroom. 'Are you cold?'

She shakes her head; she feels hot, peeling off the layers. It's not exactly erotic, but she can't remember how to be alluring. You're supposed to tease, aren't you? It feels a bit late for that. And besides, he's seen it all before.

If she weren't quite so pissed, she thinks, she would be worried about all the bits of her that were firm last time they did this, over twenty years ago, and now aren't: the fact that she has a tummy pouch that held her babies, faded stretch marks, saddlebags.

He does not seem to notice or care – and it's dark, and he is in a hurry, pulling down his jeans and taking hold of her again before he's even got them off properly – is reassuring.

You've drunk enough for this not to matter, she thinks.

He says, again, 'You sure about this?' as if he's expecting her to throw him off suddenly. He is sober, after all.

She feels a surge of something: hunger, frustration, desperation. 'Just fuck me,' she gasps.

He does.

Sarah wakes up and it's still dark.

Her mouth is dry, her tongue like a lump of rubber, because she has been sleeping on her back with her mouth open. Most likely snoring, too, although since there is nobody but the dogs to hear it that doesn't matter.

Aiden, if he was really here, has gone.

She lies still for a moment, thinking about the pub. How much did she drink? It hadn't felt like a lot, at the time, but Sophie kept topping up her glass and telling her it was good that she wasn't driving for a change. And she had been nervous, too, about introducing Aiden to everyone. She needn't have worried, of course. He's such a charmer. Everyone seemed to love him.

She sits on the edge of the bed for a moment before she trusts her legs to support her; goes to the loo and washes her hands, which feel sticky. Then she drinks a whole glass of cold water, straight down, gasping at the end of it. She refills the glass and takes a few sips, turns off the bathroom light and takes the glass back to the bedroom.

The clock tells her that it's half-past three.

Outside, the wind has picked up again and she can hear it buffeting the window. The weather is always noisy up here; even with double glazing, the wind is always pushing against the walls and the glass and trying to get in. It moans and sighs and catches something in the mortar, ending on a tuneless whistle. She settles down again in the warm bed.

She remembers Aiden holding her hand; she doesn't remember going outside. She remembers sitting in the car outside the house, inviting him in. She remembers the feel of him, hard, strong, against her.

He kept asking her if she was sure, didn't he, as if he wanted to back out but wasn't quite brave enough to do it himself.

Shit, she thinks. *I'm never drinking again. I'm not confident. I don't remember how this works.*

Aiden's car is gone when Sarah takes the dogs for a walk. She wonders if he has done a runner – decided against staying after all and gone to London, or to stay with friends, or something. She wouldn't blame him. In the dull, greyish daylight, showered, fully dressed, everything she can remember about last night feels horribly awkward.

For most of the day her brain feels solid, dense, like cream that has been whipped too far; she carries a bottle of water to the studio and sips it as she stares at the illustration she has been working on for *The Candy Cotton Piglet at the Circus*. No animals in her circus, of course, at least, not in the traditional sense. Her acrobats are mice, her ringmaster is an elephant, the clowns are a flock of crazy seagulls. She thinks the seagulls aren't working; considers that they really should be monkeys. But she hates being predictable.

It feels pointless, today. It won't sell.

Eventually she puts the sketch to one side and ends up copying a picture of Louis as a toddler, one of her favourites, in which he's holding up an empty snail shell, his brows drawn together in a frown of scientific discovery. Seconds after the picture was taken, his two-year-old fingers had squeezed a bit too hard and shattered the shell. He'd been inconsolable.

She has a drawer in the studio full of sketches and watercolours of her children, at every age of their lives, some copied from photographs, some from memory.

There are more pictures of Louis than there are of Kitty. It wasn't that she favoured her son, more that his expressions fascinated her: everything about him was curious, open, delighted. Kitty had been much more of a challenge as a small child. She had some delayed speech, and as a result spent much of the time seething with barely repressed fury at being unable to express herself. Tantrums were frequent, often inexplicable, and exhausting. For several months Sarah barely left the house, having spent so much time and energy apologising and eventually not even bothering to do that, so fed-up was she at the looks on people's faces. *Bad mother*, they all thought. *Spoiled her, let her get away with it. Nip it in the bud, that's the way to deal with behavioural issues*. Louis had always loved his sister, from the moment she was born; but even he had seemed baffled as to how to react to the fury.

In the end, staying at home with Kitty had helped where going out had not. In her home environment Kitty was calmer; she had the time and the space to make choices, to get things for herself. And gradually, with the peace and quiet, her speech had developed and the tantrums became less frequent and eventually stopped altogether. But Sarah remembers them well: the stand-offs, the red cheeks, the brows knitted together, bared teeth, screams so ferocious your ears rang with them afterwards.

Strange, then, that it's now Kitty she can turn to; Louis who has stopped communicating.

At lunchtime she tries to call her daughter. She has essay deadlines frequently and Sarah tries hard not to interrupt, but much of every day is spent imagining what she's doing. If she's not in lectures; she'll be in the library, or working in her room. Sarah has left two voicemails since Aiden arrived, and Kitty has done the same.

'Mum! At last. I keep missing you.'

'I know, you've been busy. How's it going?'

Kitty has just started her second term. Since Christmas things have been noticeably better for Kitty, and noticeably worse for Sarah. Last term Kitty had been homesick; she'd phoned almost every day. But by Christmas she had made friends, had joined a film-making club and was writing scripts for them, had started running with another girl from her shared apartment. By January she had been desperate to get back and Sarah, facing the prospect of several months before Kitty was planning to come home again, felt hollow with the loss of her.

'It's good.'

'How's the flat?'

'Oh, it's fine apart from the bloke upstairs with his bloody drum kit. We're all going to talk to him, though; Oscar thinks it's way too loud.'

'Oscar?' This name has cropped up a few times recently, but, if he was bothered by the drumming, it meant he'd spent time at Kitty's flat.

'Yeah,' Kitty says.

Sarah can hear the smile in her voice. Wants to ask, but decides to leave it for now. If there's something to say, Kitty will share it when she's ready. *Change the subject.*

'I've got a new neighbour, by the way.'

'Really? What do you mean?'

Kitty is probably expecting Sarah to tell her that she's adopted a goat to keep the grass down in the field. This has been an ongoing plan which has never quite come to fruition.

'You remember Aiden, Dad's and my friend from uni?'

'Vaguely.'

'He's back in the UK, so he's staying in the cottage for a while.'

And we fucked last night, she almost wants to add, just to make it real. Of course she doesn't want to say this. Kitty doesn't need to know. She'd be horrified.

'Oh,' Kitty says. 'That's nice for you. Is it? I mean, he is all right, is he?'

'Of course. Anyway, I'm not going to see much of him; he's got his own space. I think it's good to have someone nearby, though. It's incredibly quiet without you home.'

'You're kidding! You've got Basil and Tess, and I can't imagine for one minute that Sophie's not round every five minutes. You were always complaining you never got a moment to yourself.'

Sarah laughs. 'I know, I know. How's the workload? Are you exhausted yet?'

Another swift change of subject, neatly done. The next ten minutes is taken up with Kitty listing her responsibilities, reading lists and everything else she's got on – although there still appears to be time in the schedule for nights out.

Sarah feels relieved that she's managed to explain the Aiden situation at last. It's felt odd, having something so dramatic happen to her without having discussed it with her daughter first. It feels as if Kitty is slipping away.

After the call ends, Sarah tries Louis's mobile. There's no reply, and no option to leave a voicemail. Louis conducts his business entirely by email and text, not that he ever replies to her. She sends him a message anyway.

Hope you're OK. Call home if you get a chance. Love Mum xxx

She knows he won't respond. This does not seem to matter as much as usual.

At four, a little past their regular time but she is only just feeling up to it, Sarah feeds the dogs and takes them out to the back field. It's not much of a run but with the aid of a ball she can ensure they get a fair amount of exercise. As usual, Basil chases the ball with manic enthusiasm, as though this is what he was put on the earth to do. Tess steals the ball from Basil when he drops it, then she runs away and abandons it, leaving Basil to complete the cycle and bring it back to Sarah to throw again. It's almost as if Tess enjoys teasing him.

At the top of the field Sarah walks the length of the dry stone wall separating her land from the moor beyond, checking for loose stones when the mood takes her, until it becomes almost too dark to see. The field is too big for her, really. When the weather warms up, George's gardener will come over twice a month with his tractor to cut the grass back and collect it. He charges her £10 for the privilege, and sells the grass on. She should think about letting it out for grazing, but it's nice to be able to walk the dogs up here without worrying about them chasing livestock, or rolling in muck every few paces.

The valley begins to light up as a hundred kettles are boiled for a hundred post-work cups of tea. The cottage is lit. The car is back; perhaps he's going to stay, after all.

She has not been hungry all day but Sarah forces down a piece of toast, listening to the news. She thinks about going back to the studio, although it's raining now; she can hear it against the window. Thinks about ringing Kitty again. What she really wants to do is call Sophie, tell her about Aiden, get it all out there like a proper confession. Is that what it is? Does she need to be cleansed? But Sophie and George have gone to some constituency dinner tonight, planned for months. She won't be home until the early hours.

In the end she runs a bath, hoping that it will make her sleepy, because now she's started thinking about it – Aiden – she can't stop. She undresses slowly, automatically, folding her clothes and putting them on to the chair. As she leans forward and slips off her bra, the soft cotton brushes lightly across her breast, and instantly the exposure reminds her of last night and a rush of liquid heat floods her.

The shock of her arousal is followed within seconds by a dangerous prickling behind her eyelids. She invited him in. She was drunk. She shagged him. He didn't stay. He hasn't come over to see her, hasn't texted, even though he's just a few yards away he might as well be back in Japan, or wherever it was he's been all this time.

She sits up in the bath, sniffing, trying to contain it. Here it comes, the wave of misery; tears pouring from nowhere. She rests her face in hot, wet hands, sobs.

You bastard, she thinks. *I'd forgotten what a shit you are.*

Aiden

There are many things you have resolved in the past week. Your life has changed irrevocably, and at times it's hard to keep up with what's going on. Who you are supposed to be. How you are supposed to behave.

You have resolved that you are not going to tell her. You will not tell her anything. Already this is becoming difficult. You wondered how much Jim had said, and you are certain now that she knows nothing at all about why you left, where you've been, what you've been doing. This gives you all the more reason to keep quiet about it. To say anything now would do no good at all, certainly not for her. It might make you feel better. Briefly.

You have realised that you have no control over your feelings.

You have decided that, perhaps, if things progress you might have to start again: a new life, a new career, something legitimate. It's time to put the past behind you and earn your money doing something that you can actually discuss in polite conversation, even if it's not going to earn you nearly as much. You need help to do this. Sarah Carpenter can help you. She doesn't know this yet.

You have realised that acting all the time is incredibly difficult, and downright exhausting.

You tell yourself that if you act it long enough, it will become a habit and then it will be easy. One day at a time. It's the only way you can do this.

You put on a sweatshirt and head out into the darkness to see if the fresh air might help. It's insanely dark here at night; the nearest street-lights are down in the valley, pinpricks of orange light. Up here there is nothing but the lights shining from Sarah's upstairs windows.

You follow the path round to the garden, up a steep, grassy slope, hoping for some sort of a view of the valley; but when you reach the dry stone wall you nearly fall over it. Looking back, there is nothing but the darkness, the lights in the valley, and the black outline of the house, hunkering down into the hillside.

You are not going to fuck Sarah Carpenter again. It was a mistake; you lost control. That cannot happen. You need her as a friend. You can't expect her to help you if you're going to dick around with her feelings the way you did last time.

A light comes on in one of the windows and you watch as Sarah runs a bath. You stay still, watching, even as she undresses.

You watch her from the darkness of the garden under her window, and you realise that, if the opportunity does arise to fuck her again, you are probably not going to be able to stop yourself.

Part Two

Sarah

Sarah sees Aiden's car parked outside the cottage when she takes the dogs out, first thing. The curtains are closed, the lights are off, but it's still early, not quite seven. All the way up the hill she thinks about whether to knock on the door later, about nine maybe, offer him a coffee. She's got a dentist's appointment at ten, which gives her the perfect excuse to make it quick. Just a little chat to smooth things over, yes?

Look, she can say, *I'd had a bit to drink. Let's pretend it never happened, shall we?*

She practises saying it in her head, brightly, with a smile, because this is what she thinks he probably wants to hear. He regrets it, he must do, otherwise why would he leave her while she was asleep? Why would he not come round the following day, or call or text? It's the sort of fucked-up way men behave, she thinks, or maybe not all men but certainly Aiden – that's how he operates. Why on earth should she have thought he might have grown up a bit in the last twenty-something years?

Tess and Basil have disappeared over the top of the hill. When she gets there the sun bursts through the clouds, bathing the valley in a rich golden light that is so unexpected it takes her breath away. She can see everything, the whole world laid before her: tiny houses, fields, the snaking road with miniature vans and cars and Matchbox-sized lorries trundling away towards York.

I don't need him, she thinks. *I was doing fine before he got here.*

But then, there is the not insignificant matter of the money that was deposited into her bank account the day he arrived: one thousand, six hundred pounds. Needless to say, it has fallen into the pit of her unauthorised overdraft, but it has at least filled it almost to the brim. Next month, she might be able to start paying back some of the money she owes on credit cards.

And it's nice to feel that someone is there, just in case. She promised him that she wouldn't ask him to fix the septic tank, but it's not that she worries about. Sometimes it feels like a long way from the nearest human being, up here. If she screamed, nobody would hear.

This thought makes her laugh; over in the cottage, Aiden probably wouldn't be able to hear her if she screamed anyway.

Best not to start screaming, then; it won't do any good.

Basil is running up the track towards her, something hanging out of the side of his mouth. Tess trots along behind him, grinning in the sure and certain knowledge that he's about to get into trouble and not wanting to miss it.

'Basil! Drop it! Drop!'

He waits until he's close, like the good gundog he thinks he is, sits and deposits the wing and well-rotted carcass of a big black bird, a crow or a rook or something, neatly at her feet. Wagging his tail cheerfully as she retches and turns away.

As she heads back down the hill, stumbling awkwardly because she has put Basil on his lead to stop him going back for his find, Sarah's phone rings. She juggles lead and phone and gives up, unclipping Basil. He's either forgotten or he's desperate to get home, because thankfully he scampers downhill.

'Hiya,' she says. It's Sophie.

'Hey. You free for a coffee later?'

'Love to. What time? I've got the dentist at ten.'

'How about eleven? At Barker's?'

'Super. I'll call if I get held up.'

Basil is already waiting at the back door when she reaches it, his tail half-heartedly wagging in case she's going to give him permission to go back and fetch his prize.

At twenty to ten, breakfasted and ready to go out, Sarah stands at the kitchen sink looking out of the window at the cottage. The curtains are drawn. She thinks about going over there anyway, waking him up – after all, what time is this to be still sleeping? – but if she's going to confront him it would be better if he was at least wide awake, fully dressed and not grumpy.

Better to wait?

Aiden

You're woken up by a knock at the door, loud enough to suggest that the person knocking has been doing it for some time. You look at your watch. It's nearly ten. You get out of bed and walk barefoot to the front door.

It's Sarah's friend, Sophie. The one with the dark hair and the eyes that miss nothing.

'Oh, I'm sorry,' she says brightly. 'Did I get you up?'

'Don't worry,' you say. 'I was working late. Do you want to come in?'

You don't expect her to accept – after all, you're in your boxers and a T-shirt that should really be thrown away – but she smiles and comes in, her heels making an authoritative clatter on the tiled floor.

'Tea?' you offer. 'Or coffee?'

'Coffee would be great,' she says. 'Black, no sugar.'

You fill the kettle and put it on to boil. She probably wasn't expecting instant, but for the moment that's all there is.

'Make yourself at home,' you say. 'I'll be back in a minute.'

Jeans, a clean shirt, socks. Deodorant. At least you feel a little less exposed.

When you come back into the kitchen, Sophie is making the coffee. She is undeniably very attractive – beautiful, in fact. But there is something unspoken between you, and you wonder if it's about to be brought out into the open.

'I thought I'd pop over,' she says, without turning round. 'Sarah's gone to the dentist.'

'Oh,' you say. 'I haven't seen her for a day or so.'

'Really,' she says, putting two mugs down on the kitchen table, without any pretence at surprise. 'How are you settling in?'

'Fine.'

There is a pause. You get some milk from the fridge and add it to your mug. She is sitting at the table now, watching you.

'I feel we might have got off to a rather bad start,' she says candidly.

'Did we?'

'You know we did. And you also know exactly why, so you can stop the act.'

You sit opposite her, your expression neutral. She's right, there's no point pretending. Not when it's just the two of you here, facing each other. Sarah isn't here. If you can't be honest now, when can you? In fact, it's almost a relief.

Sarah

Sarah is so lost in thought that she only realises her name is being called when she is almost back to her car.

'Sarah! Sarah!'

It's Will, calling her name from across the car park. He jogs across to her, which gives her a few moments to arrange her face into an appropriately cheery expression. Across his back a guitar case is slung, which bumps against his backside as he runs.

'I'm sorry,' she says. 'I was miles away.'

'How are you?' he asks. 'I had such a great time the other night.'

In the pub? With all those boring old farts? 'I'm glad,' she says, vaguely. 'I'll tell Sophie; I'm just off to meet her now.'

He gives her a smile that, later, she will think is slightly odd. 'Aye,' he says, 'tell her I said hi. And thanks.'

'Where are you staying?' she asks, and then regrets it immediately.

'Oh, I'm going to be house-sitting for some friends of Sophie's in the village,' he answers. 'They're going on holiday to Paris. So I've got a nice place for a weekend. After that, who knows?'

'And your mum? How's she doing? I meant to ask, the other night.'

The smile slips a little. 'She's doing okay. Last I heard. Emily is in the school band.'

'Ah, what does she play?'

'Trumpet.'

'Takes after her big brother,' Sarah says, looking at the guitar. 'Musical.'

The smile comes back, briefly. 'Yeah. Guess so. I miss her.'

'And your dad? And Robert?'

'Don't hear from them as much, but they're okay. My uncle opened up another garage in Paisley, so my dad's managing that. Robert's moved over there too.'

The wind has picked up while they have been talking, and Sarah can feel the first spots of rain. 'I'd better get going,' she says. 'Nice to bump into you again.'

'I'll see you soon, then,' he says.

She watches him go, jogging across the square towards the Co-op. Waiting, despite the rain that's getting heavier by the moment, because she wants to see Sophie by herself today, doesn't want him gatecrashing this particular get-together.

When he is out of sight, Sarah turns and heads through the little alley that leads to a courtyard containing Barker's Tea Rooms, their favoured daytime meeting place. Sophie is already there, sitting on the dark leather sofas at the back. Sarah unwraps her wool scarf and peels off her jacket, which is wet; hangs it up on the coat rack.

'I got you a tea,' Sophie says, giving her a hug. 'They've got fresh scones if you're peckish. I've just seen them coming out of the oven.'

'I've lost my appetite a bit,' Sarah says.

'Don't tell me,' Sophie says, 'it's Aiden.'

Sarah frowns. 'What makes you say that?' She's right, though, of course. It's either Aiden, or the tail end of her hangover, or Basil's decomposing half-bird.

There is a pause. Sophie stares at her, weighing up her approach. 'Thing is, I thought I recognised him.'

'What?'

'In the pub. He looked familiar.'

Sarah considers this, pouring tea from the pot. It's proper tea, dark, brewed. 'You must be confusing him with someone else,' she says. 'He's got one of those faces.'

'I'm good at remembering people,' Sophie responds, 'you know I am.'

It's true. Sophie never forgets a name, or a face. It's partly what makes her such a great partner for George: she can turn on the charm like a lightbulb, making everyone feel as if they must be incredibly special to be remembered by her, when they only met the once.

'But he's been in Japan,' she says, lamely. She takes a gulp of tea. 'Or somewhere.'

'I remember you telling me that he was abroad. I remember you invited him back for Jim's funeral, didn't you, and he didn't come? But he must have come back for a visit, at least once,' Sophie says.

'Where did you see him?'

'It was a few years ago, in London. It was when I bumped into Jim in town. Do you remember, I told you about it? He was in the restaurant at the Athenaeum. I was meeting Lois Buckingham?'

'Vaguely.'

'Jim was with this guy. I went over and said hello, what a surprise, all of that. And he said he was having lunch with a friend and introduced me to the man he was with. It looked like a business thing, they were in suits – I didn't think any more of it. I didn't pay attention to his friend at all at the time. But it was him. Aiden.'

'When was this?'

'It must have been a couple of months before Jim's accident. It certainly wasn't any longer than that.'

Sarah wants to insist that she's mistaken, that it must have been someone else. Aiden hasn't been back to the UK in years. Why would Jim have met up with him in London and not told her about it? It doesn't make any sense at all.

'Sarah? Are you okay?'

'Yes,' Sarah says. She feels odd, hot. When she puts her teacup down on the table it gives a little rattle.

'I went to see him earlier,' Sophie says, 'when you were at the dentist.'

'What?'

'I told him that I'd recognised him. He didn't deny it. He says he met up with Jim a couple of times a year, sometimes more often.'

'Why – I don't understand. Why wouldn't Jim have told me?'

'I asked him that. He said he didn't know, but he was lying.'

'This is crazy.'

'I know, that's exactly what I thought. I've got some good news, though.'

'What's that?' Sarah says, wondering what on earth's coming next.

'He might be hiding something, and I think you need to be a bit careful with him, but actually I've decided I rather like him.' And she giggles, the good old Sophie giggle that Sarah knows and loves.

'Oh, so you don't think he's a psychopath? That's great.'

'I never thought that. I just didn't know what to make of him, that's all. But now I've had a chance to meet him properly I think he's all right. And you know what else?'

'Go on,' Sarah says.

'He likes you.'

'Well, I should hope so,' she says, 'given that I'm putting a roof over his head.'

'No, I didn't mean like that. He really likes you.'

'Whatever gave you that idea?'

'I asked him.'

'Oh, God! Sophie, you didn't! Please tell me you didn't.' Sarah rests her head in her hands and groans. This is worse than being back at school. 'That's so awkward. He'll think I asked you to say something. After the other night...'

She stops, but Sophie is too quick for her. 'What happened the other night?'

Sarah takes a deep breath. 'After we got back from the pub... I invited him in. I was a bit drunk.'

'You were definitely drunk. So what happened?'

Sarah can't even bear to say it.

Sophie's eyes widen. 'You little saucepot!'

'Oh, don't. It was such a mistake.'

'Why?'

'Because he left before I woke up and I haven't seen him or heard from him since. I think he's avoiding me.'

Sophie chews her lip. 'Maybe he's just been busy.'

'Don't make excuses for him. I told you what he was like when we were at uni. He did the exact same thing: slept with me and then disappeared. But back then it wasn't an issue, because Jim let me cry on his shoulder, and then I got together with him instead. Only now...'

'There's no Jim. And you deserve better.'

Sarah breathes out, pours out the last of her tea. There is a dark film on the surface of it but she needs something to do, something to drink, an opportunity to change the subject.

'I feel like I'm too old for it. Which reminds me – I saw Will. I meant to say... just before I came in here... and he said you've set him up with some house-sitting?'

Sophie doesn't answer, which makes Sarah look up. Her friend's cheeks are flushed under her make-up, her eyes bright.

'What is it?' Sarah asks immediately.

'Oh, God. I don't know where to start. Sarah, please don't breathe a word of this, will you?'

'Of course I won't,' she says. 'You know you can trust me. What is it?'

Sophie leans across the table. 'I snogged him.'

'What?'

'At the pub. After you left.'

'You didn't!'

'I went to the loo and when I got out he was waiting for me, and he took me by the hand and we went outside, out of the back door...'

'Bloody hell.'

'... and round to where the bins were, and I was a bit wobbly and thinking where the fuck are we going, and then he just... well. He kissed me.'

'But George was there! In the pub!'

'I know. But it was... sensational. I've not been kissed like that in decades.'

Sarah stares at Sophie, who has her hand over her mouth, eyes wide, as if she regrets the words that have spilled out and wishes she could put them safely back again.

'And you just called *me* a saucepot! Honestly!'

Then Sophie laughs, and Sarah does, too, and suddenly Aiden not being in contact doesn't seem such a big bloody deal after all. And Sophie, who should know better, has snogged a lad little more than half her age with her husband mere yards away.

'So what happened? Did you say anything?'

'The back door opened and Paul and Amy came out. It was dark; I don't think they saw us. They got in their car and went. But it kind of killed the moment. I wanted to go back inside.'

'And that was it? Just a kiss?'

For a moment Sophie doesn't answer. But Sarah knows her best friend. She immediately thinks that something has happened, that actually she has seen Will since then, done more than kiss him. It crosses her mind that Sophie might even have seen him this morning – that, maybe, Will had just got out of Sophie's car when she saw him in the square. Then she remembers that Sophie was too busy confronting Aiden this morning to be misbehaving somewhere with Will. She is reading too much into it, she thinks. Besides, this is Sophie: Will isn't her type at all, is he? She has sophisticated taste. In fact, Aiden is far more likely to appeal to Sophie than Will.

'Look at us,' Sophie murmurs. 'We're like a pair of bloody teenagers.'

Sarah is about to say something along the lines of how at least *she* is single, bites the words back just in time. But then Sophie says something almost as tactless.

'I'm glad for you, though. It must have been so difficult, after Jim. Three years without sex? I'd just die.'

Now it's Sarah's turn to go quiet. It's not three years, she wants to say. Not quite. And Sophie doesn't need to explain how it feels to be kissed by Will, not to Sarah.

Sex is like a transaction. It's a business arrangement, between two or more individuals who give pleasure and take pleasure and then go their separate ways.

I don't think about it, I just do it when the opportunity presents itself, and afterwards I always wonder about these people who say it's good, that there's a connection, rubbish about souls meeting and setting each other on fire. It's all nonsense. It's an animal thing, designed to stop the species dying out, and anyone who says otherwise is kidding themselves.

It's a surge of endorphins that ends as soon as it begins.

I watch people having sex all the time, and I don't see any evidence of a connection.

But then, it's the same thing with every human interaction, all these little episodes of life that I see through kitchen windows and bathroom windows and at bus stops and in supermarkets; arguments, sympathy, laughter.

We are all just little lost bodies floating in a vast sea, bumping off each other but never quite managing to cling on.

Because, the moment you cling on to someone, you both drown.

I know that. I've seen it.

Sarah

It's just starting to get dark by the time Sarah turns into the driveway. Still early, but the clouds are gathering ominously overhead, blocking the sun and what's left of the winter daylight.

She has delayed going home to give herself time to think. Going on to Thirsk and trailing round the supermarket, then stopping in the town centre for a trawl around the charity shops for something to do, has given her a few clear hours to talk herself round in a circle. Aiden is a grown adult, after all. He can behave in whatever manner he chooses; it doesn't mean she has to fret and feel guilty about what happened.

Just as well, she thinks, that she has composed herself and gathered her thoughts, because, as she parks the car in the open-sided barn opposite the cottage, she notices his front door is open and – damn it, no getting away from it – he is standing in the doorway.

'Hi,' he says, brightly. As if nothing has happened. 'Here, let me give you a hand.'

Before she can respond he has taken the shopping bags from her and is carrying them towards the house. Even this, helpful as it is, makes her cross. She managed to carry everything perfectly well before he got here.

Still, it means she has a hand free to open the door, and it's starting to rain so it's just as well. She shuts the boot of the car and follows him. Having barked at Aiden and inspected him, Basil moves past him to greet her, tail wagging. He turns around again as soon as he feels the rain. *Fair-weather dog*, she thinks.

'Haven't seen you for a while,' she says.

He is unpacking the shopping on to the kitchen table, as if he's trying to help but doesn't want to go as far as trying to guess where everything goes.

'I've been working,' he says, folding up the shopping bags as he empties them. 'Busy couple of days.'

'Tea?' she asks, half-hoping he'll say no.

'Great,' he says. 'Want me to do it?'

'Go on, then.'

She carries on putting things away as he fills the kettle and puts it on to boil, finds mugs. 'I saw Sophie earlier,' she says.

'Yes,' he says, 'she said she was on her way to meet you.'

He's not going to try and wriggle out of it, then. That's something.

'She said she saw you, in London. A few years ago. Meeting Jim.'

'Yes.'

She does not reply. The shopping has been put away. For want of something to do, she gets the biscuit tin down from the cupboard and puts it on the table. The kettle boils and she takes over the tea-making, pouring water into mugs and stirring. He hasn't taken his eyes off her.

'Jim was helping me out,' he says. 'Financially, I mean.'

Sarah puts the two mugs down on the table. Aiden pulls out a chair and sits down. For a moment she stays with her back to the sink, and then she gives in and sits down.

'Why didn't he tell me?' she asks.

'Maybe he thought you wouldn't approve.'

At this Sarah pulls a face. 'Why the hell wouldn't I approve?'

'It wasn't illegal, or anything like that. I don't know why he didn't want to tell you.'

'How much money are we talking about?'

'Ten thousand pounds.' He hesitates, then adds, 'It's all paid back, years ago.'

'A successful venture, then,' Sarah says, raising her mug in a salute. *Ten thousand pounds.* The thought of it makes her feel sick.

'It is.'

'It's still going?'

'I'm still using the profits from that enterprise to fund new ones.'

She wants to ask what the enterprise was, but in that moment she hears a muffled buzzing sound and Aiden pulls a phone out of his back pocket.

He looks at the number. 'I need to take this,' he says. 'Do you mind?'

'Of course not,' she says.

He gets up from the table and goes to the front door, lets himself out and shuts it behind him before he answers. In the silence of the kitchen she can just about hear him, outside, talking. Nothing of what he's saying, just the tone of it, and then a laugh. Her head is fizzing with it. The money, oh, the money. Did he really pay it back? Was that why he hesitated? In any case, it certainly isn't there now. Jim must have invested it in other things, or spent it.

It's only a few minutes later that he comes back inside. 'Sorry about that.'

In a small, quiet voice, she says, 'Jim trusted you.'

'He did.'

'I just wonder why he didn't trust me.'

He doesn't reply for a moment. He finishes his drink instead, as if pondering his next move.

'Don't be too hard on him, Sarah. I think he was just trying to keep us apart. I think he thought I might try and steal you away.'

Sarah snorts at this.

'You think? Like I'm not able to make decisions like that for myself?'

She's cross at the assumption, and it takes her back to the moment when Thursday's hangover was wearing off and she realised that the Aiden she'd been fantasising about all these years was still the lad who'd played her for a fool.

'I'm sorry,' he says. 'I didn't mean to imply that.'

'No, it's fine,' she says.

'You're angry,' he says. 'It's not fine.'

Then she just can't help herself any more. 'I am angry. I'm cross that Jim didn't trust me, and I'm cross that, even though you and I were friends years ago, good friends, and more, you didn't think that it might be something I should know about. And that you wouldn't have told me, even now, if Sophie hadn't recognised you.'

He looks as if he's going to interrupt and disagree with this, but she doesn't give him a chance.

'And as if all that's not bad enough, we slept together on Wednesday night and you left while I was asleep and didn't so much as text me to say hello after that. That's just rude, I think. So you regret it, I don't even care, but if nothing else we are supposed to be friends and it wouldn't have killed you just to say as much to my face instead of leaving me to feel like some slapper you'd picked up for the night in a club.'

Sarah finally runs out of breath, and energy, and anger. She can't bear to look at him. After a moment he places his hand over hers, warm and firm.

'You're right,' he says, quite calmly, 'that it was very rude of me to walk out and leave you like that. But you're wrong if you think I regret what happened.'

'Oh,' she says.

'It feels like something I've waited half my life for.'

Now, finally, she can look at him. Normally so measured, so laid-back as he is, there is something in his eyes she's not seen before. He looks – sad. And then, just as quickly, it's gone.

Sarah watches as he crosses the yard to the cottage and goes inside. At her side, Tess gives out a tiny whine.

'All right, girl, I know.'

She feeds the dogs, and in the thirty seconds it takes them to eat what's in their bowls she has pulled on her boots and her waterproof coat. Having been left on their own for most of the day, they are more than ready to go out, scampering around her feet and nearly knocking her over.

Above her, the hill rises in the gloom, dark clouds scudding across the summit and making her feel giddy. She doesn't fancy being up there today. It's too high, too windy; she feels too fragile. She whistles for the dogs and lets them through the gate to the path that runs around the side of the hill. Overjoyed at this unexpected change to the routine, they race ahead of her, barking.

She doesn't usually come this way. The path crosses a stream about half a mile further on; in summer it's fine, but often in winter the stream becomes a rushing torrent that floods the path. Beyond that, the track opens up into a series of fields in which a variety of livestock are grazed. It means putting the dogs on their leads, something she does rarely these days. But maybe she won't take them that far.

Not for the first time, she wonders whether she has done the right thing by inviting Aiden to stay. It was a foolish thing, a spur-of-the-moment thing. It's the sort of decision she would have made as a twentysomething, ruled by her heart, expecting nothing but the best from people and riding the wave of being young. Aiden's return has made her feel like that again, bursting with possibility and the glorious *what if*, because nothing bad can happen, and, even if it does, well, she'll cope, won't she?

But now the bitter wind is stinging her cheeks, the mud heavy under her boots, making her slip and catch herself: she's not twenty any more. She has a house, and debts, and, while she doesn't need to worry about the children any longer, it's a hard habit to break, worrying.

Aiden gives her a glimpse of the Sarah That Used To Be. Back then, at university, she had a series of half-relationships, friends who came with benefits, friends who were defined by the few things she had in common with them – Cath from her course, Josie from the Art Soc, Leanne and Davy who drank in the Star on Thursdays; and none of that mattered because everyone knew that was how it was; everyone did the same thing. She never gave herself long enough to form any sort of real attachment, and at the same time there was an odd sort of hollowness about it all that seemed like an unconnected thing, a side-effect of being young. But the hollowness swelled like an injury, grew into disgust at herself, and then into a fear, a dull panic that her whole life was going to be defined by a series of failures and false starts, and that, whatever she was going to face, she was going to have to do it on her own.

And then Jim came along, and suddenly it all made sense. She didn't even love him, then. He said to her that he would promise to be there for her forever, and it was the permanence that attracted her. The idea that, whatever lay ahead, she would have Jim.

Now he's gone, and all he's left for her is the house, the debts, and his ex-best friend.

As soon as the sun goes down behind the peaks she turns back, but, even so, it is almost completely dark by the time she heads back down through the field. She wishes she had left some lights on.

'Tess!' she calls. The dog is nowhere to be seen. 'Tess!'

Basil sits in the doorway, tongue lolling. It's not often that Tess is the one being shouted at, and it looks as if he's enjoying it.

Sarah is about to go back up the hill to look when she sees a flash of pale fur and the dog shoots down the hill towards her. Her tail is between her legs. Sarah checks her over for injuries; perhaps she has got caught somewhere. She runs her hand down the dog's back. Tess is trembling.

'What is it, girl? Where did you go?'

Tess gives a barely audible whine.

Sarah looks up towards the hill, which looms up as a dark shape against the lighter black of the evening sky.

'Come on, both of you. Inside.'

She should go and look, but there is something about the darkness, something about Tess's whine and the tremble in her body, that makes Sarah want to be inside, with the door shut behind her.

Sarah has just come back into the kitchen when she hears a noise outside. The dogs hear it too; both of them go to the front door, barking. Basil is wagging his tail.

She opens the door, expecting to see Aiden, but no one is there. Nevertheless Basil and Tess both rush out into the yard and disappear into the shadows. The security light, attached to the side of the workshop, comes on. Sarah thinks it might be a fox, although they do not often appear this far out of the village.

'Hello?' she calls. Just to make sure.

Then she can hear a voice and a man steps out of the shadows near the side of the house, both dogs scampering around him. Tess leaves him and comes back to Sarah, runs into the house.

It's Will.

'Hi!' he calls cheerfully.

'Hello, Will,' Sarah says. 'What are you doing here?'

'Well,' he says, finally pushing Basil out of the way and reaching the door, 'I could say I was passing, but that would be... you know... a bit of a fib.'

'Come in,' she says, because she can't leave him outside on the doorstep, can she?

He is wearing a thin hoodie, and has his guitar slung over his back, along with a rucksack. As he removes the guitar case and then the bag, she gets a sense of the weight of it from the way his arm strains, placing it gently on the floor. Basil sniffs at it hopefully and wags his tail. 'Nothing in there for you, matey,' Will says, rubbing the top of the dog's head. 'Sorry, old lad.'

'Would you like a drink?' Sarah asks. 'Tea?'

'That'd be great, thanks. If you were making one.'

He pulls out a chair and sits at the dining table.

'I thought you were house-sitting?' she asks, because it's patently obvious from the bag that he isn't.

'Ah,' he says, 'I got the dates wrong. Really awkward – it's next weekend, not this weekend.'

'And they can't put you up in the meantime?'

He pulls a face. 'It seems they can't, no.'

She puts a mug on the table in front of him, and he wraps his hands around it. Already Sarah knows where this is heading, and at the same time as trying to fend it off, think of an excuse, she's already feeling sorry for him. He's only a little bit older than Louis, for God's sake. She can't turn him out, can she?

'Have you got nowhere else to go?'

He looks down into his tea forlornly. Doesn't speak.

'Will,' Sarah says, 'look at me.'

He shakes his head, and doesn't look up.

A second later he covers his face with his hands.

'Hey,' she says. 'It's okay.'

Sarah places a comforting hand on his upper arm, waits for him to recover. It takes some minutes. He doesn't make a sound, doesn't look up, but his shoulders tremble. Even through the hoodie he feels cold to the touch.

Eventually he wipes his eyes roughly on his sleeve, breathes in, and presents her with a smile. 'Sorry,' he says. 'Sorry about that.'

'It's okay,' she says again.

'Yeah,' he goes on, brightly, 'so I was wondering whether I could be really cheeky and sleep on your sofa for a couple of nights.'

He doesn't look at her while he asks, as if he is already expecting her to say no.

'I don't have anyone else I can ask,' he says, 'and I know it's a big deal but I know you've got that separate cottage, and I wondered if you might need someone to – you know – keep an eye on it for you?'

She goes to speak, but he hasn't finished.

'I'm good at fixing things, you know – I can do painting, decorating; I can wire up electrics. Whatever you need doing.'

'I know you're good at fixing things,' Sarah says; 'you helped me with the guttering when you stayed here before, remember?'

'Aye, I did,' he says, proudly, as if he'd forgotten.

'But the thing is, Will, I've got a friend staying in the cottage at the moment. You met him, last weekend at the Royal Oak. So it's not free. I'm sorry.'

'Oh, right, I see,' he says, but looks as if he doesn't. A second later he drinks some of his tea and goes to stand up. 'I'll be on my way, then. I don't want to trouble you, Sarah. You know you were always very kind to me.'

'Hang on!' Sarah says. 'You don't need to rush off.'

She doesn't particularly want him staying in the house with her, on her own, but she can't imagine sending him out into the darkness again with nowhere to go. But then, she's not on her own, is she? Aiden is there. He is just a few yards away.

'I can sleep in the workshop,' he suggests. 'I don't mind. I won't disturb anything.'

'Don't be daft,' she says. 'It's not exactly warm out there.'

'I've got my sleeping bag,' he says. 'Seriously, don't worry – anything's better than the bus shelter.'

He says that as though he's done it before. The thought of it makes Sarah want to weep.

'Look,' she says, 'you can have the spare room tonight...'

He looks up, overjoyed, his bright blue eyes shining, 'Serious? Are you serious? Thank you, thank you so much...'

'... but tomorrow we need to find you somewhere better, okay?'

'Aye,' he says, but looks doubtful again.

'We'll worry about that in the morning. Are you hungry?'

He is, of course he is. And he needs a bath. While the oven's warming up, Sarah goes upstairs to put clean sheets on the bed in the spare room, the one at the back of the house. She turns the radiator up while she's in there. Normally she leaves it just about ticking over. Seems little point in keeping the whole house toasty when it's just her here.

When Sarah gets back downstairs Will is asleep, his head resting on his arm. He is breathing deeply. She does not wake him but puts the pot of chicken casserole she had defrosted into the oven to heat through, prepares some vegetables. Even the chopping and the boiling pan don't disturb him. She goes into the living room while the vegetables are cooking, switching on the television. The news is just finishing and the weather report indicates that heavy rain is due overnight. There is a risk of localised flooding. *Not up here*, she thinks, *thank goodness*.

When the oven timer sounds to remind her about the dinner, she goes back into the kitchen. Will is awake now, sitting back in his chair.

'That smells so good,' he says.

She wants to object, reply that it's only chicken, that anything would smell good if you were as hungry as Will clearly is, but instead she smiles and accepts the compliment as it has been given. She fills a plate and puts it in front of him. Then she dishes up her own portion and sits at the table to eat with him. It's nice having company. It does feel a little odd that it's just the two of them, especially after what's happened with Sophie. She wonders whether to bring up the subject, considers that he might be too tired – and too emotional – to talk about her now. It can wait, she thinks. After all, Sophie doesn't even need to know he stayed here. He will probably be gone in the morning, or certainly after the weekend.

'This is great,' Will says. He has nearly finished already.

'You want some more? There's a bit left. Help yourself.'

He gets up from his seat and takes his plate over to the Aga, spooning the last bit of casserole out. The last few mouthfuls he tries not to rush. She watches him while he eats, and when he catches her looking he smiles at her. He really is beautiful, she thinks; it takes her by surprise. Under the tangle of short curls, he has clear skin, and that makes the blue of his eyes even more vivid. A pierced nose – not so common in young men, but not at all effete, because he has a good strong nose that suits a silver stud, and white, even teeth. A beautiful boy, he is.

No wonder Sophie is attracted to him, she thinks. No wonder she was, herself. But she isn't going to think about that right now. She told herself she wasn't going to think about it again.

She doubts that he even remembers.

Sarah stands at the bathroom door with an armful of dirty clothes, while Will sinks into the warm water with a blissful sigh.

'I've put the clean clothes on the dresser there,' she says. 'Just some things of Louis's. They might not fit, but, you know, better than nothing.'

'That's great, thanks,' he says. His eyes are closed.

She turns to go, shuts the door behind her. Well, that was awkward. She had brought the clothes to the bathroom door, suggested he hand the dirty clothes over and swap them. The door was wide open and he'd just stripped off, there and then, before she could even say anything.

Even so, she had tried to avert her eyes as he passed over the pile of clothes with a smile.

Downstairs, she puts Will's clothes in the washing machine with the other things he has dragged out of his rucksack, adds detergent, and sets the machine running. She rinses the dishes and loads the dishwasher, and then sits down.

She needs to clear her head, to think.

A few minutes later, Will comes down the stairs and pads into the living room on socked feet. He is much taller than her son, and the jogging bottoms are a little short, but they will do. His hair is wet but he looks much better, so much more relaxed. 'I was going to offer to make you a cuppa,' he says.

'That's kind. I'm okay, though. You want to make one for yourself?'

He goes through to the kitchen and comes back with a mug of tea and his guitar, sits cross-legged on the sofa with the guitar on his knee.

The memories of it, what happened, surge up inside her, sour like vinegar. She thinks he doesn't remember; he cannot, surely, because if he did it would all be too much to bear; and then he starts to play 'Killing Me Softly' and she realises he does.

Aiden

At five past ten there is a knock at the door; Sarah is there, the wind tugging at her hair and the cardigan she's wearing.

'I'm sorry it's late,' she says.

'Don't worry. Is everything all right? Have you got a visitor?'

You saw him crossing the yard, or, rather, loitering for a while in the barn as if he was trying to pluck up the courage to knock on the door. You watched him for a while, recognising him as the young man who'd been talking to Sophie in the pub. Finally he skirted the yard, keeping close to the wall of the workshop, and knocked on the front door of the house.

'It's only Will. He's kind of homeless. I think he's supposed to be house-sitting for someone in the village, but they've not left for their holiday yet. He didn't have anywhere else to go.'

You pour her a glass of wine without asking if she wants one – it feels too late for tea – and she takes it. She follows you to the living area, sits down with you.

'If you're worried about him being in the house with you, you can send him over here; he can always sleep on the sofa.'

'No, it's fine,' she says. 'I think he's been sleeping rough for a few days. It's only because it's been raining that he came here. His clothes were all damp.'

'You can stay here, if you like,' you say. 'I'll have the sofa. Or I'll go and sleep in the house.'

'It's not that,' she says quickly. 'It's not that I mind. He's stayed over before, lots of times.'

'What, then?'

'Something happened between him and Sophie.'

You wait for her to continue. She is chewing gently on her lower lip, as if she is unsure of what to say. Sarah does not talk about her friends. She does not gossip. Or, at least, she never did when you knew her, all those years ago.

'You know you can tell me, Sarah. Whatever it is. It's just between us.'

'She says she kissed him,' she says. 'After we left the pub, the other night.'

As she says it she looks up at you again and there is something in her eyes, some distant hurt. You wonder about Jim. You wonder whether they went all those years being faithful to each other; whether their marriage was happy. You don't feel you have the right to ask.

'I've never seen her like that,' she says. 'She's normally so measured, so careful. She seemed – I don't know – thrilled by it, I suppose.'

'And you don't approve?'

'It's not that. George is – Christ, I shouldn't be telling you all this; for God's sake don't repeat it – well, he's never been faithful to her. I just didn't think she would do the same to him.'

'You think something else happened?' you say.

'We used to talk about everything,' she says. 'It did feel as though she wasn't telling me the whole story. And I didn't press her. I don't know why I didn't.'

But then she puts a hand to her mouth, her fingers pressing against her lips.

'You do know why,' you say.

'What?'

'You know. You're just not sure you want to tell me.'

She laughs, a short bitter sound. 'Why do you always have to be so bloody perceptive? Are you psychic?'

'Yes,' you say seriously. 'Of course I am. I know you, Sarah. I know everything about you. I know exactly how your mind works.'

She kicks you gently with the toe of her shoe. 'Stop that.'

You laugh to ease the tension. She thinks you're teasing, which is fine with you. The truth is, you do know everything about her. Everything.

'Sorry.'

'That's just it, though. I haven't been honest with her. There's something I should have told her, right at the beginning, and I didn't.'

You wait for her to carry on. This isn't something you can rush.

'I feel embarrassed about it now,' she says. 'But I had a – a thing – with him. Years ago.'

'A thing?' You can't help yourself.

'At Louis's birthday party. His twenty-first. Will was there, and everyone was drunk, I was drunk. It was only a few months after Jim died; I don't know if that's why I behaved the way I did. Everything felt strange back then, as if I wasn't really myself any more. I guess it was – maybe it was part of the grieving, I don't know. I was determined to have a good time if it killed me, for Louis, and I'd managed it until really, really late – most of them had crashed out and I'd woken up a bit, and I went outside to get some fresh air and think, and Will followed me out. We were just talking and laughing, and he rolled a joint and we shared it. And then he played me some tunes on his guitar, out there in the garden with just me and him, and the next thing I knew he was kissing me.'

You don't speak. You wait for her to continue.

'It was just that once. In the morning he did all the washing-up and tidying up downstairs, and then, when all the others who'd slept over got up, they all went down to the village for breakfast and I didn't see him for ages after that. He's never said anything, never made me feel weird about it. It was just one time, and you know what? It felt great. It made me feel as though my life wasn't over.'

There it is. That explains why he looked so comfortable with her, in the pub. That explains the way he was looking at her. You hate that self-assured swagger you see in other men, that triumph, that entitlement. No wonder you took an instant dislike to him.

'You didn't tell Sophie?'

'I was a bit embarrassed. I mean, he's nearly twenty years younger than me, for God's sake... not that Sophie would have cared about that. But I knew, I kind of already knew, that it would just be that once. So there was no point telling her, was there? It was just a moment that I had, and he had, and it was great but that was it.'

'And you think maybe he told her that he'd already slept with you? When they were together?'

'God, I hope not. I can't really ask without telling her everything.'

'And you can't tell her, now?'

'Not if she's fallen for him. If I tell her that I slept with him, it will look as if I'm – I don't know – jealous, or something. And besides, it will probably all burn itself out, won't it?'

There is a long pause. She has finished her wine. You go to top it up but she stops you, her hand over the glass – she is taking it easy tonight. She doesn't want to get drunk with you.

'So now, with him turning up here, do you think he wants – you know? Sorry to put it crudely. You think he wants a rematch?'

She looks up at you. 'I don't think so. It was years ago, and besides, he's interested in Sophie now, not me.'

'Would you, though? If you go back, later, and find him in your bed?'

You're putting words in her mouth now, aren't you? What you want to believe. You don't want to think that maybe, just maybe, she wants to fuck him again, even more than he does her. Because that would hurt. That would cut you deeply.

She shakes her head. You've gone too far; you can see it in her eyes. Something has grazed against her and she is holding herself still, upright.

'I should be getting back,' she says.

You look at her for a long while. It feels like the wrong moment, when you've just pushed her, made her uncomfortable. But you can't help yourself.

'Stay,' you say.

Women are strange creatures.

They are uncomfortable in their own skin, baffled by their own body, never quite happy with what it's doing, as if it is something separate from themselves. They shave and pluck and conceal, diet and tone and sculpt, and all you can think of is the effort it takes, and how, if they put a fraction of that effort into something else, the world would be a different place.

I always think the funniest part of it all is how squeamish they are about being naked. I mean, why? It's just skin. It's just muscle, and fat, and hair. They're so judgemental about themselves, they project it on to other people. Spoils it, every time.

No wonder I can never connect properly with any of them.

Strange, too, when they are supposed to be creative vessels, nurturing, whatever. You'd think they'd be kinder to the body that's designed to procreate.

I don't understand why they do this to themselves, and to us. They demean us just as much, as if our opinions are invalid and not worth their consideration. It's like when you tell them they're beautiful, and they just give you that look like you're taking the piss.

They misjudge me, all of them.

Or perhaps I should say they underestimate me. I should be used to that, by now.

Everyone does it.

Sarah

It's not that she doesn't want to stay. She wants him, and perhaps it's because the conversation about Will and their encounter in the garden, and his reaction to it – was he actually jealous, or did she imagine it? – was strangely arousing.

It's not the way I want it to be, she thinks. His hand is stroking the small of her back. She has never felt anything like it; she can feel it through her whole body, as if there is a collection of nerve-endings there that have never been discovered.

This time, he goes slow.

This time, as if he is aware that she is pretty much sober and therefore might need time to relax, he undresses her piece by piece, paying attention to each new section of her body as it's revealed.

At any moment she could tell him to stop. She thinks this, all the time, wondering if she's going to do it, or if she is actually going to go through with it.

It's not the same as really wanting it but perhaps it's just her mind that isn't sure; her body is certainly responding and there is a tipping point, when his hands, warm and firm, circle her waist and pull her down the bed, closer to him, that she gives in.

He knows what he's doing.

Sarah is ticklish, and often found Jim's gentle touch more distracting than arousing. She likes to be held and touched firmly, and either he knows this – perhaps he even remembers? – or maybe this is just the way he does it. It feels – she searches for the word, in her head – safe.

She likes that he uses a condom.

She likes how it feels when he fills her.

She likes the orgasm that takes her by surprise, and that he lets her pause for breath afterwards and then, without asking, carries on with the same pressure and pace to help her to a second climax, which is longer, more intense.

She likes that he knows when to stop.

She likes that, afterwards, when she is tired and sleepy, he tells her to lie on her front and massages her shoulders and her back, ending it with a long, slow, sensual stroke from her neck to her tailbone that goes on and on until she is almost asleep.

In fact, she must have fallen asleep for a moment, because she opens her eyes and she can tell from the feel of the mattress that he is gone. She lifts her head and she can hear him in the living room, talking to someone.

For a moment Sarah is disorientated, but then she realises he is on the phone. She pulls the covers over herself, turns on to her side, closes her eyes.

I'd like to, yes, definitely... perfect... You know me, I never forget things like that...

When he comes back to bed a few minutes later, she keeps her eyes closed for a moment before she moves and stretches sleepily. She doesn't want him to think she has been eavesdropping.

He kisses her, strokes her cheek.

'I should be getting back,' she says.

'You said that before,' he laughs.

'No, really. I don't want to leave Will in the house on his own.'

Aiden pulls a face but doesn't try to stop her as she gets up and finds her clothes. She thinks, perhaps, that she should say something about what just happened but the words won't come. What were you supposed to say? It's been years since she did this 'new relationship' thing, if that's what it is.

What she wants to say is 'thank you'.

A few minutes later Sarah is crossing the yard and shivering, hoping that the dogs aren't going to bark when she opens the door, and wake up Will. Tess raises her head and wags her tail sleepily when she comes in. Basil, snoring in his bed, doesn't even stir.

The house is quiet.

She stands in the kitchen for a while, listening to the clock ticking, the wind outside. She turns off the lights and puts Will's clothes into the dryer in the utility room. Then she heads upstairs, feeling her way in the dark, trying not to make the stairs creak too much, although chances are Will is so fast asleep nothing will wake him.

At the far end of the corridor, the door to the guest bedroom is closed, no light showing under the door.

Sarah uses the bathroom, washes her hands and cleans her teeth, then goes into her room and shuts the door before turning the bedside light on. The room she sleeps in isn't the master bedroom. It feels too big, too empty these days. The only time she ever uses it is when there are visitors, when she has a houseful. This room is much smaller, too small for a double bed really, but just enough room to have a bedside table and the built-in wardrobe. Also it has a view over the back, the side of the hill rising away from the house, so, when she is in bed and the curtains are open, all she can see is the green of the grass and she feels safe, secure, held by the landscape. On the other side of the house, the master bedroom has a double aspect: the smaller window looking over the yard, then a big window showing the incredible view over the valley. It had been part of the reason why they had bought Four Winds Farm, that view.

She lies in her bed and thinks she can hear a guitar playing softly, somewhere, but then, when she sits up and turns in the darkness to look at the door – as if that will make the sound clearer – all is quiet. She must have imagined it.

It feels weird, knowing that Will is here and nobody else, no Louis, no Kitty. But Aiden is just across the yard; she is safe, safer than she usually is when she is on her own.

The digital clock on the bedside table tells her that it is half-past midnight.

Thinking through the events of the evening, it occurs to her quite suddenly that it's very late to be making a phone call.

It takes her a long time to sleep. So many years, she thinks, wondering about Aiden; so many years with Jim, thinking she was happy when actually he was always second best. Did he know? Was that why he didn't tell her that Aiden came back to England?

Of course it is. She never was very good at hiding her feelings. And now Jim is gone, and what is left is this unending *what if, what if…*

Aiden

You lie awake for a long time. Some time after midnight it starts to rain, gets heavier, the wind racing up from the valley and blowing it against the bedroom window.

You should be feeling relaxed after that, shouldn't you? But you're not. Even while you were watching her, starfished on your bed and flushed, her breathing slowing, you were wondering if she ever came like that with Jim.

You can't help it. Something in you can't leave it alone, picking at the thought like a wound.

And the thought of Sarah alone in her house with a stranger, a lad, with whom she shared a drunken fuck many years ago, is unsettling. You wish she had stayed here, or better still asked you to go and stay with her in the house. You wish she felt comfortable enough with you to ask. But you're not there yet.

It crosses your mind to get dressed, to let yourself in through the back door and check that they are both all right. That they are in separate rooms. That they are asleep.

You listen to the rain.

You feel the anger growing inside you, starting as an itch, spreading into a burn, directionless. You don't even know why you're angry. It's him, the lad, turning up unannounced and landing on his feet; getting her to feed him and wash his grubby clothes and give him a warm bed to sleep in; that he also expects her to want to fuck him too. The arrogance of youth, you think. And then you remember that you turned up here just last week and she offered you the same hospitality. And more.

The more you think about it, the more the parallels emerge. It was a long time ago, longer than the few years since she had her 'special' night with the lad, but you have been there too. You wanted, and got – how did you put it? – a rematch.

Is that why you're so angry about it? Because she doesn't see you as anything special?

But then, the whole thing has taken you by surprise, hasn't it?

This isn't what happens to you when you meet a woman. It's a challenge, an intrigue. You don't get involved. You don't fall for them. You don't think about them, once they've gone. Sometimes – let's face it – you don't even like them, particularly. You're good at hiding that.

And, above all else, you don't need them. You've made mistakes, haven't you? And you've got away with it, so far, until this last time. Someone died, and you just walked away.

Outside, the rain has stopped. You sit up on the edge of the bed. Your phone buzzes with a text message. You ignore it.

You are not going to lose her. You cannot let that happen. Not this time.

Sarah

When Sarah opens her eyes the next morning it is barely light. She can hear Basil's tail thumping against the carpet; she can see a pair of brown eyes staring hopefully into hers, doggy breath wafting across the edge of the bed towards her. He rests his chin on the duvet and licks her hand.

She sits up and turns, looking towards the door, which was closed last night and now is wide open.

She dresses quickly because it is cold in her bedroom. She glances down the corridor to the door at the end, which is still firmly closed. She must have not shut her own door properly after all, she thinks. Or Basil has pushed it wide. She goes downstairs and uses the bathroom next to the utility room so as not to wake Will, then pulls her boots on and her coat, and takes the dogs out. They run off immediately, chasing rabbits and whatever else they can find, sniffing the perimeter of the garden and then out into the field. Heavy rain has fallen again overnight and the ground is boggy with it. The wind has dropped, but it is still blowing from the north and feels icy now. She had hoped to work on some new drawings this morning but it might even be too cold for the workshop.

By the time she gets back to the house her hands are stinging with the cold. In the porch she toes off her boots and hangs up her coat. The dogs follow her as she puts the kettle on to make tea. She wonders if she should cook up some bacon, or sausages, and make him a sandwich. That used to be the trick to get Louis out of bed.

In the end she makes a pot of tea, drinks a mug of it and goes to the utility room to get the clothes out of the dryer.

It's empty.

She goes upstairs. The door at the end of the corridor is wide open now. The bed has been stripped, the sheets and duvet cover neatly folded at the end of the bed. On the bare mattress is a single sheet of paper.

It says, simply:

THANKS AGAIN SEE YOU SOON

And he has scrawled his mobile number beneath it. Sarah sits on the edge of the bed and stores Will's number into her phone.

An hour later, Sarah is in the workshop, tidying up her desk before starting work on the next illustration for *The Candy Cotton Piglet at the Circus*. She has already done nine out of the standard twelve pages of the book, and she has made preliminary sketches for the whole thing. At this stage, the Candy Cotton Piglet usually throws some kind of wobbly and she ends up having to make dramatic changes.

It's hard to keep motivated for this book. After all, no one is waiting for it. The last two books in the series, complete, illustrated and reworked, have not been published. Her agent has tried to place them with various publishers, but, despite the early successes, none of the books she has done since Jim's death have sold. Sadly, the new drawings lack the vibrancy and spirit of the original books in the series, her editor said. Meanwhile, sales of the vibrant, spirited first books have dwindled to almost nothing. No new editions have been suggested following a large quantity of returns after the last one, and it looks likely that they will soon be out of print.

Perhaps you should try something new? her agent ventured. *A new character – something a bit livelier?*

She could do this. But for some reason the Candy Cotton Piglet won't let her. She has tried to draw other creatures – a dog, and, for a while, a hare called Arabella – but each time she ends up coming back to the Piglet and drawing more adventures. She cannot finish anything, now, because if she does she will have to show someone and that will inevitably lead to more rejection. Nothing she does is any good.

And yet, she persists.

The workshop always takes a while to warm up, even though there is an oil-filled radiator in here which is kept on at all times, to prevent the pipes from freezing – not to mention her paints.

Unexpectedly, the sun is shining through the skylights, bright shafts slanting across to the workshop floor. In each of the two rectangles of glorious light, a dog lies sprawled. She stands and stretches. The workshop has a kitchen of sorts, a butler sink in which she cleans her brushes and a work surface that has a kettle and a coffee machine that she doesn't use because it takes an age to build up enough pressure and then produces a single shot of muddy-looking coffee that is never quite hot enough. In the workshop, it's usually tea. She flicks the switch on the kettle and walks the length of the workshop while she is waiting for it to boil.

Her mobile phone rings. Usually if she is working she switches it off, but as she hasn't started yet it trills and starts skipping over the work surface. It's Kitty.

'Hello, beautiful girl! How are you doing?'

'Hi, Mum! I'm all right, how are you?'

'Fine, fine. What are you up to?'

'I'm just walking up to the library, then I'm going to meet up with Oscar and Suze later. Nothing too exciting. What are you doing? Are you working?'

Sarah can hear the sounds of traffic, hopes that her daughter is paying attention when she crosses the road.

'Haven't started yet. So how's Oscar?'

'Oh, he's lovely. I can't wait for you to meet him, Mum.'

Sarah smiles.

'So can I assume from that that Oscar is more than just a friend now?'

'Well... yes, I guess he is.'

'In that case I can't wait to meet him either. When are you coming home?'

'Next weekend, if that's all right? That's what I'm ringing about. Is it okay if I bring Oscar?'

Kitty has a boyfriend. Oscar isn't her first, of course. She had a few boyfriends at school, only one of them lasting longer than a few months.

'Of course,' she says, after a beat. She thinks Kitty is going to ask if Oscar can sleep in her room. She has thought about this before; with Jim gone, she has tried to think ahead, tried to make these decisions in advance.

Jim would have argued that he did not care what Kitty did when she was away from home, but under his roof she should behave appropriately, and that meant separate bedrooms.

Sarah would have replied that they were both adults; Kitty was undoubtedly having sex, and to force them apart at home was to treat her like a child.

Jim would have countered that to agree without even having met this Oscar was a risk; what if he turned out to be a druggie? What if he was bossing her around, jealous, possessive? Would Sarah still be happy to have him sleeping with Kitty under those circumstances?

Sarah argues back that she trusts her daughter to make adult choices. That she needs to make her own mistakes, but that she is, has always been, a child who is wise beyond her years. She cannot see Kitty going out with someone who is jealous and possessive. And if he turns out to be like that, well, then, they will deal with it.

Imaginary Jim falls silent.

When he does this, Sarah feels a little spark of triumph at having outsmarted him, out-argued him, until she remembers that he is dead and she is putting the words in his mouth. Of course she is going to win every argument. Poor Jim, poor dead Jim, does not stand a chance in these discussions any more.

Part Three

What am I, to them? Am I an interloper, or the glue that's holding them together?

Sometimes I look at them with their expensive houses, their shells of respectability, and wonder why I want so badly to be a part of something like that. Sophie with her designer lifestyle, Sarah with her cosy home, built around her like armour-plating.

Is this what being part of a family does to you? Is this what it means to belong?

I wouldn't know, of course. I don't belong anywhere.

I never really had a choice in the matter, of course, and that is always there, that stink that follows me around: being paid off. Being sold like a piece of meat.

Blood on my hands, that's what they say, right? Good job none of them knows about that. None of them knows what they are dealing with.

They don't understand danger because they've never been afraid.

I'll show them what fear feels like.

I will make them feel it and then they will understand.

Aiden

You are in York city centre, in the bar of the Grand Hotel. It's Monday, early afternoon, and the bar is empty apart from an elderly couple and a man in a suit talking loudly into his mobile phone. After five minutes you know everything there is to know about his portfolio, and how fucked it will be if Henry doesn't pull his finger out.

You check your phone for messages. It is already turned to silent but until she turns up you want to keep an eye on it, in case of problems.

You like to be early. It gives you a chance to set up everything you need, to get into the right frame of mind.

The man in the suit gets up to leave, throwing a tenner on to the table and not so much as casting a glance at the woman behind the bar. You give her a sympathetic smile. She looks at you and smiles back.

You think for a moment that she is about to come over and talk to you, but luckily she does not, because in that moment Jane Christie enters and you stand and smile and kiss her on both cheeks.

'Would you like a drink?' you ask.

'Definitely. Do they do cocktails?'

You hand her the cocktail menu, which you have already looked at, trying to guess which one she would go for. You have put a theoretical fiver on the Vesper Martini.

'I'll have a Vesper Martini,' she says, to the waitress who has approached your table.

Jane Christie is not her real name. You have known her for nearly four years, met her maybe a dozen times, and she has no idea that you know this about her.

You know many other things, too, but this is the one that amuses you most of all.

It's only afterwards, when you're heading back to your car, that you think about what it is you're doing here. You've managed to push Sarah to the back of your mind for the past few hours, but the result is that now you can think of nothing but her.

Is this what you really want?

Sarah

Sophie and George live in the Old Rectory. Sarah has always thought this is odd, since the church is right at the far end of the village, half a mile away. The churchyard has sheep grazing in it. This strikes her as odd too, seeing the ragged-looking hill sheep wandering between the gravestones, munching. But the graves are all very old, and it saves the vicar having to spend church funds on employing someone to cut the grass.

Genuine rectory or not, Sarah has always liked Sophie's house. Outside it looks like a typical early Victorian functional building, grey stone walls and a porch, a gravel driveway; inside, it has been designed and decorated up to its rafters. It has even featured in a magazine, one of those ones Sarah thinks exist to make you feel inadequate.

'It's not me, darling,' Sophie has said more than once. 'If it were up to me, I'd be happy in a messy old place with muddy kitchen floors and piles of dust everywhere.'

Sarah doubts this is true, but appreciates the sentiment nevertheless. She parks the car at the top end of the drive where she can be sure not to block in any of George's vehicles. It's been raining most of the weekend, and rather than easing up it seems to be getting heavier again now that she has to get out of the car.

Sophie opens the door of the conservatory, or orangery as George insists on calling it, to save Sarah walking round to the front of the house.

'Do you need a hand?' she calls.

'I can manage,' Sarah answers. 'No point both of us getting wet.'

She is holding two cake carriers stacked on top of each other; the top one holds a chocolate cake; the bottom one is full of cupcakes. She has spent most of the morning baking on Sophie's behalf, for the Women's Institute sale which is taking place tomorrow. Sophie is a member of the WI; Sarah has always managed to avoid it.

'You're a lifesaver,' Sophie says, taking the two plastic containers out of her hands while Sarah wipes her feet and then, to be on the safe side, takes off her trainers.

The kitchen, which is twice the size of Sarah's and a vision of chrome and black granite, smells of fresh coffee. Sophie lifts the lid on the cake box and takes an appreciative sniff. 'Lucky buggers,' she says. 'Can't we just eat it now?'

'Have a cupcake,' Sarah says. 'I did an extra one.'

In the end they share it, half each, cut down the middle with a dinner knife. They take their coffees into the snug at the front of the house where Sophie has lit a fire. Even in here, everything co-ordinates, from the silver-grey sofa to the glass coffee table with art books and unlit candles arranged on the centre of it. But at least it's warm.

'Where's George?' Sarah says.

'Away this week,' Sophie answers, 'thank God.'

'Why?'

'He's being grumpy as anything. No idea why. How's the tenant?'

Sarah swallows the bite of cake she's just taken. It's too sugary, she thinks, wishing she'd gone easy on the icing. This is the WI, not a city bakery – they don't do excess. So much for helping Sophie out: comments will be made.

'I keep missing him,' she says, truthfully. 'He seems to go out a lot.'

'Has he shed any light on the mystery meeting with Jim?' Sophie adds, when Sarah doesn't immediately reply.

There is a little pause. Even right before she opens her mouth, Sarah thinks she isn't going to tell; but this is Sophie, her best friend, and who else can she confide in?

'He says Jim loaned him some money. He says he's paid it back.'

There. She's said it. It feels as though the words are hanging in the air like bubbles; she wishes she could scoop them back in.

Sophie raises an eyebrow. 'And that's why they were meeting?'

'Apparently.'

'And you believe him?'

Sarah thinks for a second. 'I've no reason not to.'

'What did he say the money was for?'

'Funding some projects, when he started up.'

'Hm.' Sophie pulls a face, drinks some of her coffee.

Sarah thinks it would be good to change the subject. 'What's up with George? Do you think he's worried about something?'

Immediately she regrets phrasing her question like that. Last year, when George was confronted by Sophie about his infidelity, the only excuse he could come up with on the spur of the moment was that he was worried about the general election.

Sophie smirks at the thought of it. 'I don't know. I don't even care, to be honest. He's still at least trying to be discreet.'

'Oh, Soph. It's not fair.'

'It's entirely fair. After all, I've not exactly behaved impeccably either,' she says, and gives Sarah a little wink.

Sarah frowns. *Really?* Sophie kissed Will, maybe more than that, but she can't remember anything else...

'You've forgotten Armando.'

Sarah laughs out loud. 'That was different, wasn't it? You just – ' she stops herself, lowers her voice, although there is no one here to overhear ' – you just paid him for a massage, didn't you?'

'And the rest,' Sophie purrs.

'But it wasn't a *relationship*,' Sarah insists. 'You weren't seeing him... were you?'

'No, of course not. It was a transaction. He provides a service – entertaining and diverting as it is – and then goes away again.'

Sophie visits London often, meeting friends, shopping, theatre trips, events with George. She's down there at least twice a month, often staying over. And once or twice that included someone called Armando, who visited her in her hotel room and provided her with a therapeutic sensual massage. Stress-busting, she called it.

'You're not still seeing him, are you?'

'God, no! I couldn't get over the way he kept calling me "baby". Not to mention that fake exotic accent. I think he was from Swindon.'

'I'd forgotten all about him,' Sarah says. 'How strange.'

'It was years ago,' Sophie says. 'Like going to a spa, he said. Not quite the same thing, really.'

Sophie is a veteran spa-goer, an enthusiastic partaker of facials and treatments. Sarah has tried it once or twice, usually using a voucher that had come her way at Christmas, but she has never quite got the point of it. Especially facials: being slathered in five different substances and having them wiped off again has always felt rather odd. And the intimacy of being touched on your face, she thinks, by a complete stranger. It made her feel uncomfortable. Even back massages, nice as they are when you've been working hard, bending over a desk... you have to get dressed again afterwards, oily and relaxed.

She thinks of Aiden, of him stroking her back. The endless patience in the way he touched her. The care he took over it. And then the phone, buzzing in the pocket of his jeans, on the floor.

'You're worried about him,' Sophie says. She sits next to Sarah and puts her arm around her shoulders. 'Come on, my lovely. It's fine. Don't be upset.'

'It's not that,' Sarah breathes, 'it's got nothing to do with me, he can do whatever he wants to. It's just...'

'What?'

'It feels as though he's lying to me about something, and I can't work out what, or why.'

Afterwards, as she is driving slowly back up the hill, Sarah realises she didn't tell Sophie about Will staying on Friday night. Sophie has not mentioned Will either; perhaps he has been forgotten, in which case it's just as well she didn't bring the subject up once again. The wind is fierce, and she can feel the strength of it as she drives out of the village and up the hill, where it is more exposed. The road is full of detritus, washed down the hill by the heavy rain last night, rivulets of water rushing down to the bottom. She slows down as the Land Rover is buffeted on the narrow lane. Where the road bends to the left a figure appears, straddling the narrow ditch, and she brakes abruptly. It is her closest neighbour, Harry Button, apparently wrestling with something heavy. He waves at her and she pulls into their driveway.

The wind snatches the car door out of her hand and flings it open. She climbs down and pushes it shut again. Walking back to Harry, she finds she has to shout to get his attention.

'Bit breezy!'

He doesn't answer but acknowledges her with a nod. He is bent at the waist, struggling to lift what looks like a canvas sandbag.

'Here, let me help.'

'No, no, lass, I can manage.'

He clearly can't. But this is Yorkshire; you don't just take over a man's job.

'Is everything all right? What are you doing?'

'Spring's burst through. Gone under t'wall. Garden's flooding.'

His white hair is blowing all around his face. Sarah finds herself wondering inexplicably if the wind has somehow caused the spring, which flows down the hill all year round, following the ditch by the side of the road, to burst its banks. But she sees quickly that the ditch is clogged with leaves and branches at the sharp bend in the road, and that as a result the water has backed up and flowed through a gap in the dry stone wall.

With a final heave, Harry manages to lift the sandbag against the dip and the rush of water changes course, channelling everything it's got down the hill once more, over the blocked gully and out across the road.

He is in the ditch up to his knees, and, as Sarah stands there on the road, watching helplessly, he loses his balance, wobbles and regains it again. Sarah looks up over the wall to the picture window of Cragside Cottage, where Moira Button is standing watching them both.

'Harry,' Sarah says, 'you'd be better sandbagging the other side of the wall. Come out of the ditch, will you? That'll hold for now. I'll go and get help.'

Harry looks confused, but it's almost with relief that he takes Sarah's offered hand to help him out of the ditch. At the age of eighty-nine, or whatever he is, he is still a tall man, an upright man. His corduroy trousers are soaked beyond the tops of his wellington boots. He can scarcely lift his feet. He holds her shoulder, lifting his feet out of each boot in turn and draining them of muddy water.

'You must be freezing,' Sarah says.

'It i'n't all that bad,' he says, speaking up against the howl of the wind.

Sarah looks up at the scudding grey clouds and wonders when it will snow. The ditch that normally has the spring trickling through the bottom of it is a raging torrent that has crested the bank and is now flowing fast down the road.

'Go inside,' she says. 'You get dried off. I'll go and see if my friend's in.'

She looks at the garden, which has been terraced and therefore does not properly match the slope of the hill. Despite living in such a challenging place for a keen gardener, he has made it a labour of love. Year-round, the lawn is green and carefully weed-free. From here, it looks like a giant brown puddle.

'Aye,' he says. 'Thank you, Sarah. Very grateful to you, for stopping an' all.'

'Don't worry,' she says. 'Your garden's dealt with worse over the years, I'm sure.'

He walks slowly off up the driveway towards the house and Sarah sees Moira move from her position at the window, heading towards the back door. No doubt to make sure Harry doesn't enter until he's stripped off the wet and muddy garments.

Sarah climbs back into the Land Rover and drives another hundred yards up the lane, pulling in through the gate of Four Winds Farm. She drives into the barn, and then heads straight to the cottage. The car is outside, and in the cottage a light is on even though it's barely lunchtime. The clouds are coming over, promising more rain at any moment. If it rains, it seems unlikely that Harry's single sandbag will hold.

'Hi,' Aiden says, opening the door.

'Aiden,' Sarah says, the words snatched from her mouth by the wind, 'do you think you could give me a hand with something? You'll need wellies. And a waterproof. Have you – '

'What's up?' he asks, but he's already pulling on a black ski jacket.

'Have you got boots?'

'No,' he says.

'Come on, I've got a pair of Jim's still.'

Without waiting, she heads to her back door. As she opens it the dogs burst out, chasing each other around the yard, barking. She lets them, concentrating instead on sorting through the tangle of boots in the cupboard. Eventually she finds a matching pair. Aiden is behind her.

'What size are you?'

'Nine-ish.'

'These are a ten; they'll do.'

He kicks his way out of his brown leather boots and wraps his jeans around his calf, before slipping his socked foot into first one wellington boot, and then the other. Sarah hopes no spiders or mice have taken up residence since they were last worn, but it's too late now.

'My neighbour's had a bit of bother with the spring,' Sarah says, calling to the dogs. Tess comes readily enough, but Basil ignores her for a moment, scampering around, pretending to be deaf. 'It's burst through the wall into their garden.'

'Right.'

With both dogs safely inside – she doesn't want them running around on the road – Sarah sets off back down the hill, Aiden by her side. 'They're both in their eighties,' she says. 'Been here all their lives.'

'Are they your nearest neighbours?'

'Only neighbours, until you get down to the village,' she says. They have reached the Buttons' driveway. There is no sign of the elderly couple, which is probably a good thing.

The sandbag, slung against the bottom of the dry stone wall, is holding, but the water is forming a deep reservoir at the top of the spring. At any moment, it will back up to the edge of the dry stone wall and from there it will flow down the Buttons' drive towards the house.

'We need to clear that blockage,' Aiden says, heading towards it. Sarah's hair has escaped from the band holding it back, and she struggles to gather it all up again so that she can see. By the time she has joined Aiden at the bend in the road, he has moved a large branch and a tangle of bramble with his bare hands.

'Christ,' Sarah calls, 'I should have got you some gloves!'

He is extricating himself from the bramble, throwing it on to the road. It starts to tumble down the hill so Sarah catches it, and moves it to the other side of the road.

The rain starts, and as it does so the wind picks up even more, howling and gusting around them, blowing heavy drops of icy water into their faces. Aiden works quickly, straddling the ditch precariously, heaving bundles of dead leaves, litter and twigs out of the way. The water rushes around him.

Briefly, he looks up as he hands Sarah another armful of rubbish. 'You realise,' he shouts with a grin, 'any minute now I'm going to slip and fall in?'

'You'd better not,' Sarah responds. 'You'd likely slide on your arse all the way down the hill to the village.'

'Hold on,' he says, reaching down into the black, swirling water, 'there's something big stuck in here.'

Sarah grasps him by the elbow to counterbalance him while he bends almost double, his arm in the water almost up to the shoulder. She can feel the muscles tense as he pulls and tugs, and then, with a triumphant, 'Aha!' and rushing gurgle of water, he pulls out a black plastic bucket, a big one, missing its handle.

‘That was wedged in there,’ he says, panting with the effort. ‘No wonder it was backing up.’

Already the water level in the ditch is subsiding, the stream flowing fast around the bend in the road. Sarah helps Aiden get out of the ditch and back up on to the road. It is getting dark. Sarah can see the sandbag Harry Button had put against his wall. It is about two feet clear of the water now, and the level is still dropping.

They head back up the hill as quickly as they can. Aiden is soaked to the skin, and shivering. So much for the boots, Sarah thinks. He might as well have gone swimming in it.

Aiden

You have been skiing in Finland and the Alps and you have never in your life experienced cold the way you are now. You sense you are losing focus, although the shivering is at least keeping you from slipping into unconsciousness.

Sarah is talking all the way up the hill, striding at a pace to match your own. You cannot hear her. The wind is blowing what feels like sheet-ice horizontally into your face, making it difficult to see or breathe.

At last you turn into the gate and the wind drops slightly in the shelter of the barn.

'I'd better get changed,' you say lamely.

'Come and have a bath,' she says. 'Warm up properly.'

'No, no,' you respond through chattering teeth, 'shower's fine, honest.'

She laughs, and you think you look a mess, dirty and wet.

'All right, if you're sure. I'll make some soup. Come over, when you're ready?'

You nod and open the door of the cottage, get inside, shut it behind you. The noise of the wind all but disappears, and you're left standing in the hallway of the cottage, your face numb, dripping on to the rug. You strip everything off, there and then, emptying your pockets on to the kitchen worktop. Your skin appears as a mixture of white, bright pink, and bits that have a vaguely blueish tinge. You leave the clothes where they are, the trousers hanging out of Jim's boots, and go straight to the bathroom.

The shower is so hot it stings, but at least it's making you feel alive again. When you've warmed up, and got all the mud off your hands and face, you get dressed in clean jeans. Back in the living room, you're thinking about lighting the fire when there's a knock at the door.

The pile of wet clothes and the muddy boots are still there. You drag the laundry basket over and dump everything but the boots in that. 'Hold on,' you call out. 'Just a sec.'

It's Sarah, of course. Who else would it be? As you open the door and her face drops to your bare chest, your jeans still unbuttoned, you find yourself reacting.

'I'm sorry,' she says.

'Come in,' you say, because the wind is blasting into the cottage and your skin stands up in goosepimples all over again. 'I'm nearly done.'

'I was getting worried; I thought you might have collapsed or something.' She's looking everywhere except at you.

'No, I just spent a while warming up. Have a seat. I'll just be a minute.'

You go into the bedroom and pick out a clean T-shirt and jumper, doing up your jeans with a grin. By the time you get out there, she has put your dirty, wet clothes into the washing machine and is watching them turning in the drum.

'I'm sorry,' she says again, with a short, self-conscious laugh. 'I guess I've been a mum too long. Can't leave a pile of dirty clothes alone.'

'That's okay. Thank you.'

'No, thank you for helping out. I didn't think it would be that much of a drama. I made chicken soup.'

'That was quick.'

'No, no, I made it the other day. Feels as though you need it after an ordeal like that. Do you want to come over?'

Her hair is still damp so she must have showered, too; it's scraped back into a clip. She looks pale.

'Sure,' you say at last.

As you leave the cottage, the Royal Mail van turns into the yard and performs a neat circle in front of you so it's facing the right way to leave. The postwoman gets out and hands Sarah a pile of envelopes, then drives off before you've reached the door of the house. It's stopped raining again but the wind is still howling around the buildings, and you're glad to get into the kitchen and the warmth of the range, the delicious smell of soup and the slight tang of damp dogs. Sarah puts the pile of post on the kitchen table and you sit down. Basil ambles over, leaning against the side of your leg. You rub his head and he lets out a contented sigh. Sarah busies herself pouring soup into two bowls, and cutting thick slices of wholemeal bread from a misshapen loaf.

'So, other than rescuing neighbours, what have you been up to since I last saw you?'

'I met up with Sophie this morning,' she says. 'That's about it.'

She sits opposite you, picking up the pile of post, opening it mechanically, and putting it to one side after barely glancing at it. There is something about the way she is sitting, some tension in her posture, that alerts you. She is uncomfortable about something. Her movement has a deliberate casualness about it, and instantly you find yourself staring at the letters, now discarded and just out of your reach. What is it she doesn't want you to see?

Her cheeks are flushed and she looks miserable now, even though she's chewing on a piece of bread, dipped into the bowl of soup. For a while you watch her while she is deep in thought, while you eat your soup, which is as incredible as you thought it would be. You can feel yourself thawing.

'So how is Sophie?'

'Okay,' she says.

Her hand is on the table in front of you, loosely furled. You notice she doesn't wear her wedding ring. You place your hand over hers, surprised to find it's cold. You close your fingers around it, and she looks up at you in surprise.

'Tell me what you're thinking,' you say.

She starts, and there is the merest flicker of her eyes towards the pile of letters.

'Nothing in particular. Thinking about the laundry.' Her tone is quite sharp, but she's not pulling her hand away.

It's a lie. You let go of her hand, reach for the letters and she doesn't stop you, even though it feels like an intrusion of the very worst kind. You flip through them. They look ordinary enough, official, but the sort of mail everyone gets every day – bills, statements, estate agents' details. She reaches across and takes them from you before you can do more than glance, puts them face down out of reach.

'What is it?'

'It's nothing, really. I mean – I don't need looking after, thank you. I really don't.'

You let go of her hand. 'I wasn't trying to do that. But we're friends, Sarah. You can talk to me if it will help. About whatever it is.'

'I said it's nothing.'

Her look, now, is challenging. Her blue eyes meet yours. You find yourself longing to take her hand again, to ask her when and how she got those walls built up so high that she won't even let you sympathise.

'Anyway,' she says, standing up so suddenly that the chair rocks back against the uneven tiled floor, 'I must be getting on. Glad you're all right, anyway.'

She picks up the two empty soup bowls and clatters them into the sink, her back to you. For a moment you watch her, giving her some space. Then you stand up and go over to her, close behind her, not touching but thinking about it. You close your eyes, thinking about sliding your hand across her bare neck, over her shoulder, then round her waist, pulling her against you. Thinking about kissing the back of her neck. You're lost, for a moment, in some scent that is coming off her, subtle, fresh – maybe it's her shampoo or even, who knows, it might be the washing-up liquid.

When you open your eyes again you realise you can see her reflection in the kitchen window. She's staring at you.

This isn't the right time. You take a step back.

'Thanks for the soup,' you say. 'It was perfect.'

You follow her to the door. Outside the wind is still howling, but the rain is holding off, for now. 'Is it often like this?' you ask.

She pulls her thick cardigan tighter around her chest. 'This is nothing,' she says cheerfully. 'Wait till the temperature drops.'

Sarah

It's none of his business, she thinks. *He has no right to waltz back into my life and take up root in it, and start to interfere.*

She stands, holding on to the sink, looking out over the yard, even though he has long since gone into the cottage and closed the door. The smile has dropped from her face. When she looks down at her hands the knuckles are white.

The letters are still on the kitchen table, unread. Whatever they say, they can wait until teatime when it's going to be too late to do anything, and then she can sleep on it and think about it all tomorrow.

In the past, she would have balked at the notion of not dealing with something financial straight away. She hates debt, hates it. But most debt is like a rising flood, isn't it? Like standing at your back door watching the water rise and creep across your beautiful green lawn. And, when that happens, you go and get the sandbags and move everything upstairs; you act, like Harry Button; you do something to help yourself.

But this – this wasn't a rising floodwater; this was a tsunami. While Jim was in hospital, unconscious, helpless, Sarah had opened the letters addressed to him because she had to, and there she had her first inkling that there were things he had not told her. Bad investments, business loans, all the money from the sale of his internet start-up which she'd thought he had safely stored for their future – not where she thought it was.

Luckily, back then, she'd still had a good income from the first books. That had helped a bit: a bucket to bail herself out for a while. But now – now that nobody seems to like her work any more, her income has all but dried up, and the little that is coming in feels a bit like dabbing a tissue at the waves lapping at the back door.

She should have sold the house as soon as she realised the extent of it, got it over with – at least there wasn't a mortgage. But back then property wasn't selling well, particularly isolated farmhouses with mediocre broadband coverage; and in any case there were Kitty and Louis to consider, and her own sanity. She'd thought she might be able to get a mortgage on the house to cover the debt, but, as a freelancer with no guaranteed income, already in her forties, and with Jim in hospital, none of the banks would offer her anything. And even then, being pragmatic – and naïve – she'd thought that one of two things would happen: either Jim would survive, in which case they'd be able to discuss it, face it together; or he would die, and then there would be life insurance, and that might not be enough to cover it all but it would certainly help.

A tsunami of debt.

No life insurance.

And Sarah, grieving, spent too long ignoring it, and now denial has become an ugly habit that she cannot talk about. Not to Sophie. Certainly not to Aiden.

Before Christmas, she got a couple of the local estate agents to do a market appraisal on the house. The letters they sent are sitting in her ignored pile of mail. The valuations suggest that the proceeds would be enough to cover the debt with some left over; maybe, if she's lucky, to buy one of the modern two-bed flats they're putting up in Thirsk. That's if the house manages to sell. For now she has left it as a last resort.

The only hope for her is to write something brilliant, something that will sell worldwide, garner merchandising deals that will clear the debt and keep her going while she sorts her life out. It's a hope that feels fainter every day, but it drives her back into the workshop and forces her to get her pens out. She has to keep going. There is no other option.

Next morning, Tuesday, Sarah has a meeting with the customer adviser at the bank. They have been asking her for a meeting and she has been putting it off for weeks, keeping them at bay by paying in small amounts when she can – money she gets from Sophie for baking cakes and keeping quiet about it; royalties.

She is there early, as if that might make it better. The woman who calls her in is possibly the same age as Kitty, maybe younger.

'We really want to do everything we can to help,' she says. 'But the situation is getting more serious. We need to look at ways in which you can pay off at least some of the debt, because otherwise it's just going to keep growing.'

Sarah's smile is hurting her cheeks by the time she comes out of the bank. She has a bag full of leaflets about debt consolidation and a number for the Citizens Advice in Thirsk. The woman wanted her to sign up for something there and then, of course, but she thinks she has managed to put her off for a little while thanks to the news that Sarah now has a regular income from a tenant.

For a moment she stands on the pavement, taking deep lungfuls of air. Above the noise of the traffic she can hear music.

Will is standing in the doorway of the wholefood shop that closed down at Christmas, playing his guitar. He is singing too, but she cannot quite make out the song. His guitar case is at his feet, and as she crosses the road towards him she can see coins in it. A bit of silver, some coppers. A man passing him gives the guitar case a soft kick, making the coins jump, and offers some comment.

Will does not look at him.

She puts her hand into her pocket and finds the pound coin she uses for supermarket trolleys, puts it down into his case. He reaches the end of the song and strums a final chord.

'Thought it was you,' she says. 'How are you?'

He is pale under his beard, and his eyes look tired, but he still manages a smile for her. Sarah wonders where he has been sleeping.

'Not bad,' he says. 'I'm sorry I left without saying goodbye the other day. Felt a bit awkward, like.'

'That's okay. Have you got time for a cuppa? I was just going to get one.'

She wasn't, of course; she had been planning to head straight home again. But she can't get over the thought that Will has been sleeping rough somewhere.

'That'd be great, thanks.'

She waits while he packs his guitar away and they go into Della's, a tea room that caters for the tourists for most of the year and is grateful for any winter custom. The tables are tiny, crammed in, and today there are only three other customers. Sarah asks him if he wants a cooked breakfast, and he says he has already eaten, which she assumes is not true. She goes to the counter and orders a pot of tea for two and teacakes, and then sits opposite Will in the window.

'I really fancied a teacake,' she says; 'you'll have one with me, won't you? I'll feel guilty eating on my own.'

'Thanks, yeah,' he says. 'The smell's made me hungry now we're in here.'

He lifts his teacup with both hands. Sarah can't be sure, but it looks as though his hands are shaking.

'I spoke to Louis,' he says, out of nowhere.

'Oh?'

'Aye, I rang him,' Will says.

'How's he doing?'

'Yeah, yeah, he's okay. Seems like he's doing quite well for himself. He was telling me he's got a new contract, some big hotel near Pickering.'

'Who would have thought that salad leaves could turn out to be so profitable, eh?'

Will laughs, and it lights up his face. 'I know! I think he's growing other stuff now, too, not just the leaves.'

Her son, the horticulturist. Louis had dropped out of university after a year that had been ruined by Jim's accident, six months of torture with Jim in hospital in a coma, then his death. Louis had come back to her angry and traumatised, monosyllabic. Eventually he had been offered the tenancy of a patch of land with some polytunnels already in place, and had started growing vegetables for something to do.

'But he's well?' *Did he ask after me?* she wants to ask, as though he's an ex or something.

'Aye. Seems just the same. Quieter, I guess. Didn't say that much.'

Sarah drinks her tea to give herself time to think.

'I'd like to call him,' she says, 'but he doesn't answer when I do ring. I tried going to his flat a few times but he was never there.'

Will lays a hand over hers, gives it a little squeeze. 'He'll come round. He just needs a bit of time.'

'It's been years!'

The teacakes arrive, which gives her a moment to compose herself.

'So,' she says, watching Will tucking into his. He looks hungry, and thin. 'Where have you been staying?'

'I found a B&B,' he says. 'It's okay. It's just for a few days.'

'Have you spoken to Sophie?'

An odd little smile plays across his lips. 'Maybe,' he says, chewing.

'Did you meet her husband at the pub? George, his name is,' Sarah says. Why did she say that? It feels like a cruelty.

'Yeah, I didn't talk to him, though. He's an MP or something? What's he like?'

Sarah wants to say that he's a pompous git who doesn't always treat Sophie well, that he neglects her and cheats on her, but what she actually says is, 'He's okay. He's a good cook.'

That makes Will laugh. He has finished his teacake, wipes his mouth on the napkin.

'You want that other half? I can't manage it,' Sarah says, pushing her plate towards him.

'Only if you're sure,' he says, but he's already picked it up. 'Thanks.'

She watches him eat, thinking of Louis. Wondering if Louis skips meals, if he's warm enough in his flat.

'I really like her,' he says, and she hears it again. Something in his voice. 'She's...'

He hesitates, and Sarah wonders what it is he wants to say, waits. But he doesn't finish.

'She's my best friend,' Sarah says decisively. It sounds like a warning.

'Don't worry,' he says. 'I care about her. And you, of course.' He has finished the second teacake, and the teapot is empty.

Aiden opens the door of the cottage.

'Well, this is an unexpected surprise. Come in.'

Now she's here she feels silly. All the way home, thinking about the bank, and Will and Sophie, she has been holding on to the thought that she can go home and see Aiden. She needs him, she thinks. Needs the distraction.

They are standing in the hallway and she looks across to the open door of the bedroom.

'I needed to see you,' she says.

Aiden gives her a slow smile.

But he gets the message, quicker than some men would. Perhaps women come on to him all the time. She doesn't need to spell it out, which is a relief, because what can she say? *I need you to take my mind off things*?

He walks towards her purposefully and eases her gently backwards until her back is against the wall. He's close and yet still he's looking right at her, right into her soul. She thinks he can see everything; can see right through her. Everything she is ashamed of, every last mistake. Every fantasy.

She waits for him to kiss her but he doesn't move. He's still watching.

Sarah thinks he wants her to say something, to ask for it maybe, to give him permission. She is trying to find the right words because his gaze is intense, curious, analytical. The frustration of it is clutching at her inside, and then, just a second before he kisses her, she sees what it really is.

He is keeping himself under control – right before he lets go.

In the bedroom he helps her undress, then strips off his clothes while she waits for him. The bed is cold and it takes her a moment to relax again. His hands are warm against her skin, and for now he is just holding her. His fingers on her shoulder, and then his lips following them, planting a kiss on her bare skin.

She feels him, hard, against her thigh. She grips him tightly, and he responds with a gasp against her mouth. He moves his fingers across her hip, across her belly, before sliding between her legs. He knows what he is doing, she thinks. There is something deft, expert, confident about the way he does it. She does not need to concentrate or fantasise in order to build her arousal. He is doing it all for her. She gives in, lets him, while he kisses her. For a moment she opens her eyes and is alarmed to see how he is focused on her face, watching her, gauging her reaction to what he's doing. She closes her eyes again quickly.

'Don't think,' he says. 'Just relax. Let me do it.'

'Oh...'

After a while he says, 'I want to see you come.'

And then, almost unexpectedly, she does.

It feels like belonging. That she is able to visit him in this place that was hers and is now his, to walk in here and ask for this. He is familiar and yet different. Just as she was all those years ago, she is attracted to him in a way that is almost visceral. Being with him feels as if she has come full circle, come home.

'Hey,' he says, softly. 'Where did you go, just then?'

He has stopped moving against her and his hand is on her face, stroking one finger down her cheek.

'I was just thinking about... back then. You know.'

Something clouds his face. 'I think about it all the time.' His finger traces a line down her cheek, her hairline, down to where it meets her ear. 'I got everything so wrong.'

'No,' she says softly. 'You didn't. You really didn't – I did. And then you just disappeared...'

'I hated myself for years because of that. I should have been here. If not before, then definitely when he had the accident. That must have been... I can't even imagine.'

'It was all a bit of a blur, to be honest,' she says.

'What happened? Can you talk about it?'

Sarah thinks: she has been asked this so many times that it has become an anecdote, and just for once she wants to remember it properly.

'We were at a party, for New Year. I was supposed to be driving, but when it was time to go I wasn't feeling well – I had a rotten cold – and he said he'd only had a couple, it would be fine. It was only a couple of miles. He was going too fast, and the road was icy; the car skidded and hit the wall at the bottom of the hill. He hit his head. That was all.'

'You weren't hurt?'

'Just bruises.'

He strokes the side of her face, tenderly. 'I'm sorry.'

'I thought he'd be fine. I mean, he'd cut his head, I could see that, but you know, when there's no broken bones, you sort of expect…'

'He never came round?'

'No. It took six months, lots of ups and downs, and then he got pneumonia.'

'How did you manage? With the kids?'

'Kitty was amazing, considering how young she was. She was just so sensible and brave. Louis – he took it really badly. I always felt that he blamed me, because I was supposed to be driving. And he was right – it was my fault. I shouldn't have let Jim drive.'

'Sarah, it was an accident.'

She smiles. 'I know. It took a long time, but I've stopped hating myself. Not sure about Louis, though.'

'I should have come back. Jim – ' he says, and then stops himself.

'Jim what?'

'He'd told me I should stay away. But, once he was gone, I should have come back.'

Sarah looks at him, her heart thumping. She knows this already. In fact, she knows all about it, because she found the evidence in Jim's papers when she was clearing out his desk. But she wants to hear him say it. She wants to hear his side.

'I know,' she says.

'He told you?'

What Jim had told her, of course, was something quite different. *He ran*, Jim said. *He took off, the cowardly bastard. He couldn't face the fact that he'd dumped you… and he should have treated you better than that, and now he's just fucked off and left us both behind.*

And the rest. The litany of Aiden's failures. *Bastard left us both behind. My best mate! I thought he was worth more than that.*

All of it lies, of course. Aiden hadn't run away from anything, had he? They hadn't been in a relationship. He'd had no responsibility towards her whatsoever. Just because her feelings ran much deeper than his, why should she expect him to stay?

He is gazing at her now and she doesn't want this moment to end, doesn't want to spoil it, this intimacy, this connection. She's waited so long for it, longed for it, to be honest about things now can't possibly help. And yet – is it going to remain hanging between them forever?

'He paid you,' she says. 'Didn't he?'

And, from the look in his eyes, she instantly knows that it's true.

'Yes,' he says.

He doesn't apologise, and she doesn't want him to. It doesn't matter now, anyway, does it? At the time – finding the scrap of paper in Jim's things when she had been clearing through it all – she hadn't even been angry about it. Jim was lying unconscious in the hospital; it was just another layer of hurt and betrayal to add to all the other ones. Uncovering all the lies, bit by bit.

'How did you find out?' he asks.

'I found the contract,' she says. 'Or whatever it was. Fairly sure it wouldn't have been legally binding if you were to have challenged it in a court of law.'

She thinks he is going to laugh but he doesn't. 'I can't believe he kept it,' is all he says.

So the friendship that had been so strong in their years at university had fractured at the end of it; many friendships did. Aiden went off overseas, Jim got a job, Sarah got a job;

life started to fall into place. When Aiden didn't come back, Sarah didn't think of it as anything personal. Not for years. Not until she found that stupid bit of paper.

Even the writing was wobbly, although, other than Aiden's scrawled signature, it was still unmistakably Jim's. The paper – the back of a flyer for a band performing in the Union Bar in June 1990 – was crinkled, stained with brown circles from the beer glasses.

I, Aiden Joseph Beck, do solemnly promise to fuck off somewhere and not come back ever and to leave Sarah and Jim in peace.

Signed: A. J. Beck

I, James Carpenter, hereby promise to give Aiden Beck the sum of two thousand pounds to fuck off somewhere and not come back.

Signed: Jim Carpenter

'You know, if I'd thought for one minute that I could have given you a decent life, I would have told him what to do with his money.'

Sarah laughs. 'No, you wouldn't. You were desperate to go off and see the world. You didn't want a relationship with me at all, Aiden, don't pretend now that you did.'

'Is that really what you thought?'

'Of course. You were a complete hedonist. You didn't want to commit to anything. I'm not saying that's a bad thing; I used to envy you. How free you were.'

He is frowning and for a moment she wonders if she has got everything completely wrong, after all.

'I wanted to ask you to come with me, but you'd already decided. I could see it. It wasn't about the money, it was about not hurting you any more.'

'If it wasn't about the money, why did you take it?'

'I spent some of it on the air fare to Thailand,' he says. 'Then I gave a chunk to an orphanage in Phang Nga.'

She almost doesn't believe him, but it doesn't even matter. It's the sort of thing Aiden might do. And in a way she likes the fact that he has stayed away all this time, because her life was good and she hasn't been unhappy through any of it, except for the last three and a half years. And even then, if he had come back after Jim's accident, would she have been ready for all this? Probably not.

But perhaps she is ready now. Kitty and Louis don't really need her any more. Nobody needs her. She is free to do whatever she chooses with her life, and at this moment, this precise moment, she is ready to start again, Aiden is here.

He is kissing her again and brave, grown-up Sarah wants him, badly – not just his fingers and his mouth, skilled as they are, but his hard body and his incredible, complicated mind; everything he has, everything he is. She reaches for one of the condoms he has helpfully left on the bedside table, pleased at her own boldness. When she is done, she straddles him and he smiles, watches her as she impales herself, slowly. She likes the way he looks at her.

She thinks she likes being watched.

I can tell she likes being watched.

She wants an audience, now she's relaxed, now she has finally let go of all the body issues and whatever else it is – the history, the experiences with other people. She's putting on a show for me and that's enough to get me aroused enough to finish, so great and thank you Sarah Carpenter.

One of many I've been watching.

One of many I'm playing with.

Aiden

There is a moment when Sarah falls asleep in your arms. You watch her as she drifts off.

The first time you saw Sarah Lewis was when Jim Carpenter, who had the room next door to yours in the hall of residence and who from day one had been technically your best friend, demanded you go to the second floor of the main library to check her out.

Jim was not the type of person you were accustomed to hanging around with; he was what you'd have called dependable. Went to a local grammar school, his father a history teacher, his mother a logistics entrepreneur. Jim was the eldest of four, the eldest by far. He had been responsible his whole life, and it had made him self-reliant but also just a bit too sure he was always right.

You, on the other hand, were always outgoing. Jim used to say you had the knack of putting anyone at ease – especially the girls.

In reality, looking back, Jim had been good for you. You had been good for each other. He was ballast to your tendency to play too hard; you got him out of the library. He would go along with you to crash parties at the weekend, to gigs, film screenings. A lot of the time he paid, and pretended he would ask for the money back from you later.

So what did he get out of it? Well, Sarah. That's what he got. Because you were the one who got the girls, not him. You were the one with the winning looks, the twinkle in the eyes, the confidence and the charm, the way with words. And Jim tagged along, happily joining in once you'd done the groundwork. After only a couple of weeks, you'd established some sort of team protocol.

That was when he first caught sight of Sarah.

He sent you up to the second floor of the library. He described where she was sitting, taking notes from a whole series of books. She had blonde hair, he said. Petite.

Of course, as soon as you saw her you knew. The desk light was making a halo of her hair, making her skin glow. She was the most beautiful person you had ever seen.

As was the plan, you went up to her and introduced yourself. From her friendly smile and the way she leaned back in her chair and stretched, you correctly surmised that she was tired and bored with reading. You asked what she was working on, she tried to describe the essay she was trying to get her head around – history of art – and after less than five minutes you'd asked if she wanted to come to a gig with you and your mate tomorrow. She said yes, asked if she could bring her flatmate, Helen. You said yes. You took her number, offered to meet them at the pub on the corner.

And then you left her to it. Walked away with your cheeks burning, trying to arrange your face into a neutral expression before Jim twigged what had happened to you.

'Well?'

'She's coming to the gig. We can meet her at the pub at half-seven tomorrow. She's bringing her friend Helen. I got her number.'

'Fantastic!'

Helen had turned out to be a livewire, a girl with long, dyed black hair and piercings. She was a good laugh, and Sarah was too, and, while you tried really hard to see her as the one Jim fancied, and therefore off-limits, she wasn't the sort of girl who saw herself as belonging to anyone.

For a long time she resisted Jim's attempts to get her to commit. She worked hard, though, she was serious, and Jim's affection for her seemed to be solid whether she was willing to go out, or whether she was insisting on staying in to work.

She's right, of course: you weren't ready for a relationship back then. Who knows if you are now? You are not even sure if you know how to accomplish such a thing. Monogamy has always felt like something done by other people, for no other reason than to make them feel virtuous.

It comes as something of a relief that she doesn't seem bothered about it now, either. You have noticed that she hasn't asked you any more questions about your job. Perhaps she's got over it.

Sarah moves, and breathes, and turns over in bed, turning her back on you. You take the opportunity to ease your arm from under her neck. For several moments you lie still, thinking of Sarah, and Helen, and Jim. You wonder where Helen is now, whether Sarah is still in touch with her.

Helen.

There was another Helen, years later. Helen who told you everything about her life, none of it true. She wasn't a business executive; she was a head teacher. She wasn't single; she was married. She wasn't even from Brighton; she was from Camberwell, not that it should have mattered. None of that usually does; it's all just conversation, time-wasting. The important things, like the sweet spot on the inside of her thigh that made her gasp when you stroked her there – all of that at least you knew to be real. But Helen was complicated, wasn't she? Orgasms without penetration were frustrating her, she said. She was insistent about exactly what it was she needed – sex – and you resisted it for a long time.

You should have listened to your instincts, but in the end you gave in.

And a week later she told you the truth, all of it, looking at you with shining eyes and then seconds later adding that she was leaving her husband for you, that she'd already told him all about you and that her car was outside with her suitcase in it.

Five days later, she had died from an overdose in the bathroom of her three-bed semi and her husband was trying to find you with the intention of removing your head and other extremities, and you were driving north to self-imposed exile in Yorkshire.

You sit up, slowly, find your clothes and dress. In the kitchen you make tea, and a few minutes later she emerges from the bedroom, her hair a cloud of fine gold.

She smiles.

'I'm sorry I fell asleep,' she says. 'How rude of me.'

'Not at all,' you say. 'It wasn't for long. Want some tea?'

'No,' she says, 'I need to get back. The dogs will want to go out. Thank you, though.'

'Have a cup of tea at least,' you say. 'Don't rush off.'

Just for a change the sun is shining, setting over the valley and flooding the living room with golden late afternoon light. Even so, the wind is blowing fiercely outside.

'Kitty is coming home at the weekend,' she says.

'That's good to hear. You must miss her.'

'I do.'

'I'll keep out of your way,' you say.

'Oh, please don't. I'd love you to meet Kitty. Besides, she's bringing her new boyfriend. I don't want to spend the whole weekend being a gooseberry.'

'Ah, that's it. You're just using me again. First it's sex; now you want an excuse to escape.'

She smiles, but her cheeks are pink.

'That was out of order,' you say. 'Sorry.'

'Is it a bad thing?'

You know what it is she means; she doesn't have to say it.

'Of course not. Unless it makes you unhappy.'

'I thought it was going to, but actually there's so much else going on, it seems like a small thing in comparison.'

Your phone vibrates in your back pocket. You should have turned it to silent, as you usually would when you were with someone, but Sarah took you by surprise.

'I'm sorry,' you say.

'Don't worry,' she says, standing up. 'I need to get back.'

She shuts the door behind her, just as you swipe to accept the call.

'Hello, beautiful,' you say. 'Long time no speak.'

Sarah

It's almost dark by the time Sarah gets back from walking the dogs. She has been thinking about the bank, about the option to consolidate the debt, and she has decided to go ahead.

It's a strange sort of arrangement she has with Aiden but she thinks that she trusts him. Something has changed with their dynamic; what she feels for him now is not that girlish infatuation that has kept her fantasies going intermittently over the years. There is a mutual sexual attraction, perhaps the same as there always was between them, and behind that is a framework based upon mutual respect and friendship. All those years ago she would have called him a friend with benefits, although that phrase didn't exist then, she's fairly sure; but, whatever it was, it worked.

Why had she been so upset, then, when he had not called her that last time? Was it because of Jim, telling her she deserved better?

She is standing at the top of the field, looking down over the croft, the house, the valley beyond. The sun has set and the temperature is dropping, a chill spreading up her body from the cold, wet ground.

Where Jim is concerned, she feels as if the foundations have been constantly shifting without her fully realising it. The money; the way he treated Aiden, his own best friend.

It's as though she has spent her lifetime at sea, and has only recently, now that Aiden is back, learned what solid ground feels like.

She is making a sandwich for her supper while the dogs eat their dinner noisily in the corner. She's just sitting down to eat when there is a single knock at the door, and then it opens and in comes Sophie.

'Hello,' Sarah says, as Sophie unpeels her winter coat, takes off the thick scarf and pulls off the woollen hat. From under it, her hair falls down into a dark, shiny wave.

'You don't mind me calling in? I should have come earlier – I meant to. Sorry.'

'Not at all. I'm pleased to see you. Would you like a sandwich?'

'No, thanks, love. I'm eating later. I just wanted to say we made nearly forty quid at the bake sale.'

'That's great news!'

Sophie does what she always does, almost through force of habit: gets two glasses down from the cupboard, fetches the corkscrew from the drawer, and looks in the fridge for a bottle. 'You need topping up, darling,' Sophie remarks, nudging the fridge door closed with her backside. 'I'll bring you a selection next time, shall I?'

'You don't need to do that,' Sarah says.

'It's me that drinks it all,' Sophie says. 'So it's only fair for me to top it up again.'

'How about tea?'

Sarah pours two mugfuls from the pot she made twenty minutes ago. It's a bit stewed, but it will do.

'So how's George?' she asks gently.

Sophie drinks and wraps her fingers around the mug thoughtfully. 'Honestly? Okay, then. He's sullen, childish, rude, ungrateful and charmless. And drinking far too much. How's that for starters?'

Sarah eats the last of the sandwich and pushes her plate to one side. 'Isn't he always a bit like that?'

This, at least, makes Sophie smile. 'It's got worse.'

'Why?'

Sophie pulls a face. 'I don't know. I'm sick of it, to be honest. He's away tonight, and then most of the weekend on a golfing thing. But it's fine. I'm almost past caring what he does.'

'I saw Will today,' Sarah says, watching her friend's face.

The shutters have gone up, but they have been inexpertly constructed. 'Oh?'

'It's none of my business,' Sarah says. 'But he seems... very keen.'

Sophie breathes out. 'He is. You're right.'

'So you're seeing him?'

'I wouldn't put it quite like that.' Sophie sighs and stirs her tea. There is a scum on it, brown shapes shifting like tectonic plates. She drinks it anyway.

'I'm not judging. God knows you've been through enough with George. Does this feel serious?'

Sophie is thinking about it, weighing up her response. After a moment she says, 'I'm not sure. It's – he's refreshing, you know? He's gorgeous, and hungry, and full of life and spirit and adventure. He's making me feel as though I've just woken up.'

'Wow,' Sarah says.

For the first time in several minutes Sophie looks up and catches Sarah's eye, and it's as if a light has been switched on in there. She smiles and it's almost erotic, the charge that's coming off her. 'I know it's almost funny,' she says, 'but for the first time I can really see why George does it.'

'Are you going to tell him?'

Sophie frowns a little as if this is a crazy thing to suggest, but then the idea sinks in and she can see the logic behind it. 'I might,' she says. 'I don't want to hurt the poor old bugger, but really I wish he'd just been honest with me about his affairs, if he absolutely had to have them. It's all the suspicion and the lies that hurt, worse than the act itself. He always seems to come back home, dirty old stray cat. He's not going to leave me. I'm not going to leave him. It feels like the adult way to behave, to just tell him what's going on.'

'How do you think he'd take it?' Sarah asks.

Sophie barks a laugh. 'He'd go fucking insane, probably. Storm around and shout a lot, then he'd probably sink half a bottle of single malt and take me to bed to remind me how it's done.'

Sarah puts the kettle on to make a fresh pot of tea.

'Tell me how the kids are,' Sophie says. 'How's Kitty getting on with Oscar?'

'She seems all right,' Sarah says. 'Some lad upstairs has bought himself a drum kit. That has kind of brought out her militant streak; there's a bunch of them trying to persuade him to follow a strict schedule for his practices, if he has to do it at all. She's coming home at the weekend; you can ask her yourself. Want to come over for a meal?'

'I love Kitty's militant streak,' Sophie says. 'She's so fierce.'

Just as the kettle boils, there is a sudden sharp knock and the door opens. It's Harry Button.

'All right, Harry?' Sarah says. People do not necessarily wait to be invited in round here; at least partly because the chances are high that the house occupant might be 'out back' or even not at home at all. Sarah has lived here for most of her adult life and still hasn't really got the hang of walking into other people's houses. 'Come in, have a seat.'

'Hello, Harry,' says Sophie.

'All right, lass?'

'How's it going?' Sarah asks.

'I'll not stop long,' he says, easing himself slowly into one of the kitchen chairs. 'I just came to say that spring's proper gone down now.'

'Oh,' Sarah says, 'that's good to hear.'

'So you and your friend, like, well we're very grateful. Moira sends you all her thanks too; she's cooking you summat. Says she'll bring it over tomorrow.'

'That's very kind of you, but there's no need, really.'

Harry stares at her for a moment. 'Well, we're both right thankful to you.'

'Let me know if it builds up again.'

'Have I missed something exciting?' Sophie asks.

'There was a blockage in the ditch yesterday, with all that rain,' Sarah says. 'Just needed a load of weeds and rubbish pulling out, but the water was going all over Harry's beautiful garden.'

'Aye,' Harry says. 'It were a right mess. But you sorted it all out, like I said. Very good of you.'

Sophie checks her watch, squeals abruptly and gets to her feet. 'I must dash,' she says.

The three of them head over to the doorway. Harry gets there first.

'Love to Moira,' Sarah says, as the old man ambles off down the driveway, his boots shuffling against the cobbles. The wind has dropped. In the yard, for a change, it's quiet and still. The clouds are patchy and the moon is shining brightly, showing Sophie's blue Audi parked at a nonchalant angle.

'I'll call you,' Sophie says. 'Let's have lunch, shall we?'

'That would be wonderful.'

Sarah watches her climb into the car, grateful for once that her friend will be driving down the hill with nothing inside her but tea. It's only when the tail-lights disappear around the corner that Sarah realises she didn't answer the question about coming over when Kitty's here. She'll want to see her: Kitty is one of Sophie's favourite people. No matter – they will see each other before the weekend, and Sarah will ask again. Saturday night, she thinks. Or maybe Sunday: she will do a roast.

Busy tonight, over at Four Winds Farm.

Lots of people coming and going.

Sophie and Sarah in the kitchen, gossiping over a teapot, although I'm willing to bet Sophie would rather have wine. She's drunk it all, probably. Drunk her way through Sarah's wine cellar and now Sarah doesn't have the money to buy any more. Not that she's told Sophie. She's ashamed of it, being up to her neck in debt, otherwise she'd have asked her for help and probably got it.

She doesn't like to borrow money from her friends – shame she has to keep borrowing it from the bank, isn't it? All those letters, piled up on the kitchen table and ignored. Naughty Sarah.

And how it must bother her, when Sophie is loaded. It must itch every time they see each other, every time she sees the latest designer thing Sophie's wearing, the new car every six months, the holidays booked.

She thinks Sophie doesn't realise, which is what makes it funny. Sophie is no fool; she thinks she's helping, asking Sarah to bake her cakes and not let on to the WI. Giving her cash, as if it's some legitimate business.

They dance around each other with their secrets, their pretences, their games.

And, after Sophie, there's the old man from down the hill, come to say hello.

He's not going to stay long.

But it's all right; they're all on their feet, coming out. Sarah waving to Sophie as she gets in the car.

Hurry up, Sophie.

You're late.

Sarah

After Sophie leaves, Sarah takes the dogs out up to the field but quickly regrets it; the rain starts off as drizzle and a few minutes later is needling into her cheeks, carried on an icy wind. By the time she is halfway up the hill the wind is strong enough to make her lose her balance on the tussocky grass. The dogs slink around the edge of the field, keeping to the shelter of the wall; they do their business quickly and Basil starts heading back down towards the house. The driving rain becomes sleety and quickly gives way to snow; the wind tugs at her waterproof hood and the flaps of her jacket. Her waterproof trousers whip around her legs.

When she calls to Tess, her voice is snatched away and disappears so quickly that it is as if she never opened her mouth.

'Tess!' she tries again, louder this time, holding a hand up to her eyes to shield them from the needle-like snow.

There is no sign of the dog.

'Tess! Where are you?'

She looks down the hill to where Basil is crouching against the side of the back porch, waiting for her to get back. She half-expects Tess is down there somewhere too, so she heads down the hill. It is getting slippery; the snow is coming down in earnest now, turning the grass tussocks white and making every step awkward and hazardous.

Back at the house, there is no sign of the dog. Sarah lets Basil into the utility room, rubs him down roughly with the towel, and shuts him in there. Outside, the wind blasts at

Sarah the second she steps out from the shelter of the wall. She heads up the garden, keeping close to the low wall as she can.

'Tess!'

The wind moans. She strains to listen, thinks she can hear something else above the noise of the wind: howling?

She continues up the hill, turning her head into the wind, seeing nothing but her wellies trudging through the wet white snow. After another twenty steps she stops, turns, shouts again. This time she hears something – a bark, from behind her, higher up the hill.

'Tess! Where are you, you bloody dog?'

Another fifty paces and she hears it again, barking, each sound carried away on the wind. Out of the darkness a white shape looms up ahead. It's the croft, the half-derelict shepherd's shack. The door, which is usually half hanging off its hinges, is shut, and the snow is piling up against it.

'Tess?'

Another bark, louder this time.

Sarah reaches the croft and pushes at the door. It's jammed, warped from years of rain, and for some reason it has slammed shut. Sarah pushes harder, feels it give slightly. The wood creaks under her gloved hand. From behind the door, frantic barking. This time she uses her shoulder, one big shove, and the door bursts open, slamming back on itself.

Sarah is propelled into the dark space, sprawls across the floor. Her shoulder bashes into something solid and she feels a burst of pain.

Tess bounces around her, barking, stopping to lick her face, barking again.

'Christ, Tess! How did you get in here?

The door is pushing against her foot, already trying to slam itself shut. The croft is small, two tiny rooms, and the roof is caving in in places. When they moved into Four Winds

Farm, Sarah and Jim had talked about renovating it, making it into a summer house or a log store, but in fact this far up the hill it's too far away to be of any real use. A few items of furniture ended up here, an old kitchen table, a chest of drawers – against which Sarah has fallen – but as her eyes grow accustomed to the darkness Sarah realises there are other things here too. The fireplace has ashes in it, as though someone has built a fire. And a piece of plywood has been fixed, somehow, across the small broken window. In the corner, under the table, is an old dirty mattress and a sleeping bag. Next to it is a blue plastic plate and a flask. Sticking out from the bottom of the mattress is a newspaper and a magazine. Sarah reaches for them, pulls them free. It is too dark to see any of the text.

Tess is sitting in the doorway, looking anxiously from Sarah to the hill outside, back to Sarah again. When she gets to her feet, Tess starts barking again. She is looking into the darkness of the croft, baring her teeth, growling.

Sarah is jolted by a sudden fear that she is not alone. She looks behind her into the room, at the closed door that leads to the second room.

'Tess? What is it, girl?'

Tess jumps, paws braced against the stone slabs. There is nothing in the room, nothing other than a faint bad smell – rotting food, damp clothes – and surely nobody could be in here? It's freezing, bitterly cold. But then, there is the second door. Closed.

Sarah decides she is safe with Tess here, and walks the few paces to the door. Tess follows her but is going mad, barking and jumping in circles, and as Sarah approaches the door the dog jumps at it.

'All right, girl. It's all right! Tess, down!'

Hand on the door handle, Sarah's bravery falters. 'Anyone in there?' she shouts. 'I'm coming in with the dog.'

She pushes open the door.

Even in the darkness, Sarah can tell the room is empty. Tess runs in, races around it once, whines, scratches at the floor behind the door. It must have been a rat, a rabbit or something. Now that she thinks about it, maybe that's what the smell is – fox or rabbit wee.

Behind her, the main door to the croft crashes shut again without her foot to hold it open, and she is plunged into complete, icy darkness.

It feels, just for a moment, like drowning. Sarah has to remind herself to breathe, as she feels around the walls, knocks against the chest of drawers and kicks the plastic plate away with a clatter. She can hear something – breathing, a snuffling – and something brushes against her leg. Panic grips her for a second until she hears a whine and remembers Tess. And then she finds the door. She tugs at it but once again the wood has scraped tightly against the doorframe and it's stuck. She yanks at it, her shoulder hurting, terror making her strong, until it jerks free and she is out in the howling wind and the swirling snow once more.

'Tess! Come *on*!'

The dog casts one last anxious look into the darkness and runs off down the hill. Sarah lets go of the door and the wind snatches it away, slamming it shut again.

She half-runs, half-falls back down the hill, slipping at least twice. The snow is so fierce now she can hardly see. Eventually she reaches the back porch, heaves the door open against the snow which is drifting against it, and stumbles inside. Tess follows, still turning in mad circles and barking. She pushes the door shut behind her and the noise of the wind suddenly dies.

'Tess, for God's sake, shut up!'

Basil is whining, crouched against the door to the hallway. Sarah catches Tess by the collar and drapes her in the towel, rubbing her as dry as possible. Through her thick fur Sarah can feel that she is trembling. She opens the door and Basil rushes off, presumably to sit in front of the Aga. Tess doesn't move. She sits by the back door, looking up at it intently while Sarah peels off her sodden coat and pulls her frozen feet out of her wellies, as if at any moment the dog is expecting the door to open and someone to walk in.

That night Sarah sleeps fitfully and wakes again before dawn. She lies in the dark listening to the house, wondering what has woken her. There is nothing, no sound; but now she is awake her brain has started fretting about the stresses that will form the shape of her day.

She must phone the bank. She cannot put it off any longer.

The snow has gone, except for a few sparkling patches on the summit of the hills; it's a beautiful day, bright, chilly, full of promise. By nine she has walked the dogs, made toast and coffee and is in the studio, thinking about starting work. It's cold in here despite the heater. Once upon a time this was Jim's workshop, the place where he pottered and tinkered and hoarded power tools. He had cabinets on the walls with hooks holding hand tools, pencilled outlines so that if something was missing he would know what it was; a red tool chest containing spanner sets, plastic tubs with spares and broken things, a collection from a lifetime of keeping things that might one day be fixable or usable. When he died she spent one fraught weekend clearing it out, stowing the red chest out of sight in the barn, putting pictures of all the power tools up online and not paying much attention to how much money they sold for. She regrets that now. He must have spent thousands accruing it all; when it was empty she was barely eight hundred pounds better off.

She had wanted it all gone. There was so much to do and everything around her had reminded her of Jim. She wanted to remember, but, if there was a fresh start to be had, she wanted it to start now. By that time, she had had a growing awareness of the financial problems and, despite knowing that it came from Jim's attempts to keep his business afloat – loans taken out against other loans, contracts fulfilled at a loss to keep clients happy – she was angry at it, at him, at the idea of his spending money on power tools he was never going to use, and, worst of all, at his not having given her the slightest hint of the spiral of debt he had let them all be sucked into.

Louis had seethed at the clearout. Kitty had been gentle, tearful at times, begging her not to be too hasty. Sarah has often thought that she should have just been honest with them about the money; but back then she was anxious to preserve the memories they had of their dad, happy ones. And she'd thought she was being careful about what she was expunging from the house – nothing personal, nothing with specific memories attached, at least not at that early stage. But what was left behind was more about her than it was about Jim; the essence of him, his clothes, the things he touched, were all disposed of. He wasn't the type of man to leave notes, and he was more often the one taking the photos than in them. And so, without fully realising it, she had pushed him away.

What is left now is a fragment, a shape without colour and form – like the workshop, whose walls and windows remain the same, but which inside is now painted, carpeted, with a big desk and bookcases from IKEA, their old sofabed, new cushions, a throw. If she stares at the walls hard enough she can just about imagine it the way it was. But nothing of that remains.

And she has produced good work in here; she believes that some of her finest illustrations have been born in this room since it became her space. The trouble is, nobody else seems to feel the same way.

It's hard to keep going under those circumstances. It's no wonder she's struggling.

She tries to call Kitty to find out what train she is getting on Friday, but there is no answer. She sends a text instead, finishes her coffee and tapes a fresh sheet of watercolour paper to the board. She has had a new idea: animal superheroes. They don't know they have superpowers. She is going to start with a pigeon who has phenomenal strength and no clue; the pigeon is responsible for pot holes and fallen trees. She sketches out a few scenes on her pad. Quickly the pigeon is joined by a supersonic goat named Carnage. She hasn't thought of a good name for the pigeon yet; all that comes to mind is Bob.

An hour later, she has twenty or so quick pencil sketches. In each one, Bob the pigeon looks baffled; the goat looks vicious. She rests her head in her hands, pulling a face. It feels hopeless.

Her phone buzzes with a text and she snatches it up, relieved to have an interruption. There is a message from Kitty:

Sorry I missed u mum. Will call later xx.

This time Sarah senses something at the same time as the dogs do; from their respective positions on the floor of the workshop they both look up, ears pricked towards the door. Basil moves first, barking, tail wagging. Tess looks less certain.

What happened in the croft has unnerved her, she thinks. It's broad daylight, the sun is shining, and yet the hairs are standing up on her arm.

She opens the door and Basil bursts through it, running straight for the house and barking at the door. Tess follows him, her head down, ears back. It's not Aiden coming back, then; the car is still missing from its usual spot.

Sarah crosses the yard to the house and has her hand on the door when it opens from within, making her jump.

'Christ!'

'Ah, there you are! I was just leaving you a note.'

Will stands aside to let her in. He is all smiles.

'I did knock,' he says. 'Thought you were out with the dogs.'

'I was working,' she says, and almost goes to apologise but stops herself. 'What's up?'

'I've got something to show you,' he says. 'We'll need to take your car.'

'Where are we going?' Sarah asks, again.

Will is sitting next to her in the front passenger seat of the Land Rover. He looks fresh and he's fidgety, like a small boy with a secret, something that she finds a little disconcerting.

'Surprise, I told you,' he says. 'Keep driving.'

They are headed into the moors, and, while it is a sunny day for a change, Sarah is in no mood for a mystery tour. She keeps thinking of the work she should be doing. A text interruption is one thing, but not an hour's trip.

'I guess Sophie told you,' he says quickly.

Sarah glances across to meet his searing blue eyes, which are studying her face for any reaction.

'That you're seeing each other? Yes,' she says.

'And?'

'And what?'

'What d'you make of it?'

She is surprised that he is asking. It's not really any of her business, after all. 'She seems happy,' she says, in the end.

'Yeah,' he answers, still smiling. 'I am too. She's amazing.'

'Just – you know – be careful,' Sarah says. She can't help herself.

'I won't hurt her, if that's what you're bothered about.'

'I don't want either of you to get hurt. It just seems like it's the sort of thing that can't possibly go anywhere.'

For the first time since she saw him in the town centre, the smile has dropped from his face and he looks thoughtful. He goes quiet for a bit and, not for the first time, Sarah thinks again about what happened at Louis's birthday party. The details of it are hazy; the feelings that were left behind are anything but. She wants to ask if he has told Sophie; wants to assure him that she will not. But to ask would be to bring the subject up, and she cannot be sure that he hasn't, in fact, forgotten all about it after all. If he has, that's the best thing for all of them.

'You need to take the next right – there, look.'

'What – here?'

The only right turn is through a metal five-bar gate into a field.

'Aye, that's it. Turn in there.'

The Land Rover bumps over ruts and dips, finding an overgrown track at the edge of a ploughed field. They follow the hedgerow to the end and there is another gate standing open, leading into a rough, partly concreted yard.

'I'll just wait in the car, leave you to it.'

'What? Leave me to what?'

Then she looks. There is a row of five polytunnels, a Portakabin, an old timber barn and a newer one made of breeze blocks and corrugated iron. Tucked behind the barn is a concrete yard on which a dark green Jeep is parked.

Sarah doesn't need to ask where they are, or what they are doing there. Will's huge smile has returned, and as she turns off the engine and looks at him she has just one question. 'Does he know I'm coming?'

She finds Louis in one of the polytunnels. He is wearing a black bodywarmer over a grey sweatshirt, sleeves pushed up to his elbows. *He looks thin*, is the first, difficult thing that crosses Sarah's mind.

'Oh, it's you,' is his greeting. He doesn't smile.

'Hello, Louis. How are you?'

'Okay. How'd you get here?'

'Will showed me where it was,' she says, by way of explanation. 'It was a surprise.'

'Right. Where is he?'

'He wanted to wait in the car.'

'Bet he did.'

'So all this is yours?' she says, looking around. There are trestle tables to the end of the polytunnel, long rows of seed trays all showing bright green foliage. 'What is it?'

'These are all salad,' he says, staring at her as if she has asked a stupid question. And of course: she has. She has grown lettuce in the garden. She knows what lettuce looks like, for God's sake. Why is it so hard to talk to her own son?

'Have you spoken to Kitty?' she asks. 'She's coming home on Friday.'

'Yes, I know.' He hasn't moved, but now he lifts one of the plastic trays near to the door. It's full of lettuce heads, glistening with water. 'You can bring that one if you want to help.'

She picks up a second tray and follows him out of the door. He heads over to the barn and does not speak on the way, which gives her a chance to think of things to ask him, things to talk about. In the barn, a wheeled cage of the type used in supermarkets is waiting on the concrete floor. He slots his tray into it, and then takes hers and adds it.

'I miss you,' she says. Even to her ears it sounds desperate, lame.

He stops, briefly, but does not answer. Instead, he pushes the trolley towards the open barn door. The wheels make a tremendous clattering noise which prohibits further conversation until he stops.

'If you'd just answer your phone sometimes,' she tries, 'or even send a text every now and again. Just to let me know you're okay.'

He does not look round, but slams the metal gate of the trolley shut with a clang that echoes off the walls. 'As you can see, I'm fine,' he says.

She follows him out of the barn. He is heading towards the Portakabin, which she imagines is where his office is.

'I'm finding it really tough now Kitty's gone,' she says.

He looks up, meets her eyes, finally. His gaze is cool, not quite hostile but not far off it. 'Hindsight is great, isn't it?' he says. 'Dad should still be here. Then you'd have someone to talk to, and you could bloody leave me alone.'

Outside the Portakabin is a Formica table with metal legs, three fold-up picnic chairs. Judging by the fag butts and the bin full of crisp packets, this is where the workers – whoever they are, wherever they are – take their breaks.

'Have you got lots of people working for you?' Sarah asks, in an attempt to make conversation.

After Louis's stinging comment in the barn, she had wanted to get straight back in the Land Rover and head for home, but then there was Will to think about, and to walk away when he'd gone to all the trouble of bringing her here would have felt ungrateful.

'Not many,' Louis says. The table has a mug on it, half-full of what might be coffee. He throws the liquid into the weeds growing around the base of the cabin. 'It's only busy at certain times.'

'And you're selling it at the farmers' markets?'

'Hotels,' he says, 'mainly.'

'Really? That's good going. How did you get into that?'

He doesn't answer this, and she doesn't blame him. She's trying too hard.

'Would you like to come over for lunch?' she says. 'On Sunday, maybe, before Kitty goes back? I know the dogs would be pleased to see you.'

'Oh, for God's sake,' he says, slamming down the empty mug, heading back towards the polytunnels. 'See yourself out,' he calls.

The tears burn Sarah's cheeks and she rubs them away with the heel of her hand. When she gets back in the car, Will notices. He says, 'Hey,' and puts his hand on her shoulder as if he's going to give her one of his hugs, but she raises her hand to ward him off.

'No, I'm fine, I'm fine,' she says.

'Ah, try not to worry,' he says. 'He'll come round. At least you've seen him. It's a good start.'

'Really? How'd you work that out?'

'He's talking to you, isn't he? Better than before.'

'If you say so.'

Driving back up the lane a few minutes later, Will says, 'I'll keep working on him for you, if you like. He's not a bad lad. He's just been through a lot.'

'I know that,' she says.

They are back at the main road. Sarah indicates left, even though there is probably not another moving vehicle within five miles.

'Done well for himself,' Will says. 'Not bad going, for a few bits of salad.'

But Sarah isn't listening; she is thinking of her baby boy, her son, smiling and laughing and running towards her, his arms raised for her to pick him up.

Aiden

Karine Hoffmeier is relaxing in the lounge area of her hotel suite. You left her, briefly, to prepare the bedroom.

You have known Karine for about seven years, and you're pleased to see her again. She lives in an eight-bedroomed town house in York city centre, with her husband and their three dogs. They have children – four of them – at various private schools and universities around the world. You have never met any of them, although you have seen photos. Identical, beautiful golden-haired children of various sizes. You like Karine: she is not any trouble. She always knows exactly what she wants out of your encounters. Usually, it's a quick, fast orgasm, followed by a long, slow massage, which usually brings about at least one other climax. Her husband knows about you, that Karine meets you sometimes – whether he approves or not, you haven't a clue. You suspect Karine would not tolerate his disapproval.

She was two minutes late, proclaiming that she couldn't find the hotel – her Teutonic sense of punctuality clearly put out by having to travel out into the sticks. Your previous encounters have all taken place in London. Nevertheless, when you tell her that you have moved to the area, she positively beams with pleasure.

'I would have brought you some champagne, darling, if I'd known,' she purrs, as you start to help her out of her clothes.

'I've got some for us, later,' you tell her.

She's still half-dressed, bum up on the dressing table, when she grabs you by the wrist and pushes your hand under her skirt. You hold her tightly – she likes a firm touch; not to be pushed around exactly, but to feel as though someone else is in charge. She spends her whole life in control, of her husband, her household, her finances, and for these few moments part of the deal is that she gets to relax.

'You're ready for this,' you say, murmuring it into her ear.

'Yes,' she says, the word ending on a groan.

Not for the first time, you marvel at the seemingly limitless variety of the female orgasm. To you, that makes it a beautiful thing, a thing of wonderment and awe. Every woman comes in a different way, and you consider it part of your skill that you do not presume to know how to bring any woman to that stage. It involves conversation, discretion and a little bit of intuition.

Karine is ready for you, as she usually is. You wonder about the anticipation, the fantasy that lies behind the readiness. The fact that she needs hard fingers pushing into her, your other arm supporting her upper body. Her hands are gripping the edge of the dressing table. One of your legs between hers, keeping her knee apart. This bit requires no talking. She makes a noise, stifles it. When you've met before in London hotels she has been vocal, even yelling. Today, for some reason, she is clearly feeling inhibited.

'Yes,' you say, encouraging, 'come on. Shout for me if you want to.'

She gasps. 'I can't…'

'Yes,' you say. 'You can and you will. I'm telling you it's time for you to come.'

That does the trick. Well. You have found a new thing to add to your repertoire for Karine. Normally she wants you silent for this bit – just a firm, authoritative hand – but now you know you can order her to come. Not only is this effective, it's exceptionally effective. Moments later she comes, wetness flooding into your hand, her knees giving way. You hold her up. She lets out a long, vocal groan, ending in something that sounds like a sob.

'Shh,' you say, holding her. It's not an instruction but a reassurance. 'That's it. You needed that, didn't you?'

'I did.'

She shudders. You peel away her jacket, unbutton her blouse. She goes to help you, but you push her hands away. They are shaking. 'You're all right?' you ask, just to check.

She nods, dumbly. Eventually she undoes her skirt and steps out of it. Every item of clothing you've taken from her slowly and folded, leaving it neatly on the chair. This is part of your routine with Karine. You did it the first time and she liked it, so, ever since then, you undress her. When she's naked, she lies on the bed on the towels you have put down in preparation. You run your hand from her neck to her lovely feet. You have always liked her feet, dainty, with little painted toenails.

'Now,' you say, 'it's time to relax. Right?'

'Mm.' Her face is turned away from you.

'Warm enough?'

'Uh-huh.'

You pour oil into your hands, smoothing them over her body. It's easy to lose yourself in this part, the rhythm of it, the pressure, varying the speed. Feeling the muscles under the skin, loosening the tension, untying the knots. You can feel the stress as it leaves her body. She sinks into the towels beneath her. Around her shoulders she is particularly tense, as she invariably is. You think of her carrying the weight of responsibility on her shoulders, and bit by bit you take it away from her. Little pieces of pressure, self-doubt, the wearying nature of having to maintain control, all of it slowly melting away. It's hypnotic, and beautiful.

You tell her this. Talking is part of what makes this work for Karine, this bit of it anyway. 'I'm learning more about your body every time I see you,' you say. 'I love the way you feel under my hands.'

She doesn't acknowledge you.

'Does it feel good,' you say, 'letting go? Does it feel better?'

She murmurs her assent.

'When you go home, you'll feel all brand new again. You come to me, and I fix you.'

She is poured out, liquid, her body one long pause. Your hand, running up the inside of her thigh, dips into the cleft between her legs. Her lips are still swollen with the pleasure of her earlier orgasm and the sensitivity of it makes her jump a little.

'Relax, Karine,' you say.

She pushes her hips towards you.

'Not yet,' you say. 'You have to wait for it this time. My rules.'

She shivers, but not with cold: her skin is hot, alive, tingling under your oiled hands. Again, you slip down, with more purpose this time.

She arches her back slightly, pushing towards you. As a punishment, you move away from her bottom – firm and tempting as it is – to her shoulders, relaxing away the tension that has once again built up.

'You're a tease,' she says.

'Yes,' you say, 'I am. But you only come when I let you, Karine, that's the rule.'

Half the challenge is in the timing. You want to make her wait for it until the optimum moment, the point at which her orgasm will be utterly amazing. If you get the timing wrong, if you take her too far, she will be frustrated and then the satisfaction will be more of a release, which is disappointing. But you know Karine, you know her body, you know how much it can take. Her fingers have gone from relaxing to tense again, clenching and relaxing. You return to her legs, more oil here so that your hands are slippery with it. Between her legs she is wet enough. Your fingers slip between her lips and inside, stretching her. Gently this time, soothing.

'Yes,' she says, '*yes.*'

'Slowly,' you say. You massage her purposefully now, just for a minute. You can feel her clenching around you. 'Turn over.'

She obeys, shifting awkwardly. Her chest is flushed. She smiles up at you, her eyes closed. 'You're getting better at this,' she says. 'Every time I see you, it's better.'

'No talking,' you say.

'Mm.'

'And I think it's nearly time for you to come again. But not quite.'

It's easier this way; you can see her face, the concentration on it, even with her eyes screwed tight shut. Your rhythm is strong, with pauses when you slow down. You build it up to a point when you think she's there, bring her back from it. There's an edge. You need to find it.

You see her hands clenching around the edge of the massage bed, her knees coming up, her bottom rising off the bed as she pushes herself against your hand.

'Uh-uh,' you say. 'Not yet. Not quite yet.'

'Aiden!' she gasps. 'Please...'

You speed up for her. Her body tightens around your hand. 'Now,' you say. 'Now you can come...'

And, a moment later, she does. Her body lifts off the bed, her toes clenched into a point, her head thrust back. She grips the towel. Seconds pass. You keep the pressure just there.

At last she relaxes, falls back. She laughs with it, pushing her hair back out of her eyes with one hand. 'Aiden, you kill me. You really do.'

Your hand is resting on her belly, the pressure firm and reassuring. You can feel her taut abdominal muscles under the skin. 'You've been working out,' you murmur. She's always kept herself fit. You wonder if she's feeling the pressure of age encroaching – she must be, what? Fifty? Older? You find it difficult to tell, and you've never much cared. One woman in Sydney told you proudly that she was seventy-three. You wouldn't have guessed.

With your other hand you stroke her cheek, soothing. You brush the stray hairs out of her eyes, waiting for her to come back to the room. After a moment she opens her eyes. 'That feels so good,' she says.

'I know. You ready for some more?' you ask.

'I think I'm done for today. I don't think even you can top the last one.'

'In that case,' you say, 'would you like a back massage?'

'Oh, yes.'

She turns over again and you add fresh oil to your hands. This is going to be different, a therapeutic massage this time, the pressure gentle. You feel her relaxing again. A good place to end it. You continue until you think she might actually be close to falling asleep. You lay a fresh towel over her, and a coverlet that has weight to it, up to her shoulders. You place a hand in the small of her back.

'Relax for a bit,' you whisper. 'Come and have a drink in the lounge when you're ready.'

If you're in a hotel, and the client can afford it, you always opt for a suite. It gives you space to leave the client to relax; and if there is any noise, on one side at least there is a whole room between you and the neighbouring guests. You have also found that hotels are less likely to ask questions if they've been paid the top whack.

You have only been confronted once, and that was in London. The night manager stopped you early the next morning as you were leaving, pointed out that the hotel was not the place to conduct 'overnight business meetings'. You supposed, perhaps, that he recognised you; it was a hotel you had visited several times. You asked if he would prefer it if you advised your clients to go elsewhere. He backed down, then, saying that your clients were always welcome; hoping that you would continue to be discreet. You reassured him, shook his hand, and never went back to that hotel.

You close the door quietly behind you, leaving Karine lying on the bed. Only then do you check the time. Your session so far, from her arrival to now, has been an hour and three quarters. Actually this is about right. You estimate another half-hour or so for her to relax, dress, and drink something with you in the lounge. Once that's done and she's out of the door, you can phone Sarah. While you would not think of her while you're with someone else – for some reason this feels unprofessional – now that you've closed the door on Karine you can think of nothing else.

There is an element of sexual frustration that comes with this career you have chosen for yourself, and it is a frustration born of your own boundaries. You could, of course, fuck these women if they wanted you to, and if you felt comfortable with it. Many of them would. But, with most of them this is the line you do not cross. And the result is that often, having spent hours caressing smooth, naked skin, running your hands over curves and seeing women laid waste by their own sexual release, you are so aroused you can think of nothing else. In the past you have gone home and masturbated, sometimes several times, to release this tension. Sometimes you do it before you go to meet women, just so you don't have that distraction between you, but you have found that it helps to be turned on. You are alert, focused and more intuitive if you are hard yourself. If you've just come, you are drowsy and distracted.

Now, you are aroused. You think this is because you know you are going back to Four Winds Farm later, and Sarah is there, and maybe you will fuck her tonight. You start to think about it, about taking her clothes off – it starts off slow but in your head, possibly as it will be in real life, you're tearing them off her and pushing them aside within moments.

The door to the bedroom opens and Karine comes out, dressed in her sharp business suit and killer heels. 'Hey,' she says, smiling.

'What would you like?' you ask. 'Champagne? Or coffee?'

'Oh, definitely champagne, darling.'

You pop the cork, pour it carefully into two glasses, brought with you for the purpose. She sits on the couch, watching.

'Cheers,' you say, clinking her glass. You sit next to her, close enough for you to touch if she wants you to. Technically, your session isn't over until she leaves. This is important to you, that your clients don't ever feel rushed. You give them your full, undivided attention because that's what they are paying you for. Massage, orgasm, it's all incidental. What they actually want, all of them, is someone whose sole focus is them.

Sarah

Sarah drops Will off in Thirsk on the way back. He is meeting a friend, he says. She leaves him in the Market Place and drives out towards Sutton Bank, pulls over in a lay-by and cries, great gasping sobs racking her body. There is nobody to see. Cars and lorries whizz past her. She forgets, of course, how bad things are with Louis. When months pass with no contact it's almost easy to believe he is off somewhere, too busy to call. Being forced into that situation with him so cold – so *cold* – has made her realise just how angry he still is.

Now she has hiccups, and that stops her crying because she is cross at herself. It's all so pointless; crying isn't going to make anything better.

Back at home she takes the dogs out and thinks about going doing some more work, but she can't face it. She stands shivering by the back door, watching as Tess sniffs suspiciously around the croft. Whatever freaked her out yesterday has gone; she gives the shack one last disgusted look and heads back down the hill, wagging her tail. Basil, tanks emptied, is already waiting to go inside.

The phone is ringing in the house. Thinking it might be Kitty, Sarah kicks off her boots and runs to the kitchen to pick it up.

'Did I catch you at a bad time?' Aiden says, chuckling at how breathless she is.

'I just got in with the dogs,' she replies.

'I'm heading back now,' he says.

She wonders why he is telling her. Presumably he's been out working somewhere, doing whatever it is he does, setting up franchises. 'Um, okay. Where are you? York?'

'Harrogate. I was thinking of you today.'

'Were you?' she asks, surprised.

'Couldn't stop.'

She is not sure if him thinking about her is a bad thing or not. She is still pondering it as she goes into the kitchen, a few minutes later. Distracted, she makes a cottage pie big enough for six people, and leaves it to cool down. Doing that has used up an hour. Normally she would separate it into portions for freezing, but this one will do for Friday night's dinner. She has shown herself to be incapable of cooking a fresh meal for one. Each time she attempts it, she cooks too much; now, five months after Kitty left, she has given up trying and instead gone back to her old, familiar amounts – the family plus leftovers – freezing it in plastic tubs she has bought from Yorkshire Deals in Thirsk. The freezer is already full – soups, curries, casseroles – but she has a need to cook. It distracts her from the empty house, makes her feel as though she has a purpose.

Kitty's room is almost exactly as she left it, when she headed back to uni after Christmas, a week earlier than she needed to; citing work and the need to get into the library. Only the dirty clothes and linen have been removed, the cups and the dishes Sarah found under the bed. Otherwise, it's all there; everything is lined up waiting for Kitty to return.

Sarah sometimes sits there, on Kitty's bed, looking around the room at the posters and the corkboard with photos of her friends, gig tickets, doodles stuck to it. But she does not stay for long. It's too quiet.

Louis's room is empty; all that remains are a few oily stains on the wallpaper where posters were stuck to the walls. It looks like what it is now: a spare room. He took everything with him when he went.

It is dark outside but she notices the light is on in the cottage; so Aiden is home. She had wondered if he was going to come over, but he has not. Probably it's tiring, whatever it is he does.

When she has finished eating her bowlful of cottage pie she washes up and leaves the plate on the draining board. The dishwasher, that's another thing – by the time she has enough crockery to fill it even moderately full, everything has dried on, and gone a bit manky. She had started rinsing everything assiduously before putting it in there, but quickly realised it was even easier to just wash it by hand and be done with it.

It's these unexpected things that hit her hardest. The quiet in the house, the not having anyone to talk to – she'd considered the impact that would have, thought she had dealt with it by bracing herself. But it's the repetition of doing her own washing, cleaning her own crockery. Things still being in the place she left them. And the lack of purpose! Nobody calling out that extended 'Mu-u-um?' when they needed her.

Nobody needs her now.

At nine, wondering if it's too early to go to bed, the phone rings again – it's Kitty.

'Hey, Mum,' she says.

'Are you out somewhere?' In the background, Sarah can hear the noise of a bar – clinking, tinny music, layers of voices, laughter – and instantly the wave of mum-worry washes over her. She frowns at her own reaction. Kitty can take care of herself.

'Sort of. I wanted to stay in but Oscar's meeting a friend so I said I'd come along. Going home in a bit, though.'

Kitty sounds as if she has had a drink, or several. Perhaps it's Sarah's imagination.

'How are you getting home?'

'Don't worry, Mum. Oscar's going to walk me back.'

'That's good,' she replies, simultaneously thinking *is it*?

'I'm going to try and get the 16.56 on Friday.'

'Is that the one that gets in at half-past six?'

It's the briefest of conversations, and it leaves Sarah feeling worse. Before it can take hold, she distracts herself by letting the dogs out the back for a last wee.

When she shuts the door again, she hears a noise in the house; Tess barks at it and then Basil does too, and she follows them into the kitchen. Basil is scratching at the door and then she hears a knock.

Aiden is outside.

'You can just come in,' she says. 'I told you, it's not locked.'

There is something about the way he is looking at her. Inside her, something fires.

Aiden

You want to talk to her.

You want to tell her about Karine, about how suddenly your life feels different, because of her, but when she opens the door all the words evaporate.

'You can just come in. It's not locked.'

You are not listening. You do not wish to be reminded that you could just walk in at any moment. The thought of that is just too, too tempting.

You knock on the door and you will continue to do so because you have this feeling, this sixth sense that she might be there with that kid, that they are fucking or whatever, that you will see something now that you will never be able to unsee: her in the arms of a man who is not you. The sight of her happy with someone else. You saw that before, didn't you, when she started seeing Jim? You had to run away to the other side of the world to try to get over it.

In the kitchen you hold yourself in check for as long as you can. To prove to yourself that you can resist. You have control.

But then the need to kiss her is too strong. You are expecting her to resist, to flinch, but she does neither. In fact to your surprise and relief she is responding, her hands at your back, pulling at your sweater, slipping up underneath to touch bare skin. She makes a sound, like a groan, and you pull away from her again to see her face, to check she is all right.

She smiles at you.

You push her back against the kitchen table and her fingers are fumbling at your belt buckle, struggling with it until you take over. She undoes her jeans and without any hesitation slips them down, off, spreading her knees so you can get between them, and within a second or two you are pushing inside her. Her hands on your backside, pulling you closer.

Yes yes yes.

The feeling is indescribable. You try not to move too fast, because, if you do, this will all be over; but she is pulling you in, and you can't help it, thrusting because it's the only thing you can do. And you can hear her breathing fast against your neck, and something else, a sound like pain or something, a little squeak.

It's enough to make you stop, to pull her face towards you so you can see her eyes. You have also realised with a shock that this is the first time you've not worn a condom.

'You stopped,' she breathes. 'Don't stop, Aiden, don't...'

So you stop thinking and fuck her hard, fast, losing control until you feel it building inside you and then you spin over the edge; holding it for a second, holding your breath, then pulling out because you have to, coming between her thighs and then it's over.

She is holding you, both her arms around you.

You're aware that she is leaning back against the kitchen table in a way that must be uncomfortable. You hear a soft whine and look down to see Basil sitting at your feet, looking up at you in confusion.

'Oh, my God,' you say, and laugh. 'Sorry, Basil.'

She laughs too. She is breathing hard.

'I think I just traumatised your dog.'

'Good job he can't talk,' Sarah says.

You look at her face, flushed, her eyes shining. Then you kiss her, tenderly this time, tasting her.

You move away, and she pulls her jeans on, standing awkwardly. A second later, and you are both fully dressed again.

'I'm sorry,' you say. 'That was – '

'Do you want a drink?'

'Sure,' you say.

'Can you help yourself? I'm just going to, um...'

She disappears upstairs. You're angry at your loss of control. You have never done that before. You cannot let it happen again.

You find a bottle of wine in the fridge and two glasses, make a mental note to replace it. It's probably in there ready for her visitors this weekend. Still, it will do for now, and you need something to take the edge off. When you pour the wine you realise your hand is shaking.

She is standing in the doorway.

'What is it?' you ask.

Sarah gives an odd little laugh. 'Nothing. I just thought you'd be gone by the time I got back.'

'Is that what I do?' you ask.

'Yes,' she replies. 'You're always running away.'

'Ouch.'

'It doesn't matter. I'm not trying to stop you.'

'What if I want to stop?'

You offer her a glass and she takes it and leads you into the living room, curling up into the corner of the couch. You sit next to her, where you can place your hand on her knee.

'I saw Louis earlier,' she says.

'How is he?' you ask.

'Hostile,' she says, drinking her wine.

'Are you going to tell me what happened between you?'

She gives a short, humourless laugh. 'I'm not even sure. He blames me for Jim's death, that's part of it. He didn't agree with the decision to not resuscitate. He blames me for the accident too, like I said. So for most of that year he was barely speaking to me.'

'He loved his dad very much,' you say. 'He must have found it tough. It's not right that he took it out on you.'

There is a pause. She is thinking about everything she says. You wonder if that's because she still doesn't trust you.

'I thought it was. I blamed myself, too. Which meant it was very hard to find a way to reach him. And, in any case, he just wanted to get away. He wanted to escape from it all. After his birthday – ' She stops short, thinks, and drinks some more wine.

'What were you going to say?'

'Just that he left home.'

That wasn't it, you think; or, if it was, it reminded her of something she had forgotten.

'But you saw him today?'

'Will turned up this morning. He found out where Louis works, I don't know how. So we had a weird kind of road trip out to where Louis has this farm. Lots of polytunnels.'

'And? How was it?'

She looks at her hands, bites her lip. 'Pretty grim, actually. Still. It was nice of Will to go to the trouble. I think he knows I'm finding it tough without Kitty.'

You are surprised by this, by her calm acceptance of what you would call interfering, especially from someone she hardly knows.

'Are you?'

Sarah takes a deep breath in. 'I'll manage,' she says. 'It's nice that he cares.'

'You're not on your own any more, though.'

You know instantly that it's the wrong thing to say, and you wish you could take the words back. A cloud has crossed her face. You cannot interfere, or imply that she needs you.

'It's late,' she says.

'Sure.'

You take your wine glass through to the kitchen, rinse it under the tap. Sarah is standing in the doorway. 'I would ask you to stay,' she says. 'I'm not very good company at the moment, though. I'm sorry.'

'It's okay,' you say, smiling at her to reassure her that you mean it.

'I didn't even ask how your day went.'

This time your smile is genuine. 'It was fine. But I was glad when it was over and I could come home.'

A few minutes later you're shutting the door of the cottage. It's cold in here because you've been out all day. The door has a deadlock on it, and you have not been bothering to lock it, once you're home. But now you stare at it, thinking about Will and how he invites himself in, surprises people, interferes in friendships and relationships that are none of his business.

You lock the door.

Perhaps Sarah should start locking her door, too.

Sarah

Sarah finds it difficult to get to sleep.

She should have had a bath to warm up a bit, to relax, because, lying in bed, she has the darkness for company and there's nothing to stop the thoughts; they crowd over her, jostling for space.

Even taking into account the money Aiden is giving her for rent, it's not enough. She doesn't want to resort to bankruptcy, or raising money on the house through an equity release scheme, because Sophie would find out about it and then she would demand to know why Sarah didn't ask her for help. She could, of course, actually ask Sophie for help. But there is no way to pay Sophie back, and, even though the debt is not her fault but Jim's, she cannot bring herself to talk about it with her friend.

The thought of it makes her think of her father, who died from a heart attack in his early fifties. He was a proud man, and money was personal. He would sooner have squatted in the corner and had kittens than discuss financial concerns with anyone, much less a friend who was well-off. Then there is her sister, Kay, who lives in Devon with her own family and is, these days, scarcely ever in touch. Could she ask her? It would be a very difficult conversation. Sarah has never got on particularly well with her, and they barely manage Christmas cards.

And then there is the other option, much closer to home. Louis, who seems to be doing well now. Will mentioned a contract with a big hotel. And now Louis has a team of people working for him. Maybe, if she can manage to stay in touch with him, he might give her some work? She could even take the dogs with her.

But it is no use. Even if she could bring herself to ask Louis, which she cannot, what if he said no? How would she ever be able to repair things between them then?

She closes her eyes against the darkness and breathes deeply, slowly, trying to relax, trying to force all thought of money from her mind.

The wind roars outside, wrapping itself around the house and tugging at the loose stones, pushing its way in through the gaps and cracks and mouse holes. That's the other thing to consider: the house is in need of serious repairs. Even if she were to find a buyer for a grey stone farmhouse hunkering into a cold, damp hillside miles from anywhere, whoever was mad enough to make an offer would probably take one look at the structural survey and pull out.

A sudden noise – not the wind, something close by – makes her eyes snap open again. She sits up. The door to her bedroom, the one that she pushed almost closed, is ajar. She hears a soft whine, and Basil's tail thumps against the carpeted floor. He usually sleeps downstairs, but tonight perhaps he has sensed that she could do with company. She holds a hand out into empty space, hears him padding across to her, feels a warm lick on her fingers and then a heavy doggy sigh as he settles down next to the bed.

Sarah closes her eyes again and thinks of other things: Kitty, drunk, walking home alone because Oscar, whoever he is, has gone off with someone else... Louis, mad with fury, shouting at her on the morning after his twenty-first birthday... and Jim, in the car beside her, unconscious, blood on his face.

Part Four

Sarah

Kitty's train is due at six-thirty. Sarah heads into the village in the late afternoon because it's market day and she can stock up on fresh fruit and vegetables cheaply just as the stalls are closing. After that she drives to Thirsk and stops at Yorkshire Deals to get washing powder and toilet rolls. Once the car is loaded up she heads back out of town, past the racecourse, to the station, where she parks and waits.

It's dark, early evening, and Sarah keeps checking her phone for messages from Kitty or Sophie. Earlier this afternoon, she sent Sophie a text asking if she wanted to come over for a drink later to see Kitty and meet Oscar.

There has, so far, been no response, which is not like Sophie.

She looks up through the windscreen to see people emerging from the bridge over the platforms and she looks for her daughter, suddenly desperate to see her. It has been the longest time they have ever been apart. And then, there she is! Her beautiful girl, long golden hair under a beanie, holding hands with a man, both of them carrying rucksacks. Kitty waves, and Sarah gets out of the car. Kitty drops her boyfriend's hand and runs towards Sarah, and Sarah rushes forward too and they crash together, laughing, in a hug that's tight enough to hurt.

'Hello, Mum!'

'Hello, my darling! I am so pleased to see you...'

'Mum, this is Oscar.'

Sarah takes a moment to size up the boyfriend. He looks nice, she thinks, if a little sullen. She holds out her hand, and it takes him a second or two to respond. His handshake is a little feeble.

'Hi, Oscar,' she says. 'Lovely to meet you.'

Kitty beams, looking from one of them to the other. 'Did you bring the dogs?'

'No, I've been to the market, I'm afraid.' She opens the boot and the rucksacks are piled in next to the bags of shopping.

Kitty gets in the passenger seat next to Sarah, leaving Oscar to climb in the back. As they drive through the traffic, such as it is, around Thirsk's one-way system, Kitty is full of excitement about her second term at uni, the sports clubs, the film club she's joined.

Sarah begins to feel sorry for Oscar, on his own in the back. 'How about you, Oscar? How are you finding things?'

Through the rear-view mirror Sarah can see that he is looking out of the window at the houses as they pass by.

'Oscar's a second-year,' Kitty says before he has a chance to speak. 'He's already been there and done that. He knows everything already.'

Sarah bristles and then tells herself to give the boy a chance, even though he has barely said a word. To be fair, even if he did speak it would be difficult to carry on a conversation with him in the back and concentrate on the road, so she makes a mental note of all the things she wants to ask him, saving them for later.

'How is Sophie?' Kitty asks.

'Oh, she's fine,' Sarah says brightly. 'I'm hoping she'll come out for a drink tonight. But she's not answering my text.'

'That's not like Sophie,' Kitty says, knitting her brows.

'Who's this?' Oscar asks from the back seat.

'Mum's best friend. She's the most glamorous person you'll ever meet. Her husband's an MP. He's a bit of a tit, though.'

'Kitty!' Sarah says.

'He is, Mum. You know he is. He's quite friendly really – I'm just never sure what Sophie sees in him. She's far too intelligent to be a trophy wife. She should be the politician, not him.'

Sarah's phone chirps with an incoming message. 'That'll be her. Can you read it for me?'

Too late, Sarah remembers Will and hopes that Sophie hasn't messaged her something horribly intimate, or even Aiden – but it's too late to stop Kitty fishing through Sarah's bag for her phone.

'Oh,' Kitty says. 'That's a shame.'

'What's it say?'

'It says: *Sorry re this weekend, got lots on. Love to Kitty. Talk next week.*'

'Really?' says Sarah. 'That is a shame.'

But Kitty is distracted almost immediately, planning a night out for Oscar tomorrow with her schoolfriends, who seem to have conspired to all be home for this weekend. The car is full of Kitty's laughter and Oscar saying things from the back that Sarah doesn't catch.

All she can think about is Sophie. She had said that George was going to be away this weekend – golfing, wasn't it? So it's unlikely Sophie will be going with him. What is she planning to do all weekend that's so important that she can't get away to see Kitty, even for a quick drink?

And then, of course, the answer to her question presents itself.

Will.

I've always been a people-watcher.

In the city this means sitting outside a café with a latte and a book you're pretending to read. I can't be arsed with all of that.

I've always liked watching people when they are exposed, raw, vulnerable. The woman crying on the train, who thinks nobody can see her. The man counting out his coins before he goes into the pub. And then counting again, because he knows he hasn't got enough. The girl playing with her phone, waiting, waiting for someone to call. She keeps checking. There is still nothing.

But this isn't the city, is it? After dark, there aren't any people on the streets, nobody hurrying home from work; everyone's back in their homes, burrowed away, safe and warm like so many little country animals, all their little secrets tucked away.

And they all feel so safe, don't they? They're not scared of anything. In the city everyone's suspicious, expecting to get their purse snatched or be threatened by some random drunk. Everyone is tense, fierce, ready to react.

Not here. They're all asleep by ten.

But that's good. I like it.

I can wander through the village and not meet a soul; I can stand outside in their gardens and observe them, watching the football or the news or Corrie*, cosy and safe with their* *curtains wide open, oblivious to the dark night. I try to understand them, but the only thing that keeps coming back to me is this...*

These people are not my people.

I do not belong.

Sarah

The dogs launch themselves at Kitty as soon as Sarah opens the door, and Oscar, who is carrying both rucksacks, is taken aback.

'Are you okay with dogs, Oscar?' Sarah asks.

'Sure,' he says, but without any real enthusiasm. Sarah wonders if this is as excited as he gets, and then thinks generously that maybe this makes him a good match for Kitty, who is always happy and has boundless energy at any given moment.

Sarah is about to push the door open once again with her knee, holding one of the bags of shopping too, when it opens from inside. Her first thought is that Sophie has changed her mind and come after all, to see Kitty and at least have a drink. But it isn't Sophie.

Will smiles widely and a bit apologetically. 'Hi again,' he says.

He stands aside to let them in. Kitty, who is clearly hyped up to maximum excitement by being home, by seeing the dogs and probably by having Oscar here, throws her arms around his neck and kisses his cheek. 'Hello! How are you? What are you doing here?'

Will has the grace to look a little embarrassed. 'Long story,' he says, 'tell you in a minute.'

'Will, this is Oscar, Oscar, this is Will.'

The two men shake hands. Sarah sees appraisal in Will's eyes.

'And you are...?' Will says. He has not let go of Oscar's hand yet.

'I'm with Kit,' Oscar says.

'Let's put the kettle on, shall we?' says Sarah.

Kitty takes Oscar on a tour of the house, apparently having already accepted Will's presence without any concern.

Will is leaning against the kitchen table, looking infuriatingly relaxed.

'Well,' Sarah says, 'this is a surprise. Aren't you supposed to be house-sitting?'

'Oh, aye. I am. I'm not stopping, don't worry. I just thought I'd come to say hello to Kitty. Not seen her for ages.'

Sarah frowns at this, and that her assumption that Sophie was with Will has clearly turned out to be wrong. 'Perhaps you could have given us a call, Will.'

His face clouds over. 'Oh... right. I'm sorry. I thought you'd be here by now, anyway, and the dogs were barking, so I thought I'd settle them...'

Upstairs Sarah can hear running feet, creaking floorboards, laughter. At least Oscar seems to be relaxing a little.

'Look, I'd really rather you didn't just let yourself in, that's all.'

He looks at her and then looks at the table. 'I'll go.'

'No, no. You're here now. I'm not telling you off,' she says, although she is, she wants to, but she can't bear the thought of upsetting him for some reason that she can't fathom. 'I'm just saying. Come round any time, but let me know first, okay?'

'Sure,' he says, his head still down.

At that moment Kitty and Oscar come thundering down the stairs. 'Are we going out for dinner?' Kitty says. 'I'd like to show Oscar round the village.'

'I've done a cottage pie,' Sarah says. 'Perhaps we could go out for a drink after?'

'Okay,' Kitty says. 'Are you staying for dinner, Will?'

Will looks up at Sarah. 'If I'm invited,' he says.

'Course you are,' Kitty replies. 'Mum always cooks far too much. That's right, isn't it, Mum?'

In her head Sarah resists for a fraction longer, then wonders what it is she's fighting against. 'Of course.'

'Well, if you're sure. Thanks. I can... you know, perhaps I can do the veg or something? I don't mind helping.'

'We'll all do it,' Kitty says. 'What about your friend, Mum? Is he coming over too?'

'Aiden? I can ask him, if you like.'

In fact, now that Will is staying for dinner too, Sarah suddenly longs for company of her own age to balance things out a little. It's not an intimate supper getting to know Kitty's new boyfriend any more, so she might as well ask Aiden.

She gives them all tasks to do and the atmosphere is almost jolly. Will stands at the sink scraping carrots; Kitty is putting the cottage pie into the Aga. Oscar is set to work laying the table.

The dogs follow her out into the yard. Aiden's car is there, thank goodness, and the lights are on. But when he opens the door he looks almost surprised to see her.

'I'm sorry,' she says. 'Am I interrupting anything?'

'Not at all,' he says. 'Coming in?'

'No; I just came to ask if you wanted to come and have dinner with us. Maybe come out for a drink afterwards, too? My house is full of young people and I'm feeling left out.'

His smile – it melts her. 'I'd love to. Give me two minutes? I'll come straight over.'

The kitchen is full of noise and chaos. Tess immediately retreats to the living room, curling up by the sofa. It's been a long time since it was this noisy. Kitty is flicking water from the sink at Will. Someone – Kitty – has brought out a portable speaker and put on music. Oscar is watching Will warily.

He has still scarcely spoken. Sarah decides maybe he is just shy. 'Kitty says you're doing engineering too. I didn't realise you were in the second year.'

'Yeah,' he replies.

'Oscar's been, like, mentoring me,' Kitty says, her hand on his shoulder.

Sarah wants to say something about how Kitty has known Oscar just a few short weeks. Such a short time that it cannot, realistically, even be measured in months.

'Mu-u-um...' Kitty says.

The drawn-out syllable implies that something is coming. Sarah thinks she is going to ask whether Oscar can share her room, although if she's been upstairs she must have seen that the spare room is not made up.

'Mum? I was thinking – wondering whether maybe I could invite Oscar to come to us for Easter? I know it's a long way off yet...'

Sarah is momentarily speechless. This isn't something she has thought about and she flounders for something appropriate to say. Even Will looks round, surprised, glancing from Kitty to Oscar to Sarah, trying to gauge the mood, as if he is sensing tension.

'What about your own family, Oscar?' Sarah says eventually.

'It's okay,' he says, 'I understand: it's a big deal. I wish you'd waited a bit, Kit.'

Oscar suddenly goes up a peg or two in Sarah's estimation, but he isn't finished.

'My parents split up,' he continues. 'My mum lives in the States, and my dad lives in Bolton, and he's married again and he's got a new family with his new wife and she hates me.'

He laughs at this, as though it is funny.

'So, um, yeah, I don't like to impose, so feel free to say no.'

'If you say no, Mum, he'll be spending two weeks in a bedsit in London on his own.'

Emotional blackmail – she wants to put her foot down. But Will is looking at her and she remembers what he was like, years ago, when he first started hanging round with Louis for much the same reason. Displaced, unwanted, homeless.

'Of course you can come, Oscar,' says Sarah. She would have invited him anyway, because she cannot bear to think of someone being on their own like that.

'Thank you,' Oscar says. Kitty beams. In that moment, the door opens and Aiden comes in, bringing with him a blast of cold air. They all turn to look at him. Kitty reacts first, giving him a hug that he's probably not ready for. Aiden shakes Oscar's hand. Will stares.

There is something in the room, a brief thrill of something uncomfortable, unpleasant. Sarah can't identify what it is and for a moment she wishes she hadn't invited Aiden over. But seconds later, with Kitty laughing and joking and putting everyone at ease, whatever it was has gone.

'Let's eat,' Sarah says.

The Royal Oak is crowded, as it always is on a Friday night, but that just makes for a lively atmosphere. Aiden buys the drinks and Kitty proposes a toast: to new beginnings. Sarah thinks she is talking about Oscar, who is starting to relax. He has a beer in front of him and for the first time Sarah takes a moment to study him properly. He's not quite emo – maybe he was at one point, earlier in his teenage years, but now he's grown out of it. He has dark hair that's longish and untidy and not in any sort of style; pale skin and dark eyes. He has uneven teeth and hides them frequently, touching his mouth or not speaking unless he has to. But Sarah notices the look in his eyes when he is watching Kitty; he gazes at her when she's talking, as if he's listening intently. He has his arm casually around the back of her chair, but every so often Sarah sees him stroking her shoulder with his thumb.

Meanwhile, Will is looking uncomfortable. He has chosen to sit with his back to the room, opposite Sarah, keeping his head down.

When Kitty and Oscar are deep in conversation about a mutual friend, Sarah asks him if he is okay.

'Yeah, yeah, sure. Why?'

'You look a little – I don't know. Out of sorts?'

He tries to look defiant. 'Feels a bit like I'm taking advantage,' he says. 'You giving me dinner, taking me out, you know.'

'Why shouldn't you come with us?' Kitty asks, diving in. 'You're practically one of the family.'

And Aiden, who was quiet and thoughtful all through the meal, has still hardly said a word. It's making her feel twitchy, that he doesn't feel able to join in, that he's barely spoken to Kitty. She wants badly for them to get on. When Will gets up to go to the bathroom, and Kitty and Oscar are deep in conversation, she also asks *him* if he's okay.

'Sure,' he says. 'Why?'

'You're very quiet.'

He grins. 'I like watching people, that's all. I like trying to work out what's really going on.'

'That sounds deep. What do you mean?'

'It's nothing sinister. There's always a subtext, that's all. Other things.'

'Such as?'

He glances to Kitty and Oscar, who are on the other side of the table. He puts his arm over the back of the chair and gets close enough to Sarah's ear to murmur, 'She likes him much more than he likes her. He's not ready for the sort of relationship she wants. But he doesn't want to hurt her.'

Sarah frowns at him. She could probably have guessed at something similar, judging by Oscar's reticence, but – really? To categorise people like that? It makes her wonder what he thinks about her. In that moment she feels picked apart, examined. It's not a nice feeling.

'You think you're such a good judge of character, don't you? But you don't know everything about everybody.'

'Well, I do think Kitty is doing a good job of winning him over,' he says, surprised. 'So who knows?'

He's looking at her carefully, as if he's trying to work out what he's said to upset her.

'What about Will and Sophie, then?' she says challengingly.

Aiden looks over in the direction of the Gents'. 'I wouldn't like to say.'

Moments later, Will is back, and for a change she is pleased to see him.

'I'd better get going,' he says. 'Thanks for the drink. I'll see you soon, yeah?'

'Do you need a lift anywhere?' Sarah asks.

'No, it's just up the road. I'll be fine. Thanks again.'

Sarah watches him go. Aiden removes his arm from the back of her seat. She wonders if Kitty noticed it had been there. She has not dated anyone, since Jim died. The subject has come up, once or twice, and Sarah has batted it off with vague exhortations that she's too busy, or can't be bothered, or that decent single men are a bit thin on the ground in rural North Yorkshire.

Then he says, 'But there's something he's not telling us. Something big. I can't work it out,' and she realises he is still thinking about Will.

Sarah parks the Land Rover in the barn and everyone climbs out. Kitty and Oscar go ahead, arms round each other.

'You want to come over later?' Aiden asks.

Kitty opens the door and the dogs rush out, dancing around them. Oscar looks a bit less alarmed this time.

'I don't think so,' Sarah says.

She looks across at him. It's dark, but the security light above the workshop has lit up enough to see the disconcerted expression on his face.

'I'd better take the dogs out,' she adds.

'Shall I come with you?'

'I'll be fine,' she says. He gives her a little backwards wave to acknowledge it, and Sarah whistles for the dogs.

It's very dark on the hill and it takes a while for Sarah's eyes to adjust. She keeps her head down, thinking about Aiden. She had been looking forward to him getting to know Kitty, and for her to meet him; and yet all he'd done with the evening was to pick imaginary holes in Kitty's new relationship.

Sarah is suddenly aware of something right in front of her and she stops, gasps in shock: but it's only the croft, the shape of it unfamiliar in the darkness. Tess is at her side, sniffing at the doorway, and Sarah thinks she is going to have a go at it again, but after a cursory examination the dog skirts the wall and runs off into the darkness.

Sarah stands still. Everything looks different in the gloom; the only light comes from the moon, which is full but mostly hidden behind high clouds. The door to the croft is a dark rectangle against the grey stone, a black mouth, beckoning her in. She takes a step forward, places her hand against the wood. It is cold, rough against her palm. She gives it a little push. The door holds firm. Close to the croft, the air still, her breathing echoes back at her, making it sound as though there is someone standing right behind her.

She turns, quickly, but of course there is nobody there.

But now she doesn't want to be out here any more; she wants to be inside, with Kitty. She starts back down the hill, calling the dogs, looking down at her house with all the upstairs lights on; how bright and cheerful it looks!

She stops dead.

The window to the bathroom is illuminated and she can see, clearly, Kitty standing next to the bath, tipping a bag full of what is probably dirty laundry into the basket. Oscar comes up behind her, wraps his arms around her waist. Kitty turns and kisses him.

Aiden's wrong, she thinks; he likes her too. He's just shy about showing it yet.

She should be uncomfortable about watching them when they are so clearly unaware of her presence but for some reason she can't tear her eyes away. They're both fully dressed, they are just kissing – admittedly it's pretty full-on – but it feels good to see Kitty's happiness and Oscar's affection. Then they turn and leave, and abruptly the light snaps off, leaving a dark square.

The spell is broken, and Sarah shivers.

She was in a crappy mood earlier. I could tell, I could feel it coming off her in waves. Women are like that, they change like the wind, trying to fool you; one minute they're smiling at you and the next, they've got a face like stone and you've said something wrong.

I wanted to tell her: you don't get to treat me like that.

You think I don't know people, I wanted to say – see through their façades, their lies, the way they cover up? Well, I do. I've been away a long time and I've seen some things you wouldn't believe; the things people do to each other.

I am the keeper of your secrets, I wanted to tell her. I know you. I know everything about you, what keeps you awake at night, your jealousies, your hurts, your petty little insecurities. I know what makes you cry. I know the noise you make when you come.

I keep all of your secrets tucked inside me, and you know what? It makes me powerful. It makes me hard.

I wanted to fuck her there and then against the car, fuck her hard to take her mind off it all. If I'd insisted, she would have gone along with it. She needs it, she needs to be told what to do.

But for now I can let her think this is all her idea; that she's calling the shots. Play her silly game.

I can wait.

It'll be fun when I take over, when all of her secrets come tumbling out for everyone to see.

If only she had a clue.

Sarah

Sarah is lying awake, listening.

The house is perfectly quiet. She glances across at the bedside clock. Nearly half-past one.

She wonders what woke her, and she turns in bed because she has a sudden sense of a draught, a breath, a movement; but nothing is there. The door to the hallway is still closed, the way she left it. The curtains are open so that she wakes with the daylight, but for now it is just the moon shining through her window and leaving a bright pale patch of light on the duvet. She strains to hear sounds coming from Kitty's bedroom, wondering if something there has woken her up; but again, there is nothing. Not even a snore.

Sarah closes her eyes, turns over and pulls the duvet up to her chin.

She waits.

It's no good: she is not sleepy any more. Perhaps it's the hour she spent with Aiden, earlier; she'd stayed up and chatted to Kitty and Oscar, hoping they weren't waiting for her to go to bed first. But Kitty had drunk enough wine to be tired, and Sarah wasn't surprised when she headed up the stairs just before eleven. To his credit, Oscar had waited for a moment, as if he was about to ask Sarah where he was allowed to sleep.

'Anything you need?' she had asked.

'No, just, um, thanks...' he said, and unexpectedly gave her a hug.

Then he turned and scooted up the stairs.

She had cleaned the kitchen, washed up their wine glasses and stood for a moment at the kitchen sink looking out over the dark yard outside. The lights were still on in the cottage. She couldn't leave things the way they were. Without thinking about it any further, she had gone over there and knocked on the door.

They hadn't spoken much; there wasn't anything to say.

It's easy to do these things, she thinks; it's only afterwards that she starts to worry that she's doing it all wrong. Is she using him? Is she in love with him? It doesn't feel as though it ought to matter that much, but it does.

With a sigh she gets up and pulls on her dressing gown; it's chilly up here. She opens the door and looks out into the dark hallway. Kitty's door is firmly shut.

She steps across the creaky floorboards into the bathroom and locks the door behind her. She doesn't turn on the light; the moon is shining in, lighting the bath like a stage set. She doesn't flush. The cistern, a high Victorian one, makes enough noise to wake the whole house. She lowers the lid and reminds herself to do it first thing in the morning.

When she opens the door again it's hard to see anything at all; the hallway is dark. She can just about make out the square of grey light bisecting the landing from her open bedroom door.

She goes back into the bedroom and closes the door firmly, making sure it's properly fastened, before climbing back under the warm duvet and curling up into a tight ball with a sigh.

Even so, in the darkness, the warmth, in the silence, it takes her a long time to fall asleep.

Aiden

You have spent the last half-hour on the phone making plans for next week, and when you end the call it rings again almost immediately. Your heart sinks; you had been about to turn it off.

But, when you look at the number, you see it's Sophie.

'Hello?'

'Hi. Sorry to ring so late. Is it a bad time?'

'Well, I was just about to go to bed...'

'It's important. Look – hold on a sec.'

She is whispering, as if someone else is there, someone who shouldn't hear their conversation. You can hear a door opening and closing, footsteps, and then a moment later she is back on the line.

'Sorry about that. I'm back.'

'Is everything okay?'

'Yes, fine. Look – have you had a chance to talk to her yet?'

'No, not yet. Kitty's home this weekend.'

'I know,' she says. 'I just – I think you need to get it over with, Aiden.'

You have been through this in your mind, many times. You are not quite sure of the reason why you are holding back. It's not easy, this, and the reason is that it matters. It's important. If you get it wrong, it's likely things will never be the same between you.

'It's not that straightforward,' you say.

'I don't like subterfuge.'

'Sophie – '

'It's not a threat. Just please think about what you're doing. The next chance you get, yes?'

'Fine.'

'So either you tell her, or I will, okay?'

Sarah

In the morning Kitty and Oscar take the dogs on a long walk. They intend to hike over the other side of the hill, and follow the course of the river to the lake – some seven miles in total. Sarah has promised to go and pick them up when they phone her. They are planning to have a pub lunch somewhere, possibly meet up with friends later.

It's all suitably vague. Sarah had almost forgotten what it was like having Kitty here; the memories are flooding back now.

The house is echoingly empty with everyone gone. She tidies up and then finds herself standing in the kitchen looking out over the yard.

Aiden's car is not there.

She had begun to think she was falling in love with him. It's not hard to think like that when the man you're with has taken the time to develop a deep understanding of your body and how it works; how to give it the greatest soaring pleasure you've ever experienced. There are moments, following the prolonged eye contact, the slow, deep kisses, the hand-holding, when it feels like love. But how can it be, when he has been here less than two weeks?

But now, with the wind causing dry leaves to dance and spin through the yard, she reminds herself that he has given no indication that he feels the same way about her. He has secrets, things he has not been able to divulge. He and Jim met up without telling her. Jim gave him money. She feels as though she has only just felt the edges of something vast, buried between them like an unexploded mine.

Is it a bad thing? Can she sustain a relationship when there is no trust?

It's all right for now. But one day it will break her, and she knows that when that happens it will hurt far worse than it does now.

So: this has to end.

And she has to end it, because he won't. At the end of the weekend, she decides, when Kitty has gone, she will tell him.

The clock ticks; the house waits, listening to her breathing.

Sarah is just in that difficult, chaotic moment when all the elements of a Sunday roast dinner are coming together at the same time when there is a knock at the door.

This in itself is surprising, and the dogs bark and begin scrabbling at the door which doesn't help, so Sarah shouts, 'Come in!' and then, when nothing happens, yells for Kitty, who is laying the table in the dining room.

She thinks it is probably Aiden, who still can't manage to walk in without being invited.

She carries the roast potatoes through, oven gloves on, the heat still searing through to her fingers.

But it isn't Aiden.

When she gets back to the kitchen, it's Louis being hugged by his sister, the dogs jumping up at both of them in ecstasy.

'Louis!'

And this time – maybe because Kitty's there – he actually gives her a brief hug.

'Hi, Mum.'

She has a moment to look at him – he looks well, and he's smiling, actually here in her kitchen and smiling at her... then she remembers the vegetables still boiling and going soggy.

'I'm just dishing up,' she says. 'Kitty – can you take this through? And go and introduce Louis to Oscar…'

A few moments later they are all seated around the dining table and helping themselves to roast potatoes, Yorkshire puddings, vegetables. Sarah loves him for coming, for putting his issues to one side to see Kitty.

'Let's start before it gets cold,' Sarah says.

'This looks great,' Oscar says.

'What are you studying, Oscar?' asks Louis.

'Civil engineering, same as Kit,' he says.

Sarah notes that he doesn't ask what Louis studied; Kitty must have briefed him. That's good of her. The conversation flows naturally as they eat and drink, and afterwards there is apple pie, or a slice of chocolate cake with tea. Everyone has cake.

They move to the living room and Sarah begins to stack the plates.

'I'll help you, Mum,' Kitty offers.

'Don't be daft, it's your last day. Go and relax.'

'I'll help, then,' Louis says.

Sarah is about to instruct him to go and sit and talk to his sister but, actually, the opportunity to have a moment alone with him is too good to pass up. 'Thank you,' she says.

'No probs.'

'No – thank you for coming. I'm so glad you did.'

'Well, you invited me.'

He takes the plates through and comes back for the empty vegetable dishes while Sarah puts clingfilm over what's left of the cake.

'Will phoned me. Again,' he says.

'Oh?'

'He told me you're in trouble.'

Sarah stops what she's doing and looks at him. 'What?'

'He says you're thinking of selling the house.'

Where did that come from? How on earth would Will know that? It can't be from Sophie; she's never said anything to her about it. Sarah is too shocked to speak.

'Is it true?'

She can't lie to him, not now that he's seen the expression on her face. 'Yes. Maybe not just yet – I'm waiting to hear if the stuff I'm working on will make me enough to carry on. But yes, things are... a bit tight.'

'I can help,' he says. 'If you'll let me.'

She is not about to let him see her cry, so she concentrates on the cake again, stretching another piece of clingfilm across and trying not to squash the icing. He can't possibly have any idea of how bad the debt is – a couple of grand isn't going to scratch the surface.

'That's a very kind offer. You don't have to,' she says.

'I know that. But I can help if you're desperate. If you're going to sell up.'

'Thank you,' she says. 'Really. Thanks.'

'Let me know. We can talk about it again. After all, this house is Kitty's and my inheritance. I don't want to see it going for a pittance and you pissing away the proceeds, do I?'

The sudden cruel twist of his words, when she had thought he was being kind, makes her feel sick. As she goes through to the living room a few minutes later with the fresh pot of tea she feels a little drunk, in fact, as if the ground has shifted under her feet.

But it's all about to get much worse.

Louis is sitting on the arm of the chair as if he's ready to leave – which he probably is. Lord knows he wouldn't want to get comfortable, would he?

'Thanks, Mum,' Kitty says, moving cake plates out of the way. 'So what happened to Aiden today?'

'Aiden?' Sarah asks. 'What do you mean?'

'Didn't you ask him?'

'Ask him what?'

'To lunch.'

'No,' Sarah says. 'I expect he's doing something.'

'Did you know Mum's got a new tenant?' Kitty asks Louis.

Louis frowns. 'What? Who's this?'

'Aiden Beck,' Sarah says, trying not to sound defensive. 'He was a friend of your dad's – well, and mine, really. We were all at uni together. Anyway, he's just come back from living abroad, so I offered him the cottage for a bit.'

Sarah looks up and catches Louis's eye. He is staring at her, frowning. 'Well, I bloody hope he's paying you rent,' he says.

'Louis!' Kitty says. 'Mum's being really kind.'

'He is paying rent,' Sarah says. *Not that it's any of your business.*

Louis gets to his feet. 'I'd better get going,' he says.

'Already?' Kitty asks.

Sarah says nothing. She has the sense that if Louis stays longer he will say something else, worse, in front of Kitty.

'Thanks again for coming. You're an ace big brother,' Kitty says, tiptoeing to wrap her arms around Louis's neck. He shakes Oscar's hand, heads for the kitchen.

Sarah follows.

He is rubbing Basil's ears and fussing over Tess.

'Louis – ' she says, not quite knowing what it is that she wants to say but just that she must say something.

'Don't,' he says. There is a tone to his voice, low, angry. 'It's fucking bad enough that you've spent all Dad's money. That's one thing. And now you've moved your new bloke in as well? Jesus.'

'What?' Sarah is genuinely horrified at the thought. 'Aiden's just a friend, for goodness' sake.'

'That's not what Will said.'

'Will?'

Louis's lip is curled into a snarl. 'You know what else he told me? About your so-called friend?'

'Look, this isn't – '

'He's a male prostitute.'

Sarah opens her mouth to speak, horrified. 'He's not – I mean – for God's sake, Louis, this is crazy.'

'He has sex with people for money.'

'No, of course he doesn't!'

'What *does* he do for a living, then?'

'He's – he does something setting up franchises, therapy, I don't know.'

'Right. Perhaps you should ask him.'

Sarah's hand flutters over her mouth. What can she say that can possibly make this better? He's not going to listen if she tries to explain. He is not going to understand the subtleties, the nuances of this new relationship she explored and has now decided to end.

He stands up, pulls on his coat. Sarah feels suddenly faint, the room lurching sideways. 'Louis, please.'

'You've got form for this. Shagging around. Haven't you?'

'What?'

'I saw you,' he says, his voice icy. 'I saw you, in the garden with Will at my birthday party. You complete slag. Dad wasn't even cold in his grave, and you were drunk, shagging a kid half your age.'

Sarah stares, unable to move.

'Not got much to say now, have you? No. And you wonder why I find it so bloody difficult to be anywhere near you? Well now you know. You disgust me,' he says, and slams the door behind him.

Sarah rinses the plates, slowly, and puts each one carefully into the dishwasher, while breathing in gasping, jerking breaths and trying not to cry. If she cries, even briefly, Kitty will see and ask and she doesn't know what she can possibly say.

She cannot even think about what he said to her. How could anyone have misread the situation so completely?

Her hands are shaking.

She puts a plate slowly back into the sink before she drops it, leans against the work surface, looking out of the window. Deep breaths. Slowly. *You can do it*. She mustn't cry. Mustn't spoil Kitty's last day. She has to keep it together.

When she feels strong enough, she goes back into the living room. Kitty and Oscar are watching the rugby. Kitty is sitting sideways on the sofa, her legs across Oscar's lap.

'I'm just going to have a bit of a lie-down,' Sarah says lightly.

'Are you okay, Mum?' Kitty asks, craning her neck over the back of the sofa.

'Yes, I'm fine. Just a bit of a headache. It'll go away if I have a nap. You don't mind?'

'Of course not. Is there anything I can do?'

'Don't let me sleep too late? Call me if I'm not up by four. I don't want you to miss your train.'

'Will do.'

Already she has turned back to the television.

Sarah goes upstairs and the dogs follow her, confused when she shuts the bedroom door. She stands for a moment, stunned, wondering what she's doing here, what she can do next.

This isn't me, she thinks. *This isn't the person I am. I am better at holding things in.*

If Aiden's car had been outside when Sarah returned from dropping Kitty and Oscar at the station, she would have gone in and spoken to him there and then.

As it is, she sits in the car for a while, looking at the cottage, thinking about Will and Aiden and what a complete mess she has made of everything.

'*He's a male prostitute...*'

He can't be, he just can't. He would be going off to meet women, perhaps bringing them home with him. She's not seen him with anyone. She would know, she would be able to tell – wouldn't she?

It's rubbish – just another thing Louis has made up, to hurt her.

Isn't it?

The shock of the confrontation with Louis left her unable to sleep, this afternoon. She lay still in the darkness, trying not to cry, trying not to make a noise, trying to think of something else to distract her. In the end she gave up and went downstairs, sat in the living room with a cup of tea trying to make sense of it all while Kitty and Oscar were getting their things together.

Louis saw her, with Will.

The thought of it is horrible, but now it's out there she can think of nothing else.

Louis hadn't even wanted a party for his twenty-first; it was Kitty who persuaded him. She told him that his dad would have thrown him the biggest party he could imagine, which was true. It had been the worst possible year for all of them and nobody felt much like celebrating, but Sarah knew they had to start somewhere. And Jim's death wasn't Louis's fault – why should he miss out on his special birthday?

And in the end it had been okay. Kitty had organised it all through Facebook with Louis's friends and hers; everyone had been drunk. At Louis's insistence, there was no food more elaborate than pizza. The dogs were staying at Sophie's house. The music was loud, it was dark, and Sarah had retreated out into the garden.

And Will followed her, with his guitar. She remembered talking to him about nothing much. He was kind. He said she was a beautiful person, and that made her want to cry. He put his arms around her, and he kissed her.

She hasn't thought about this bit in detail for years; perhaps she has blanked it out. She has always told herself that she was drunk, that it was a one-off, that it was a bit of a mistake.

The truth is, she had needed it. She had needed someone to hold her – even awkwardly, lying on the grass at the back of the garden – and tell her that she was doing okay. That she wasn't bad. That, whatever Louis thought, none of it was her fault. In fairness she could happily have stopped at the gentle hug and the kind words, and maybe at the bristly bearded kiss that tasted of cider and weed, but when he put his hand under her top she didn't stop him.

At first it was the shock of it, coming out of nowhere – what did he think he was doing? And then it was almost funny – *this is Will, I'm old enough to be his mother!* And then, seconds or perhaps minutes later, when his hand moved inside the waistband of her jeans and she still hadn't stopped him, still hadn't pulled away, she thought, perhaps, *oh, well...* and, *I'm drunk. I'll say I was drunk. It's too late to back out now.*

In the past few years, when she has thought of it, it has been with the clouded fondness of an event you've decided you cannot allow yourself to regret. She has pretended it was nice. She told herself she needed it, needed to feel human again, to remember that she was a woman and still young enough to do spontaneous, foolish things.

But now, in the car, staring out over the grey yard and the drizzle and the darkening sky, she remembers it differently.

In her mind's eye she goes back to that summer night and stands in her garden, looking down at the woman and the young lad who is fucking her hard on the grass.

She is drunk and feeling queasy. Will is on top of her and his fingers, rubbing at her in a juvenile attempt at foreplay, are rough. The ground, baked by days of sun, is hard underneath her, a stone grazing her shoulder. And when she is in that position – pale legs spread awkwardly, jeans still hanging off one ankle, Will, more or less fully dressed, on top – Sarah from her imaginary position looks away in disgust and sees that Louis has come out of the house, lurching, looking for Will or looking for her or maybe not doing anything but getting some fresh air. He stops dead, catching sight of the two pale shapes moving in a way that cannot be misinterpreted. A slow grin spreads across his face and he creeps forward to see who it is.

The woman's head is turned away, towards the hill, perhaps because the lad's breath has got too much or perhaps because she doesn't want to look at him any more. But Will hears the clumsy footsteps and turns towards them, not stopping; in fact he is fucking her even harder – she even makes a noise, something like a cry, something like pain. And Will sees Louis's face. And grins, and winks.

Sarah drops her head to the steering wheel.

Oh, God.

Aiden

When she says it, she is quite cold.

'I think we need to just be friends,' she says.

You are sitting in the living room of the cottage, on Monday, and a chilly winter sun is filtering through the windows. You offered her coffee or tea; she declined both.

She won't look you in the eyes but she is not upset; her head is up, her eyes focused on a spot on the white wall in front of her.

'Did something happen?' you ask.

She doesn't move, doesn't speak, and you wonder if she's even heard you.

'Sarah? What is it? What's wrong?'

'What is it you do for a living?' she asks, and for the first time she smiles, just briefly. 'I don't think you've ever told me.'

That's it, then, you think. She knows – or at least, she knows something, and now you have to find the right words really fucking quickly, and try to fix it.

'I'm a sensual masseur,' you say.

She nods, as if she was expecting you to deny it and she is at least a tiny bit less angry with you because you haven't.

'Louis said to me that you're a prostitute.'

The laugh is out before you can stop it, a loud 'Ha!' because it's not the first time you've heard that. And then you realise the context and you wish you'd managed to keep it in. 'It's very different from that.'

Sarah takes a sharp, shuddering breath in. 'Why didn't you tell me?'

Yes, you think, why didn't you? You fucking coward. Why didn't you mention it on day one? She even asked you, didn't she, in the car on the way to the pub where you met Sophie, and you sidestepped the issue by telling her she looked beautiful.

'I know you must be angry,' you say. 'I'm sorry I didn't tell you sooner. I didn't want to upset you.'

'I thought we were friends. Friends don't keep secrets from each other,' she says coldly.

Really? You want to remind her about the small matter of her not telling Sophie about that one-night stand with Will. We all keep secrets from each other, all the time, and we kid ourselves that they are tiny ones, that they don't matter, right up until the moment that we are found out and we realise it matters very much.

'No,' you say. 'You're right.'

'Louis said that Will told him,' she says. 'How did Will find out?'

You could lie, or at least just tell her that you don't know, but you don't want to make things worse. Perhaps she already knows the answer to this question and is testing you.

'I think probably Sophie told him,' you say.

She nods again. 'Right. So I'm the last person to know. Thanks.'

You take a deep breath in. 'I know it feels as though this is a big deal, but it really isn't. It's just a job.'

'We had sex,' she says. 'I thought that meant something. I didn't realise I was just getting a freebie. Were you going to send me a bill at the end of the month? Take it off the rent?'

She is deliberately trying to wound you now, but she is close to tears so you don't bite back. She is being so strong, so dignified, and any second now she is going to lose it and break down.

'It meant something,' you say.

'It's too late,' she says, without expression. 'This is going to make everything awkward; I can't do it any more.'

Your baseline for understanding situations like this one comes from your career rather than your personal life. Clients have said similar things to you, in the past. *We have to stop seeing each other. I cannot carry on like this. It isn't working out. It's not you, it's me.*

As though it's a relationship, despite everything you've discussed, not a business transaction.

Whereas this: this is a relationship, or rather you had hoped that was what it was becoming. Perhaps, as she said in the pub, you aren't as good at reading people as you think you are?

Usually, clients stop seeing you because someone has found out about your arrangement and it has become awkward for them, or embarrassing, and all it takes is for you to challenge gently whether it's really what they want, and they cave in and hold out their hand for you to take, or they cry and you hold them, or they just go away and think about it and the next week they're phoning you for an appointment.

Sarah is, you remind yourself, not a client. She is fierce, hands clenched into fists in her lap, teeth gritted.

You want to take her by the shoulders, force her to let it out, the anger, so that you can comfort her and get past this. But she is holding it in, and you have to let her do it. You have to give her the space to come to terms with everything you've told her. It's going to take time, and you can't interfere.

'Okay,' you say. 'So we are friends?'

She looks at her hands. 'Yes, of course.'

'That's good,' you say. 'Because I'm happy to be whatever it is you need me to be.'

That, too, seems to be the wrong thing to say. She stands up suddenly, makes for the door.

'Sarah?'

'Just – just leave me alone…'

And she's gone, slamming the door behind her. The sound echoes on the bare walls. Your heart is thudding with it.

You got that wrong, didn't you?

You got that one completely wrong.

Part Five

Sarah

Sarah is lying on the bed like a corpse, feet together, hands clasped over her tummy, looking up at the cracked ceiling and listening to the sounds of the house creaking and settling.

She is properly alone now.

She has pushed everybody away by being naïve and stupid, and now she has nobody. Aiden isn't the person she thought he was; and nor is Sophie. Her best friend has been laughing at her behind her back – *sweet, silly Sarah, she doesn't understand things like this* – and Louis, oh, God, Louis, so traumatised by what he saw that he's still furious about it three years later…

There is only Kitty left, and she is miles away, out of reach.

Sarah holds her breath, listening.

There's no point staying here. With a sigh, she sits up on the edge of the bed. She is still fully dressed, and she is in the master bedroom because she didn't think she would be able to sleep in the bed where she had been with Aiden just a fortnight ago. This bed isn't even made up – the bedspread hides a bare mattress, but she hadn't bothered to get the sheets out because she already knew that she wouldn't be able to sleep.

From somewhere in the house, Sarah hears a muffled bang. Her head spins towards the door as if she will be able to see what it was. Nothing moves. She listens. The house settles and waits with her.

There it is again; a door banging? Maybe Kitty has left a window open somewhere.

She does not move. Something is gripping her, something she is not used to: she is afraid. It crosses her mind that she could phone Aiden, ask him to come over, but she cannot bring herself to do that; and besides, her mobile is downstairs, charging, and the landline up here doesn't work.

Bang.

This time she hears Basil give a short warning bark immediately afterwards – it must have woken him up, whatever it is. The fact that the dogs are downstairs gives her a fresh burst of courage and she crosses to the door, takes a breath and yanks it open, half-expecting to find someone standing on the other side of it. The landing is dark and empty.

Downstairs, all is quiet. Basil gets up from his bed and greets her, wagging his tail sleepily.

'What is it, Bas? What's up?'

A cold draught comes from somewhere, creeping over the back of her neck and raising goosebumps on her arms.

It's coming from the back door.

The utility room door is closed. It isn't usually closed, unless she's trying to contain a muddy dog; perhaps the draught has blown it shut? She hesitates for a moment with her fingers on the door handle. From the tiny gap under the door, an icy breeze blows over her bare feet.

She breathes in, and out, and then pulls open the door quickly. The back door, which is unaccountably open, slams shut with a bang that rattles the glass in the windowframe.

Sarah squeals in sudden panic, her heart hammering in her chest.

No one is there.

She is alone.

She spends the rest of the night on the sofa, curled under Basil's blanket, watching crappy middle-of-the-night repeats of reality shows.

When the breakfast news programmes start she gets up, stretches, and goes to feed the dogs and make coffee.

She feels numb now, feeble; all the anger has dissolved and all that's left is sorrow. If only she hadn't been quite so furious, perhaps she could have talked rationally, worked out what was going on and why. Despite his admissions, Sarah can't help but think that there is more that Aiden hasn't told her.

At seven she takes the dogs out of the back door – closing it firmly behind her – and walks them around the field, distracted enough to barely notice where they go. She's not out for long. It's freezing cold, and the rain starts again, turning quickly from drizzle to an insistent, misty rain that drenches her quickly.

She keeps her head down, stumbling back down the hill, and as a consequence does not see the dark figure standing in the doorway at the back of the house until she is almost there.

She gasps with the shock, clutching her chest.

Basil is all over him, tail wagging.

'Sorry,' Aiden says. 'Didn't mean to make you jump.'

She is about to say that he didn't, but then she notices the dark circles around his eyes and realises that he probably hasn't had much sleep either.

'You coming in?' she asks.

In the kitchen, the dogs dried, the coffee brewing – it feels as if they both need something strong – Aiden sits with her at the kitchen table and asks her if she is okay. 'I wanted to explain, about my job,' he says.

He is looking at her, right into her eyes. She is too tired for another argument; perhaps he knows this and that's why he's come over early.

'The official version is that I provide a traditional massage in the comfort of people's homes, or hotel rooms, with or without clothing.'

'The official version?' Sarah repeats. She feels, suddenly, spectacularly stupid. 'What's the unofficial version?'

'I do other things, pretty much on a case-by-case basis. Some women only want to talk or have a standard massage; some women want to be touched more intimately. Some women want me to help them come.'

Sarah is finding it difficult to breathe. Oh, God. He's a prostitute.

She still hasn't moved. She is staring at him. This man she thought she knew, this man for whom she has had such intense longing for most of her adult life, is someone utterly unfamiliar.

'Say something,' he says gently.

'I... can't.'

'I wanted to be honest with you,' he says.

At last she finds her voice. 'You have sex with strangers for money?'

'It's very rare for me to have actual sex with them. It's more about opening them up physically and emotionally, becoming attuned to their needs through touch. Just like traditional massage, except that the touching is intimate and often leads to orgasm. And they aren't really strangers. I get to know them first. I mean, I wouldn't exactly call them good friends – but they're not strangers either. They're clients. Like any other service business, you do best when you know exactly what it is your client needs. That takes time, conversation, agreement between all the parties. Mutual understanding.'

'You make it sound as if you're selling them jewellery or mobile phones or a new set of hair straighteners.'

'I'm selling them happiness. Contentment. Self-confidence.'

'You're selling them self-confidence? They're paying for a hand job; that says to me that they must have pretty low self-esteem.'

Ouch.

She catches the expression on his face. 'I'm sorry. That came out wrong.'

Aiden smiles at her. She can't quite tell if it's genuine. 'It's hard to explain. I don't blame you for thinking badly of me, of them. But it isn't like that. My clients are well-off, usually professional women. Some of them are in loveless, sexless relationships but don't want to risk having an affair with someone they don't know if they can trust. Some of them are single, and don't have time for a relationship. I can give them what they need, when they need it, and then I leave them alone when they don't. It's a business transaction, but it is one that's designed to serve their needs perfectly. Every client gets a bespoke service.'

'It sounds as though you take this very seriously.'

This time, she can see that his smile is genuine. 'I do. That's what makes me good at it. I do genuinely enjoy taking the time to make sure they get good value for their money. Some of the men in my line of work, well, you wouldn't believe it. And they still end up making a killing. But I guess they don't get the repeat business.'

'You get lots of repeat business, then?'

'I have some clients I've been seeing for more than ten years. Sometimes a long time will pass between calls, but they always seem to come back to me.'

'Do you keep notes?' Sarah asks. The mechanics of this industry she has never heard of before are suddenly fascinating to her, and she has almost forgotten that it is Aiden who is confessing this secret life to her.

'No,' he says.

'How do you remember them all?'

'I have a very good memory. I've trained myself to remember everything. To be fair, in the past few years I haven't taken on any new clients. I was making enough from the regular clients I already had. They're like... I don't know... like old friends.'

'Like old girlfriends,' Sarah says.

'Perhaps.'

She appreciates his honesty. He is answering all her questions, not holding back.

'Is it well paid, then?'

'Not at first,' he says. 'But in the past few years, yes. Very well paid.'

'What about the risks?'

'I have very strict boundaries. For everyone's safety, not just mine.'

'What boundaries?'

He pauses for a moment, as if deciding on the best way to approach it. Then he says, 'My clients always call me; I never – ever – call them. I never take calls from withheld numbers. Clients pay me up front. I don't do relationships, so there is no grey area. I was never anyone's boyfriend. I have a list of things that I will do and things I won't when it comes to restraint and physical discipline. Back when I first started, I did a few sessions with couples, but I stopped doing that very quickly because it's too complicated.'

'Complicated how?'

'If there's just the client, I check all the way through whatever we are doing that she is happy and comfortable. If there's three people, then it becomes more difficult to check consent because there is an existing relationship between the two clients that has its own nuances and subtleties. I had a couple where the man's fantasy was to see his wife with a stranger. She went along with it to make him happy, but the whole time it felt really awkward. She wasn't comfortable with it. So I didn't go through with it; I gave them their money back and left. The bloke wasn't happy, but then neither was I.'

'Have you ever had bad things happen?'

A shadow passes over his face. 'Not really,' he says.

'Not really?'

He hesitates. 'The worst thing is when clients get a bit too attached. A few times women have wanted to start a proper relationship.'

'What did you do?'

'To start with, just remind them gently of my boundaries. Sometimes that's all that's needed. If that doesn't work, I tell them I can't see them again. You have to do it all really carefully, because sometimes my clients have emotional needs they are trying to fulfil with this transaction, and, if I can't fulfil them because of the boundaries I have in place, then I need to be careful how I tell them that. I don't want anyone to get hurt.'

'And has anyone ever got hurt?'

'Happened twice. The first time, she got bored eventually when I wouldn't answer her calls.'

'The second time?'

There is a pause, then he says, 'The second time was... bad.'

He looks as if he doesn't want to say any more, but he has aroused her curiosity now and she pushes him further.

'What happened?'

'I was trying everything with her, and it wasn't working. It was frustrating for both of us. I wanted to suggest she try working with someone else, but she insisted that all she needed was penetrative sex. I told you, I don't normally do that – but in this case I thought maybe it would help her.'

'But it didn't?'

He hesitates. 'It was too personal.'

'For you, or for her?'

But Aiden doesn't answer.

Sarah cannot think of anything else to ask, for the moment. She looks at the table and then, when he gets up to fetch mugs, she watches him move. Thinks of how she always thought he was gorgeous, but now she sees it differently. It's the way he moves, she thinks. It's the way he holds himself; confidence without arrogance. Such a rare thing.

Then it comes to her – the big question. The thing she should have asked at the beginning, when he first told her about this.

'And Jim knew about this?'

'Yes. You see now why he might have been a bit reluctant to tell you.'

The coffee machine gurgles and rumbles. She looks at him, thinking. Her head, suddenly, feels clear: cold water, refreshing, tumbling through her thoughts.

'What was the money for?'

He stops, looks at her.

'What money?'

'The loan, from Jim. Ten thousand, you said.'

For a moment, he stares. She thinks she has crossed a line; asked something too personal. But the overheads for this business – if that's what you can call it – there can't be many, can there? How much does a job lot of condoms and baby oil cost, anyway?

'Various things,' he says. 'Travel mostly – I had to pay that up front. Hotel rooms. And I needed a flat, for a while. And a car.'

She doesn't push him further. She thinks, perhaps, she doesn't want to know.

'What about Sophie?' she asks.

'Sophie?'

'You told her about all this?'

He puts a mug of coffee in front of her and the aroma of it makes her feel a little better.

'You remember she came to see me, when you were at the dentist? She asked about Jim, and I told her. She asked the same question – what I needed the money for – and I told her what I was doing to earn money. I don't usually tell people, but you know Sophie – she has a way of looking at you that's frankly quite terrifying.'

'What did she say?'

'Funnily enough, she didn't seem surprised. I didn't need to explain it in too much detail.'

Armando, Sarah thinks. *Sophie was talking about him just the other day.*

'She used to see someone like you, in London,' she says.

'That explains it, then.'

'Even so – why didn't she tell me?'

'I asked her not to. I wanted to tell you myself.'

'But you didn't.'

'No.' He looks down at his coffee. 'I wasn't expecting us to get on quite so well, to be honest. I thought there would be a good moment for me to mention it casually, but... well. We kind of got past the talking stage early on.'

Sarah is looking at him and it feels as though she is seeing him for the first time: the dark stubble because he hasn't shaved, the lines around his eyes, the strong jaw. She feels a lurch of something that might just be love.

'Well, we've established that you should have told me,' she says. 'Now the question is, what do we do next?'

'If you want me to leave...' he says.

'No, of course I don't.' Sarah is surprised by how certain of this she is. She doesn't want him to go. What she wants is for him to not be what she knows he is.

And then something occurs to her that makes her laugh out loud.

'What is it?' he asks.

'It explains why you're such a good fuck,' she says.

'I've had a bit of practice. With the foreplay part, anyway.'

'Clearly.'

'It's different, though,' he says, looking up. 'And not just because I don't actually fuck my clients. Even the rest is different. I know you might not believe me.'

'How is it different?'

'Well, as I said yesterday, it means something. And at first, yes, I know what to do, I'm trying to see what feels good for you, just like with them; but then there's a point at which it all dissolves and it's just me and you, like it was before, and it's...'

'What?'

'I was going to say "perfect".'

'You smooth-talking bastard,' she says, and laughs.

'I know I got things wrong,' he says. 'But I can't help hoping that we might be able to get past it.'

Sarah breathes, thinking. She is too tired to make decisions.

'I'm not ready,' she says.

He sits still for a moment, watching her, as if trying to think of something else to say. Then he finishes his coffee, gets to his feet. 'You should call Sophie,' he says. 'You know what she did was with the best of intentions. She's a good friend.'

He kisses her on the top of her head, says goodbye, and leaves.

The house is quiet.

She sits in the kitchen for a while, listening to the clock ticking, the wind and the rain outside. It has changed direction; it's coming from the north.

Sarah spends the rest of the day trying to pluck up the courage to ring Sophie, to let her know that she knows about Aiden, and that, actually, it's not as big a deal as she thought it was; but in the end, next morning, it's Sophie who calls first.

'I'm sorry,' is the first thing she says.

'It's okay,' Sarah answers. 'I wish you'd told me, though.'

'I know, me too. Look, can we meet for a drink? Talk about things properly?'

Sophie is waiting for Sarah in the bar at the Black Swan. It's past seven when Sarah finds her, in one of the snug alcoves tucked away in the guest lounge.

'I've been round here twice already,' Sarah says. 'Who are you hiding from?'

'Marjorie Baker,' Sophie says, kissing her cheek. 'I saw her going into the Ladies'. She's going to ask me to do something for the Summer Fair.'

There are two apple martinis on the table in front of Sophie.

'Soph, I'm driving,' Sarah says.

'Go on, you can manage one. We're going to be here a while.'

'Are we? Why? What's happened?'

Sophie mouths the word: *Will.*

'He came round on Friday,' Sarah says. 'He had dinner with us, came out to the Royal Oak for a drink. He said he wanted to see Kitty.'

'Oh, did he really?'

Sophie says it with a smile on her face but there is something under the surface, like a punch to the skin before it has time to bruise.

'Tell me,' Sarah says.

She had been grateful to hear from Sophie earlier: she needed to talk to someone, needed to see a friendly face. But, now she's here, it seems that Sophie needs support even more than she does.

'You know he was house-sitting?'

Sarah nods.

'I sorted that out. Fool that I am. I've been giving him money to stay at a holiday let in Thirsk, but I heard that

Shona and Richard were going to Paris for the weekend and I told them I'd got someone who was reliable and good with animals. They were a bit reluctant, but I told them I'd keep an eye on things too.'

She reaches across for her cocktail. It's already half-gone.

'Anyway, I thought it would be... fun. I could stay over. I've been, you know, seeing him.'

'In the holiday let?'

'When I could get away. That was all right, although it's bloody expensive even off-season. A B&B would be cheaper but you know what those places are like; they're hardly what you'd call discreet.'

'I guess not.'

'On Friday he sent me a text saying he was in the Royal Oak. I was going to meet him at Shona and Richard's, but he insisted he wanted me to meet him in town. I got there and saw your car in the car park. I sent him a text to say I was outside.'

'He was with us,' Sarah says.

'I know. I told him to stop playing games. He wasn't happy. I don't know what he's playing at; it's like he wanted some kind of confrontation, some kind of embarrassing scene.'

'Why would he want that?' Sarah asks.

'I don't know. I think he likes to stir things up. To make trouble. He gets off on it.'

Yes, Sarah thinks. That's exactly it – all the times he has turned up, with nowhere to go. He could go anywhere, couldn't he? Why come to Four Winds Farm? It's as if he's enjoying seeing her reaction when she finds him there.

'But you like him?' Sarah asks.

For a moment Sophie doesn't reply. There is something she is hiding, something she doesn't want to say.

'Soph?'

Sophie leans forward in her seat.

'It was okay when it was just about sex. But now – it's more than that. He wants it to be something more serious. And he's so persuasive, so passionate about everything. Sometimes it's a bit scary, that's all. I don't think he likes to hear the word "no". Anyway. How was Kitty?'

The abrupt change of subject says more about Sophie's need to distract herself than about her concern for Kitty; but Sarah doesn't mind. She needs distraction herself, after all.

'She's fine. And Oscar seems all right. Quiet. Kitty seems very keen on him.'

'Did you get much of a chance to talk to Kitty on her own?'

'No, not really.'

In that moment Sarah realises that, even if Kitty and Oscar don't last, from now on it's likely that there will always be someone else in Kitty's life. Their relationship has undergone a major shift. Things will never be as they once were. Kitty is not hers any more.

'Will said Louis was thinking of going over on Sunday,' Sophie ventures.

'Oh, Will! Bloody Will. I wish he'd keep his nose out.'

Sarah sees Sophie's face and wishes she could take it back. 'I'm sorry. It's just that it feels as though he's interfering. I'm sure he's just trying to help, but he's making things worse.'

'Things with Louis?'

'He said Will had told him that I'm having financial trouble and I'm thinking of selling the house. And, as if that wasn't bad enough, Will also told Louis about Aiden's job, so he took great delight in passing that on to me. So that's how I found out.'

'Shit,' Sophie says. 'God, I'm so sorry.'

'It's bad enough that you didn't tell me, Soph, but to tell Will...'

'I know, God, I wish I hadn't. I was drunk, he was asking about you and Aiden... it just slipped out. I'm sorry.'

'It doesn't matter now. It's all out there; we can't take any of it back.'

'Still. Shit. And is that true? About you being in financial trouble? Selling the house?'

'Not exactly. I mean, maybe – but it's something I've been thinking about, not something that's definitely going to happen. And Louis was so *angry*. He was so... cruel. I've never seen him like that before. He said some horrible things, Soph. I can't even tell you.'

She pulls herself together quickly because the waiter has appeared, taking away the two empty martini glasses – did she really drink the whole thing? – and asking what they want next. Sarah hasn't even looked at the cocktail menu.

'Two passion fruit bellinis,' Sophie says.

By the time the waiter has gone again, Sarah is feeling better. *Deep breaths.*

'George wants me to do a fucking dinner party,' Sophie says. 'On Saturday. Please say you'll come.'

'Another one? What's this one for?'

'He's going to try to tap Ian for some party funding. He thinks Ian controls the purse strings at the City office.'

'Does he?'

One arched eyebrow. 'It's Ian. Do you think he looks like someone they'd trust with the money?'

'And you want me there? What if I say the wrong thing, like last time?'

'Darling,' Sophie says, 'that's what I'm hoping for. Your political rants are endlessly entertaining.'

'Well, all right, then. I'll do my best.'

'Bring Aiden,' Sophie adds. 'He can soften Ian up by talking about cricket. If it's not golf, George hasn't a clue.'

'If you're sure,' Sarah says.

'Sarah, he's not going to start offering his services to Diana and Becca.'

The thought of Aiden peddling his business amongst the good ladies of the village Women's Institute is amusing for a moment, but then Sophie asks, 'Is he okay?'

'I think so,' Sarah says, and then adds, because Sophie and Aiden have clearly been happily chatting without her knowing, 'Haven't you spoken to him?'

'I had a bit of a go at him last time we spoke. I just felt so bad that you'd been left in the dark about everything.'

'I think he's fine.'

'Thing is...' Sophie says, 'thing is, I could see that you were falling for him. Even that first phone call, when he'd first arrived, I could hear it in your voice. You've been so down, especially since Kitty left, and after Christmas... and suddenly you were full of life again. I couldn't do it to you. I didn't want to be the one to take your sparkle away.'

Sarah walks back up the hill an hour or so later, thinking about Sophie and Will, and Aiden. Sophie offered to drive her home, but Sarah told her she would get a taxi. This was a fib – she'd rather save the money – and, besides, the walk gives her time to think.

It has been a good night. She went feeling miserable and now she feels buoyant, full of love for her best friend and her exceptional positivity, the way she turns the most grim situation around and makes it hilarious.

But there is something about it that's troubling her, a phrase she said or Sophie said that reminded her of something she'd forgotten, or blanked out.

Aiden.

He thinks he understands, Sarah thinks. *He thinks he knows how people's minds work, he thinks he is empathetic, but really he isn't. He doesn't get it at all.*

It's like a heightened level of arrogance.

In that moment, walking up the hill in the cold, dark, the road sparkling with frost illuminated by the wide moon overhead, she thinks that he has always had it, even at university: this sense of being untouchable, being entitled, better than everyone else; the cool observer, the connoisseur, the expert.

And now, now that she has seen it with this sudden cold clarity, it feels dangerous.

It's what draws you to him, and at the same time it's what repels you.

Aiden

You are in the passenger seat of Sarah's car, being driven slowly down the hill towards the village. It's Saturday evening, and you have been invited to dinner by Sophie and George, or rather, you've been invited by Sarah.

'Is it someone's birthday?' you asked.

'No,' Sarah said. 'Just a dinner party. Sophie wants you to talk to Ian about cricket.'

Of course you said yes. You want to spend time with Sarah, and, if this is what you have to do to get that opportunity, so be it. In truth the idea of spending the evening talking about cricket is less than appealing; but food is involved, and Sarah's adamant that it's her turn to drive, so you can have a glass of wine or maybe two.

The house is impressive; a number of cars are already lined up in the driveway, a brand-new Lexus SUV at the top of it. They are not short of money, this lot.

Sarah rings the doorbell and, as the chimes echo through the space inside, you can hear Sophie shouting something as she crosses the hallway to the door. The door opens mid-sentence. '... not with salmon, darling, for fuck's sake... hello, you two, come in.'

Sophie kisses you on both cheeks. Her soft hair brushes your face, smells citrus-clean.

'Fabulous, thanks,' Sophie says, taking the bottle of Sancerre you have brought with you. 'Come through; we can sit in the kitchen while George finishes off.'

Sarah had said that they might have got caterers in; if it's a business thing George apparently often does, but it seems today he has taken it upon himself to cook.

'Sarah, what can I get you?' George asks. He is pink-cheeked in the steam rising from a stainless steel pan on the stove. 'Gin? Wine? Beer?'

'Whatever's open, thank you,' Sarah says. 'How are you both?'

Sophie is already pouring wine from the bottle open on the granite breakfast bar.

'Everything is wonderful,' she says. 'Peachy.'

You realise she has probably already had several glasses.

George says nothing. He's surrounded by bubbling pots and the sink is full of chopping boards and knives. He and Sophie are staring at each other and you wonder what you have just interrupted.

'Let's go into the living room, shall we?' Sophie says, picking up both glasses.

You offer George a sympathetic smile as Sarah slips off the bar stool, but he's already turned away.

Their living room is huge, high-ceilinged, beautifully decorated – easily three times the size of Sarah's living room. The whole of your cottage could probably fit inside it. A fire has been lit, and there are scented candles on the glass coffee table.

The doorbell chimes and Sophie jumps up to get it.

'What do you think?' Sarah asks, smiling. 'Isn't it a fabulous house?'

'It's enormous. Is it just the two of them in here?'

'George has two grown-up daughters, from his first marriage. Sometimes they visit, bring the grandkids.'

'How does she cope with that?' you ask, quietly, although you can hear Sophie cheerily welcoming someone in the hall. 'Sticky fingers and crayons everywhere.'

'You'd be surprised. She adores the little ones; it's their mums she struggles with. She calls them the Weird Sisters.'

You drink your wine, listening to Sophie's raucous laugh. You half-turn in your seat, ready to smile and say hello to whoever it is, but the voices trail off. They've gone into the kitchen, to get drinks.

After a minute or two, the doorbell chimes again. You can both hear Sophie in the kitchen, laughing and talking, so Sarah gets up and opens the door herself.

You follow her. It's Becca and Daniel, Sophie's friends from the village.

'Oh,' says Becca, smiling, 'have we come to the wrong house?'

'Come in,' Sarah says, 'Sophie's in the kitchen.'

'Hello, Becca,' you say, kissing her on the cheek even though you only met her the once and even then are not even sure if you spoke to her at all. You shake hands with Daniel.

They both take off their jackets and, for want of something to do, Sarah takes them and hangs them up in the cloakroom. Everyone is in the kitchen. She retrieves her wine glass from the hall table and goes in to join them, leaning against the doorframe. As well as Becca and Daniel, already furnished with wine, Sophie is holding court to Diana and Ian. When Sophie sees you, she gives you a nod towards Ian, who has launched into what sounds like a political discussion with George, who's busy plating up what look like tiny quiches on to a lamb's lettuce garnish.

'Want me to take those through?' Sarah offers. 'You're running out of room.'

'Oh, fabulous, thank you,' George says, without looking up. 'Of course they don't want the hassle,' he adds to Ian. 'The party's not going to want to stir things up too much before the next election...'

The dining table is laid for eight.
Sophie smiles at you.
'Let's eat, shall we?'

George has been having jovial, red-faced conversations with Ian, who is seated next to him; and Sarah, who is sitting on the other side, is chatting with Diana. That leaves you with Daniel, whom you didn't get to talk to at all in the pub, but who turns out to be all right. He's a doctor, currently working obscene hours at the hospital in Middlesbrough. You have an interesting talk about the plight of junior doctors and how the NHS is being covertly dismantled under everyone's noses.

This makes you both glance across at George, defender of the NHS; an unlikely warrior in a pink tailored shirt.

George has been plying Ian with some seriously expensive wine; if that wasn't a mistake, Ian is clearly playing him. It's obvious to you that he has no financial influence in his firm at all, or, if he has, he has no intention of arranging any donation to the Labour Party. But it's not up to you to stop George from making a tit of himself, is it? Besides, you're too far away. Maybe after the meal is finished you can intervene.

Sophie could do it – subtly – and you look down to the other end of the table where Sophie is pretending to listen to Becca talking about the local am-dram's latest production, but actually is watching you. Or perhaps she's watching George and has merely glanced across to you in that moment, because she looks away again without acknowledging you. She is nodding, and keeping a weather eye on George. Sarah catches her eye, raises an eyebrow. Sophie rolls her eyes and gives a tiny shake of her head. She knows.

George is rat-arsed.

Sophie is pretty drunk, too; in fact almost everyone is apart from Sarah. She stopped after one half-glass of white and refilled it from the tap.

'I'm glad we got to have this chat,' Daniel says. 'I didn't get the chance when we saw you in the Royal Oak the other week.'

'No,' you say, 'it was a busy night. Will was there, wasn't he? Wonder where he is tonight.'

'Will? You mean Bill's lad?'

'I guess so.'

Daniel smirks, swirling his wine glass. 'This isn't really his type of gig. I was surprised to see him in the Royal Oak, to be honest.'

'How come?'

'He disappeared a couple of years ago, finally. We all thought we'd seen the last of him. Thought he'd gone to live with his mum in Morecambe, but apparently she'd moved house and hadn't told him her new address.'

'Really? That sounds a bit rough.'

'Oh, he was a proper handful when he was a teenager.'

Even so, you think. Your mum not telling you where she lives? That's what you might call an overreaction. Unless he was more than a handful, and even then – your own son?

'What on earth did he do?' you ask.

'Nothing anyone could prove. It was all low-level nuisance stuff: stealing things, pranks, criminal damage. Everyone knew it was him. It's a village; stuff like that doesn't stay a secret.'

'But then he disappeared?'

'He said he was going travelling. I don't think he did. Crossed my mind he'd been inside for a stretch, but after a while everyone forgot all about it. Anyway, he's back now, so maybe he's grown up a bit since then. Let's hope so.'

'Sophie was talking to him quite a lot,' you say, 'so I'm guessing he's capable of holding an adult conversation.'

Daniel laughs at this. 'Maybe. But Sophie's one of those magical people who can hold a conversation with anyone and make them feel special. Why do you think George is so desperate to keep her happy?'

Is he? You want to ask it, but you hold your tongue and look across to Sophie, who just for a moment looks lost. She has pushed her food around on her plate but eaten very little, and she has stopped drinking, too. When she meets your eyes across the table, you smile at her.

Later, when the plates have been cleared, the guests disperse to the living room. You head to the kitchen to help tidy up, expecting to find Sarah in there, but there is only Sophie, rinsing crystal glasses.

'Let me do that,' you say.

'Really? Thanks,' she answers, handing you the cloth and drying her hands on a tea towel. She carries on scraping plates into the bin and stacking them into the dishwasher. 'I'm glad you came.'

'Well, it looked as if George was managing. You didn't need my cricket expertise after all. Probably just as well, since I know about as much about cricket as I know about politics.'

She laughs, looks across the vast kitchen to the door leading to the living room. You both hear George's meaty guffaw. 'Everything okay?' you ask.

She doesn't answer for a moment, and you are about to repeat the question when she straightens and looks you in the eye and says, 'Not really, if I'm honest.'

'What is it?'

You like Sophie. Various phone conversations have followed that morning when she turned up at the cottage and demanded to know what you were doing with Jim in London when Sarah believed you hadn't set foot in the UK for years. You assumed, quickly, that the best way to deal with Sophie was by being unflinchingly honest, and it has proved the best course of action at every turn.

Now, she seems unable to speak, and above the pink cheeks tears are welling in her eyes.

'Sophie,' you say, 'tell me.'

She blinks the tears away and gives a tiny, tight smile. 'It's fine. There's nothing you can do. Honestly, I'll be all right in a minute.'

You take a step forward, put a hand on her upper arm, and she moves towards you, rests her head into your neck, your arms around her. She is shaking.

'I'm afraid of him,' she whispers. 'I've never really been scared before. I don't like it.'

Sarah

Sarah has been listening to Becca and Diana talk about village things for the past twenty minutes, while keeping an eye on George, who is doing his best to have one last go at Ian.

It's not looking good. Ian has one of those tight smiles on his face that suggests everything has just become horrifically awkward. Sarah excuses herself and goes looking for Sophie, to warn her. In the kitchen she finds her with Aiden. They are standing quite close, holding a glass of wine each. Inexplicably, she is certain that she has just interrupted something.

In that moment George comes through from the living room, russet-faced. Sarah thinks – not for the first time – that he looks like a heart attack waiting to happen.

'Fucking shitcunts,' he says.

'George! For fuck's sake!'

He is, luckily, still sober enough to look behind him before he continues, 'Now he fucking tells me he's got nothing to do with the money. At all. End of.'

'I told you,' Sophie says.

The fact that Sophie clearly did tell him, and has turned out to be right, is like pouring petrol on George's furnace. He puts his hands on the granite worktop and seethes.

Deep breaths, Sarah thinks. *Come on, George*.

'I fucking gave him the Margaux, too. Bastard.'

'Oh, come on,' Sophie says. She's at least as drunk as he is, and that means placating him is going to take second place to winding him up even more.

'I can do without your input, thank you.'

Sarah, embarrassed, looks across to Aiden, who is pretending to be serious. By the way he is looking from one to the other, he is loving this display: marital strife at its most amusing. Probably, she thinks, he doesn't get to see this first hand. Or maybe he does. Maybe his clients invite him to dinner parties regularly, claiming he is a colleague or a client of theirs, not the other way round. *He'd like that,* she thinks. *He thinks he's a good actor.*

Having regrouped, a few moments later Sophie and George head back into the living room with brandy and glasses. They are all smiles.

Sarah goes to follow them, but Aiden catches her arm.

'Wait,' he says.

She turns, but does not raise her eyes to his. She thinks she knows what's coming.

'I know what you said, about us being friends.'

Here we are, then, she thinks. *Here it comes. 'Do you mind if I have a go at Sophie?'* At least he has the decency – such as it is – to ask her first.

He moves closer to her, close enough that she can feel the warmth radiating from his body, smell his scent. 'I know what you said. I know you must have your reasons, and I respect them. But I wanted to tell you something. I'm not trying to change your mind. I just need to tell you.'

'Tell me what?' she asks, and now at last she looks up into those green eyes and fights with everything she can muster to keep her composure.

'I love you,' he says.

They are in the car, driving up the hill. Two hours have passed and Sarah has said nothing to him, nothing at all, short of a brief 'thank you' when he helped her into her coat. There was nothing she could think of to say. She has fantasised about him saying those exact words many times over the years. She has imagined that scene taking place everywhere from an airport hotel to a beach to a windswept hillside, thought about what she would say and what he would do, and, most of the time, it would end in a kiss at the very least. She never once thought of him saying it in Sophie's kitchen, much less that what she would feel about it when it finally, actually happened was nothing stronger than disappointment. After all these years, to be offered the thing you believed you wanted most in life and to find it is not what you thought it was. He is nothing but a shadow, a shade, a cardboard facsimile of the man she held in her heart.

More than ever she wishes Jim were still here, because, even with the debts, the lies, the way he clearly, she realised after he died, made huge life decisions without talking to her, at least he was *real*.

All she really wanted was to get blind drunk and pretend it hadn't happened; but she couldn't do that because she had to drive home. And so instead she chatted to and laughed with everyone but him, flitting from person to person, while Aiden sat in the corner, nursing a glass of George's single malt, and watched.

When she parks the car in the barn he gets out first. He is already halfway to the cottage before she can call out to him – 'Aiden!' – but even that is half-hearted.

Let him go.

Anger is loss of control. It doesn't happen to me.

Nevertheless, tonight it almost did and it took me by surprise.

It's white-hot, raging, consuming everything I've taken so much time and effort to create.

And all because of her?

Fickle, selfish, desperate, crazy fucking beautiful woman that I've fallen in love with.

How do I deal with that? How do I get control back, now?

Next time she treats me like that, I'll draw blood.

Sarah

Sarah stands at the kitchen sink, holding on to it tightly as if the room is spinning. It isn't; the house is quiet, the dogs are asleep, Basil is even snoring, but Sarah's life is unravelling piece by piece and there is nothing left that's solid.

Aiden's car has gone and has not come back, not even overnight; she thinks, maybe, he might be looking for somewhere else to live. She wouldn't blame him if he were.

Sophie called earlier to ask if she had happened to notice George's car on the way out.

'No,' Sarah said in reply. 'We were parked right down the bottom of the drive. Why?'

'Some piece of shit keyed it,' Sophie said. 'George is beside himself.'

'Keyed it? On the driveway?'

'It's not an accident. They've scratched the word "cunt" into the bonnet.'

'What? Who the hell would do something like that?'

Sophie didn't – couldn't – answer, but there was an echoing, unspoken name hovering in the cold air between Sarah's house and Sophie's.

'Want to come over?' Sarah asked.

'Not today,' Sophie responded. 'I'm busy trying to peel George off the ceiling. He's still on the phone to the insurance people. He's back in London tomorrow. Maybe we could do lunch on Tuesday? I'll give you a call when things calm down.'

Now, Sarah is looking out over the yard and wondering if there's any point going over to the workshop. She needs to work – she has to, especially now things are clearly ruined with Aiden and he is probably going to move out. Without the rent, she will undoubtedly have to sell the house, and fast. She will have to take whatever anybody offers her.

The thought of it makes her feel sick.

What am I supposed to do, when she decides to stop talking to me?

Do I pursue her and risk making it all worse?

Or do I do the thing I am best at: take a step back, observe, work out the next move and all the possible parameters before I act?

So she is no longer my 'friend'.

That always leaves the other one, right?

Fickle, fickle man I am, that I can move on so easily… don't make me laugh. I'm not leaving her behind. I'll never do that. She's mine; she has been mine since the first time I saw her.

Everything, everyone else is only there to play their part in getting us back together.

If she will have me, I will even change. Maybe.

But one thing's for certain.

I am not finished with her yet.

Aiden

You are sitting drinking wine with Sophie McCormack in the conservatory of the Old Rectory at half-past twelve on a Monday. It feels very decadent.

'How are you feeling?' you ask.

'Much better,' she says. 'I have to admit it's been a stressful couple of days.'

'George?'

'Oh, he's all right. He's full of bollocks but he always comes round in the end.'

She told you about the Lexus being carved up on the phone, yesterday. You told her you hadn't seen anything, of course. She told you about George's fury at it; the car has now been driven away to the dealership in Leeds. She suspects Will is to blame.

'Why would he do that?' you ask.

She smiles and shakes her head, as if she has already made a mistake by mentioning his name. You want to tell her to be careful, but this is not the right moment to do it.

You need all the friends you can get.

'How's Sarah?' Sophie asks, pouring another glass of wine. The bottle is almost empty. In the time it has taken you to drink one glass, she has drunk three.

'You should call her,' you say, which is your way of being discreet. Besides, you don't want Sophie to know that somehow you've fucked things up with the woman you claim to love, all over again.

'I said I'd take her for lunch tomorrow.'

'You'll probably see her before me, then. I keep missing her.'

'You need to give her time,' she says.

'Maybe.'

She is doing her best to look happy, but something is troubling her. She is as beautiful and groomed as she always is, but under the smooth, 'barely there' make-up she is pale. In your experience, you cannot push someone like Sophie. The more you ask, the more she will retreat. What will work is to wait.

'Did you tell her all about it? What you do, I mean?'

'Eventually.'

'It's not as seedy as it sounds.'

'It's not seedy at all,' you add, but of course that's just your opinion.

'Quite.'

'You didn't seem surprised, when I told you.'

She laughs. 'Well, I was. But at least I know that such things exist.'

Ah, you think. Here we go. Sarah said as much.

'You've seen a masseur,' you say, as if you didn't know already.

'Once or twice.'

'Any good?'

'Fairly crap, if I'm honest. The idea of it was much better than the real thing.'

'I'm sorry to hear that. There are quite a few guys doing it now.'

Sophie finishes her wine, looks at the bottle and knits her brows, as if she hadn't realised it contained so little. You can tell she wants to go and get another one, but it's broad daylight outside – although the clouds are dark grey, scudding overhead – and even Sophie has her principles.

'I can imagine you'd be better. You strike me as a... professional. Someone who takes it seriously.'

'I do,' you say. 'I take pride in my work.'

'Making women come,' she says.

'Making women aware of themselves, how incredible they are.'

She laughs. 'You're a charmer.'

'I'm not saying it to be charming. It's the truth. I watch my clients – how they are – and I honestly think, if women had any idea of the power inside them the world would be a completely different place.'

She doesn't smile at that. That look is back, whatever it is: watchful, thoughtful.

'If you had any idea,' you say, 'for instance.'

'I don't feel powerful,' she says. 'I feel...'

'What?'

Here we go, you think.

She reaches out a hand to you. 'I feel foolish,' she says, 'and old. And sometimes a little bit terrified.'

I saw them together

And her all smiling and flirting, it made me want to punch her in the face

And now the anger's back, and it's so fierce this time it HURTS and I can't even see straight

How dare she, how dare she…

I will show her

I will show them who they are messing with

Sarah

On Monday evening, just as Sarah is thinking about going to bed, Kitty phones. Sarah knows instantly that something is not right. Kitty is too quiet, bunged up – she's either caught a cold or she's been crying. Kitty never gets colds.

'What's the matter? What's happened?'

'I'm okay,' she says. 'Can I come home for a bit? I've only got one lecture next week, the tutorial got cancelled, so I wouldn't miss anything.'

'Kitty, of course you can come home. You know that. But why, what's up?'

Kitty launches into breathless sobs and Sarah catches the odd word – Oscar, of course. Eventually it all comes pouring out, Oscar being distant, telling her he needs space, seeing someone else.

'Oh, Kitty, my poor darling,' Sarah says. 'Are you on your own? What about tonight, will you be okay?'

'Kul's taking care of me,' Kitty sniffs. 'She said I can go round to theirs.'

'Good. When are you coming home?'

'Wednesday. I'll text you when I know what train I'm getting,' Kitty says. 'Thanks, Mum.'

Later, lying in bed waiting for sleep, Sarah thinks about getting in the car and driving through the night to go and get Kitty and bring her home. She cannot do this; Kitty is an adult. She has to keep reminding herself. Outside, the wind howls and now it's started to rain again. The temperature has hovered just above freezing and it feels more likely that there is snow on the way. Sarah listens to the wind, and prays to whoever might be listening that the snow will hold off until Kitty's train gets in the day after tomorrow.

The next morning Sarah walks the dogs early. It's still barely light; the wind is cold and bitter and an icy sleet is falling intermittently, blown around by the swirling wind. At the top of the hill the sleet becomes more defined, and the valley is shrouded in white cloud. The snowfall is brief; by the time she is back at the house, the dogs ahead of her, it has stopped again. Ahead the sky is a dirty yellow-grey; more snow is coming.

Back in the house, she tries to call Sophie to ask about meeting for lunch; but she isn't answering and her voicemail, unusually, fails to kick in.

Then she tries to call Kitty, leaving a message, and then Louis. There's no point in leaving a message for him; she doesn't know what to say, in any case.

An hour later, Kitty calls back. She sounds brighter than she did last night, but not by much. She is going to go straight to the station tomorrow after her last lecture.

'How are you feeling today?' Sarah asks.

'I'm worried about him, Mum,' Kitty answers.

Sarah hadn't asked how Oscar was, but that was what Kitty heard. Typical of her daughter, to be thinking of someone else even when she's hurting.

'He's just gone very quiet. He's really sensitive, you know? He really feels things. I'm worried that he's working too hard; he's trying so hard to please his dad and it's not doing him any good, honestly.'

'Oh, Kitty, I'm sure he'll be fine. Just because you can breeze through work, you have to realise other people work at a different pace...'

'I know that! He's been quiet ever since we got back from seeing you. I think it's the whole family thing, you know – he really feels it with his family fractured the way it is. Same as with Will. How is he, by the way?'

'I don't know,' Sarah says. She has not thought about Will for days.

'I was quite worried about him. He looked so thin, and pale, didn't he? It was nice of you to let him come out with us. Where's he staying? I wondered if he might have been sleeping rough.'

'He was house-sitting for someone the weekend before last. He's probably found somewhere else by now. Don't worry, I think he's good at taking care of himself. He's managed up to now, hasn't he?'

'I suppose. He looked troubled. You must admit he looked like he had something going on, Mum.'

'I think, maybe, he's been having some relationship problems...'

'Relationship problems! I didn't know he was in a relationship. Who with?'

'I don't know,' Sarah fibs. 'I don't even know for sure it's that. Just something I picked up on. I thought he looked a bit heartsick.'

'God. I just can't imagine him in a relationship, can you?'

'He's quite sweet,' Sarah says.

'Mum! You're old enough to be his mother!'

'Not quite,' she answers indignantly. 'Anyway, that's not what I meant. I just meant his heart's in the right place; he's had a rough time of it. He deserves a bit of happiness. Don't you think so?'

'I do, yes, but Oscar didn't like him.'

'Really? I thought they got on okay.'

'Yes, when you were watching. When you left the room it was quite awkward.'

'Was it?'

'He sat down next to me on the sofa, too, when there were the armchairs to sit on. Oscar sat the other side but he said that Will was trying it on. He said Will was flirting with me. I had to tell him that Will's practically my brother, that's just not something I would ever consider, but he didn't get it. I told him Will was Louis's friend, not mine, but that didn't work either.'

'Try not to worry about it,' Sarah says. 'Men are like that. Hormones worse than ours, although they won't admit it.'

But now, even after she's put the clean sheets on Kitty's bed and made herself some soup, Sarah can't get Kitty's words out of her head. She thinks about Oscar, the silent, sullen young man who had hugged her and thanked her for letting him stay; about Will and his relationship with Sophie, which has somehow changed from a bit of fun, a fling, into something that has left both of them ragged; and about these two young men left to live in the space between broken families, finding their own way in life and having no positive role models to learn from. What hope was there for either of them?

In the early afternoon, Sarah tries Sophie again, this time the landline in case Sophie has lost her mobile. It's happened before. After just a few rings George answers. His gruff voice is unmistakable.

'Hi, George,' Sarah says chirpily. 'Is Sophie there? I've been trying her mobile but she's not answering. She said she was coming over this afternoon and I wondered what time.'

There is a moment's hesitation. 'No, she's not here.'

'Oh. Any idea when she'll be back?'

'Not really, no.'

Sarah thinks for a second. There is something odd, guarded, about the way he's speaking. Sarah has a sudden horrible sense that Sophie is there, telling him to pretend that she isn't.

'George, I'm just a bit worried I might have upset her somehow. Can you ask her to call me?'

'No, I can't do that.'

'Why not?'

'She's gone off for a few days' break.'

It's like a cold shower. 'Oh? Like a spa break?'

'Something like that, I expect. She's probably turned her phone off. You know what these places are like.'

There's something about the way he's phrased it that sounds odd. 'You expect? You mean you don't know?'

'She left a note,' he says. 'She said she'd be gone for a few days, and not to worry.'

'You mean you don't know where she is?'

There is a long pause.

'George?'

'When did you last see her?' he asks.

'At your party. But I spoke to her on Sunday.'

'And she was okay?'

Sarah thinks of the best way to phrase it. She doesn't want to bring up the subject of George's car. 'She was all right, I think...'

George doesn't wait for her to finish. 'No idea where she might be?'

'No. I mean – I could ring round a few people?'

'I've already done that,' George says.

Sarah is used to him sounding impatient, even though he really isn't. 'Are you worried about her? I mean – if she left a note...'

'She's been under a lot of stress,' he says.

George is the sort of man who doesn't believe in stress. He uses the word in the same tone of voice that he might use to describe an evening of spiritual guidance, or meditation.

'George, I'm sure she's fine,' Sarah says, although she's not sure about that at all.

'Do me a favour,' he says. 'If she calls you – will you let me know?'

'Did you have a row? I mean – tell me to mind my own business, but – '

'Mind your own business,' he says. 'I mean that in the nicest possible way.'

Sarah is stung. But he's right – it's nothing to do with her.

'All right,' she says. 'If she calls me, I'll ask her to phone home, how's that?'

'Thanks,' he says, and rings off.

Immediately Sarah checks her own mobile phone. There is nothing; no message from Sophie.

After speaking to George Sarah tries calling Sophie again, but the calls go unanswered. Whether it's the bad weather, the wind making the dogs restless, or Kitty, something has made her afraid for her friend. What if Sophie has been in an accident? What if she's turned over the Audi in a ditch somewhere, drunk, driving too fast?

Sarah is tempted to go out in the Land Rover looking for her. She thinks of all the places Sophie might have gone, all the people she might be with. Most of them George will already have tried. She turns the phone over and over in her hand, looking at it, before reaching that decision.

And then she dials his number.

He answers after about the tenth ring, by which time Sarah was expecting voicemail.

'Sarah,' he says.

'Hi, Will,' she replies. 'How are you?'

'I'm good.'

Sarah is relieved to hear that, wherever he is, he is indoors. She cannot hear the wind howling, and he sounds relaxed, calm.

'I just wondered – I know this is a bit out of the blue – I just wondered if you've seen Sophie.'

'Sophie? No, I haven't. Why, should I have?'

'I spoke to George just now. She's gone off somewhere – left him a note. He doesn't know where she is.'

'What?'

'I thought he might have called you, but, you know, in case he didn't I just thought it was worth a try. I think he's worried.'

'She's not here,' he says, although Sarah notices he doesn't give any indication of where 'here' is.

'Oh, well, that's okay, then,' she replies, keeping her voice light. She doesn't want to spark off any sort of panic.

'She didn't tell you where she was going?'

There is something about the tone of his voice that Sarah doesn't like. It's jokey, a little bit challenging, as though he thinks it's amusing that Sophie and Sarah aren't as close as they let on. The emphasis is on the 'you'.

'No, I haven't seen her for a few days.' *You knew that,* she thinks.

'She's probably gone off with one of her fancy men,' he says.

'Will, really. That's a bit...'

'A bit what? Near to the truth?'

Sarah doesn't reply. She wonders if he's been drinking, or taken something. This isn't like him. He sounds wired.

'Sorry,' he says then. 'You're right. I just don't know why you're asking me.'

'Look, I know you were seeing each other. You told me that yourself.'

'Right,' he says. 'Only, turns out she's not that bothered. She doesn't want to be tied down to the likes of me. She thought it was a casual thing, she said. She thought it was just a bit of fun. Did she say that to you?'

'I didn't realise,' Sarah lies. *A bit of fun*; that was almost exactly the phrase she herself had thought about Will and Sophie. She tries to change the subject. 'So did you find somewhere to stay?'

'I've got somewhere for now. Something else is coming up soon. Much nicer.'

'Whereabouts?'

'Not too far.'

'That's good,' she says. 'Sounds nice. How long for?'

'A while.'

Why is he being so evasive? She wonders if she's offended him somehow.

'You on your own?' he asks.

Sarah doesn't answer, wondering what he means. He's got somewhere to stay, so he isn't looking for a bed for the night.

'I'm fine,' she replies, not answering his question.

'Yep,' he says. 'Anyway, if there's nothing else...'

'No – it was just – you know, if you do see Sophie, ask her to call George? He's very worried.'

'Course I will,' he says warmly, and that's more like the Will she knows. 'Bye, Sarah. I'll see you very soon.'

And he rings off.

Outside, the wind howls and moans. And, for no apparent reason, Tess starts barking.

It takes her a long time to get to sleep that night. She leaves her mobile phone on the table next to the bed with the sound turned up, in case someone calls. Sophie. Or Kitty. Or even Louis.

She wakes up suddenly, from deep sleep to wide awake in a second, her heart thumping.

She does not move, listening.

The wind has dropped and the house is silent.

She wonders if Tess barked again, if that was what woke her, or if she was dreaming about something.

She can hear breathing, looks up and gasps.

Someone is sitting on her bed.

Part Six

Sarah

Sarah reaches for the light switch. 'Will! What the hell are you doing?'

'I didn't mean to wake you. I was just checking you were okay.'

She sits up in bed, clutching the duvet around her as if it might afford some sort of protection. Her heart is thumping, so hard that she fears that she is actually having a heart attack.

'I didn't mean to scare you,' he says, his bright blue eyes wide. He looks so young, just for a moment, and she almost forgets that he is actually a fully grown man. He looks like a boy who has just woken up in the middle of a nightmare.

'Well, you did,' she says. Her voice sounds high and panicky. She tries to lower it, tries to sound authoritative. 'Please get out of my bedroom, Will.'

He stands up, quickly. 'Yes, of course. I'll – I'll wait downstairs, shall I?'

'Yes,' Sarah says. 'You do that.'

She watches as he leaves the bedroom, head bowed like a kid who's just been told off. When he shuts the door she breathes out, her hand clamped over her mouth in case she starts screaming. She wants to yell at him to get out of the house and not come back, but having him wait downstairs is better. She needs to make sure he's gone.

She dresses in jeans and a jumper, all the while wondering why the dogs didn't bark. What on earth possessed him to let himself in? In the middle of the night? Why didn't she hear him? Why didn't she wake up? She pulls back the curtains. It's still pitch-black outside.

Thick socks on, she pads down the stairs.

Will is in the kitchen and smiles brightly at her when she comes down. He is boiling the kettle.

'I don't want any tea,' she says sharply. 'I want you to leave.'

'Oh,' he says. 'I'm really sorry, Sarah, I didn't mean to – I didn't want to scare you, I was just checking you were okay.'

'I told you on the phone that I was fine. Why wouldn't I be? What made you come out in the middle of the night, for heaven's sake?'

His face crumples. He sits down at the kitchen table, puts his head in his hands.

'It's Sophie, I'm really worried about her.'

'So am I, Will. But she's a big girl. She's probably just gone away with a friend for a few days and has forgotten to tell George. Or she's told George a while ago, and he's forgotten. I'm sure she's fine.'

'She didn't tell you, then,' he says. His voice is muffled by his sleeve.

'Tell me what?'

He lifts his head, looks at her with dry eyes. 'About Aiden. She's been seeing him, behind your back, and mine.'

'What do you mean?' she asks.

'I saw them. I was going round to see her, as a surprise, like, because she'd told me George was going away again. And he was there, with her, in the conservatory. They were all over each other.'

Sarah wants to explain. She wants to tell him that Aiden and Sophie get on well and she's fine about that, but it's the middle of the night and, besides, it isn't something she wants to talk about.

'Aren't you angry?'

'He's not my boyfriend. We are just friends.'

Actually, she thinks, *not even that*.

'You should be fuming,' he says, and there is something in his tone that feels dangerous.

'Please, Will. It's late.'

Abruptly the anger dissolves into misery. 'I love her,' he says; 'it wasn't just a bit of fun for me, it was serious. I felt like I belonged with her. I wanted her to leave George and she played along with it; she... she...'

'All right,' Sarah says. Perhaps she will make a cup of tea after all. 'Come on. Take some deep breaths.'

'She told me I was the right man at the wrong time...'

Will is sobbing so hard he is becoming incoherent, wiping his face with his sleeve. Sarah fetches him a pack of tissues from the kitchen drawer. 'Here,' she says. The kettle is taking a long time to boil. 'Blow your nose.'

'George was... he was going to kick her out...'

'What? Why?'

''Cos he knew she was messing around,' he says. 'He said he was going to kill her.'

'George wouldn't say something like that!' Sarah cannot help herself. It feels as though Will is making things up to justify his misery.

''Cos she was planning to leave him,' he says. 'She was going to come away with me.'

He is a fantasist, she thinks. He has invented this relationship that, if you'd paid any sort of attention to Sophie in the past few weeks, you would know bears no relation to the one Sophie thought she was having with Will.

'She wants to have a baby,' he says.

'What?'

'She always wanted to be a mum. But George has had the operation – he doesn't want any more kids. Sophie said she could have kids with me. We were going to go away together.'

As he speaks his voice rises into a wail and he lifts his head to the ceiling.

'I told her I'd... take care of her... but she didn't... she didn't want me to... I can't, oh, God, Sarah, I can't...'

And then she can't stand it any more, the pain in his face. She puts her arm around him and he turns in his seat and clutches at her in desperation, sobbing into her shoulder.

'I was so happy... I thought... we were going to be... a proper family...'

'I know, I know. It's okay.'

She holds him gently while he cries, listening as his breathing gradually calms, until the sobs subside into the occasional shudder. His arms are around her back. One of his hands has found its way under her jumper, and when it moves Sarah realises he is touching her bare skin. He begins stroking her, as though it's him comforting her, not the other way round.

She pulls away from him. 'All right now?' Her best 'mum' voice, full of authority. *We are coping with this. Everything is fine*.

He nods, wiping his face. 'I'm sorry, I'm sorry. I haven't told anyone.'

'No,' she says. 'Good for you.'

'She told me she was going to leave him,' he says again. 'That she was going to tell George.'

'So where has she gone?'

He shakes his head. 'I don't know.' He looks as if he is going to start crying again.

'You can't stay here, Will. I know things are difficult for you, but I did tell you not to just let yourself into my house again. Didn't I?'

'I said I'm sorry,' he says. 'I was worried about Sophie.'

'I know, you said. But you could have phoned me if you wanted to talk. I don't want you to just turn up again. Okay?'

He nods. And then stands up, abruptly, making the chair squeak against the tiled floor. 'I'll go now.'

She sees him to the back door, watching as he sets off across the yard. It is just starting to get light. She watches until he is out of sight behind the cottage, thinking about him walking down the hill on his own, hoping he will keep to the edge.

Oh, Sophie, she thinks. *What the hell has been going on?*

Aiden

You are in the car on the motorway when your phone rings: it's Sarah.

'Hi,' you say, activating the hands-free. 'Can you hear me okay?'

'Yes,' she says. 'Where are you?'

'On my way back home. Is everything okay?'

'Sophie has gone missing.'

At first you think you can't have heard her properly. 'What?'

'It's Sophie. George says she's gone, he doesn't know where. I thought maybe you might know.'

'Me?' This isn't the time for discretion, you tell yourself. It's force of habit that makes you sound evasive. 'I saw her on Monday. She was fine.'

'She didn't say anything about going away?'

'No. She said she was going to meet you for lunch, yesterday.'

'She didn't call me, so I rang George and he said she had gone somewhere. It's odd – it's like he wants to be worried but he knows it's quite likely she's just gone off for a bit. I think they must have had a row about the car.'

'He doesn't think she did it, surely?'

'No, of course not. But he has put two and two together and assumed it's a friend of Sophie's.'

'Will?'

'That's my guess.'

'Is Sophie not with Will?'

'I don't think so. He came round last night – he seemed really upset about her. He thinks George has done something to her. I don't know what to think.'

'Where is he now?' you ask. Your heart has started to beat faster, and getting back to Sarah has suddenly become urgent.

'I don't know. He left first thing this morning, went off the way he always does. Why?'

'Sarah. Did he stay the night?'

It's the wrong way to phrase it, and you can hear by the tone in her voice that she has misunderstood.

'Not in the way you mean. He turned up, we sat in the kitchen talking, he went off again. Not that it's got anything to do with you.'

'You're right, I'm sorry. But please be careful with him. Don't let him in when you're there on your own...'

She sighs. 'Not that it matters now, but I didn't let him in; he just showed up. He doesn't seem to be able to get that particular message, no matter how many times I ask him not to.'

'Wait – he let himself into your house in the middle of the night?'

'He says he didn't want to wake me. Look, I know. I know it sounds really bad. But I've known him since he was a teenager. And it's obvious he trusts me.'

She trusts him, but she is wrong. This isn't the sort of thing you can tell her over the phone while you're in a noisy car doing seventy.

'I'll be back in an hour, maybe two. I know things have been a bit awkward between us. Could we sit and have a coffee or something? Please?'

'I've got to go and get some shopping,' she says.

'Later, then. Please?'

'All right. Kitty's coming home tonight.'

'Don't worry, I'll make sure I'm out of the way.'

'It's not that. She's upset. I just – I think I need to spend some time with her.'

'Sure. I'll see you later, okay?'

She rings off.

You look down at your speedometer; without realising, you've been accelerating, and now you're travelling at just a shade under a hundred miles an hour.

Sarah

The night's events feel very unreal. Speaking to Aiden has been little comfort; there is no message from Sophie; and George does not answer the phone when Sarah tries the number.

She takes the dogs for a half-hearted walk in the bitter wind, then goes into the village to pick up some groceries for Kitty's visit.

An hour later, turning back into the driveway she sees a figure waiting on the doorstep. She takes a moment to realise it is Harry Button, hands on his hips, motionless. Of all the people. She could do without a social call right now.

'Hello, Harry,' she says.

'Yer door's locked,' he says accusingly.

'Yes,' she says.

'Thought summat had happened.'

'Is everything all right, Harry? No more floods?'

He pushes his thick white hair out of his eyes. 'Oh, aye. Not calling about that. Just that we're going away for a few days.'

'Oh, right. Are you going to your daughter's?'

'Aye. Going tomorrow, before the weather gets any worse. Snow's coming, later.'

It certainly doesn't look like it at the moment; there is bright sunshine, despite the cold wind, blue sky overhead. The field is almost all green. Glancing up at the hillside, Sarah catches sight of the grey stone of the croft, squatting like a troll in the green tussocks. She makes a mental note to go up there again with the dogs again, have a proper look at it while it's still light. Sophie won't be there, though, will she?

'Yes, it's a long drive for you, isn't it?'

'We don't mind that so much. We take a flask and sandwiches. None of that motorway service station muck. Takes about six or seven hours, thereabouts. Any road, do you think you could keep an eye on t'place for us again?'

'Of course,' Sarah says. 'Anything in particular you want me to do? Just get the post in, check the pipes?'

'Aye. We've got the lights set on a timer – not that it matters much up here, you know. You've got our Jenny's number still, haven't you?'

'I saved it in my phone last year. She's not changed it?'

'No, no.' He looks pointedly at the locked front door, at the scrabbling of claws behind it. She doesn't want to invite him in for tea, he'll be here ages.

'You're not going away or owt?'

'No plans to. Kitty's coming home later, just for a few days, I think.'

'Oh, aye. And what about your friend?' Harry points at the cottage.

'I'm not sure what he's doing,' she answers.

In the end she unlocks the front door because the dogs are going berserk, but, while she stands there with Harry expecting them both to burst out and greet them, it's only Tess who comes rushing towards her. 'Where's Basil?' Sarah says, more to the dog than to Harry. 'Basil?'

She whistles into the house, but Basil doesn't appear. She gets an unexpected whiff of something foul. Forgetting about Harry Button for a moment, Sarah runs into the kitchen. Basil is lying in his bed. There is diarrhoea all over the kitchen floor, Tess's footprints running through it, dog shit all over the back of the door where Tess has jumped up.

'Basil!'

Sarah goes to him, trying to avoid the mess. As she approaches, he lifts his head and whines, then drops it again. He is drooling, his eyes rolling in his head.

'Christ almighty,' Harry Button says, holding his hand over his face. 'He don't look too bright, that 'un. Best get him to t'vet.'

Sarah can hardly see through her tears. 'Basil,' she is saying, 'it's all right, it's okay...'

Harry finds an old rug and helps her carry the Labrador out to the car. She lays him down in the back. He barely moves.

'Do you want me to go with you? I'll need to go and tell Moira...'

'No, really, Harry, it's fine, thank you.'

Tess is sitting in the porch looking at her expectantly.

'Oh – Tess...'

'Now don't you worry about t'other one. You take that 'un and I'll make sure the other one's indoors waiting for you.'

'Thanks, Harry.'

She reverses slowly to turn the car around. Harry stands, his hand scratching the top of Tess's head. Sarah gets to the gate and turns gently, trying to avoid the pot holes in the lane. She is crying, hard. 'Don't worry, Basil, hold on, old boy. Just hold on for me.'

Harry has called ahead for her, and so, when she pulls into the car park behind the veterinary surgery in Camp Lane the veterinary nurse has opened the back door to the surgery and is waiting to help her carry Basil inside.

'I'm so sorry,' Sarah is saying. 'Thank you, thank you.'

Her face is red and puffy and wet with tears; she must look such a state. And yet all she can think of is her beautiful boy, her lovely Basil, who lies like a dead weight in her arms, and just lets out a single low whine as she hands him over.

'I just found him like that,' she says. 'He was fine this morning, when I went out. When I got back just now, there was diarrhoea everywhere and he was just lying there.'

'Any chance he could have ingested something?'

Sarah stares at the vet, eyes wide. Trying to think about the kitchen, about something Basil might have eaten. 'No, not that I can think of. I didn't see him eating anything when we were out walking this morning, everything was normal...'

The vet is listening to Basil's chest, which is rising and falling in shallow little breaths. Sarah stares at her as she palpates Basil's stomach. Basil lets out a groan.

'Okay, let's do some bloods, get Basil on a drip. Have a seat in the waiting room, Mrs Carpenter, and I'll be out to see you in a few minutes.'

Sarah lets the nurse lead her out into the waiting room. The hard plastic chairs surround a coffee table with a few magazines in a neat pile in the centre. An elderly woman is waiting with a cat in a basket; the cat is yowling. Sarah does not know the woman, tries not to make eye contact, suddenly aware of what a state she must look, but this is not enough of a deterrent to a conversation.

'Bad news, is it?' the old lady says hopefully, leaning across and patting Sarah's knee.

'I'm sorry?'

'You look a bit upset, my dear. Is it...?'

Sarah looks up, wipes under her eyes with a tissue that the nurse handed to her earlier. It's sodden.

'My dog,' Sarah says. 'Basil. I think he must have eaten something.'

'Poison?'

Oh, God. Really? 'I don't know. I can't think how he might have got it.'

'It's the farmers,' the woman says, knowingly. 'My dad were a farmer. He used to put down rat poison but one day our old dog got hold of some of it. Proper foaming at the mouth, he were. Terribly sad.'

'Did he…?'

'Oh, aye. Nowt the vet could do, by the time we got him down there.'

Sarah looks despairingly at the door behind which Basil's life apparently hangs in the balance.

'Mind you, that were thirty-odd year ago; they can do marvellous things now, these vets. Your'n'll be right as rain, you mark my words. They'll patch him up right enough.'

A second door opens and another nurse looks expectantly at the waiting room. 'Tootsie Rowbotham?'

'Aye, here she is,' says the elderly lady, and stands, swinging the cat basket around as she does so. Sarah catches sight of an angry-looking black and white face, whiskers and a set of yellowing fangs.

The door shuts again and Sarah is left to wait in silence. She stares at the top magazine, a months-old copy of *Your Chickens*, trying to think of everything that has happened in the last twenty-four hours and at what point something might have happened to Basil. He was fine last night, she thinks. He was all right in the early hours, when she was sitting in the kitchen with Will – she remembers him lying with his head on her foot, the way he always does when she is at the kitchen table. She remembers him going back into his bed when she locked the door behind Will. And he'd been fine this morning, eating his breakfast as usual, going out with her around the garden and the top field – a bit reluctantly, because it was still freezing and Basil was never keen on the cold, not like Tess, who was racing around as fast as she could go – but he'd been *fine*, she was sure of it.

Now there's no one to see, she breaks down again, sobbing quietly into the shreds of tissue, only stopping when her phone begins to buzz in her back pocket.

It's Aiden.

'Hello,' she says.

'Hi, Sarah. Just got back. Are you still in town? I could meet you there if you like.'

Sarah cannot reply. She is both intensely relieved and distressed to hear his voice, sounding so normal after everything that's happened.

'Sarah? What's wrong?'

He can tell, even from the sound of her breathing.

'It's Basil,' she says, taking in a deep, shuddering breath. 'I'm at the vet's with him...'

'What's happened?'

'I don't know, they're doing tests... I think he might have eaten something, but I don't know... Oh, Aiden, what am I going to do?'

'Do you want me to meet you there?'

Sarah collects herself. 'No, no, it's okay. If you're home, would you mind looking in on the house and checking on Tess? She looked all right when I left, but now I'm worried in case she's eaten something too and it hasn't affected her yet.'

'Of course. I'll phone you in a bit, okay? Or you can ring me if you have any news.'

'Thank you, that sounds so good.'

'You take care. Don't worry about Tess. I'll see you very soon.'

She is just putting the phone back in her pocket when the vet appears in the doorway. 'Mrs Carpenter? Would you like to come in?'

Sarah gets to her feet, suddenly and inexplicably certain that Basil has just passed away on the vet's table.

Aiden

You can hear Tess barking frantically as you cross the yard. She doesn't sound ill, you think, and when you open the door she rushes out towards you, barking, crouching, baring her teeth. There is an overwhelming smell of disinfectant coming from the house.

'All right, Tess, it's only me...'

It takes a few moments before her tail, clamped between her thighs, starts a half-hearted wag. She approaches, head down, as if she's expecting to be told off.

'It's all right, girl. Have you had a rough day? Yes, me too. I know. All right, then, come on.'

The kitchen floor is damp, freshly mopped. On the table is a handwritten note. In a neat, but wavering script, it says:

Cleaned up a bit. Hope dog all right. Let us know, if you can. M x

You have no idea who M is. You put the note back on the table, and fetch some dog biscuits from the cupboard for Tess, who parks her bum instantly and looks gleeful when she sees the bag of treats.

'Good girl,' you say, offering her a bone-shaped delight. It's gone in less than a second. 'Well,' you say. 'What are we going to do with you?'

You pull out your phone and send Sarah a text, letting her know that Tess seems fine. There is no immediate reply.

The house is warm, warmer than the cottage, but it feels strange being here without Sarah. You wander through to the living room, Tess following you. On the table beside the sofa is a framed picture of Sarah and Jim on their wedding day. You weren't there, although you heard all about it from a mutual friend. It was an extravagant, showy wedding, which you thought was typical of Jim. A stately home, two hundred guests, fireworks, the lot. And yet, in this picture, you have to admit that they both look happy. Sarah looks beautiful, the way she always does, her hair held back with some kind of diamante hair clip. She is laughing and tilting her head back, while Jim is turned half-towards her, holding both her hands, looking at the camera. He looks into your eyes and it feels as though he is gloating.

'Who's laughing now, Jim, old mate?' you say quietly, into the room.

Tess, sitting at your feet, looks towards the hallway and whines.

From upstairs, you hear the sound of the floorboards creaking.

Someone is up there.

Sarah

Basil is to be kept in overnight for observation, but the vet describes his condition as 'stable'. They have given him activated charcoal to absorb any remaining toxin. He has perked up a little after being put on a drip. The X-ray revealed no unexpected blockages or foreign objects. The blood results won't be back till tomorrow, but they will indicate whether, as seems most likely, he has been poisoned.

'Labs eat everything,' the vet tells her. 'If you're out in the sticks, chances are he's picked up some poison somewhere.'

'Poison?'

'It happens sometimes, I'm afraid. If we knew what it was he'd eaten, we could get some specialist help from the Poisons Line. But you don't remember him eating anything, while you were out walking? Perhaps you could ask the neighbours, see if anyone's put something down?'

Sarah thinks about Harry and Moira Button. They wouldn't set out poison. And the nearest farm buildings are a few miles away. 'I'm sorry,' she says, 'I can't, I just can't think how he could have...'

'Don't worry,' the vet reassures her. 'He's stable now, anyway. We'll keep an eye on him overnight. If anything happens we'll let you know, but for now all we can do is wait and see.'

Driving home without him, Sarah feels numb. She keeps going over and over it in her head, the walk this morning. Last night, what was Basil doing while Tess was sniffing around the croft? He was sheltering down by the back door, wasn't he? Maybe he picked up something out of the bins? Maybe he found a rabbit, or a rat, that itself had eaten something? He looked guilty, didn't he? But she hadn't thought that at the time. He'd looked cold and wet and fed up.

And, in any case, he was fine this morning. If he'd eaten something last night, he'd have been showing symptoms by this morning, wouldn't he?

Back at home, Tess is pleased to see her but subdued, sitting in her bed with her tail at only half-wag.

'I know, girl,' Sarah says, rubbing her ears. 'Basil is a silly boy. You're much too clever to eat something bad, aren't you?'

The kitchen is unexpectedly spotless. There is a note on the table in a handwriting she does not recognise, but the 'M' can only be Moira. She thinks about going across the road to see the Buttons but they will be busy; she doesn't want to interrupt preparations for their journey tomorrow.

She half-expected Aiden to be in here, but he must have gone back to the cottage. She will go and look in a minute. He promised her a coffee, didn't he?

Sarah sits wearily at the kitchen table, checks her phone, just in case, but there is nothing. She drops the phone to the table and looks at Tess, who has jumped to her feet and is staring fixedly at the door to the living room, which is open. Beyond it, Sarah can see nothing but the gloomy room, dark because the curtains are still drawn.

She strains to hear, but there is no sound other than the wailing and moaning of the wind outside. Tess licks her nose and looks up at Sarah, then back to the door. Maybe it was the wind? Maybe something got knocked over, or a door shut in the draught? It doesn't seem likely. It never has before. Sarah reaches down to stroke Tess behind the ears. The dog is rigid, tense, trembling ever so slightly.

And then she hears something too, looks up sharply.

Will is standing in the doorway.

'For Christ's sake, Will!'

Sarah gets to her feet, because she doesn't want to be sitting down to have this conversation. 'What the hell are you doing in here *again*?'

'I came to see how you were,' he says, simply. He is dressed in a shirt and jeans, his hands shoved casually into his pockets. 'And if you'd heard from Sophie. I've been worried about her.'

'How did you get in?' she asks.

'The door was open, same as it always is,' he says.

'I asked you not to come in here without being invited. Do you remember?'

He smiles, his big, open, wide smile showing those lovely white, even teeth. 'I did knock,' he says.

Oh, well, that's all right, then.

'And I didn't answer,' she says. 'You shouldn't have come in, Will, you just shouldn't.'

He looks around. 'Where's Basil?' he asks.

Sarah stares at him. 'He's at the vet's; he's not well.'

Will saunters into the kitchen, as if he owns it. Sarah realises her heart is still thumping. It's not just the shock, she thinks. She doesn't like him being in here when she's on her own. Why ever not? He's harmless, isn't he? That's what she's been telling everyone.

'Sorry to hear that,' he says. He crouches down next to Tess, rubs her ears. Sarah notices her tail is not wagging.

'I've got lots to do,' she says, 'so if you don't mind I'd like you to go.'

He looks up at her from his position, down on his haunches. He is smiling but he looks pale.

'Sure,' he says. 'Have you heard from her? From Sophie?'

'No,' she says, 'but I'm sure she's fine. I think she probably just needed a break from everything.'

'A break from George, you mean.'

'George is all right,' she says quickly, at the same moment wondering why she's leaping to his defence. She's never been particularly fond of the man. And Will is quite possibly right.

'She's afraid of him, you know,' Will says. He stands up abruptly, in one fluid move; a young man with strong legs, no effort involved at all. He is taller than Sarah, and standing so close now that he towers above her. As if realising that she is alarmed, he takes a little step back. 'He threatened her,' he says. 'Like I said last night. He told her that if she left him he'd kill her.'

'What?'

'She was in a state about it. I thought it was hormones, you know, making her irrational. Why didn't she tell you any of this?'

'I don't know,' Sarah says.

'She liked keeping her secrets,' he says, nodding. 'Even from me. But it looks like she was keeping secrets from you, too. Her best friend.'

He comes closer again. Sarah moves back, fractionally, and her thighs hit the edge of the kitchen table. She has nowhere to go. She can feel his breath on her forehead. Her eyes remain fixed on his chest, the buttons of his check shirt, the white T-shirt underneath which, close up, looks as if it needs a wash.

'I kept my secrets too,' he whispers. 'I never told her about us, you know.'

His hand lifts and touches her upper arm. Sarah flinches a little, then tries to relax as he strokes his hand up to her shoulder.

'I never told her about that night we had together. She would have been so upset, Sarah. She would hate to think that you and I had something so special… and it was special, wasn't it? That one night. You were so good. You were… wild.'

'Will,' she says, trying to keep her voice firm, 'don't.'

'You were such a good lay, Sarah. You know that?'

'Stop it!'

Her voice is high and querulous, but something about the force of it stops him dead. He drops his hand and takes a step back, gives her a nervous smile. 'I'm sorry, really, I just…'

Sarah folds her arms tightly across her chest. 'Just go, Will. Aiden's in the cottage. If I call out, he'll come over.'

Will laughs, gives her a look. 'Oh, aye, Aiden? Your friend? The one who sells himself to poor, lonely women?'

She breathes in sharply.

His smile widens. 'You think he can hear you from here?'

'I only came to get the dog,' she says. 'He's waiting for me to go over there. If I don't appear in a minute he'll come looking for me. I don't think he'll be impressed that you let yourself in, either.'

'No,' he says, after a moment's pause. 'You're probably right. I'll just – get my jacket. Cold out there, you know.'

He saunters into the living room, all the time in the world. Sarah looks at her phone, snatches it from the charger. It has one bar, not enough to rely on.

Will is back a few moments later, pulling his jacket on.

Sarah takes a deep breath, stands a little straighter. In case he is about to argue or come close to her again. But he smiles and passes her, heading for the door.

'Your friend,' he says, turning with his hand on the latch. 'Give him my best? I don't think he likes me very much. I think we got off to a bad start, me and him.'

Sarah's heart is beating. She manages a casual shrug. 'Maybe.'

But Will just grins. 'I'll see you later, then,' he says, and opens the door, walks out and pulls it to behind him.

Sarah goes to the sink and watches him crossing the yard towards the gate. As he passes the cottage, he turns to look at it. Stops, for a moment, and stares at the door. Then he turns, looks directly at Sarah, and waves before he heads off towards the road once more.

Sarah looks down at her hands. They are shaking.

Sarah waits five minutes before calling the police non-emergency number. It feels like an emergency, but, in the same way that Sarah prefers not to go to the doctor unless she's actually at death's door, it probably isn't.

'I'd like to report someone for harassment,' she says, when she eventually gets through.

She spends the next twenty minutes telling the operator all about Will turning up unexpectedly, letting himself into the house when she has specifically asked him not to.

'Can you make the house secure?' the operator says eventually.

Sarah has a vague sensation that she is being told off. She might be imagining it, but then that's what she would say too. If one of her friends told her about someone repeatedly walking into their house, she would tell them to lock the bloody door and not be so daft.

Well, the operator is right: she can stop Will getting in by locking the doors, and that's what she will have to do.

When the call is finally finished Sarah looks in the wooden bowl for the spare keys to the front door.

Tess looks expectantly at the door.

'You want a walk, Tess?'

It seems like the best thing to do, the thing she always does: get out of the house, get into the fresh air, walk it off, think it through. She goes to the utility room and pulls on her waterproof jacket and her boots. As she shuts the door of the utility room behind her, she remembers her new resolution to lock the back door. But there's no key on the inside. She can't remember the last time this door was properly locked; when she goes away, she bolts it from the inside and then leaves by the front door. She doesn't want to take the dog out and come back in through the front, though; there will be mud all over the place if she does that.

There is a key for the back door on one of her key rings, isn't there? She goes back to the kitchen, Tess following her impatiently, and hunts through the bowlful of keys, thinking that half of them must be for doors and locks from previous addresses, until she finds one that looks likely.

The key turns stiffly in the lock, fastening the door firmly. She slips the key into her jeans pocket, then sets off through the garden to the gate which leads out to the field. As she rounds the corner and emerges from the shelter of the wall, the wind takes her by surprise, almost knocking her off her feet.

The clouds overhead are heavy and dark, and tinged with yellow. She can smell the snow on the wind. She hopes Kitty is on her way to get the train by now. If the snowfall is heavy, and settles, the trains might stop running for a while. If that happens, she would rather Kitty were here, with her, than on her own and miserable in her hall of residence. Especially if, as has happened before, the phone lines go down. The mobile signal up here isn't really good enough to be relied on.

Tess races ahead, barking, skirting the edge of the wall.

Sarah has a sudden thought that whatever Basil ate might have been hidden there, by the wall. After all, that's where Basil was last night, wasn't he? Sheltering from the weather?

'Tess!'

Her words are snatched away by the wind as soon as she says them. Tess has sped off up the hill. She is heading straight for the croft.

'Tess!' Sarah breaks into a run uphill, as fast as she can given the rough terrain and her heavy boots. It takes her several minutes to catch up.

The door to the croft is shut fast. Tess is crouching outside it, barking, then scrabbling at the bottom of the door. Sarah has to get hold of her collar and drag her away. 'Come on, you daft dog. You're as jumpy as I am.' As she heads back down the hill, her mobile phone buzzes in her pocket. It's a text from Kitty:

Am getting 15.57 train. Tried to call but no answer left message xx

Up here where, sometimes, the mobile works, she thumbs a reply:

Will meet the train. Love you xxx

When she finally gets back to the house, she has to wrestle with the key for several moments before it finally turns. She will have to put some WD-40 on it, try to ease that lock.

She rubs Tess down with the towel. Now she feels better. Now, she has a plan. She will phone the vet's, get an update on Basil, then head out to Thirsk to get in some groceries and wait for Kitty's train to arrive.

Kitty is coming.

Everything will be all right.

He tried to talk to me but it was too late for that. Let's be reasonable about this, he said.

I know you've got a bit of a past, he said. I know you've done things, that you've hurt people, he said.

Oh, mate, I thought. You have no idea. No idea at all what I've done.

No idea what I'm going to do to you, either.

You can stop all this now, he said. You just have to go away, far away, and leave us all alone. If you don't go away I'll call the police. I know you've been taking advantage of Sarah, she deserves better, he said.

He said that!

Sarah will be back any minute, I said. Let's go and talk in the cottage.

Off he trotted with his back to me, and I was thinking this is easy, this is going to be so easy.

But he didn't talk. I was very patient, under the circumstances. I gave him so many chances, not to make me angry. People shouldn't make me angry. That's when I lose control.

But he just kept shaking his head.

Sarah

Outside the station, the snow is falling heavy and fast, and settling.

Sarah has been listening to the weather report on the radio. A wide band of heavy rain has changed course and intersected with a cold front coming directly from the Arctic; there is going to be more snow tonight. A lot of it. Disruption has been forecast. People are being urged not to travel unless absolutely necessary.

Sarah wants to get Kitty and get back up the hill before the snow gets any worse. If they are lucky, the timing of the snowfall will be okay. She has enough food to see them through; the oil tank is fine, so they are not going to be cold. Basil is quite safe where he is, in the vet's – if he'd been at home and taken a turn for the worse there, she might not have been able to get him any help.

And it's at the back of her mind that the heavy snow will put Will off paying her any more unexpected visits.

Sarah watches as the train pulls in, its brightly lit windows fogged with condensation; she can see people standing, pulling on coats, as the wheels squeak and grind to a halt.

A few moments later people start pouring from the bridge over the platform, finding taxis, or heading to the car park. A brave few trudge off towards the town on foot.

She keeps a close eye on the last few people emerging, wondering if Kitty missed the train after all. The next one is due in an hour; that's if it's running.

Then – thank goodness – there she is. She is walking along while fiddling with her mobile phone, the tiny screen lighting up her face. Sarah gives the horn a quick, short blast; when she looks up, Sarah waves.

Moments later, the back door opens and Kitty slings her rucksack inside, slamming it shut. Then the passenger door opens and Kitty climbs in, bringing with her a gust of icy air and a swirl of snowflakes. Kitty's nose is bright pink, her cheeks pale under her thick beanie. She throws herself into Sarah's arms.

'Oh, Mum,' she says, 'I'm so glad to be home.'

'I'm glad you're home too. I thought you were going to get stuck somewhere.'

'I just made it. I think the next train has been cancelled.'

'Well, thank goodness, then. Come on, let's get home. You can tell me all about it.'

Sarah pulls the car out into the rush-hour traffic. There isn't usually this much, even at this time of the evening; everyone's trying to get home all at once, while they still can.

'He went all weird on me, Mum,' Kitty says, her voice breaking.

Sarah reaches across for her gloved hand. 'What do you mean? What sort of weird?'

'I think he was seeing Elle; he was all awkward around her and then he said why couldn't I be more like her, and then he didn't talk to me for, like, three days… and when I asked him what was wrong he said he wasn't sure he was ready, and I said ready for what, it's not like I've been pressuring you or anything, and he said he wasn't ready to be faithful to one person.'

Sarah thinks about Aiden and herself, back at uni. How similar he and Oscar sound, in many ways. But, unlike Kitty, she always understood that, back then. Understood that it wasn't the right time for them both.

'... and I said, well that's a joke because it's not even as if we're sleeping together, not, like, all the time anyway. And he said he wasn't happy, and I said well I'm not really happy either, but that wasn't true because I *had* been happy, Mum, he made me feel *so* happy and now... and now... I'm just so sad...'

They reach the road that takes them out of town and up the hill. Already the snow has settled, despite the gritters, and if it were not for the 4x4 she would not attempt this gradient. Others are not so wise, and she has to go slowly to negotiate around the cars that are stuck, already, the ones that have been abandoned, pulled at an oblique angle into the side of the road. Higher up, the snow is heavier and fewer cars have cleared a path; Sarah has to concentrate to stay on a straight line, up what she thinks is the road. On both sides, the black outlines of the dry stone walls are already becoming harder and harder to see as the snow is blasted against them by the wind.

Kitty has stopped talking for now, letting her concentrate. Sarah has the local radio station on low, the announcer listing the roads that are already closed, and the ones that are becoming treacherous.

It's a nightmare of a journey, and it takes them a full hour longer than the same route would normally take in good weather, but at last they make it to the village. The road here is clearer, as more cars have driven up and down it, and as they pass Sophie's house Sarah wonders whether Sophie has made it home by now. She'll phone George, later, once Kitty has gone to bed.

The turn-off up the hill towards Four Winds Farm is easy to miss at the best of times, but with drifting snow making everything look different it is particularly hard to spot. Another 4x4 is following right on her tail, so Sarah slows right down as she approaches the lane, indicating right. The car behind beeps loudly and speeds past in a cloud of snow.

'Knob!' shouts Kitty.

Sarah laughs, turns her attention back to the hill. She knows this road intimately, but now it looks strange, alien – full of bumps and dips that shouldn't be there. The wind is blowing the snow horizontally through the arcs of the headlights, and turning on the full beam results in a total whiteout. She snaps it back to normal again quickly.

Three minutes later and a dark shape appears to the left; it's the Button house. Thank goodness. They round the bend, turn in through the gate, and finally pull up in the yard.

'You run for it,' Sarah tells Kitty. 'I'll put the car in the barn.'

'Don't be daft, Mum, I'll come with you.'

'No, go on. No point you getting covered in snow. Here – you'll need this.'

From her coat pocket Sarah fishes out the front door key.

'What? You locked the door?'

'Go on, you get going. I'll bring your bag.'

Kitty finally relents; jumps out of the car. Sarah watches her legs wading through the snow. It's already about a foot deep in places, and this is in the shelter of the yard.

Once she's got the door open, Sarah reverses the car awkwardly back until she can line it up with the oak beams of the barn; then she drives straight into the shelter. She switches off the engine and takes a deep breath. That journey was scarier than she cares to admit.

She opens up the boot; she had forgotten about the shopping. Slinging Kitty's rucksack awkwardly on to one shoulder, she lowers the bags to the ground and shuts the boot lid. Then she manages to fit three carrier bags in each hand before heading out into the wind.

The cottage, as she passes it, is in darkness. The car is nowhere to be seen. Somehow, she had expected this. She hopes that this time at least Aiden is somewhere safe and warm, in a friend's flat, maybe. Or with a client, in a hotel.

So much for that coffee, she thinks. *So much for the chat.*

Kitty has already put the kettle on to boil, turned on the television and is in the process of trying to light the fire, Tess by her side, tail wagging frantically.

Despite the locked doors, Sarah is almost surprised to see that Will isn't here. She was almost expecting to find him sprawled across the couch, guitar in hand, picking out a melody.

She unpacks the shopping, half-listening to the news, which is reporting widespread disruption caused by heavy snowfalls in the northeast of England and Scotland. *No shit, Sherlock*, she thinks. The south is experiencing a light smattering of sleety drizzle and the reporter is standing outside a gritting depot outside Croydon, talking about the council's plans to keep the roads clear. Good for them.

Sarah opens the oven and puts in a casserole that has been defrosting all day. It's still half-solid, but she'll leave it in an extra half-hour and it will be fine. Just as she is opening a bottle of wine, which feels especially well deserved, the phone rings. 'I'll get it!' Kitty shouts from the living room.

A couple of moments later Kitty appears in the doorway. 'Mum? It's the police for you.'

Oh, God.

Sarah takes the phone from Kitty and hands her the bottle of wine. 'Hello?'

'Mrs Carpenter? It's DC Amy Foster from Thirsk police station here. I'm calling about the offence of harassment you reported earlier today. Is it a good moment to talk?'

'Um, yes, I guess so.'

Sarah takes a glass of wine from Kitty, who is perched against the kitchen table, arms crossed, mouthing, *What's up?*

Sarah shakes her head and waves her towards the living room. And then again, insistently. Kitty makes a face, but goes.

'I just need to ask you a couple of questions, if that's okay,' says Amy Foster. 'I'd come out to see you, but the weather... you know.'

'No, it's fine. It's rough out there, isn't it?'

'Yeah, nightmare. Okay, then. So you know this Will Brewer?'

'Will is a kind of a friend of the family. He's stayed with us before, over the years, but I'm here on my own now and just recently he's been turning up and letting himself into my house. I've asked him not to do it, and yet this morning when I got in he was in the house again.'

'I see. So he has a key?'

Sarah bites her lip. *Here we go*, she thinks. 'No, I've always left the doors unlocked. I've started locking them now, though.'

There is a pause. Sarah can hear DC Foster hammering away on a keyboard.

'And, when you've come home and found him there, is he threatening towards you in any way?'

'No, not as such.'

'Not as such?'

'He – well, he makes me feel a bit uncomfortable.'

More keyboard-battering. 'Has he ever taken anything, while he's been in the house? Or damaged anything?'

'No. Not that I'm aware of. He's read my mail, I think; he knows things he could only have known that way.'

'What is it he wants, when he turns up?'

Sarah thinks about this for a minute. It's a good question. What does he want? Why does he keep showing up? It could be all about Sophie, about how hurt he is, about how he needs attention and comfort and maybe just to be as close to her as he can possibly get – by talking to her best friend. But then, she probably isn't Sophie's best friend, is she? After all, Sophie keeps her own secrets, Sarah knows that now.

'I'm not sure. It's just somewhere to go, I think. But I just have this feeling that he likes that I'm getting upset about it.'

'What makes you say that?'

'Just that he keeps doing it. It's my own fault, isn't it? Because I've let him stay here sometimes, he thinks it's okay to keep coming back?'

'Mrs Carpenter, it's your house; you're entitled to have people to stay and then to shut the doors when you don't want them there any more.'

'I don't know. Look, I'm not exactly vulnerable, you don't need to be worried. You don't need to really do anything – I think I was just a bit shaken this morning when I found him here, I didn't know what else to do when he finally went, I just called the police because I was shaken up. You've got a million and one other things to do with the snow and everything; you must be really busy.'

'Please,' Amy Foster says comfortingly, 'don't worry about it, really. You were right to call us. How about if I have a word with Mr Brewer? I think by the sounds of it he just needs a little reminder about waiting for an invitation before turning up in someone's house.'

'You think that'll help? I mean, I don't want him arrested, or anything like that. He's not hurt anybody. And my daughter's here now, she's staying for the weekend, so I'm not on my own.'

'Leave it with me. I'll give you a call to let you know what happens. But in the meantime, if he turns up again unexpectedly and you're frightened, ring 999 and quote the reference number, all right? That way the operator will see what's happened previously.'

'Right. OK, thanks. Have you got his mobile number?'

'Yes, it's on your initial report, thank you. I'd be surprised if he troubles you in the next few days, anyway – looks as though we're all going to be staying put for a bit.'

DC Amy Foster gives Sarah her contact details, and rings off. Sarah goes into the living room and replaces the receiver. She takes a big sip of the wine.

'Right, Mum,' Kitty says. 'What the hell was that all about?'

'It's fine,' Sarah replies. 'Nothing to worry about. All over with now, anyway.'

'You were talking about Will.'

'Yes. It's not really a problem, just that he keeps turning up when I'm here on my own. I asked him not to, but he's still doing it.'

'Oh, God, really? What's the matter with him?'

'I don't know; I think he's just had a rough time lately. Maybe he's a bit lonely.'

Even as she says it, it sounds lame.

'I know, but even so. There are things you just don't do. What does he think he's playing at?'

'Kitty, it's fine. There's no point you getting all upset about it.'

'But you called the police! That's pretty extreme. You must have been bloody scared to have called the police.'

'It just took me by surprise, that's all. And, with Basil being sick, Tess has been really jumpy, barking for no reason. Then he just kind of... appeared, in the doorway, and it made me jump.'

'He just walked in?'

'He said he knocked, I wasn't here, and he just came in.'

Kitty has finished her wine. Sarah looks at her daughter, snuggled up on the sofa with her feet tucked underneath her. The fire crackles and roars, starting to throw out some proper warmth now. Sarah stretches out her socked feet towards it, trying to thaw them out. 'I should try and take Tess out. She needs to have a wee.'

'You're kidding! Look at it!'

The window is a black and white blur, snowflakes pattering at the glass, the wind swirling them around in the darkness.

'I won't take her anywhere, I'll just see if she wants to nip out.'

But when it comes down to it, kitted up, Sarah can't find the key to the back door. It's locked fast. She put the key somewhere safe, didn't she? It's not on her keyring, not in her pocket where she'd thought she'd put it.

In the end she lets Tess out through the front door into the yard. She disappears into the darkness, slinking around behind the workshop.

'Don't be long,' Sarah mutters, shivering in the doorway despite her thick coat. The snow has piled up against the side of the cottage, the whole yard a beautiful clean bed of white. Their footprints have already disappeared.

Two minutes later Tess scampers back, runs through the hall into the kitchen and shakes the snow from her coat, scattering the tiled floor with snow, which melts quickly into small puddles.

'Thanks, Tess, just what I needed.' This is why she goes in and out via the utility room.

Kitty has gone upstairs to have a bath before dinner. Sarah can hear it running. She takes the opportunity to ring George, but there is no answer. It rings and rings for ages. Maybe he has gone to meet Sophie somewhere, to talk things through, and got stranded. She hopes this is the case; maybe they are sheltering in a nice hotel in York.

When she hangs up, it rings immediately.

'Hello?'

'Mrs Carpenter? This is DC Foster again; we spoke earlier this evening.'

'Oh, yes, right.'

'Just to let you know I've had a chat with Mr Brewer.'

'Oh, okay. How was he?'

'He seemed surprised, but I think he understood that what he did this morning wasn't acceptable and I got his agreement that he's not going to do it again. He wanted to get in touch with you to explain, but I told him he should leave you in peace and that if you wanted to speak to him you'd call him and not the other way round.'

'That sounds perfect, thanks. I don't want to – I mean – he's only a lad, and he's been through a lot. I do feel sorry for him.'

'Even so, Mrs Carpenter, he's a grown man and he's perfectly capable of sorting himself out, by the sound of things. Don't let him take advantage of your kindness, if you do get in touch with him again.'

'No, of course. Thank you.'

'But if he does turn up, or call you, and you feel uncomfortable about it, do call us again. I'd like to think that this will be an end to it, but you never know. We're here if you need us, any time, all right?'

'Thank you,' Sarah says again, warmly.

She goes upstairs to make sure Kitty has everything she needs. At the top of the stairs she glances down the corridor to the spare room at the end. The door is firmly shut. She knows Will isn't here, because the police have just spoken to him, but it can't hurt to check.

She opens the door quickly, before she loses her nerve. The bed is unmade, the duvet neatly folded at the end of it. The radiator has been turned off again – did she do that? – and it's cold in here, draughts coming from somewhere. The room is at the north end of the house, and the wind and snow are hitting the window with a force that rattles the panes alarmingly.

She shuts the door firmly. Will is not here. She heads down towards her bedroom, then Kitty's. The door is open and already it looks lived-in, a pile of dirty clothes on the floor that have spilled from Kitty's rucksack. The lights are on and Kitty's laptop is open on the bed, connected to a portable speaker that is blasting out something with a heavy bass.

'Kitty?'

'In here!'

The bathroom door opens. Kitty is in her robe; the bath is full and bubbly and smells of Sarah's favourite hand and body wash.

Sarah sniffs pointedly.

'You don't mind, do you? Only I'm really whiffy...'

Sarah laughs as Kitty emerges fully from the bathroom and gives Sarah a big hug.

'I rang Will,' she says, into Sarah's shoulder.

'What?' She pulls back to look at Kitty, who raises her chin defiantly.

'I just called him and told him off a bit,' she says.

'Oh, Kitty, I wish you hadn't...'

'He's all right. He just didn't really get that turning up and letting himself in wasn't appropriate. He was really sorry. In fact he was snivelling a bit, I think he'd just got off the phone with that policewoman you spoke to.'

Sarah sighs deeply. 'This is all just getting a bit out of hand. I wish I hadn't called the police; I overreacted. Now he's going to bloody hate me, and you too probably.'

'I said he's fine. I might meet up with him for a coffee if the snow eases up.'

'You might not be able to get back to uni if it doesn't,' Sarah says.

'I've brought loads of work home with me, and I can log on to the site to keep up with anything I miss. To be honest, it looks as though the snow's bad there too; the place has probably gone into lockdown.'

'Well, that's okay, then,' Sarah says. 'Go and have your bath, and then we'll eat.'

The bathroom door shuts.

Sarah goes downstairs. Tess is in her bed, asleep. Every so often she lets out a little growl.

When I realised he wasn't going to talk I got excited because I knew then it was going to happen, and I was going to enjoy it because I always do; this is the fun part. It's only afterwards that you think what have I done?

In fact it was better than ever, the best yet, because this one was not some random person I fancied the look of, someone who'd got in the way. This one had made me angry and hurt people I care about and that made it personal.

And that made it his fault.

Oh, for a while there it was glorious. It went on and on and I thought he was never going to give up struggling. He's tougher than he looks, but once I've started I get stronger and stronger because it drives you on, the blood does, and I know there's no way he's ever going to be able to match me.

There was more blood this time; it went everywhere and once it started there was more and more of it. I think once there is blood on something then you just have to carry on, don't you? There's no point in stopping.

You can't clean it up properly, everyone knows that, so there's no point trying to.

Blood everywhere. All over my skin. The smell of it.

I sat there afterwards with it covering me and I didn't want to wash it off but I knew I was going to have to. That's always the shit part, like coming down off a high; you don't want to do it but you must, and it gets worse the longer you leave it.

I stripped off and found a pair of socks and put them on to get to the bathroom, then I washed off all the blood.

There was no point trying to clean up in the bedroom; it would have taken me weeks. I found some fresh clothes and I shut the door.

I won't be staying again. Not now.

You can't come back from something like this. I know because it's happened before.

Sarah

Sarah wakes up and the room is bright, a diamond-hard white light illuminating the room. She blinks, squints. The curtains are open. She sits on the edge of the bed, listening to the silence of the house. Nothing. Even the wind has dropped to a low whistle.

She stands and goes to the window, looks out. The field behind the house is uniformly white and the clouds are low, low enough that she can't see the top of the hill.

She pulls on her dressing gown and goes out into the corridor. Kitty's door is wide open; the room is empty. She goes to the bathroom and turns on the shower, waiting for it to warm up before stepping under the spray.

Afterwards she feels human again, better than she has for a long time. Having Kitty in the house has given her a good night's sleep, the first she has had in ages. And the thought of having her here for a while, not having to rush back to uni, fills her with joy.

Downstairs, dressed in jeans and a warm jumper, Sarah sets the kettle on to boil. There is a note beside it.

Taken Tess out. Too much snow on the hill so I'm going to the village. I might pop in on the way back and see how Basil is. x

She looks out of the kitchen window at the yard outside, at the vast expanse of snow, the wind blowing the tops of it like sand, swirling and dancing and drifting against the workshop.

There is a light on in the cottage. Sarah stares for a moment, and then looks at the footprints in the snow.

Her heart thumps madly.

She pulls on her boots, pushes her arms into her coat, misses, swears, fiddles with it until she finds the armholes, rushes out into the yard. The snow is deep now, up to the tops of her boots, but she trudges around the edge of it where it isn't so bad until she gets to the cottage door.

She doesn't knock.

She tries the door, and it opens.

'Hello?' she says.

The cottage is quiet. She goes inside, stands on the mat and stamps the snow off her boots.

He appears from the kitchen, carrying a tea towel, wiping a mug. His normally wild curls are damp. He smells clean. 'Hey, Sarah,' Will says. 'How's it going?'

'What the hell are you doing in here?'

He smiles, as if nothing's wrong. 'Aren't you coming in?'

She walks further into the room, not taking off her boots. She doesn't care about leaving a trail of snow and mud any more, and she's not going to wrestle with taking them off and putting them back on again. 'Will, you need to leave, please.'

'Ah,' he says. 'You didn't say anything about this place. You told me – or rather, the police told me – that I wasn't to come into your house, or contact you, any more. Haven't done either of those things.'

Sarah feels physically sick, her stomach turning over. 'How did you get in here?' she asks.

'Oh, in here? I borrowed your key. I didn't think you'd mind.'

'Well, I do mind.'

'Do you want a cup of coffee? You've got a very nice coffee machine here. Nice beans.'

Sarah has to shake her head to try and maintain a sense of reality. 'Where's Aiden?'

'Oh!' he says, brightly. 'Aiden! Yes, I'd forgotten about Aiden. The man who fucks other people's women for money?'

His eyes are wide, the irises like shards of ice, pale blue. This is the first time she has heard him swear.

Sarah doesn't answer. She is freefalling.

'He's not here, is he, Sarah? He's gone away.' He makes a strange, flighty gesture with his hands, as though Aiden is a bird that has escaped from a cage.

'You don't know anything, Will. I want you to leave. I'll call the police again, they'll arrest you this time.'

'I think they'll struggle to get a patrol car up here, to be honest,' he says cheerfully. 'And if they did happen to have a 4x4 that wasn't already busy doing other things, I'll be long gone before they get here. And then you'll just be wasting their time, won't you?'

Sarah says nothing.

'I said, you'll be wasting their time, won't you? You're good at that, Sarah. Wasting people's time. Giving yourself one minute, backing off the next; teasing people. Aren't you?'

He is really close now. She closes her eyes slowly, a single tear squeezing out and rolling down her cheek. He is breathing against the side of her forehead, hard and fast. He touches her cheek with one finger. She flinches.

'I'm not going to hurt you. I won't hurt you. I don't know what you think I'm going to do.'

'Please just go,' she whispers.

He smiles. No tears, not any more. He's together, relaxed, certain of himself.

'I don't know what you women all see in him, anyway,' he says. 'He's an old man. I mean, I can see he's good at it. That thing he does, with his hand on your fanny, watching your face, the way he makes you wait for it – '

'Shut up! Shut up!'

Now he throws back his head, laughing at her. 'You're not going to pretend you didn't know I was there? What's that all about, anyway, leaving your curtains open all the time? You love being watched. I can see you do. You loved it at Louis's party, screwing me out there in the back garden where anyone could find us. You love it. You're a complete slut; you might as well be selling it like he does.'

He comes close now, pressing his body against hers from behind. He slides his arm around her waist and his hand snakes down across her stomach, between her legs. She grabs for his hand and tries to push it away. She can feel he is hard, pressing into her back, and now she's afraid.

'I'd like to watch you again. I liked seeing the expression on your face.'

'Leave me alone!'

Sarah pushes him back. She turns and makes a run for the door, but he's quicker than she is, gets there first, blocks her in. He pushes her against the wall, knocking the breath out of her. She turns her head away as he gets close, as if he's about to kiss her. She's crying now, tears of shame, fear, panic, falling freely down her cheeks.

'It's okay,' he says, 'shh. It's fine. I just want to tell you this. You don't have to be lonely, now he's gone. I can be with you, I can look after you. Don't keep pushing me away.'

'I want you to go,' she says through gritted teeth.

And he lets her go, quite suddenly, moves away. 'All right,' he says. 'I have things I need to do, in any case. I just wanted to get this out in the open, you know? I've been keeping an eye on you, and now Kitty's here I can watch out for her, too. Okay?'

He reaches across her and opens the door.

'You go back to the house. I'll get my coat and go, okay? I'm not going to hang around.'

Sarah looks at the open door, makes a run for it. She slips and slides across the yard back to the house. Behind her, she hears him laughing.

Sarah shuts the front door behind her and takes several shuddering, panicky breaths. She stares at the door, half-expecting him to open it and walk in. She reaches up and tries to put the chain on, but it is fiddly and her fingers are numb, and somehow it won't fit in its catch.

She pulls her hand back and looks at it in surprise. It is shaking badly. 'Kitty?' she calls into the empty house. 'Are you back? Kitty?'

There is no answer.

She leaves the door, because Kitty is out there somewhere with Tess. She walks to the kitchen, stands at the sink and looks out at the yard, gripping the edge of the worktop.

The sun is shining weakly, but it looks as if the snow might be melting; it is already wet around the edges, nearest to the house, as if the warmth of the walls is penetrating into the freezing air. But then the sun goes behind a dark cloud, and the wind stirs up the soft crystals of snow, like a breath blowing spilt sugar from a table top. It's strangely beautiful, hypnotic, and for a moment Sarah watches, lost.

Then she looks down at her hands and sees that they are still shaking. She fills the kettle and switches it on, trying to calm herself.

I'm okay. It's all right.

Sarah rests her head in her hands, takes a deep breath in. Now she is away from him, it feels unreal. He's not hurt anyone, she tells herself. He's just a fucked-up kid who doesn't know what to do with himself, and she's become the victim of a game he's playing.

Calm down. It's all right.

Going into the living room, Sarah turns on the television and switches to the twenty-four-hour news channel while she cleans the grate, for something to do. The news has very little about the weather now; it's all about Syria, political responses to immigration. Eventually the report wends its way round to the weather. She reaches behind her for the remote control and turns up the volume.

'*... possibility of further snowfalls this afternoon, worsening this evening as the wind picks up again, and it's likely we could see some drifting on higher ground, particularly on the Moors and heading into Scotland. The wind in particular is strengthening all the time, with gusts of up to seventy or eighty miles an hour in exposed areas, which could be strong enough to bring some trees or power lines down. The Met Office has issued an amber warning for people living in the northeast of England and southern and central Scotland with regard to the wind, and you can keep an eye on the latest information on our website.*'

Sarah has never worried about the weather up here before. The house, crumbling though it is, is like a castle, thick-walled and safe; and with the oil tank filled up, the freezer full of food, they can ride out any storm. There isn't much of a mobile signal here at the best of times, so the only real concern is if they lose the landline. And even then, a hundred metres out towards the lane and the mobile signal is usually good enough for an emergency connection.

She tries the landline; there is a dialling tone, which is comforting. On an impulse, she dials Sophie's phone again. The mobile goes straight to voicemail.

'Hi, it's me – it's Sarah. Just wanted to speak to you. I know this must have been a bloody nightmare for you. I hope you're somewhere safe, and you're okay. Please, please give me a call back?'

After that she tries George. Again, no answer; the phone rings and rings, and, when the voicemail kicks in, Sarah disconnects.

Finally, she tries Aiden.

The number you are calling has not responded. Please try again later.

She goes back to the fireplace, lays the kindling and the logs and lights the fire. It blazes bright, and the feel of it, the smell of the logs and the soot in the chimney, is comforting. When it's well alight, she leaves it and goes to sort through another load of Kitty's laundry. There is less of a hurry about this now that it seems Kitty's staying, but, even so, it needs doing.

The phone rings while Sarah is in the utility room. She rushes back to get it.

'Hello?'

'Mrs Carpenter? It's Kerry from Abbey Vets here.'

'Hi. How's Basil? Is he okay?'

'I'm just calling with an update for you. He's doing very well at the moment, although he's still quite wobbly. The blood tests we ran yesterday show some liver function abnormality, which does confirm that he ingested some kind of poison. He's responding well to treatment, though, so hopefully there should be no long-term damage. We're not fully open today, there are just a few of us with the hospitalised animals, so I wanted to let you know in case you were concerned that we'd left him on his own.'

'It's a nightmare, isn't it? Are you having to sleep there?'

'We do have a small camp bed for emergencies, but I and the other nurse both live nearby, so we're taking it in turns to check on them all.'

'Thank you. Oh – my daughter Kitty might be calling; she's just gone for a walk down to the village.'

'Ah, right. Well, she might find the door locked, but if she rings the bell we'll let her in.'

'I'm sure she will. We've been so worried about him.'

'I think if it weren't for the snow Basil might have been able to come home later today, but given the weather forecast it might be safer to keep him here another night, if you're in agreement.'

'Yes. As long as he's okay. I do really miss him. And my other dog, Tess, does too.'

'Well, hopefully they'll be reunited soon. And with a bit of luck he won't go eating anything else he shouldn't.'

'Do you know what it was yet? Is there any way of telling?'

'No, unfortunately. That's the trouble with Labradors, though: they eat everything. No common sense where food's concerned.'

Kerry ends the call. The wind is picking up, Sarah thinks; she looks out of the window and sees that the sun has gone in. She thinks it might be snowing again, but when she looks out properly it's just the wind drifting the snow around the yard. The clouds overhead are dark and low.

The phone receiver is still in Sarah's hand. She dials Kitty's number. It goes straight to voicemail, without even a single ring.

'Kitty, it's Mum. Come home now, darling. Please. It's going to start snowing again. Please come home as soon as you get this. If you need me to pick you up, I'll come out in the Land Rover, just call me. Love you.'

For a moment Sarah watches the flames, listening to the crackle as the damp logs spit. Then she hears something else – another noise, coming from the back of the house.

Scratching, whining.

Sarah rushes to the front door, opens it and calls out. Tess comes hurtling round the house, pushes past her and inside, barking and racing round in mad, panicked circles.

'Tess? Where's Kitty?'

As if the dog can answer her. Tess barks at the door, teeth bared.

'Kitty!' Sarah yells, cupping her hands around her mouth. 'Kitty!'

She leaves the door open and pulls on her weatherproof jacket, runs back to the kitchen for her phone. Just as she reaches for it on the kitchen table, it buzzes with a text message.

Sarah looks at the phone, and for a moment she can't understand why the message isn't being displayed. Then she realises it's a picture.

It takes a long time to load. In the end, Sarah goes outside, where she gets one bar of signal. When the image finally appears, she can't quite tell what it is; it's dark, and there is a white shape, which is blurred. She touches the image to enlarge it, and when it finally comes into focus she gasps in shock.

It's Kitty's face. Her eyes are screwed shut, and her mouth is wide open, as if she is screaming.

Sarah stares at her phone, trying to process what she's seeing. The message has come from Kitty's phone. Is it some kind of joke? Has Kitty sent her the message by mistake?

She tries Kitty's number, but of course the mobile signal isn't good enough for a call, and it disconnects immediately. She picks up the landline, and dials Kitty from that. This time, it rings and rings, unanswered, until eventually the voicemail kicks in.

Leave a message, it's Kit Carpenter, bye!

'Kitty, ring me as soon as you get this – it's Mum. Ring me now. Please.'

Sarah pulls up the picture again. Why is it so blurred? She sits awkwardly back on the sofa. She has the two phones in either hand, staring from one to the other. There is only one thing she can do – something she should have done earlier.

'Emergency, which service do you require?'

'Police, please,' she says firmly. There is a short pause, then a different voice.

'Yorkshire Police, what's your emergency?'

'I think my daughter is in trouble,' Sarah says. Her voice is tight with panic.

'Right,' the operator says, 'what sort of trouble?'

'She went for a walk to the village earlier. She isn't answering her phone. And I've just received a picture message from her phone. It's a picture of her face, it looks like she's screaming.'

'Can I take some details from you, and we'll get someone to help. What's your name?'

Sarah's voice trembles as she reports her name, her address, her date of birth, Kitty's name, Kitty's date of birth... *It's all taking too long*, she thinks. *It's all just too slow.*

'Please,' she says, feeling the tears starting now, at last, because she's on her own again and she thinks she might just be going mad, might be losing touch with reality, 'please help me... I think someone has got her...'

'Why do you think that?' says the voice. There is no curiosity there, no sense of wonder. The operator is reporting facts, typing them up fast.

'I just know,' Sarah says. She needs to choose her words carefully. 'There's someone who has been watching the house. I know this sounds strange. I reported it – I spoke to a detective. Amy Foster. She told me to ring, and give you a number, only I don't know where it is now...'

'I can look that up for you. Did you give your home address?'

'Yes, yes.'

'Here we go. You reported a harassment yesterday.'

'Yes. He was here again. He was here this morning. I told him to leave. He did. Kitty was angry about it. She might have gone to find him; I don't know. She said she was going to get some fresh air, see if her friends were home, but maybe she went to look for him?'

'Can you just confirm who it is we're talking about, Mrs Carpenter?'

Sarah shudders over the name. Over the thought that he has somehow got hold of Kitty. That she is screaming.

'Will,' she says. 'Will Brewer.'

Sarah stands in the kitchen staring out over the yard, over the whiteness and Kitty's tracks, which are fading as the snow blows and swirls over them. The sun has gone in; the clouds are heavy and getting darker.

The year they first moved into Four Winds Farm, the snow was heavy, like this – heavier. The kids had been out there building a snowman with Jim. Then they'd built an igloo up on the field. There was so much snow they hardly knew what to do with it. Afterwards, they all piled back into the house and Sarah made them all hot chocolate and they warmed up in front of the fire.

There was snow every year, of course. Sarah couldn't remember them ever bothering to make a snowman again, much less an igloo. They were teenagers by then and the snow was an inconvenience, something to be trudged through, something that cancelled clubs and meet-ups and dates.

The clock ticks and the wind blows, and the landline doesn't ring. She checks her watch. Fifteen minutes have passed since she talked to the police about Kitty. They told her someone would call her back, and that it might be a little while but to rest assured that someone was dealing with it.

'It's urgent!' she'd said to them, her voice sounding high and quavery even to her own ears.

Someone will call her back. They are dealing with it. She has to trust that they are.

This is no good – what can she do, sitting here? She pulls on her boots and her coat and finds her hat and gloves. Tess jumps up from her bed.

The snow is knee-deep in parts of the yard. If she wants to get the Land Rover out she might need to dig a path through to the driveway and probably beyond. The snow piles over the top of her boots and soaks through her jeans quickly. When she gets to the gate it feels deeper; the wind has blown it across the road between her house and the Buttons', and it's only a low hump in the white expanse that shows where the dry stone wall is. The ditch must be just in front of it, but you'd never know. Underneath the snow, the stream must still be flowing down the hill.

Something looks odd about it; even with the drifts, there is an odd shape on the Buttons' drive. She trudges a few steps closer. It's a car, half-hidden in the snow. It takes a while to get to it, minutes more to brush enough of the snow away to confirm what she suspected: it's Aiden's car. She pushes snow away from the passenger window, suddenly fearful that he's inside it – but the car is empty.

Why would he leave the car here? Perhaps her driveway looked worse, and maybe he left the car here knowing the Buttons were away? But that raises another question, one that is more terrifying still. Aiden's car is here – so where is he?

There are no footprints here, no sign of life. Kitty must have cut through over the stile behind the cottage, gone down to the village through the fields.

She fishes her mobile phone out of her pocket, dials Kitty's number.

Leave a message, it's Kit Carpenter, bye!

She cuts it off. There is no point leaving another message. She tries Sophie's phone, which doesn't even ring, then

George's, then she gives up. The phone bleeps an alarm – the battery is almost gone. It should have lasted longer than that; the cold must have drained it.

The village below her is lost in a swirl of grey-white cloud. She can barely make out shapes, and then they are gone. Turning to go back to the house, she can hardly see that either; it is snowing again, and within a few moments it's swirling and drifting and hitting her face like needles. She pushes her way through, trying to match her feet into the tracks she has already made. At the gate she gets her foot caught in something and falls face-first, hands out in front of her diving through soft snow. It's difficult to stand up again; there is nothing solid to push against. In the end she gets to her knees and manages to get up.

Now it becomes urgent to get back to the house. There is something menacing about the way the sky has turned dark and now she cannot see the road, cannot see the Buttons' house, can only just make out the back wall of the cottage and the posts of the stile into the sheep field sticking up through the drifts.

'Tess! Tess!' she calls, her words snatched away as soon as they leave her mouth.

She hears an answering bark from somewhere.

In the shelter of the cottage the snow has banked up, driven by the wind up from the valley. She fights her way through it, around the corner and into the yard. Between her and the house she can just make out a figure, something moving.

At first she thinks it must be Tess, but it's too big for that. It's a person, someone wearing white, moving slowly, and nearly at the door.

'Kitty!'

She moves faster, pushing through the drifts, exhausted already, until she gets to the door too, shoves it open and shuts it fast. Even in those few seconds the snow has blown into the hall. She stamps it off her boots, tries to shake herself down.

'Kitty?'

Tess is in the kitchen, wagging her wet tail at the figure who is trying to rub her down with a towel. It takes her a second to recognise who it is, because the person is wearing white ski trousers and a grey pullover. A white ski jacket with navy blue piping along the seams is hanging, dripping, over a kitchen chair.

It's Will. Of course it is Will.

'Where's Kitty?' Sarah asks, as soon as she can speak without coughing.

'Kitty? No idea. Isn't she here?'

Sarah launches herself at Will, taking him by surprise and pushing him up against the wall. 'Where is she? What have you done?'

He laughs at her. He actually laughs.

And then he turns sideways, twisting out of Sarah's feeble, frozen grip. He stands in the middle of her kitchen, his hair wet at the ends, his blue eyes intense, hands loose at his sides. A sob that she is powerless to stop rises in her throat and she drops into a crouch, falling back against the wall and pulling her knees up to her chest.

'Sarah, Sarah,' he says, soothing. 'It's all right. It'll be okay. Has Kitty gone somewhere? What's happened?'

'She – she went down to the village... I got a text from her phone...'

He waits for her to say more but she cannot. She is shaking from the cold; her lips are numb.

'We need to get you out of these wet things. Come on.'

She resists him as he starts to peel off her coat, pulls her up to a standing position, then manoeuvres her round to the kitchen chair, where he unzips her boots and pulls them off. Her jeans are soaked.

'I'm going to find you some dry clothes,' he says. 'You stay here, I'll be back in a moment.'

He puts the kettle on, then leaves the room. Sarah listens to him going up the stairs, then hears the creak of the floorboards in her room. *I don't want him here,* she thinks. Her coat is hanging over the chair in front of her. She reaches for it, then searches through the pockets for her mobile phone.

It's not there.

She looks again, checks all the pockets, even the ones she doesn't use, checks the lining in case the phone has fallen through. Outside, the wind howls; the snow patters against the kitchen window, even drowning out the rattle of the water in the kettle rising to a boil.

'No!' Sarah yells, and rushes for the door. She must have dropped her phone outside, maybe when she fell. The wind blasts through the house the moment she opens the door. The snow has drifted against the door and it falls inside.

Strong arms catch her just as she is about to run out in her socked feet.

'What are you doing?' Will drags her back from the door and wrestles it shut against the wind. 'You can't go out again – look at it!'

Sarah presses her hands against her face. 'My phone – I must have dropped it! What if Kitty's in trouble?'

'Then she'll call the landline. Look, come on – you need to get a grip. Everything's fine, I'm sure of it. Come on, come back into the kitchen.'

She lets him lead her by the arm and sit her down again. The kettle clicks off and the wind howls around the house, rattling at the windows. She watches, almost dazed, as he makes a pot of tea, taking care to warm the pot and stir the tea around inside before putting it on a trivet on the kitchen table.

'Where did you get those clothes?' she asks. Her teeth are chattering. He looks odd, in those white ski trousers that are too big around the waist and a little too small in the leg. The braces are still on his shoulders; if he slipped them off the trousers would fall down.

'I borrowed them. Better for this weather, right?'

'Borrowed them from whom?'

Jim has a pair for the snow. They went skiing years ago, in fact the first time was at university with the Ski Soc. The three of them, her, Jim and Aiden, fooling around in Val d'Isère with all the posh kids. Jim's ski gear is dark blue, though, flashes of neon yellow through the sleeves. Sarah is shaking so much when he finally hands her a mug that she doubts she can hold it.

'Right, I'm going to help you undress now. Is that okay?'

She doesn't assent but he does it anyway, helping her to her feet and undoing her jeans, tugging them away from her skin. Her legs, when they're finally on show, are mottled and bluish with bright pink patches. He has found a pair of jogging bottoms and he helps her to step into them, a pair of thick socks. Sarah has been watching all this take place as if she is one step removed from it all, as if it is happening to someone else, and now she looks down at the top of Will's head as he kneels at her feet, pushing a thick sock, rolled up, over her toes and then pulling it up her calf. He strokes her foot firmly but tenderly, then moves to the other foot and does the same, applying full concentration to it.

He is here, she thinks. *If he's here, he is not with Kitty. She must be fine. She's safe.*

'Stand up,' he says.

She does as she's told. He pulls her sweater over her head while she raises her arms like a good girl. Under it she is wearing a vest and her bra. He has found her a T-shirt and a zipped top that she hasn't worn in years. Casually he runs his hand across the front of her chest, over her breasts, as if he's feeling to see if the fabric is wet, nothing more. When she doesn't react, he does it again, this time lingering.

She tries to fold her arms across her chest but he gently pulls them away. He rolls up the T-shirt and puts it over her head. She puts her arms through the sleeves and then takes the sweatshirt from him. 'I can manage,' she says.

'Sure.'

He sits at the kitchen table and lifts the mug of tea to his mouth, sipping it.

'Good job I'm here, right?' he says. 'You'd be in hypothermic shock now. You might have collapsed and had a heart attack.'

'Hypothermic shock' sounds like something he might have made up, just to sound knowledgeable. She doesn't want him here, wants him to go, but she is wary. She is on her own. Where is she going to go? Where is he going to go? And in any case, the police are supposed to be calling her back, or coming out to see her, if they can. She will just have to manage this the best way she can.

Stay calm. Think. Don't piss him off.

Try not to show him you're scared.

'Take your time,' he says, when she takes a big gulp of tea. It's hot and burns her mouth a little, and makes her cough. Why does she feel so dazed?

'I wish Kitty would call me,' she says.

'Where did she go?'

'She went for a walk,' she says. Perhaps he doesn't know, after all? Perhaps Kitty went to a friend's house, and they have taken a picture as a joke, sending it to her by mistake?

All of this, she knows, cannot be true. But, for now, she can continue the pretence.

She looks through to the living room, at the landline phone which is lying discarded on the sofa. 'I should try to phone her again.' She gets unsteadily to her feet but he's there first.

'I'll get it; you just sit down. You're still a bit wobbly, aren't you?'

She feels a little better, actually, but it can't hurt to have him imagining she's still unstable. He brings her the phone. As he hands it to her she notices that there is what looks like dried blood around his fingernails. His knuckles are swollen, scratched. The sight of this makes her heart pound heavily in her chest: *Kitty's blood? Is she hurt?*

He is watching her, studying her face.

There are no missed calls.

Sarah presses the green button to make a call, but there is no dialling tone. There is nothing, just the sound of her hair rustling against her ear, the wind outside.

The landline is dead.

'Well,' he says, 'that's that. We're stranded, aren't we? You and me together?'

The wind finds the tiny gaps in the window frames, whines like an animal in pain. Tess has disappeared, probably hiding under one of the beds. She can tolerate any weather, but strange noises have always unnerved her.

'We could walk down to the village,' Sarah says slowly. 'I'm sure all the phone lines can't be down.'

Will laughs.

'Go out again? What for?'

To find Kitty, Sarah thinks.

'No,' he says. 'No point going anywhere, is there? We've got other things to do, here. We need to talk.'

Even with dry clothes on, Sarah is shivering.

'Come through here, come on.'

He takes her through to the living room, holding her hand as if she's five or ninety-five, leads her to the sofa and wraps around her shoulders the blanket that Basil sometimes sleeps on. Then he busies himself with the fire, stoking it and adding some more logs. Sarah looks at his back and thinks it would be easy to do something right now, push him or hit him with something, and she gets as far as looking around for something suitably heavy, but then he interrupts her.

'I can tell you're worried,' he says. 'I know you're not happy with me being here, are you? Well, it's a bit tough, that, because I'm here now, and I'm not going away just yet.'

He stands and turns his back to the fire, stretching his arms over his head. His fingertips brush the low ceiling. Then he moves the magazines and the empty mug and the coaster from the coffee table and sits facing her, his knees touching hers.

'Now, how shall I put this?' he says, fixing her with his piercing blue eyes. 'There's going to be an easy way and a hard way, and I'm really hoping we can do this the easy way, get it all over with and then I can leave you in peace.'

He takes hold of her hand, strokes the back of it. Sarah flinches at the touch, but he's holding her too tightly for her to pull away.

'See, I know all you want is for Kitty to come home safe and well, to your lovely, cosy little family home. I know you want me to go away and not come back. All of that can happen, you know, even with the snow and the wind. I can make it happen. But if that's what you want, you have to do something for me. Are you listening, Sarah?'

Sarah nods. Tears are falling now and she can hardly see him.

'So, let's do this the easy way, shall we?' He pats her hand comfortingly, as if that'll help. 'All you need to do is tell me where Sophie is.'

She stares at him, horrified.

'I don't know where Sophie is,' she whispers.

Will looks at her for a long moment, as if trying to assess whether she's telling the truth.

'See, that's a shame,' he says. 'A real pity. I thought you were going to do the right thing, Sarah.'

'No, you don't understand, I really don't know where she is. She didn't tell me anything. She didn't tell me she was seeing Aiden, she didn't really even tell me about you, I hardly saw her – '

With no warning he hits her across the side of her head with the back of his hand, sending her sprawling on to the arm of the chair. She clutches her face with both hands, gasping with shock. Her cheek is tingling with it, her ear ringing. He has caught her earring stud somehow and it's come out, and her ear is bleeding.

'Ow!' he says, shaking his hand. 'Bloody hurt, that did.'

Tess has turned up out of nowhere and is barking furiously, baring her teeth.

'Come on, Tess,' he says in a consoling voice. 'It's okay, girl. Come with me.'

He goes into the kitchen, taking Tess with him. Sarah gets to her feet, is about to run for the door, but he returns with a wet tea towel wrapped around his hand, shutting Tess in the kitchen. He pushes Sarah back on to the sofa. She can feel a slow trickle of blood running down the side of her neck. She rubs at it, wipes her fingers on her jogging bottoms.

'Where do you think you're going, eh? Sit down.'

But now Sarah has found a gutload of courage from somewhere. He's hit her and that feels like the last straw. She stands up again immediately. 'This is ridiculous! What do you think you're doing?'

He looks startled, takes a single step back. Tess is barking like a mad thing in the kitchen.

'I've told you I don't know where she is. You're not going to accomplish anything by threatening me. Now where's my daughter? Where is she?'

She sees something in his eyes, a flicker of a little boy being told off, but then it's gone. It takes a second for him to remember who he is, why he's here, but then it's back with force. He screws up his eyes, draws back his lips in a snarl, hunches his shoulders and with both hands shoves Sarah hard, back on to the sofa, and then he's on top of her, his knees digging into her thighs, his hands around her throat.

She claws at his fingers, tries to pull his wrists off her, but his elbows are locked, all his weight pushing down on to her throat. She cannot breathe. She looks up at him desperately, then tries to reach his face, to dig her fingers into his eyes, anything to make him stop, but she can't reach.

Then there is a flurry of black and white fur, snarling teeth and barking and the pressure stops. Tess must have managed to push open the kitchen door. *Clever girl*, Sarah thinks. She heaves a deep breath in, and again, coughing and falling off the sofa on to her hands and knees. She can hear barking and Will shouting, then a yelp of pain from the dog.

'Tess,' she gasps.

The kitchen door is shut again, properly this time. Then Sarah sees Will's boots appear on the carpet in front of her and before she can move he has taken hold of her by the hair, dragging her upright. The pain in her scalp is intense, sudden, and her legs fight to gain purchase on the carpet to ease the pressure. He pulls her by the hair and by the sleeve of her jumper up the narrow staircase, Sarah's socked feet slipping and stumbling.

'Let me go! Let go!'

Her voice is hoarse; she can barely hear herself against Will's grunting as he drags her up the stairs. The wind is rattling the tiles on the roof and howling through the house, but when they reach the top of the stairs she manages a scream, manages to wrench herself free from his grip, using the last bit of strength she has to push him away.

She doesn't see his closed fist until it meets with the side of her head and her legs crumple beneath her, and everything goes black and silent.

When she opens her eyes it is gloomy. She is stretched out like a starfish in bed, in a room that is semi-dark, lit by the glow of some artificial light. Over her head she can see a lampshade that she doesn't recognise. When she tries to lift her head from the pillow something tightens around her neck, and her head throbs. It takes a second to realise that she is tied by the wrists and ankles to the bed.

She lifts her head again carefully, to see that she is in the spare bedroom, upstairs. Will Brewer is sitting on the ottoman under the window, the curtains drawn, the bedside light next to her lit. He is leaning back, one knee jiggling an anxious rhythm. He is staring at her, chewing on one fingernail. There is something almost childlike about the way he holds his hand steady with the other hand.

'Why have you tied me up?' she asks, as calmly as she can.

'You were going to run for it.'

'Well, I won't. Where can I go, anyway?'

He drops his hands to his lap, pressing his fingers to his knees as if to stop everything shaking. He takes a deep breath.

'Please, Will. You can untie me now.'

He shakes his head. 'I need to go out for a bit.'

'Why? Go where?'

'Things I need to do.'

'Where's Kitty? Where is she?'

He doesn't say anything for a moment and she thinks that he might, possibly, be about to see sense and tell her everything; that he might realise how crazy this all is, how he could get out of it even now if he could only see how stupid it was. And then she remembers the dried blood crusted around the edges of his fingernails, remembers being thrown back into the sofa by the force of him hitting her, his hands around her throat, and she realises he can't go back. He can only go forward. It can only get worse.

'You're asking the wrong question,' he says. 'Why aren't you worried about Sophie? Don't you care about her? Or do you know where she is, and you're just pissing me about?'

'I told you, I don't know where she is. Will, please just untie this – whatever it is – around my neck. It's too tight.'

'It's to stop you moving,' he says cheerfully. 'So you can't strain to pull your hands free. I saw it on a TV programme.'

'Don't leave me here like this,' she says, beginning to feel panic rising. If the noose around her neck tightens, how can she loosen it again?

With a sigh he climbs on to the bed, straddles her. The sight of him above her triggers a memory of his fingers closing around her throat downstairs and she gasps, shrinks away from him. He looks down at her with something that might be confidence, as if he's suddenly realised that she is completely under his control. His eyes wander from her face down to her chest. He touches her temple with a finger, catches the tear she hadn't realised she had shed, traces a wet line down her jaw to her throat. He moves two fingers under the ligature, whatever it is, as if he's checking a dog's collar for a snug fit. He eases it looser, just a little. Sarah swallows with relief.

He continues down her neckline, fingering the zip of her fleece, then moving across her chest, finding the bump of her nipple and stroking it until, undesired, unbidden, it reacts.

Will smiles at this, at his power.

'Please,' she says.

'Please what?' he asks. 'You want me to...? Oh, Sarah. Maybe later. When we've got more time.'

He climbs off her, and, with the weight of him pressing her down gone, the ligature around her throat loosens a little more. She doesn't move, in case he sees. It's lying on her throat. She lifts her head a little bit. Will is at the door.

'I won't be long. A few minutes.'

And then he disappears.

'Don't leave me!' Sarah calls out, because she thinks this is what he needs to hear. He is going anyway.

Downstairs, she hears Tess's barks and yelps grow suddenly louder as the kitchen door opens, and then quieten again as Will speaks to her soothingly. Please God don't let him hurt her...

A few minutes pass before she hears the front door slam. From outside, a single bark. He's taken Tess.

She waits for a few more moments, in case he has just pretended to go, in case he's still in the house, but she can hear nothing, not even the wind. The house echoes in silence, waiting for her to move.

She tugs at each binding, but it feels as if struggling just tightens the knot. Still, she thinks there may be one thing she can do: tipping her head back into the pillow, she feels the ligature ride up to her chin. It's tight across the back of her head, but at least it's not around her throat.

By wiggling, pushing her head back, gradually the knot slips up the top of her head and then, quite suddenly, it's off. Lying across her face is what could be a black stocking. She blows, shakes her head to get it off her face. Is that what he's tied her up with? If that's it, there should be some stretch in there.

At least now she can lift her head properly, turn her head to the side to see what she's up against. A pair of tights, she thinks, tied around each wrist in a double knot at the back of her hand, and then tied around the iron bedstead. They are tight, but now her neck is free she can stretch one arm tighter to loosen the other, and if she pulls hard she can almost reach round to the knot...

On the third attempt her fingers touch the knot. But that's as far as she gets – a touch. Rest for a minute. Think. How can she get out of this?

Unbidden, Sophie's face comes into her mind. Sophie, sitting opposite her in the Black Swan. *He likes to stir things up, he likes to make trouble... he gets off on it.*

Sophie knew what he was capable of, she thinks. She wasn't running away from George. She was running away from Will.

A few minutes...

The thought of Will coming back gives Sarah a surge of strength and she pulls and wriggles and twists until the ligature on her right wrist slips suddenly over the knuckle of her thumb. A moment later, an almighty tug, and it's free. The blood surges into her fingers and she sobs with relief. Her hand, in front of her face, looks white and purplish, the fingers swollen. But they are free.

After a few moments she tries to reach across to the knot on the left side, but it is too far, too high. Instead she tries to squeeze a finger under the ligature at her wrist, to stretch the fabric. It feels tighter than the other side, or maybe her hand is more swollen. The fingers on her right hand have pins and needles. She cannot feel her left hand any more.

And then she manages to get a finger under one of the layers, and pulls it away, allowing her hand to turn. She pulls and twists and wriggles and then both her hands are free. She cries with the sudden stab of pain in her shoulders, holding both her hands to her chest, rubbing them together.

She doesn't have long.

By bending her knees and edging her bottom down the bed, she manages to pull herself into a sitting position. Her socked feet are tied, with the ligature around the socks. It looks as if it should be easy to work her feet free of the socks, giving her a few millimetres of space to pull herself free. Her legs are pulled so wide apart that she cannot reach either of them without considerable effort, but by pulling and twisting she eventually manages to get both hands to her right ankle.

A few minutes later, she is free. It feels as though the whole process has taken more like an hour. She sits cross-legged on the bed for a minute, massaging her feet, which are freezing. Every joint aches, as does her head. She fingers her ear carefully, wondering if he tore something when he hit her. It feels bruised, puffy, crusted with dried blood.

When she can feel her feet enough to stand, she goes to the window and moves the curtain aside just enough to see that, outside, the daylight is fading. She wonders why he bothered to close the curtains, to turn on the light; maybe to disorientate her. It has stopped snowing, but outside is all white.

She walks carefully to the door, listening for sounds in the house, avoiding the floorboards she knows creak. The house is silent. Quickly she runs across the hallway to her own bedroom, to the upstairs phone. She clutches the receiver, goes to dial 999, but the line is dead. There is no tone, no response, nothing.

I have to get out.

First thing: proper clothes. Jeans, waterproof trousers over the top, a T-shirt, a different sweater – all done quickly with shaking, numb fingers. Clothes she's chosen herself – there is something powerful about it. It shows intent.

She slips down the stairs, keeping to the edge, just in case he is back – but the house is still quiet. Downstairs in the kitchen she glances through the window. The world outside is white, and quiet, the clouds overhead darkening. She can see the cottage, the footprints clearly leading away from the house, past the cottage. Two sets – Will's, and Tess's. She goes to the front door to retrieve her boots. They are still wet from the snow but they are the best ones she has; she tucks her jeans inside and slips the waterproof top layer over the top of them.

She stands up, feeling better now she is prepared. Another glance out of the kitchen window.

She sees the shape of a man rounding the cottage, white ski trousers. Will is coming back.

She runs for the back of the house, the utility room, pulling an old Barbour jacket of Jim's off the peg and pulling it on as she yanks at the door. It doesn't give. It's locked, of course. Where's the key? Where's the fucking key?

She pulls at the drawers, looks fruitlessly at the hooks upon which the spare keys the house has accumulated over the years are hung. From the front of the house, she hears the front door open and bang shut. She freezes. There is no time, no time to find the key. How can she get out?

Then she has an idea. She unhooks another set of keys. She hears rustling as Will takes off his jacket and his ski trousers, thinking that if only she doesn't move, if only she can keep quiet... he doesn't know she is here.

'Sarah?' he calls.

That's good, she thinks: *he is in the kitchen*.

'Sarah, it's only me. I'm back.'

Wherever he has been, he has left Tess behind. Sarah hopes her dog is safe, hopes that he has not hurt her in some way.

She listens as he heads up the stairs, listens to the creaking. As soon as she hears the second creak she moves, fast, trying not to make a sound. Hoping he will be too distracted to listen out for sounds downstairs.

He is upstairs now, heading down the corridor. Did she leave the door open? She cannot remember. In any case, she has just seconds left. She dashes for the front door, opening it and closing it quickly behind her, knowing he will hear and come running. She fumbles with the key in the deadlock, knowing it's stiff, knowing her fingers are still a little numb, and just as the lock shoots home the handle turns, the door rattles and he is right there behind the door.

'Sarah! Sarah! Open the fucking door! Open the door NOW! Sarah!'

She turns and runs through the snow, jumping through his fresh footprints, not looking back.

It won't take him long to get out. Maybe two minutes, before he finds a window that opens wide enough for him to get through. Maybe she has less than two minutes.

She moves as quickly as she can, back behind the cottage and out of sight of the house.

Whichever way she goes, he will see her footprints. Nevertheless, she has to try.

The wind has dropped completely and the sky has cleared; the sound of her shuffling through the fresh snow is amplified by the emptiness of the landscape, as are her gasping, heaving breaths.

She has just reached the gate when she hears something behind her. She stops dead, heart thumping. A wrenching, creaking sound, metal scraping. She wonders what it is and then realises it must be the patio chairs outside the conservatory, scraping against the concrete. He must have got the conservatory door open.

She has no time to get away. Keeping as close to the side of the cottage as she can, she inches her way round it, glancing around the corner.

There he is.

She shrinks back out of sight, not sure if he saw her or not.

'Sarah! Don't be an idiot! You'll freeze to death!'

And then she thinks: the cottage. The cottage has a separate landline; perhaps it is still working. Maybe it's not down because of the snow; maybe Will cut the wire or something. And, even if the phone's not working, then there is a knife block in the kitchen; she can find herself a weapon...

She holds her breath, listening. Whichever way he goes, she will hear his shuffling footsteps through the snow.

'Sarah! Do you want to see Kitty again? Do you?'

Just for a moment she screws her eyes tight shut. This can't be happening, she thinks. I'm dreaming, I must be dreaming this.

She can hear him, shuffling. The sound comes from all around her. When she looks around the corner again, he is gone. He must be behind the cottage now, coming up behind her. Quickly, quietly, keeping close to the wall which has been sheltered from the worst of the snow, Sarah makes her way to the cottage door. It opens smoothly – he didn't lock it. Thank God he didn't lock it.

She closes the door behind her as quietly as possible and runs for the kitchen. The phone should be in here, but it's just the cradle; the handset is missing. She wants to cry with frustration, her eyes flitting around the room, checking every surface for the phone.

The bedroom. The door is closed; it must be in there.

She runs across the open-plan living room and as she does so catches a glimpse of Will through the patio doors. He has seen her. Quick, then, quick, and she pushes open the door of the bedroom.

Inside is hell.

The floor, the walls, the bed, everything is dark red. The smell of it hits her and she brings her hand up to her mouth to stop the scream.

Kitty. Is it Kitty?

Something terrible has happened here. She takes a step further into the room and that's when she sees it – a leg, just the foot and some of the shin visible in the space between the bed and the window.

It's not moving.

Aiden?

Behind her, she hears the cottage door open and close.

She does not look round. He's breathing, hard.

When he speaks, his voice is low, gravelly… *oh, God* – amused.

'Want to see what's left of him?'

She moves so quickly he doesn't have time to react: she spins and pushes out as hard as she can, catches him off balance. Will staggers backwards. It gives her a second to run, and in another moment she is out of the door and racing as fast as she can across the yard towards the barn, the car. There is no point heading for the gate any more. It's a long way to the village; he'd catch up with her too quickly. At least in the barn there are places to hide. She ducks down behind the Land Rover, looking back the way she has come. Her tracks are deep and obvious, not only across the pristine snow of the yard but snowy prints all the way across the concrete of the barn, to where she is crouched. She might as well hold up a flag.

He has reached the end of the cottage, and for some reason – probably the confusing tracks leading to the gate – he carries on without glancing to his right. He is moving quickly, almost jumping through the snow.

He's going.

The snow is deep, but she could risk it in the car. At least she could lock herself in… except the car keys are in the house. Jim used to keep a spare set in his toolbox, back when they had the previous car, the VW Golf that ended up costing him his life.

And then he reaches the gate, looks down the hill towards the village, then back to the house. She ducks down behind the car again but he was looking straight towards her. He must have seen the tracks.

When she looks up again he is halfway across the yard, yomping through her footprints. He does not call out.

Whimpering, she turns to find Jim's bright red tool chest, starts tugging at sticking metal drawers, sending spanner sets scattering over the floor. The spanners are tiny, hundreds of them, wrenches, screwdrivers, all of them too small to use as a weapon. She grabs at the bottom drawer, the deeper one, and inside are plastic cases containing Christ knows what. At the back, a small plastic bag with car keys in, several of them, a lifetime's collection. And a wrench, huge and heavy and rusted.

'Sarah.'

She spins with the wrench in her hand and hits, connects with something solid, screaming with rage and fright as she does so.

Will falls heavily against the car and slumps to the floor. He does not put out his hands to break his fall.

There is a metallic clatter as the wrench falls from her hand to the concrete.

She stares at the figure sprawled at her feet. He is lying on his right side, his head and left arm behind the front tyre of the Land Rover, his legs crossed neatly at the ankle. He is so bundled up in the ski jacket that she can't tell if he's breathing. The hood is still up. Her hand is over her mouth, as if to stop herself screaming. Behind her hand she is gasping and making a keening sound.

Enough, she tells herself. *Pull yourself together.* She breathes through the panic, letting it begin to settle. *Think.*

She steps over his legs, tugs at the shoulder of his jacket so that he flips over on to his back, away from the car. His eyes are slightly open; blood has trickled from under the black woollen hat across his cheek, his temple and his forehead. Even without getting closer she can see a mist of breath coming from his mouth. He's alive, then. The hood, and his hat, must have protected him from the full force of the wrench.

She turns back to the toolbox, to the plastic bag full of spare keys. Even a quick look tells her the Land Rover key is not among them.

One last glance at Will. Then she turns on her heels and runs as best she can through the snow to the house.

It takes her a few minutes to get the keys. Her hands are shaking so much as she rummages through the wooden bowl full of house keys, workshop keys, door keys and spare keys that she drops the fob when she finds it. It skitters under the kitchen table and she has to get down on one knee to retrieve it. Tess's half-chewed rawhide bone is under there too.

She runs back through her own footprints to the barn, pressing the key fob and seeing the welcoming flash of the indicator bulbs, bright against the snow. It's dark now, and the wind has begun to stir again. A few flakes of snow drift in the sharp yellow glow of the security light; it's impossible to tell if it's new snow, or flakes lifted on the breeze.

She will need to pull him clear of the car in order to back out without running him over.

But Will isn't there.

She stares at the patch of concrete where he'd been lying just a few minutes ago. There is nothing, no trace of him, not even any blood on the floor. Immediately she spins around, looking into the dark corners of the barn, the yard, around the cottage. No sign of him.

Sarah pulls open the car door, climbs in and presses the button to lock the doors behind her.

The silence of the car envelops her. She can see her breath, clouding into the space.

There is no sound, not even something as specific as a smell, but suddenly she is certain that Will is in the car with her.

It's like an electric shock; all of her senses alert, adrenaline flooding her. She holds her breath. There is nothing, no sound. She shuts her eyes tight – *please God, no* – and when she opens them again she twists in the seat and looks behind her.

The back seat is empty, the footwells clear.

He's not there.

Now she feels comforted by the familiarity of this space, cold as it is; and the car starts first time, as she knew it would. Safe. Reliable. Radio 4 comes on; it's *PM* and suddenly she is in love with the voice of Eddie Mair.

And then there is a sudden bang next to her, and Will at the passenger window, thumping on the glass with his bare hand, leaving a bloody smear on the glass.

She screams, slams her foot down on the accelerator. The car lurches backwards and Will slips, falling into the snow.

She has never tested this car on deep snow but it feels like a good time to try.

The car backs out of the barn and crunches into the snow. She tries not to think of it backing up, stuffing into the exhaust. She glances out of the window. The snow reaches the bottom of the door. She spins the wheel and the car jerks ahead, spraying snow in wide white arcs around the yard. She cannot see him any more and she doesn't want to waste any time looking. The tyres skid and then grip and then she is at the bottom of the drive, turning into the lane.

Where is he? There is nothing, no trace; no dark shapes around the corner of the buildings.

So far, so good; but the yard and the drive have been sheltered from the worst of the weather. Out here, in the lane, it's deep; her car headlights pick out the beautiful white landscape like a feather duvet in front of her. She turns on the wipers as the snow crests the bonnet of the car and is thrown up on to the windscreen, blinding her for a second.

She steers between the hedge on her left and the dark dotted line to her right which must be the top of the Buttons' dry stone wall. It looks like embroidery, she thinks. Running stitch. Crawling forward, she sees a few rocks poking out of the snow, perpendicular to the wall. Blanket stitch.

And then they disappear completely under the whiteness, and there is only the hedge to her left to guide her. The car's headlights sometimes emerge from the drift and show her nothing but white. Most of the time they are under the snow. She creeps forward, marvelling that the car is still going.

The hedge to her left drops away and disappears and Sarah feels panic rising. Either side of the narrow road is a deep ditch; the hedge has been her only guide to where it might be. Ahead of her she can see street-lights and buildings at the bottom of the hill. There is only another three hundred yards, maybe two, until the end of the lane and the junction with the Keighley Road. She tries to remember the lane, whether there are any bends. She must have driven this way a thousand times, more. But ahead of her, between the bonnet of the car and the street-lights in the distance, is nothing but white.

It is this ditch, the one at the bottom of the lane, into which Jim drove the car. He took the corner too fast, only slightly over the alcohol limit but nevertheless not entirely sober, lost control and slammed into the wall at the bottom. Bounced off the airbag and hit the side of his head on the window.

Blood on his face.

It was forty minutes before they cut him out.

The Land Rover dives nose-first into the snow and Sarah shrieks in panic, even though the car is barely going above a crawl. But it isn't the ditch, it's the dip in the road just before the junction, and the car rises again, briefly illuminating the snow-covered pole of the stop sign.

The snow on the main road is compacted, banked up at the sides. Cars have been down here, and, judging from the deep ruts and the dark splodges of mud, tractors too. She pauses for a moment, looking left and right up the road as if waiting for a gap in the traffic. There is nothing coming. Nothing is moving.

Where am I going to go?

The answer comes to her as clearly as if someone had spoken it aloud: George. Sophie's house.

She turns left and, a few yards further on, right, into the driveway. There are tracks in the snow, footprints criss-crossing the snow, lights on in the house. She stops before she gets to the building because she can't be certain where the pond is, sliding down from her seat into snow that, here, is just about shin-deep. Already she feels as though the nightmare is over; the snow is never as bad in the village, and, even if the phone lines here are down too, George's mobile will work.

She heads to the house and rings the doorbell.

She waits, and rings again.

There is no reply.

George has gone to the pub, Sarah thinks, already knowing that this is unlikely. Sophie is missing; he cannot be anywhere but waiting for her to come back. Unless she *has* come back. Unless she's back safe and sound, because the alternative – that she has been found, but that something terrible has happened to her – is too awful to think about.

She trudges around the side of the house, through the wrought-iron gate, to the back garden. The topiary bushes look like iced Christmas puddings, the low wall and the gap in it showing her where the steps leading down to the lawn would be. In any case the snow here is not deep; there are no footprints, either. Sarah walks the length of the back of the house, past the patio doors which are in darkness, round to the glass structure that George thinks is an orangery because he's put an orange tree in it, a squat little thing that regularly sheds its leaves and appears close to death, and which even when it's revived produces flowers but never, even once, a fruit. Sarah has pointed out more than once that, whatever they are choosing to call their conservatory, this is Yorkshire.

The double doors to the orangery are locked, but she digs through the snow beside the bay tree outside to find the terracotta plant pot upturned in its own saucer. Under this is the key.

She finds it and it turns easily in the lock. The door opens and a waft of warm air hits her icy cheeks.

'George?'

There is no sound.

She shuts the door behind her, stamps the snow off her boots, brushes it from the bottoms of the waterproof trousers. The door that leads into the kitchen is closed, but, when she tries it, it isn't locked. There is a key hidden for this door too, in case of emergencies.

She is standing in Sophie's kitchen.

Something is wrong.

It's not just the silence, not just the bad smell – not rotten food, not quite like that; it's metallic, and foul, drifting on the warmth of the house. There is a phone handset on the kitchen counter. She presses buttons, even tries dialling 999 – but the phone is just as dead as hers was.

The house, silent, warm, contemplative, waits for her next move.

She doesn't call out again.

Instead she walks through the kitchen towards the door to the dining room. There is a light on somewhere in the house, the hallway probably, but here and in the next room it's dark.

She goes through the dining room and out into the hallway, which is lit by the heavy chandelier that hangs in the centre of the room. Around the curved wall the oak staircase sweeps dramatically to the first floor. The hall table, an elegant antique that George is fond of telling everyone cost over four grand, is lying on its side, letters and keys and flowers scattered across the tiled floor, a crystal vase smashed. Water from the vase has soaked into the edge of the Persian rug.

Silence.

The living room is in darkness. But even from a quick glance Sarah can see that everything is in order, from the cold, swept fireplace to the neat stack of glossy magazines on the coffee table. It's as if Sophie has just stepped out for a minute.

Upstairs, then.

She keeps to the edge of the staircase, climbing gingerly as if at any moment she expects someone to appear.

The smell gets worse with every step. And even though by following the smell she knows what she is going to find, it's still enough of a shock to make her gasp out loud when she discovers George in the en-suite bathroom, slumped wet and fully clothed in the shower tray, his legs out across the slate floor, his head near the plughole. His cropped, greying hair is covered in blood.

'George!' Sarah says, rushing to him. He is cold. Stone cold. His face is turned to the wall. She edges around the shower screen and tugs at his shirt. He is heavy, inert, and there is no room to manoeuvre – it takes a minute or two of dragging until he suddenly flops dramatically on-to his back.

Sarah gasps and lets go. His face is unrecognisable, battered and swollen, his eyes blackened and closed.

Sarah shrinks back against the bathtub, brings her knees up to her chest, both hands clamped across her face, sobbing.

Her hands are wet with his blood, and now it's all over her face and she can taste it as well as smell it.

Just as she thinks this is it, she cannot take any more, there is a sound from the shower, a sudden, gasping cough.

He's alive. *George is still alive.*

'George? George? Can you hear me?'

He's breathing, she thinks. She can hear it now, a wheeze in his chest. She grabs the grey towelling robe from the back of the bathroom door and covers him in it, trying to get some warmth back into him.

There is a grumbling sound from the back of his throat, and then he whispers, 'Sophie.'

'It's me, George. It's Sarah. Where's your phone? Where's your mobile?'

She sees, or thinks she sees, a slight shake of his head.

'Your mobile, where is it?'

'... took it...'

'Someone took it? Who did this to you?'

She already knows. What's the point in asking?

'... Sophie...'

'I'm going to go and look...'

'No... wait... don't go...'

She stops, takes a deep breath on his behalf, as if it will help him. Holding his hand, trying to bring some warmth back into it. 'I'm sorry,' she says, her voice catching in a sob. 'George, please, hold on...'

He is trying to open his eyes. The effort it's taking is exhausting to watch. The wheezing is getting worse – should she try and put him on his side? What if he's bleeding, inside? What if his lungs are filling with blood?

'I don't know what to do...'

His lips are moving. She gets close to him, close to his face, even though to look at him is terrifying her.

'Spare,' he says. 'Phone. Drawer... bedroom.'

She scrambles to her feet and runs to the bedroom. There is a walk-in wardrobe that's the size of Sarah's box room, and inside it are two chests of drawers. Both of them are in a mess; drawers have been pulled out, underwear and socks and tops and belts and scarves have been flung and discarded. Two of the drawers are upside down on the king-size bed. Nevertheless she searches, picking everything up and moving it to a pile by the door so she can see progress. She turns the drawers the right way and piles them up. It takes several minutes. At the end of it there is a pile of clothes and two sets of drawers, but no phone.

In desperation she looks around the bedroom. There are matching nightstands on either side of the bed, a small drawer in each. She tugs out the one nearest to her, tips its contents on the bed. It must be George's – cufflinks, a watch, a plastic case which looks as if it might be for a dental plate, a half-used blister pack of painkillers, a pair of nail scissors.

The other side – Sophie's side. Hers has even more in it, and the drawer jams – she tugs and pulls and tucks her hand inside to press down whatever it is that's preventing the drawer from opening. One more yank and it flies free, everything spilling all over the place. Sarah sits down heavily on the bed. Among the crap scattered all over the floor at her feet is a small black mobile phone.

She turns it on, holding her breath. It sparks into life. She whimpers with relief as the 'no signal' gives way to bars and a little, beautiful '4G'.

She dials 999 and waits.

It's only a second, but that's all it takes; she glances across at the pile of clothing by the door. Much of it has blood on it, probably George's blood, from her own hands. But she sees Kitty's scarf among the tangle of fabric; Kitty's pale blue scarf with the sequinned border, more blood on it than just a smudge. And, looking down, she can see bloody marks where something has been dragged across the carpet. Not towards the bathroom, or from it – but towards the hallway. And on the doorframe, about a foot from the floor, a small, bloody handprint, as though someone has clutched at the door before being dragged away.

'Emergency. Which service do you require?'

From downstairs, Sarah hears footsteps and then a voice that turns her cold.

'Sarah! Are you there, you crazy fucking bitch? I've got someone here who wants to talk to you...'

There is a high-pitched wail that turns into a scream.

'Mum! RUN!'

It hurts worse when he hits her this time because she is expecting it, and she flinches.

They are in the living room, which is now brightly lit. Sarah is sitting on the floor with her back to the sofa, opposite Kitty, who is slumped against the fireplace. Both of them are bound hand and foot with cable ties that are digging into Sarah's wrists. She doesn't mind. She can take anything, any pain, because Kitty is here and she is alive, and although her mouth is swollen, and her lip is bleeding a little from where he's hit her, she is otherwise apparently unharmed.

'Shut up,' Will says, although neither of them has said anything.

'You bastard, you piece of shit,' Sarah hisses.

He sits casually down on the sofa behind her, his legs either side of her, and grabs a handful of her hair.

'I told you,' he says, his voice so calm it's terrifying, 'that we should have done this the easy way. Now look at what a mess you've made, Sarah. This is all down to you. Isn't it? ISN'T IT?'

'Yes,' she sobs. Her scalp is on fire as he tugs at her hair. 'Please, let us go...'

'All you have to do,' he murmurs, his mouth close to her ear, 'all you have to do is one simple little thing, and I'll leave you both alone. Understand? It's so easy, Sarah. So easy. Just tell me where she is.'

'I don't know,' she wails. 'I don't know where she is. Please, you have to let us go. This is all so wrong, Will.'

'She doesn't know!' Kitty cries. 'I told you, I told you she doesn't... please!'

'Shut up, you little bitch!'

Abruptly he stands up and leaves the room. From where she's sitting, Sarah can't see where he has gone. Kitty is facing the door.

'Kitty,' Sarah whispers. 'Are you all right?'

'Yes, yes. Are you?'

Sarah nods. And then he's back, and in his hand is one of Sophie's kitchen knives. He holds it to Kitty's throat.

'No!' Sarah screams. 'No no NO!'

'You need to stop this right now. Stop it, and think about what you're doing.'

Sarah does not know where the voice comes from, but she's heard it before. It's her 'mum' voice, the one she uses when things have gone far enough, when someone has crossed the line, when the fun has suddenly become borderline dangerous, when people are overtired.

Incredibly, it seems to have an effect on Will. He pauses for a moment, his right hand gripping Kitty's hair, holding her head back, the knife poised against the beautiful pale skin of her throat. His hands are trembling. And, even though his face is twisted into a grimace, she can see that there are tears pouring down his cheeks.

'Put the knife down.'

He does not move.

'Will. Put the knife down on the table.'

Sarah watches as he reaches across to the coffee table, the blade pointing down as if he's about to stab someone with it. He lowers it to the table.

'That's it. You can come back from this, Will. It's going to be okay. Now let go of Kitty's hair.'

His fingers relax and he eases his hand free of Kitty's scalp. Kitty whimpers with fear. Sarah looks at her steadily, trying to make eye contact, trying to reassure her. As if she knows what she's doing. As if this is going to end well.

'Sit down next to Kitty,' she says. 'Sit down and let's talk about this properly. Let's talk about Sophie and try to think where she might be.'

Will sits, his elbows on his knees, his face in his hands. He lets out an agonised, desperate sob. Sarah lets him. Kitty's eyes are screwed shut and she is shaking with fear.

'Kitty, you need to calm down now. Everything's going to be okay. Both of you.'

Think, Sarah. She has no idea where she's going with this, but all she can think of is George upstairs and the urgent need to finish this, to get it over with, so that they can get him to a hospital; so that she can find Aiden. And still, from somewhere, she can hear barking. 'Where's Tess?' she says at last.

'In the garage,' he says, his voice close to breaking. 'I just locked her in there.'

Sarah nods and waits.

'I looked everywhere,' Will says. 'I tried all her friends, all the places she might have gone. I phoned the hospitals but they wouldn't tell me anything.'

'Wouldn't it be better to leave her in peace for a while, and let her come back when she's ready?'

'You don't understand,' he wails. 'George is a mean bastard. He wants everything his own way, and if things don't go right for him he gets nasty. You know what he did? He turned up at the place where I was staying. He told me if I didn't leave Sophie alone he'd get someone to sort me out. He's a crazy piece of shit, Sarah. He might have done something to her... maybe she can't come back?'

'Will,' Sarah says, more calmly than she feels, 'that really isn't very likely. You know Sophie as well as I do. She's probably gone off for a relaxing retreat somewhere and turned her phone off. And your behaviour towards us really isn't helping, is it? Now you need to cut these ties so we can start thinking of how we're going to put things right.'

She holds out her wrists towards him.

And then the doorbell rings.

'You need to answer the door,' Sarah says.

'No,' Will says. His face is wet with tears and there is blood on his hands, all over his shirt. 'No, no, no, I can't, Sarah, don't make me.'

'It's the only way,' she says. 'You have to answer the door, now. And then come back here and untie me. It might be Sophie; maybe she forgot her key.'

'What if it's the police?'

'Then you have to let them in and we can start to explain things,' Sarah says, as though this is easy, straightforward, as though there is nothing else to consider.

'I can't!'

'If you don't, they'll break the door down and then they won't even give you a chance to explain. Do it the easy way, Will. Have some sense.'

Despite the confidence in her words, she's surprised when he gets to his feet awkwardly. He towers over her. The doorbell rings again, and is followed by a sharp knock. He picks up the knife from the coffee table. Kitty flinches back, as if he is about to threaten her with it again.

'Leave the knife where it is.'

'I'm scared,' he whines.

'I know. But it will be okay. Put the knife down.'

'Promise?'

Open the fucking door, she wants to shout.

'I promise.'

But he still takes the knife with him.

Even with her wrists tied together, she manages to cross her fingers. As if it matters, lying to this man. Of course it won't be okay. It will never, ever be okay again. But she knows now that this is the only way to deal with him, the only way to get through to the terrified little boy who wants nothing more than for someone to love him, no matter what. Sarah gets to her knees awkwardly so that she can see over the back of the sofa to the hallway.

Will gets to the front door and opens it a tiny crack.

Sarah hears voices, shouts. Will tries to shut the door again, but he is sent flying across the tiled floor of the hallway as the door is flung open, and two police officers come into the house. The knife skitters away.

Kitty screams with relief.

'Please,' Sarah says, 'you don't understand, I need to get back to the house.'

'We need to get you checked over,' the male officer says again. 'Another patrol is going to your house, I explained that.'

'He's in the cottage, not in the house,' she says, for what must be the third time. Her teeth are chattering and she cannot seem to get the words out properly. The paramedics are dealing with George and a second ambulance has now arrived. Kitty is inside it.

'Where's Will?' Sarah asks.

But in that moment one of the paramedics approaches her; it's her turn.

'I think she's just in shock,' the police officer says.

'There's blood all over her, but I don't think any of it is hers.'

His radio starts up again and he does something to turn the volume down, leaves Sarah in the care of the paramedics. But she still hears his reply to the crackling voice, just as he walks out of the front door. 'Right... right. And is he still alive?'

Part Seven

Sarah

The police officer who seems to have been tasked with keeping an eye on Sarah and Kitty is called Aiden. Under any other circumstances Sarah might have found this amusing, but given the situation she cannot bring herself to laugh. The A&E department at James Cook University Hospital in Middlesbrough is busy, of course, but it doesn't take long before they have both been checked over and found to be in good health.

Sarah is still shaky, but now she is beginning to feel better. Kitty is here, with her, and she is alive.

She asks everyone she sees if they have heard how Aiden is, but nobody seems to know anything.

Photographs have been taken of their injuries by a forensic nurse practitioner and, once that's done, they are free to leave. The officer who has been waiting for them takes Sarah to one side. 'You were asking about your friend Mr Beck? He's been brought in; he's in resus. The doctor just told me you can go in for a few minutes – they're going to take him up for a CT scan. They're asking about next of kin.'

'I don't think he has anyone,' Sarah says.

Kitty comes too, because Sarah does not want to leave her alone. The pair of them are taken into Bay Three, where Aiden is on a trolley, lying flat with his head between blocks, a cellular cotton blanket covering him. Sarah can see dried blood and bruises and it's hard to tell where the injuries are. His right eye is black, swollen shut.

'Aiden?' Sarah says, looking down so he can see her face.

'I'm sorry,' he says. His mouth is an odd shape, his lower lip cut and swollen.

'Jesus,' Kitty says.

'It's okay,' Sarah says. She is trying not to cry at the sight of him. 'I'm sorry this happened to you. Are you going to be okay?'

'He was threatening Sophie,' he said. 'She was scared of him.'

'She's still missing, Aiden, we don't know where she is…'

And then, suddenly, he smiles, then winces at the effort of it.

'I do,' he says.

'I've forgotten your name,' Sarah says to the officer, who has been waiting for them outside.

'Oh, it's Aiden,' he replies. He looks very young, which makes her feel old.

'I meant your last name.'

'Arnold. PC Arnold. I can give you a lift.'

'Is it possible to collect my dog?' Tess has been released from the garage, and at the moment is being looked after by the police. Sarah wants her back before she gets taken to the emergency kennels.

'I'll check. Can you wait here a minute?'

Sarah stops him before he goes off.

'While you do that, I want to go and see George. Is that all right?'

'Ah...' The police officer looks at the registrar, who is finishing the notes next to him.

'I think he's been taken upstairs to the HDU,' she says.

PC Aiden Arnold offers to take Sarah and Kitty up there. George has been brought here by air ambulance, so, even though he was still in the care of the paramedics when the ambulance took Kitty and Sarah, he was in the hospital and being treated well before they were.

'I won't be long,' Sarah says to Kitty. 'Why don't you wait here with PC Arnold and I'll meet you in the foyer in a few minutes? I just want to see how he is before I leave.'

Kitty looks relieved. She is exhausted, Sarah realises, and traumatised by what's happened.

The HDU is on the first floor, and, as expected, she isn't allowed in. 'Are you a relative?' the staff nurse wants to know.

'A friend. I was with him... I just want to know he's okay.'

The nurse's voice softens a little when she sees the marks around Sarah's throat, her swollen, cut ear. 'He's stable at the moment. You can phone in the morning, if you like.' She passes over a leaflet, *Information for Patients and Visitors to the High Dependency/Intensive Care Unit*. The phone number and key members of staff are listed on the back.

'Thanks,' Sarah says.

'You're welcome. Goodnight.'

Sarah stares at the leaflet for a minute, not reading it. In truth, she doesn't particularly want to go home. Aiden is here. George is here. Kitty is safe.

'I'm sorry they won't let you in,' says a voice behind her. 'They asked me to wait a few minutes while they do something. I'm going back in a minute.'

Sarah turns to see Sophie sitting on a set of three chairs bolted to the floor in the corridor. Has she been there all along? She must have walked straight past her. Sophie looks pale and shattered, as though someone has picked her up and dropped her.

'Sophie!'

Sophie stands and Sarah rushes to hold her, squeezing her as tightly as she possibly can. Sophie is shaking and for a moment Sarah wonders if she's ill, but then she realises she is crying. They both are.

'I'm so sorry,' Sarah says, over and over again, although she's not sure exactly what it is she's sorry for. For not being able to help George. For not being a better friend. For introducing Sophie to Will in the first place.

'I'm sorry – no, I'm really sorry...' Sophie is saying, crying into Sarah's hair. 'I fucked everything up. It's all my fault, everything's my fault. And now George is... he's...'

'He'll be fine – he will. George is strong, Soph; he'll get through this. You both will.'

'I don't know, I don't know. He's in a bad way... they – they've put him in an induced coma. He's got swelling on the brain.'

Sarah breathes in. Same as Jim. She doesn't say this, of course.

'And they told me what you did,' Sophie adds.

'Me?'

'That you found my phone. That you dialled 999. You saved him, Sarah, you saved his life.'

But I never even spoke to them, Sarah thinks. When Will had shouted for her, she had shoved the phone down her top into her bra, hoping to use it later, to phone the police, and not realising that the line was still open.

They must have traced the number to Sophie's address; maybe they heard something of what was going on.

'I'm sorry about Aiden,' Sophie says. 'Is he going to be okay?'

'I think so. Did the police tell you?'

'No, Aiden did. When he regained consciousness, he got the police to call the hotel where I was staying and told me about George. He didn't want me to hear it from anyone else.'

'He knew where you were?'

'I told him about it when we were chatting once, this little place George and I used to go to. He worked out where I was, and came to see me. He was worried about you because of how much Will was hanging around the farm.'

'He tried to warn me,' Sarah says. 'I'm glad he knew where you were, though.'

'Me too. Otherwise I would still be there now. Where is Will?' Sophie says.

Sarah stares at her for a moment, wondering what she's been told. Wondering what she can possibly say. 'I don't know,' she says at last.

'He's been arrested?'

'Yes. They took him away.'

'Thank God,' Sophie says. 'Thank God for that.' She starts crying again, her shoulders shaking.

'They're taking us to a hotel for the night,' Sarah says. 'Come with us?'

'I want to stay here, with George.'

'They'll call you if they need you, won't they? He's unconscious. Come on. You shouldn't be on your own.'

'I'll come for a while,' Sophie says. 'Then I'll come back here. I want to sit with him.'

'Okay, then,' Sarah says. She threads her arm through Sophie's, and steers her towards the stairs.

It's snowing again, just a few small flakes tumbling from a dark sky, when the police car drops them off at the hotel. Tess isn't allowed, but PC Aiden Arnold has been in touch with the officers still at Sophie's house, and one of them has agreed to drop Tess off at Daniel and Becca's house. They have a dog, a cantankerous one-toothed Jack Russell called Vic, so it's not ideal, far from it, but, as Louis is not answering his phone, Sarah has no one else she can think to ask. Ian and Diana have cats. Three of them.

Sophie is too tired to object to where they've been put for the night, although she is still insisting that she is going to go back to the hospital in an hour or so. They are allocated a twin room and a double, and almost immediately Kitty crawls into one of the twin beds and closes her eyes.

'I wish I could have a drink,' Sophie says, looking at her.

'Let's go next door,' Sarah says.

While Sophie sits on the bed, Sarah fills the plastic kettle and puts teabags in the two mugs. 'I know it's not quite what you had in mind,' she says, 'but a cup of tea is better than nothing.'

'I'd still rather have a vodka,' Sophie says dolefully. 'Or a gin. Or even a tequila.'

'Me too,' Sarah says.

Sarah makes the tea, sharing one of the little plastic UHT milk tubs between the two mugs. It will have to do. She passes one mug to Sophie and sits on the foam sofa.

'Why did you go, Sophie? What happened?'

Sophie's dark eyes are wide.

'I got scared, that's all. Will was being so difficult; he'd been... I don't know... forceful, I guess, ever since that night I picked him up from the pub. He was telling me what to do, how I was going to leave George, how we were going to start a family. I thought it was quite sweet at first but then I realised he meant it: he was completely focused on this future we were going to have.'

'And you told him it wasn't going to happen?'

'I tried. He got... scary.'

'Why didn't you tell me?'

Sophie's bottom lip quivers. 'I thought... I don't know. I was going to tell you, over that lunch we never had. But you seemed to be fond of him. I thought it would make things awkward for you, too, especially with Louis.'

'Oh, Soph.'

'And besides, I thought it would just be easier if I went away for a bit, to think.'

'I was worried about you,' Sarah says. 'George was beside himself.'

Sophie manages a bark of a laugh. 'George knew where I was. It was more or less his idea.'

'What? I don't understand.'

'He was furious when he found out about my fling with Will. You know what he's like – he has to manage everything. He wasn't even bothered until the Lexus got scratched. And then, when Will started threatening me, George was fabulous. He said I should disappear for a while. We thought he'd get bored eventually, that he'd give up. We never thought for one moment that he'd get violent.'

'You know George didn't give the game away,' Sarah says. 'Even when Will hurt him, he never revealed where you were. He didn't even tell me.'

Sophie smiles again, and looks down at her fingers, clasped in her lap. 'Funny old bastard, he is. He can be a bloody arse to me, but when someone else has a go he's the first one to leap to my defence.'

'His heart's in the right place.'

'Yes, or more probably it's that being a bastard to me is *his* prerogative. You know what men are like – so territorial. They can't bear the thought of anyone pissing on their bonfire, can they?'

'Aiden didn't tell, either.'

The thought of Aiden makes Sarah feel suddenly sick. She'd thought he was dead, that Will had killed him. All that time he was unconscious in the cottage; it's a wonder he survived.

'He was kind to me, Sarah,' says Sophie, looking at her seriously. 'He's a good man.'

'Yes. He is.'

Despite her little smile, Sophie is grey-faced. Sarah is struck by how changed she is – the bright, vibrant Sophie has disappeared completely.

Sarah puts her mug down on the desk, takes Sophie's out of her hands, and folds her friend into a hug. 'It's okay now. We're safe.'

Aiden

You manage to sleep a little and that is good because then, at least, everything stops hurting for a while. When you wake up again – they are constantly checking you're not dead – the pain starts up again, everywhere at once. The stabbing pain in the back of your head is the worst of all. They have put stitches in it, and the local anaesthetic wears off far too quickly.

Still, the pain means you are still alive. You are still here.

At some point in the night they move you up to a ward, and there, at least, you manage to sleep in half-hour bursts, until finally you see daylight from the windows at the end of the bay and they sit you up and give you something to drink. Tea, toast. How are you feeling?

Awesome.

A doctor tells you you are fine. Nothing broken. Cuts and bruises. They are keeping you in for observation because of the head injury, but if you continue to look perky they will let you go home.

Home, you think. You've never properly had one of those.

The painkillers they gave you are beginning to wear off, the comforting numbness is lifting, and what's left is a thumping ache and the stinging in the back of your head. You ease yourself into an upright position, hoping to see a nurse, and instead you see a tall young man standing by the nurses' station.

He's looking at you.

When he sees you're awake he approaches, and he's familiar in a strange sort of way, ghost-like, someone you know from a dream. And then you see he has Jim's eyes, Jim's crooked smile, and Sarah's fair hair.

'Louis,' you say.

He smiles at you.

As if that isn't surprising enough, when he gets to the bed he offers you his hand.

'Your face looks rough,' he says.

'Yeah, well,' you answer.

'The police came round last night,' he says. 'After they went I wanted to go home straight away and see Mum and Kitty.'

'They've gone to a hotel,' you say. 'The police are at the farm still.'

'Yeah, and I'm too much of a coward in any case,' he says, rubbing his hand across his face. 'How are they?'

The truth, you think. Can he take it? Should you rub his nose in it, say that no, perhaps it's not his fault that his friend turned out to be a fucking psychopath, but if he'd not been behaving like a petulant child for the past three years he might have seen what was going on?

'I think it's a bit too early to say,' you answer.

'Will rang me out of the blue,' he says. 'Not heard from him for three years. Didn't know who it was at first, and then he started telling me that my mum had got a new bloke, that you'd moved in. That you were a – you know. Whatever you want to call it.'

For some reason that makes you laugh. Your head pounds. None of it seems as important any more. 'Well, whatever he said probably had some basis in truth. I'm not a prostitute, though; I'm a masseur. In any case, I'm not going to be carrying on in that line of work any more.'

Louis says, 'You've known Mum a long time. She must trust you.'

That he's willing to change the subject feels like a good sign.

'We were all good friends at university. But you know that already.'

'And you went off travelling,' Louis says.

'I ran away,' you say.

He looks surprised. You don't blame him – you're finding your new commitment to honesty a little uncomfortable yourself.

'From Dad?' Louis asks.

'From both of them.'

He doesn't press you. Perhaps he doesn't need to. It's only been a few minutes, but you like him. You didn't think you would, after everything Sarah said about him. She has made allowances for him at every turn, giving him time, giving him space, and only now do you see why.

'I miss him a lot,' Louis says. 'I was so angry that he died. He was only forty-three.'

'Yes.'

'I've been blaming Mum all this time. You know she should have been driving, that night? She had a cold, she said; that's why he drove.'

He pauses and looks away for a moment. He's an adult, a grown man; but just for a moment you can see the fatherless boy. Sarah's son.

'I don't think it was her fault,' he says. 'I was just so angry.'

'I don't know if he was any different with you,' you say, 'but the Jim I knew was a very determined man. If he got an idea in his head, there was no point trying to talk him out of it.'

'That's true.'

'It looks as if you've inherited his enterprising spirit,' you say. 'I hear your business is doing very well.'

'Yeah,' he says. 'It's not doing too badly.'

'He'd be very proud of you. Your mum is too.'

There is so much more you could say to him about Jim, but this isn't the time or the place. For now, you are suddenly desperate that fences should be mended between Sarah and Louis, This one thing is something that you might be able to fix, and it might make her feel better. You want that more than anything.

'What are you going to do?' Louis asks.

In the past you have made your decisions carefully, unless circumstances have forced you into a corner. If you needed to run, you would run. At the time you didn't feel ashamed; it was the way things were, and you always came out of it all right.

But this time is different. Running isn't what you want any more. And you don't know what Sarah wants, but it almost doesn't matter. Friend, lover, partner – whatever she wants you to be, you'll be it.

'I'm going to stay with your mum,' you say.

Sarah

It's three days before Sarah, Aiden and Kitty can go home. The wind changes direction, bringing with it warmer temperatures and rain, and, while the snow is still deep in the yard, the Land Rover can make it safely back up the hill. The three of them have stayed in the hotel, venturing out of their rooms only for meals, to visit George in the hospital and to be interviewed by the police. Will Brewer has been charged and remanded, which was a relief to them all. George has made good progress towards recovery, and has been moved to a general ward.

Sarah collects Basil from the vet's, and Tess from Becca's, before taking Kitty and Aiden home. It seems only right that they should all go together. She wants to take Sophie, too, but she has gone to stay with her sister in London for a week or two. Their house is being professionally cleaned; Sophie has generously paid for the cottage to be dealt with also.

The dogs are ridiculously excited to see each other, and as soon as Sarah opens the back of the car they both leap out and race through what's left of the snow, obliterating the remaining tracks. The police have been here, of course. The house – and the cottage – were crime scenes. She locks the door behind her.

The house is dark, and quiet, and warm. Sarah doesn't understand why it's warm, she's expecting it to be cold, but the heating is on, and with the lights turned on and the curtains closed everything is shockingly normal.

At bedtime they start off in three separate bedrooms: Kitty in her room, Aiden in the spare where Sarah has been sleeping, and Sarah in the master bedroom. After only a few minutes on her own, Sarah knocks quietly on the spare room door.

'Can't sleep either?' Aiden asks, lifting the corner of the duvet.

'I guess it's not surprising. I'm so tired, though.'

They lie quietly side by side for a moment, and then Sarah moves closer to him and his arms fold around her.

'I think I'm going to have to sell the house,' she says.

He sighs into her hair. 'It's not good to make rash decisions,' he says. 'There's no hurry.'

'I've been thinking about it for a while.'

'I know. But I'll help in whatever way I can until you know what you want to do.'

She listens to the wind outside, rattling the window frame. Less than a week ago she had been lying here and had woken up to find Will sitting on her bed.

Suddenly she feels sick, sits upright in bed.

'Sarah?'

Above the wind she can hear another sound, coming from the room next door. She reaches for her dressing gown. 'Kitty's crying.'

By two o'clock all three of them are downstairs in the living room, the woodburner lit, watching a programme about steam trains and drinking tea. The dogs are with them. Kitty eventually falls asleep with her head in Sarah's lap.

'It'll be better tomorrow,' Aiden says.

'I hope so.'

She looks up at him. The swelling has gone down and he looks more like Aiden again; the bruises are starting to change colour.

'What are we going to do?' she whispers.

'I don't know,' Aiden says, kissing the top of her head. 'But we'll be okay. You know you're stronger than anyone I've ever met. You proved that last week. So, we'll be okay.'

Kitty stirs, and sighs. Sarah strokes her daughter's hair away from her face, the way she used to when Kitty was small.

He's right, she thinks. *We will be okay. One day normal life will resume.*

The strange thing is, it does. Normal life returns with startling efficiency.

After several weeks, when Sarah is sure she's strong enough and that the university are offering the right kind of support, Kitty goes back to Manchester to carry on with her second term. Sarah walks the dogs twice a day. She tries to finish *The Candy Cotton Piglet at the Circus*, but finds she cannot. Instead she paints landscapes, dramatic skies, melting snow. Sophie thinks they are good, the best work she's ever done. She asks to buy them. Of course Sarah refuses, giving them to Sophie as a present instead. But the next ones she frames, offers for sale at the village art exhibition. They sell for fifty pounds each. It's not much, but it feels like a place to start.

Aiden has a new phone, and he has only used it to call her. He is going to train to be a physiotherapist; his healing touch will be dealing with a different kind of need, a different kind of pain. She is beginning to sleep better, and so is he.

Meanwhile the house is up for sale. Big houses don't sell as quickly as small ones, but already there have been some viewings; the estate agent promises that the market will pick up when the weather improves. The bank has, mercifully, offered her more time to repay her debt now she has a strategy in place to reduce it.

Sophie and George are back at home, and, whether it's denial or just a measure of their strength, they are bouncing back, better than ever. The press attention has died down remarkably quickly. They are planning a dinner party. Sarah and Aiden are invited.

Louis has been in touch. Explaining everything to him has been awkward, but he listens; he phones almost every day. He is coming home for a whole weekend at Easter. Sarah feels as if he is finding his way back to her.

And Tess no longer barks at the croft.

Whatever was inside it has gone.

It's always the same story for me. They all seem to like me, they all say nice things, and then when I get close they back off. Happens every time. Happened with Sarah, after Louis's party; same thing with Sophie. Like I don't have feelings. Like I don't matter.

Years ago, when my mam and dad split up, they sat down with my sister Emily and told her it wasn't her fault. She didn't understand, she had a hard time accepting it, she was crying her eyes out, but it was right what they said. It wasn't her fault, even though Amy was Emily's best friend, even though she'd been the one to introduce us. Amy didn't understand how much she meant to me and what we could be together. And the fact that her dad came round to our house to see my dad and my dad got angry and my mam blamed me for that, and they argued with each other all the time about what they were going to do with me and then it all got too much and all fell apart – that wasn't Emily's fault either. That was Amy's.

They didn't say that to me, of course. I wasn't even supposed to be there by then, I was on bail, and there was some sort of injunction that meant I wasn't supposed to go within a mile of them or their house, but I don't know why they bother doing things like that. When you're facing a court case for harassment and other stuff and you're probably going to prison, well, it's not like you can make it worse, right?

Besides, they never saw me.

I'm good at watching people without them realising. I'm good at keeping their secrets.

You get to know people properly when you watch them from the outside. It's like you're there, belonging but not belonging, a part of the household but separate from it.

Like a shadow. Like a ghost.

It's when the watching isn't enough any more that it goes wrong. When you want to be inside a place properly, inside people's lives – when you want to become a part of their lives and not apart from them – then you make mistakes; then you get angry; then you ruin it.

There's a lass here, one of the counsellors – I like her. She's only young. She said to me yesterday, You don't belong in here. You're too nice, she said.

Where do I belong? I asked her.

Safe, somewhere, she said. Safe and with people who care about you.

I'll wait for that, then, I said.

I'm good at waiting.

Acknowledgements

Never Alone has been on a long journey since the first draft of it was written during NaNoWriMo in November 2014. Many people have helped the story develop, and have provided invaluable research assistance, and I am glad to have the opportunity to acknowledge them here.

Firstly my eternal gratitude to the Myriad Editions family, particularly my outstanding and insightful editor Vicky Blunden, and publisher and friend Candida Lacey, for being excited about every draft, for improving it each time, and for your patience as I worked my way round in circles with the plot. Thank you both for your faith in me, and in the story. As always I am profoundly grateful for my genius copy-editor Linda McQueen, who spots things no one else can and always leaves me with a manuscript I can be proud of.

I am not very good at writing on my own, and so I'm lucky to have a posse of talented writing friends who have supported, inspired and encouraged me on a daily basis. For saving my sanity, making me laugh, supplying me with tea and cake and being fantastic in every way, my thanks to my cabin mates: Jo Hinton Malivoire, Denise West and Donna-Louise Bishop.

In the company of these great writers, *Never Alone* took shape in various cafés and tea rooms in Norfolk; with this in mind I recommend to you the Alby Tea Room between Cromer and Aylsham, and Henry's Coffee and Tea Store and the Rocket House Café in Cromer. Thank you for the cake, the breakfasts, the tea, and for making us feel so welcome.

I would also like to thank Gail and Mick of the Royal Oak Hotel in Helmsley, North Yorkshire, who willingly answered all sorts of daft questions about hospitals and what the roads are like when it snows.

Thank you to Jeannine Taylor and Bruce Head, who allowed me to write about their beautiful, clever dog, Tess.

Several people helped me with research and I am grateful to Charlotte Buckley for answering questions about veterinary practice (and Cath Bore for putting us in touch with each other); Ann Dunkerley, who helped a great deal with early drafts and was very encouraging at every stage; Simon Lloyd, who answered questions about massage services for women in London; Boris Starling and Sophie Hannah for explaining how cars perform in heavy snow in rural areas; Alison Murray, who, on a very intense creative writing weekend run by the brilliant Greg Mosse, told me that the scariest thing she could imagine would be waking up to find someone sitting on her bed; Yvonne Johnson for helping me choose the Margaux from George's wine cellar; Karen Gambrell for advising on banking procedure; Ben Clarke for checking my hospital scenes; Andrew Taylor for technical help; @alexisgebbie and @JFDerry on Twitter for assistance in navigating my way around York city centre (alas, you may notice that the busking scene does not now take place in Parliament Square, but thank you nonetheless). Any mistakes, omissions and applications of artistic licence are, of course, my responsibility alone.

Special thanks, as always, to my dear friends Samantha Bowles, Katie Totterdell and Greg Mosse, who always seem to be able to offer an insight into plot opportunities that I would otherwise miss; and to the brilliant Jacqueline Chnéour for providing a fresh perspective on the book. You never fail to make my books better.

Thank you to everyone who helped me with the crime scene. You know who you are; I'm not going to name names. I would not have made it this far without you.

As always I am grateful to anyone who reads my books, and to those who take time to let me know what they thought, either by email or by writing a review. In particular, the members of THE Book Club on Facebook, and to the awesome Tracy Fenton, who has been unendingly supportive of my writing, and helped me with some important changes at the last minute – you are brilliant, thank you.

Lastly but not leastly, my fabulous family who have kept cheering me on – thank you all. I love you.

Author's Note

The idea for *Never Alone* came to me when we were thinking of moving house. For many months, I spent far too much time browsing through houses for sale on various property websites, and in the course of my search I came across the property that became the inspiration for Four Winds Farm. Alas, it sold before our house was even on the market, but perhaps that was just as well. Personally, I don't think I would cope with living somewhere so remote!

Looking at the pictures of the grey stone house nestling into the hillside, the valley laid out before it, I could imagine how it might feel to be safe and warm inside when the weather closes in. From picturing safety and comfort, it's never long before I start to imagine what would be the most terrifying thing to happen next – and Sarah's story began to emerge.

I hope you've enjoyed *Never Alone*. I'd love to hear what you think of it, so if you have a spare minute please do come and say hello on Facebook or Twitter, or email me via the website – all the details are below.

The setting for *Never Alone* is central to the story, and if you enjoyed it you might also enjoy my second book, *Revenge of the Tide*, which is set mostly on a houseboat on the river Medway in Kent. Strange how the most beautiful places inspire the scariest of stories! You can read the first part of *Revenge of the Tide* here – hope you like it.

Elizabeth Haynes
July 2016

@elizjhaynes
facebook.com/elizabethjhaynes
www.elizabeth-haynes.com

Read on for an extract from Elizabeth Haynes' bestselling novel *Revenge of the Tide*.

It was there when I opened my eyes, that vague feeling of discomfort, the rocking of the boat signalling the receding tide and the wind from the south, blowing upriver, straight into the side of the *Revenge of the Tide*.

For a long while I lay in bed, the sound of the waves slapping against the hull next to my head, echoing through the steel and dulled by the wooden cladding. The duvet was warm and it was easy to stay there, the rectangle of the skylight directly above showing the blackness turning to dark blue, and grey, and then I could see the clouds scudding overhead, giving the odd impression of moving at speed – the boat moving rather than the clouds. And then, that discomfort again.

It wasn't seasickness, or river-sickness, come to that: I was used to it now, nearly five months after I had left London. Five months living aboard. There was still a momentary shock when my feet hit the solid ground of the path to the car park, a few wobbly steps, but it was never long before I felt steady again.

It was a grey sort of a day – not ideal for the get-together later, but that was my own fault for planning a party in September. 'Back to school' weather, the wind whistling across the deck when I got up and put my head out of the wheelhouse.

No, it wasn't the tide, or the thought of the mismatched group of people who would be descending on my boat later today. There was something else. I felt as though someone had rubbed my fur the wrong way.

The plan for the day: finish the last bit of timber cladding for the second room, the room that was going to be a guest bedroom at some point in the future. Clear away all the carpentry tools and store them in the bow. Sweep out the boat, clean up a bit. Then see if I could cadge a lift to the cash-and-carry for party food and beer.

There was one wall left to do, an odd shape, which was why I had left it till last. The room was full of sawdust and offcuts of wood, bits of edging and sandpaper. I'd done the measurements last night but now, frowning at the bit of paper, I decided to recheck it all just to be on the safe side. When I had clad the galley I'd ended up wasting a load of wood because I misread my own measurements.

I put the radio on, turned up loud even though I still couldn't hear it above the mitre saw, and got to work.

At nine, I stopped and went back through to the galley for a coffee. I filled the kettle and put it on to the gas burner. The boat was a mess. It was only occasionally that I noticed it. Glancing around, I scanned last night's takeaway containers hurriedly shoved into a carrier bag ready to go out to the main bins. Dirty dishes in the sink. Pans and other items in boxes sitting on one of the dinette seats waiting to be put away, now I had finally fitted cupboard doors in the galley. A black plastic sack of fabrics and netting that would one day be curtains and cushion covers. None of it mattered when I was the only one in here, but in a few hours' time this boat would be full of people, and I had promised them that the renovations were almost complete.

Almost complete? That was stretching the truth a little thin. I had finished the bedroom, and the living room wasn't bad. The galley was done too, but needed cleaning and tidying. The bathroom was – well, the kindest thing that could be said about it was that it was functional. As for the rest of it – the vast space in the bow that would one day be a bigger bathroom with a bath instead of a hose for a shower, a wide conservatory area with a sliding glass roof (an ambitious plan, but I'd seen one in a magazine and it looked so brilliant that it was the one project I was determined to complete), and maybe a snug or an office or another unnamed room that would be wonderful and cosy and magical – for the moment, it worked as storage.

The kettle started a low whistle, and I rinsed a mug under the tap and spooned in some instant coffee, two spoons: I needed the caffeine.

A pair of boots crossed my field of vision through the porthole, level with the pontoon outside, shortly followed by a call from the deck. 'Genevieve?'

'Down here. Kettle's just boiled, want a drink?'

Moments later Joanna trotted down the steps and into the main cabin. She was dressed in a miniskirt, with thick socks and heavy boots, with the laces trailing, on the ends of her skinny legs. The top half of her was counterbalanced by one of Liam's jumpers, a navy blue one, flecked with bits of sawdust and twig and cat hair. Her hair was a tangle of curls and waves of various colours.

'No, thanks – we're off out in a minute. I just came to ask what time we should come over later, and do you want us to bring a lasagne as well as the cheesecake? And Liam says he's got some beers left over from the barbecue, he'll be bringing those.'

She had a bruise on her cheek. Joanna didn't wear make-up, wouldn't have known what to do with it, so there it was – livid and purplish, about the size of a fifty pence piece, under her left eye.

'What happened to your face?'

'Oh, don't you start. I had a fight with my sister.'

'Blimey.'

'Come up on deck, I need a smoke.'

The wind was still whipping, so we sat on the bench by the wheelhouse. The sun was trying to make its way through the scudding clouds but failing. Across the other side of the marina I could see Liam loading boxes and carrier bags into the back of their battered Transit van.

Joanna fished around in the pocket of her skirt and brought forth a pouch of tobacco. 'The way I see it,' she said, 'she should keep her fucking nose out of my business.'

'Your sister?'

'She thinks she's all clever because she's got herself a mortgage at the age of twenty-two.'

'Mortgages aren't all they're cracked up to be.'

'Exactly!' Joanna said with emphasis. 'That's what I said to her. I've got everything she's got without the burden of debt. And I don't have to mow any lawn.'

'So that's what you were fighting about?'

Joanna was quiet for a moment, her eyes wandering over to the car park where Liam stood, hands on his hips, before pointedly looking at his wristwatch and climbing into the driver's seat. Above the sounds of the marina – drilling coming from the workshop, the sound of the radio down in the cabin, the distant roar of the traffic from the motorway bridge – the van's diesel rattle started up.

'Fuck it, I'd better go,' she said. She shoved the pouch back into her pocket and lit the skinny cigarette she'd just managed to fill. 'About seven? Eight? What?'

I shrugged. 'I don't know. Sevenish? Lasagne sounds lovely, but don't go to any trouble.'

'It's no trouble. Liam's made it.'

With a backward wave, Joanna took one quick hop-step down the gangplank and on to the pontoon, running despite the boots across the grassy bank and up to the car park. The Transit was taking little jumps forward as though it couldn't wait to be gone.

At four, the cabin was finally finished. A bare shell, but at least now it was a bare wooden shell. The walls were clad, and the berth built along the far wall, under the porthole. Where the mattress would sit, two trapdoors with round finger-holes in the board gave access to the storage compartment underneath. The rest of it was pale wood in neat panelling, carved pine edging covering the joins and corners. It would look less like a sauna once it had had a lick of paint, I thought. By next weekend it would be entirely different.

Clearing away the debris of my most recent foray into carpentry took longer than I thought it would. I had crates for the tools. I hadn't bothered to put them away since I'd started work on the bedroom, months ago.

I lugged them forward into the bow, through a hatch and into the cavernous space below. Three steps down, watching my head on the low ceiling, stowing the crates away at the side.

It was only when I made the last trip, carrying the black plastic sack of fabric from the dinette and throwing it into the front compartment, that I found myself looking into the darkest of the spaces to see if the box was still there. I could just about see it in the gloomy light from the cabin above; on the side of it was written, in thick black marker: KITCHEN STUFF.

I had a sudden urge to look, to check that the box still had its contents. Of course it did, I told myself. Of course it was still there. *Nobody's been down here since you put it there.*

Stooping, I crossed the three wooden pallets that served as a floor, braced myself against the sides of the hull, and crouched next to the box. KITCHEN STUFF. The top two-thirds of the box was full of rubbish I'd brought from the London flat – spatulas, wooden spoons, a Denby teapot with a crack in the lid, a whisk, a blender that didn't work, an ice cream scoop and various cake tins nested inside each other. Below that was a sheet of cardboard that might, to the casual observer, look sufficiently like the bottom of the box to deter further investigation.

I folded the cardboard top of the box back down and tucked the other flap underneath it.

From the back pocket of my jeans, I took out a mobile phone. I found the address book and the only number that was saved there: GARLAND. That was all it said. It wasn't even his name. It would be so easy to press the little green button now and call him. What would I say? Maybe I could just ask him if he wanted to come tonight. '*Come to my party, Dylan. It's just a few close friends. I'd love to see you.*'

What would he say? He'd be angry, shocked that I'd used the phone when he'd expressly told me not to. It was only there for one purpose, he'd told me. It was only for him to ring me, and only when he was ready to make the collection. Not before. If I ever had a call on it from another number, I wasn't to answer.

I closed my eyes for a moment, for a brief second allowing myself the indulgence of remembering him. Then I put the screen lock back on the phone so it didn't accidentally dial any numbers, least of all his, and I shoved it in my pocket and made my way back to the cabin.

myriad
m

MORE FROM MYRIAD

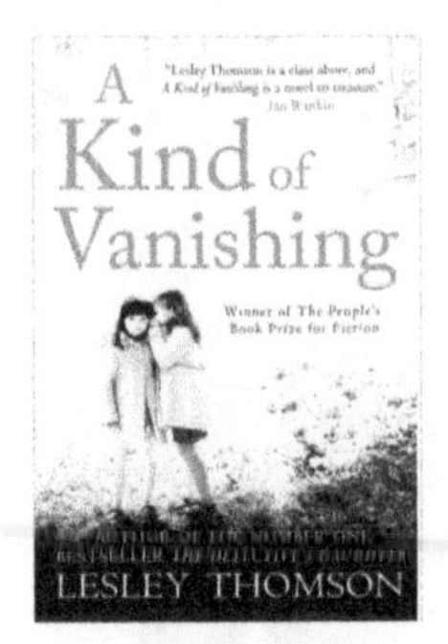

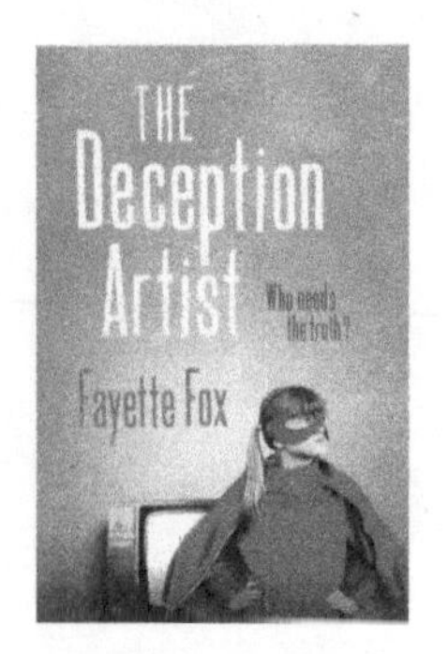

MORE FROM MYRIAD

MORE FROM MYRIAD

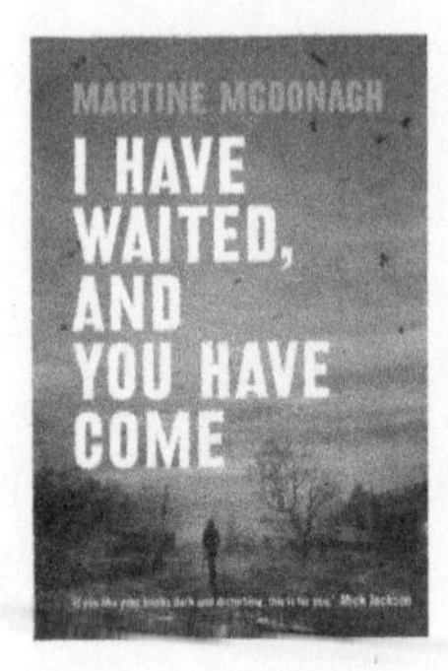

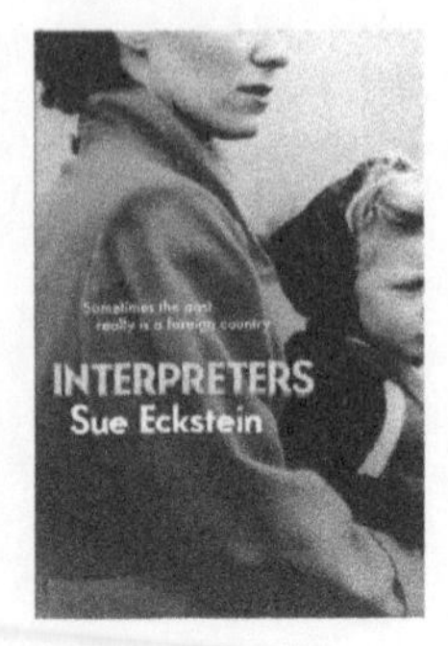

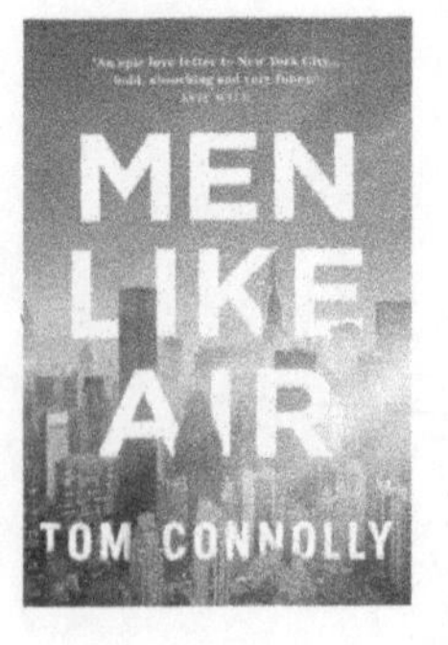

MORE FROM MYRIAD

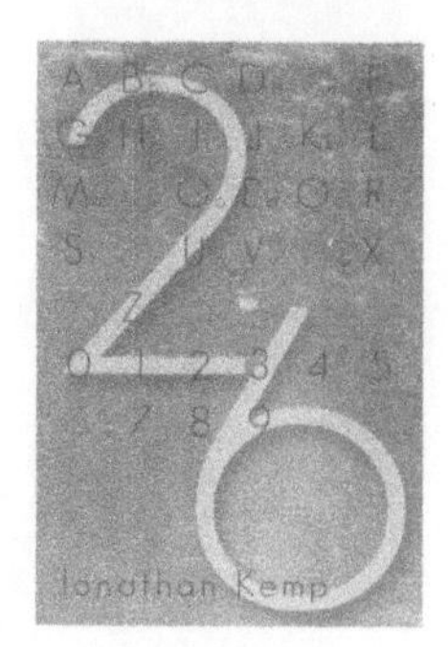

Elizabeth Haynes is a former police intelligence analyst who lives in Norfolk with her husband and son. Her first novel, *Into the Darkest Corner*, was Amazon's Best Book of the Year 2011 and is a *New York Times* bestseller. It has been published in thirty-seven countries. Her second novel, *Revenge of the Tide*, was published by Myriad in 2012 and her third, *Human Remains*, was published in 2013. She is also the author of two police procedural crime novels, *Under a Silent Moon* and *Behind Closed Doors* (Sphere).